DRUNKARD

DRUNKARD

ÉMILE ZOLA

Translated from the French by
ARTHUR SYMONS

With an Introduction by
ALEC BROWN

LONDON
ELEK BOOKS

This translation © *1958*
ELEK BOOKS LIMITED
2 All Saints Street
London N.1

Reprinted 1970

Reproduced photolitho in Great Britain by
A. Wheaton & Co., Exeter

PREFACE

LES ROUGON-MACQUART should consist of a score of novels. The general plan has been drawn up since 1869, and I follow it with extreme scrupulousness. *L'Assommoir* has come in its turn. I have written it, as I shall write the others, without swerving a hair's-breadth from my direct course. It is to this that I owe my strength. I have an aim before me, and I make straight for my aim.

When *L'Assommoir* appeared in a paper, it was attacked with unexampled brutality, denounced, accused of every crime. Is it really necessary for me to explain here, in a few lines, my intentions as a writer? I have endeavoured to paint the fatal downfall of a family of the working class, in the tainted atmosphere of our suburbs. After drunkenness and sloth, come a relaxation of family ties, the evils of over-crowding, the gradual lapse from honesty, then, by way of *dénoûment*, shame and death. It is simply morality in action.

L'Assommoir is assuredly the most chaste of my books. I have often had to probe far more disgusting sores. It is only the form that has frightened people. They have quarrelled with words. My crime is to have had the literary curiosity to pick up, and to cast in a highly elaborate mould, the language of the people. Ah! the form is the great crime! Yet there are dictionaries of this language, scholars study it, delighting in the freshness, the novelty, and the force of its figures of speech. It is a feast for the exploring instinct of grammarians. However, no one has realized that my intention was to engage in a purely philological undertaking, one which seems to me of extreme historical and social interest.

But I do not defend myself. My work will defend me. It is a work of truth, the first novel of the people which is not false, and which has the odour of the people. And it should not be inferred that the people as a whole is bad, for my characters are not bad, they are simply ignorant, and spoilt by the surroundings of poverty and hard labour in which they live. Only, it would be well to read my novels, to understand them, to see them clearly in their entirety, before bringing forward the ready-made opinions, ridiculous and odious, which are circulated concerning myself and my works. Ah! if people only knew how my friends laugh at the appalling legend which amuses the crowd! If they only knew how the blood-thirsty wretch, the formidable novelist, is simply a respectable bourgeois, a man devoted to study and to art, living quietly in his corner, whose sole ambition is to leave as large and living a work as he can! I contradict no reports, I work on, and rely on time, and on the good faith of the public, to discover me at last under the accumulation of nonsense that has been heaped upon me.

EMILE ZOLA.

Paris, January 1st, 1877

INTRODUCTION

ONE thing about Émile Zola is quite certain: too much
attention has been paid to the grand scheme of the so-called
"Rougon-Macquart novels", of which this is one. Twenty-one
in number, they are, as "everybody knows", all centred on the
members of two families. Zola did undoubtedly talk about the
effects of various supposedly inherited characteristics and of
his intention to reveal the whole gamut of this legacy in a
double family saga. But he always left one very important
factor out of his calculations—Zola the imaginative artist.
The creator Zola was in these novels stronger than Zola the
constructor of *romans-à-thèse*.

The truth is, probably, that in the whole scheme (as in
that of many other series of "saga" novels), a factor very
different from the notion of showing, on a broad canvas,
cumulative effects through the generations, was really
dominant. This force might be termed the "artist's self-
protective indolence". A more respectful designation would
be "instinctive economy of invention". The point is this: in
the minds of some creative narrators, mankind presents itself
as an infinite diversity. The characters are unlimited in
number. It is the curious difference of detail and patterning
in men's lives that fascinate such writers as Chekhov or
Maupassant. Such artists flourish in the world of the short
story. Once brilliantly drawn, their characters, even when
they do not develop them at length, cease to interest them.
When next they write, they start all over again with
new ones.

It is different with the Zolas. Not only do their characters,
once conceived, grow continuously, (often getting out of
hand), but from them and the situations they create about
them, other characters germinate. Instinctively, such writers
feel it tedious each time to invent totally new personalities,
with totally new family connections and a totally new circle
of acquaintances. In successive works they use previous
secondary personages. An important corollary to this method
is that the novelist who practises it tends to be interested more

7

in what is general and characteristic than in incidental detail, however revealing.

Thus it seems that Zola did not so much come to a conclusion about heredity and then invent a double family of personalities to illustrate it, as the other way round. From one character in his mind grew another, until the ramified families "invented" the notorious thesis about heredity—which, anyway, is never logically worked out.

As a Rougon-Macquart novel, *Drunkard* (*L'Assommoir*) pairs with *Nana*, which might be called the "sequel" to it. This one is about Gervaise (a Macquart), Lantier (a Rougon), and Coupeau (who is neither). The sequel is about Nana, the daughter of Gervaise and Coupeau. But in spite of the tie between them, there could hardly be two more different novels than this pair. The only real link is what *Drunkard* tells us about Nana's childhood. Nana's aunt (Coupeau side), does indeed appear in *Nana*, but only as a lay-figure of lay-figures. Both books contain also a lot about drinking and debauch—but in very different spheres. *Drunkard*, published in 1877 (*Nana* followed in 1880), was intended by the author to show that Nana's intense sexuality was due to her alcoholic ancestry. But Zola's artistry mastered his thesis. Or else something went very wrong with the genes, for Gervaise's daughter is both beautiful and as strong as a horse.

With the book thus defined as a very individual work, existing entirely in its own right—let us turn to the story. Colombe's Bar is the place where, when Lantier has abandoned his young washerwoman mistress with two children, Coupeau the tinsmith plights his troth with her. After that, however, the bar is relegated to a dim background. It plays no personal part. It is merely a symbol. It stands for strong liquor and the menace of alcoholism.

In its relation to the working class of the suburb in which the action takes place, the bar plays the part of the gin-palaces of England in the eighteenth and early nineteenth centuries. To make this clear, not only in the initial scene, but later, whenever the bar is mentioned (as a symbol), we have a reference to what goes on in the backyard. Here, attracting the customers, the stills are to be seen working, day in, day out, brewing the poison. By this liquor, Lantier's decency has been destroyed. In its atmosphere, Coupeau woos Gervaise. Here the whole company of characters get most of their liquor—for instance, for Gervaise's wedding-breakfast. Here, towards the end of the book, Coupeau drinks his soul away. But the establishment as such has no personality. It is not the bar, it is old Colombe's bad alcohol, that is all-important.

But is it? It would be so easy to see in *Drunkard* a Victorian moral story of the rise of a working-class household and its fall through drink. As long as Coupeau plied his trade, and highly skilled, industrious, thrifty Gervaise built up her business, this family rose in the world, but once it had reached a certain point of prosperity it fell to a lower level than it had ever known before. But through Colombe's bar? Oh no. Far from it. The matter is much more complex. Much more, indeed, like real life. Guided by genius, the "moral" story suffered a sea-change into a subtle, rich study of flaws in character, of the failure of otherwise potentially decent people to stand up to the strains put upon them by harsh social conditions.

In other words, *Drunkard* is not a *roman-à-thèse*, but an incomparably greater achievement, a combination of character study and social realism. For it is not drink that ruins Coupeau, but the sad fact that Gervaise is unable to provide the right domestic background when the man is recovering from his accident. Because she is a bad wife? No; because she is too kind and devoted.

We see this flaw in her at the outset, presented as a virtue. When Lantier has abandoned her, and she might have welcomed Coupeau's support, she is slow to accept him, even as a husband. She would rather not be "a burden" to him. And when, later, she gives birth to Nana, she goes on cooking her husband's dinner to the very last moment, eventually collapsing, to produce the babe on the living-room floor—and she is on her feet again at domestic chores a few days later. When Coupeau falls from a roof and is nearly killed, she insists on having him (now more or less abandoned by the doctors) at home, and with tireless devotion she conjures life back into him.

But one can be too good. Raised to excess, this virtue is indeed a vice. Having cured Coupeau, Gervaise proceeds to spoil him. There is the fatal, ironic flaw. When Coupeau is convalescent, Gervaise fails to provide him with that harsh, homely, wifely criticism which a loved man, when sick, will often need to put him on his feet again and get him back to work.

This same sort of character flaw is later seen working the other way round. For all his weakness, Coupeau, as the male, has always been to Gervaise a sort of moral pillar of support. With him at her side, when he was working cheerfully, steadily, skilfully, she was well able to build up a flourishing laundry business of her own. But when Coupeau begins to seek stimulus not in his craft, but in drink, Gervaise is doomed to go to pieces too. The mutual weakness of this couple drags them down. The bar is only the environment. They fail, jointly, to master it. The failure begins not with alcoholism, but with a physical accident and a woman's maternal love for her man. (After all, as one of Zola's characters remarks, Bismarck was a hard drinker. But he did not go to pieces.)

Drunkard is a story of the grandeur and horror of the slums which Dickens, with his tendency towards sentimentality, could never have achieved. It would perhaps be too horrible, were it not for another lovely feature in which it is supreme. This is the rich gallery of characters which it offers us, and the mastery with which twice Zola assembles them in great set pieces. The wedding, including the triumphal visit of the wedding-guests to the Louvre, is one huge canvas. The celebration of Gervaise's birthday in the heyday of her success is another.

These scenes remind us sharply of Zola's close association with the leading painters of his day. To an unusual extent, he thought easily in terms of shapes and colours, grouped in harmonious panoramas. There is in these descriptions, apart from the broad, yet subtle humour and the understanding of the mentality of simple people still primitive enough to enjoy a real blow-out, then to drink and squabble without any apparent loss of self-respect, a remarkable parallel to the achievement of that greatest of all descriptive painters, Brueghel.

This is a special literary form of considerable interest. More than good narration of interesting, colourful detail is required. There must be disposal of the various shapes and colours in such a way that they form a pattern of their own, a purely formal pattern, so that wherever the eye or ear rests, one is equally delighted and equally amazed.

It is not many who have achieved this quality with real formal grace. It is first found, in embryo form, in Apuleius's *Golden Ass*. It occurs in Rabelais. Flaubert achieved it in *Madame Bovary*, but, for all his efforts, Victor Hugo never really brought it off. Tolstoy succeeded more than once, but neither Dostoyevsky nor Turgeniev. And nobody, I suggest, wrote set pieces with such diversity of character and such formal colour as Zola. *Drunkard* deserves room on every household's bookshelves, if for this achievement alone

ALEC BROWN

CHAPTER ONE

GERVAISE waited up for Lantier till two o'clock in the morning.
Then, chilly from having stayed by the open window in her
white bodice, she threw herself in a heap across the bed,
feverish and her cheeks wet with tears. For a week past, as
soon as they had come out of the "Veau à Deux Têtes", where
they took their meals, he had packed her off to bed with the
children; and he would come back later on in the night,
saying that he had been looking for work. That evening, while
she was watching for him, she thought she had seen him go
into the ball of the Grand-Balcon, whose ten glaring windows
lit up the black line of the outer boulevards like a sheet of
flame; and behind him she had seen little Adèle, the metal-
polisher who dined at their restaurant, walking five or six
yards away, her hands swinging limply, as if she had just
quitted his arm, so as not to go together under the too-vivid
light of the lamps at the door,

When Gervaise awoke, about five, stiff and aching, she
burst into sobs. Lantier had not come in. It was the first time
that he had stayed out all night. She remained sitting on the
edge of the bed, under the strip of faded chintz which hung
from the bedhead fastened to the ceiling by a piece of string.
And slowly, her eyes clouded with tears, she looked all round
the wretched little lodging-house room, with its walnut chest
of drawers, in which one of the drawers was wanting, its three
cane-bottom chairs, and its greasy little table, on which stood
a dilapidated water jug. Besides that, they had had to put in an
iron bedstead for the children, and the bedstead filled up
two-thirds of the room, and blocked up the chest of drawers as
well. Gervaise and Lantier's trunk, wide open in a corner,
stretched out its empty sides, an old man's hat at the bottom
stowed away under dirty shirts and socks; while, along the
walls, on the backs of the chairs, hung a tattered shawl, a pair
of trousers clotted with mud, old clothes too bad even for the
old clothes' dealer. In the middle of the chimney-piece,
between two ill-matching zinc candlesticks, there was a
bundle of pawn-tickets, delicately pink-coloured. It was the

best room of the hotel, the first floor room, looking on the street.

The two children were fast asleep, with their heads on the same pillow. Claude, who was eight years old, drew in long breaths, his little hands outside the quilt, while Etienne, who was only four, smiled in his sleep, one arm round the neck of his brother. As the mother's glance rested on the children, she burst out sobbing afresh, then pressed a handkerchief to her mouth to stifle the little sobs that she could not keep down. And bare-footed as she was, without thinking of putting on her slippers again, she went back to her post by the window, to her night watch, her scrutiny of the distant pavements.

The hotel was on the Boulevard de la Chapelle, to the left of the Barrière Poissonière. It was a tumble-down two-storeyed building, painted dull red up to the second storey, with shutters that the rains had soaked rotten. Underneath a lamp with cracked glass, between the two windows, "Hôtel Boncœur, Proprietor: Marsouiller", could just be made out in big yellow letters, from which bits of plaster had fallen away. Finding the lamp in her way, Gervaise stood upright, still holding the handkerchief to her lips. She looked to the right, in the direction of the Boulevard de Rochechouart, where groups of slaughterers stood about before the slaughter-houses, their aprons all over blood; and the fresh breeze brought up from time to time a grim stench of slaughtered beasts. She looked to the left, following the long trail of the avenue, which came to an end, almost opposite, at the white mass of the Lariboisière hospital, then in course of construction. Slowly, from end to end of the horizon, she followed the city wall, behind which she had sometimes heard by night the cries of people being murdered; and she peered into the lonely angles, the dark corners, black with slime and filth, fearing lest she might come upon the body of Lantier—a knife through his belly. When she raised her eyes above this grey interminable wall, framing in the city with a strip of desert, she saw a broad glimmer, a dusty cloud of sunlight, out of which rose the hum of Paris in the early dawn. But her eyes turned back instinctively to the Boulevard Poissonnière; she leaned out, dizzy with the unending flood that passed between the two squat sheds of the excise—men, beasts, and carts, coming down from the heights of Montmartre and La Chapelle. There was a trampling, as of a herd in motion, a concourse of people, now and then scattered over the roadway by a sudden block, an endless file of workmen going to their work, their tools on their back, their bread under their arm; and the whole pack plunged and re-plunged, ceaselessly, into Paris. When Gervaise thought she recognized Lantier in the midst of the crowd, she leant further out of the window, at the risk of falling over; then she pressed her handkerchief tighter over her mouth, as if to keep down her sorrow.

A gay young voice behind her called her away from the window.

"Your good man not in, Madame Lantier?"

"No, Monsieur Coupeau," she replied, trying to smile.

It was a tinsmith who had a ten-franc room at the top of the house. He had his bag slung over his shoulders. Finding the key in the door, he had walked right in, with friendly familiarity.

"You see," he went on, "I am working over yonder, at the hospital. What a May! It's stinging this morning!"

And he looked at Gervaise's face, red with crying. When he saw that the bed had not been slept in, he shook his head gravely; then he came up to where the children lay sleeping like little rosy cherubs, and, lowering his voice:

"So the good man is on the loose, eh? Don't you distress yourself about that, Madame Lantier. He is so taken up with politics; only the other day, when they were voting for Eugène Sue—a good sort, I believe—he went nearly off his head. Very likely he has been spending the night with his friends abusing that brute of a Bonaparte."

"No, no," she murmured, with an effort, "it is not what you think. I know where Lantier is. We have our troubles like everybody else."

Coupeau screwed up his eyes, to show that he was not taken in. And he went off, after offering to go and fetch the milk if she did not wish to go out: she was a fine handsome woman, and she could count on him whenever she was in difficulties. As soon as he had gone, Gervaise returned to the window.

At the barrier, in the chill of the morning, that trampling as of a herd in motion, still went on. The fitters were recognizable by their blue linen jackets, the masons by their white canvas trousers, the house-painters by their great coats, under which showed long blouses. At that distance the crowd had a chalky appearance, a neutral tint, made up chiefly of faded blue and dingy grey. From time to time a workman would stand still to light his pipe, whilst all around him the others

went on mechanically, without a laugh, without a word to
one another, their cheeks pale and cadaverous, their eyes
fixed on Paris, which swallowed them up, one by one, down the
gaping mouth of the Rue du Faubourg-Poisonnière. But at
both corners of the Rue des Poissonnières, outside two wine
shops that were just taking down their shutters, some would
slacken pace; and, before entering, would stand at the edge
of the pavement, with a sidelong look at Paris, their arms
hanging limply, already given over to a day's idleness. Before
the bars, groups of men stood one another drinks, without
noticing how the time went; crowding upon one another, spitting, coughing, tipping the spirit down.

Gervaise had her eye fixed on Père Colombe's, on the left
of the street, where she thought she had seen Lantier, when a
fat woman in an apron, without a bonnet, called to her from
the middle of the road:

"I say, Madame Lantier, you're up early today!"

Gervaise leaned out.

"Ah! it's you, Madame Boche. Oh, I have a heap of things
to get through today."

"That's it, that's it, things don't do themselves, do they?"

And a conversation began, from window to pavement.
Madame Boche was the *concierge* of the house in which the
restaurant of the "Veau à Deux Têtes" occupied the ground
floor. Gervaise had several times waited for Lantier in her
little room, so as not to have to sit down by herself at table,
among all the men who took their meals there. The *concierge*
mentioned that she was going just across the road, to the Rue
de la Charbonnière, in order to find one of the workpeople,
who was sure not to be up yet, from whom her husband could
not get back a frock-coat he had sent him to mend. Then she
told how one of her lodgers had come in with a woman, the
night before, and had kept everybody awake till three o'clock
in the morning. But all the while, as she tattled away, she
peered at the young woman with an air of extreme curiosity;
and she seemed to have planted herself under the window with
the sole purpose of finding out about things.

"Is Monsieur Lantier still in bed?" she enquired abruptly.

"Yes, he is asleep," replied Gervaise, unable to keep herself
from blushing.

Madame Boche saw the tears that started to her eyes, and,
no doubt satisfied in her own mind, she was going off saying
how damned lazy men were, when she turned back to shout:

is today, isn't it, that you go to the wash-house? I have
me things to get washed; I'll keep you a place by me, and
we'll have a good talk."

Then, as if seized with a sudden pity:

"You poor dear, you'd better not stay there any longer,
you'll make yourself ill! Why, you are quite blue with the
cold!"

Gervaise remained obstinately at the window for two mortal
hours longer, till it was eight o'clock. The shops had opened.
The flood of blouses coming down the hill had ceased; and
only a few laggards hurried past the barrier with great strides.
In the wine-shops the same men, still standing, went on
drinking, coughing, and spitting. The workmen had been
succeeded by the work-girls, the metal-polishers, the milliners,
the florists, trotting along the outer boulevards in their thin
frocks; going in companies of three or four, chatting gaily,
with little laughs and bright glances to right and left; at long
intervals, one, all by herself, thin, pale, and grave, followed along
the city wall, avoiding the filth in the gutters. Then the black-
coated workers went by, blowing on their fingers, eating their
pennyworth of bread as they came along; young thin fellows
in coats too short for them, their eyes still heavy with sleep;
little old men who went swaying on their feet, with sallow
faces, exhausted by the long office hours, looking at their
watches in order to time themselves to a few seconds. The
boulevards wore their peaceful morning aspect; the people of
the neighbourhood were out sunning themselves; the mothers,
bare-headed, and in dirty skirts, dandled their babies, changing
their nappies on the benches; a whole swarm of brats, with
dirty noses, and unbuttoned clothes, hustled and dragged each
other about on the ground, with squealing, crying, and
laughter. Then Gervaise felt her head and heart grow dizzy,
as if all hope were at an end; it seemed to her that all was over
and done, that Lantier would never come back any more. Her
eyes wandered idly from the old slaughter-houses, black with
blood and stench, to the new, glaring hospital, showing,
through the gaping holes of its rows of windows, the
empty wards where death was to reap. Over against her,
behind the wall, the dazzling sky, the sunrise broadening
above the immense awakening of Paris, blinded her with its
light.

She was sitting quietly on a chair, her hands in her lap, the
tears at an end now, when Lantier entered composedly.

"It's you! it's you!" she cried, and would have thrown
arms round his neck.

"Yes, it's me; what of that?" he answered. "None of that
nonsense, if you please."

He pushed her aside; then, with an ill-tempered jerk, he
flung his soft felt hat upon the chest of drawers. He was a
young man of twenty-six, short, dark, and good-looking, with
a thin moustache that he was always twisting with a mechanical movement of the hand. He had on a workman's
canvas trousers, an old spotted frock-coat drawn in at the
waist, and he spoke with a very pronounced Provençal
accent.

Gervaise relapsing on her chair, broke into gentle complaints, in broken phrases.

"I couldn't sleep a wink. I thought something must have
happened. Where were you? Where did you spend the night?
Oh, for God's sake, don't begin over again, or I shall go mad!
Tell me, Auguste, where were you?"

"Where I had reason to be, naturally," said he, with a shrug
of the shoulders. "At eight o'clock I was at La Glacière, where
I went to see that friend of mine who is going to do the
fittings in a hat factory. I stayed on late. Then I thought I had
better stay the night. Besides, you know I don't like being
spied on. Let me be!"

The young woman began to sob again. The sound of
voices, the hasty movements of Lantier, upsetting the chairs
had awakened the children. They sat up, half-naked, pushing
back their hair with their little hands; and hearing their
mother crying, they set up a terrible howl, crying too with
their only half-opened eyes.

"Now we're off!" cried Lantier, in a rage. "I give you
warning, I'll hook it again pretty quick, and for good and all,
this time. You will *not* be quiet? Good-bye, then, I am going
back where I came from."

And he took up his hat from the chest of drawers. But
Gervaise sprang forward, stammering out:

"No, no!"

And she stifled the little ones' tears with caresses, kissing
their hair, and putting them back to bed with tender words.
Pacified in a minute, they began to laugh, and amused
themselves by pinching one another. Meanwhile the father,
without taking off his boots, had thrown himself on the bed
with an air of exhaustion, his face haggard after a sleepless

night. He did not go to sleep, but lay with his eyes wide open, looking all round the room.

"I do call this nice," he muttered.

Then, looking at Gervaise for an instant, he added, maliciously:

"So you've given up washing your mug, have you?"

Gervaise was only twenty-two. She was tall, slight, with thin features, already somewhat sharpened by the hardships of her life. With her hair uncombed, her slippered feet, shivering in her white bodice, on which the furniture had left some of its dust and grease, she seemed ten years older for the hours of anguish and tears that she had just passed through. Lantier's words drew her out of her frightened and resigned attitude.

"You are not fair," she said, emphatically. "You know very well that I do all I can. It is not my fault if we have come down to this. I should like to see you, with the two children, in a room where there is not even a stove to get hot water. It would have been much better when you came to Paris, instead of wasting your money, if you had set us up at once, as you promised."

"Look here!" he cried, "you helped to fritter the brass away, didn't you? You needn't go back on it all now, it's all very fine for you to grumble if we had a decent time."

Not seeming to hear him, she went on:

"Yes, if we stick at it, we may yet be able to pull through. Yesterday evening I saw Madame Fauconnier, the laundress of the Rue Neuve; she will take me on Monday. If you hit it off with your friend at La Glacière, the tide will turn in less than six months; we can get together some things, and find a corner somewhere where we shall have a home of our own. Oh, but we must work and work!"

Lantier turned over in bed, with an air of boredom. At that Gervaise burst out:

"Yes, that's it; you'll never die of hard work, any way. You're puffed up with ambition, you want to dress like a gentleman, and go about with your whores in silks. So you don't think I look well enough, now you've made me put all my dresses in pawn? Look here, Auguste, I didn't mean to say anything to you about it, not yet, but I know very well where you spent the night; I saw you go into the Grand-Balcon with that trollop Adèle. Oh, you've a nice eye for them. She's clean, she is. A nice one, that. She may well give herself lady-like airs. She has gone to bed with all the restaurant!''

With a bound Lantier sprang up from the bed. His eyes shone black as ink out of the sallowness of his face. Rage, in this little man, woke a very tempest.

"Yes, with all the restaurant," the young woman repeated. "Madame Boche is going to give her the sack, her and her great lout of a sister, because there is always a queue of men on the staircase."

Lantier lifted his clenched fists; then, resisting his inclination to strike her, he seized her by the arms, shook her violently, and threw her back upon the children's bed. The children began to cry once more. Lantier lay down again, muttering sullenly, with the air of a man who is taking a resolution which he has long hesitated to take.

"You don't know what you've done for yourself now, Gervaise. You'll find out you have made a mistake."

The children sobbed, and the mother, doubled up on the edge of the bed, held them both in her arms, saying over and over again, monotonously:

"Ah, if it were not for you, my little ones! If it were not for you! If it were not for you!"

Quietly stretched out at his length, his eyes fixed on the strip of faded chintz above him, Lantier paid no heed, absorbed in one idea. He lay there for almost an hour, without giving way to the fatigue that weighed down his eyelids. When he turned round on one elbow, his face set and determined, Gervaise had finished tidying the room. She had washed and dressed the children, and was now making their bed. He watched her sweeping up, dusting the furniture: the room still remained dark and dismal, with its smoky ceiling, its wall-paper half-unstuck with the damp, its three rickety chairs and chest of drawers, on which the dirt stuck hard, and went out in long streaks under the duster. Then, when she pinned up her hair, and began to wash herself before the little round looking-glass hanging from the hook of the window, which served him for shaving-glass, he seemed to be taking note of her bare arms and neck, all that he could see of her, as if he were making a mental comparison. And he made a dissatisfied movement of the lips. Gervaise limped with the right leg, but it was only noticeable when she was very tired, and let herself go. That morning, worn out by the fatigues of the night, she dragged her leg, and leant on the wall.

There was silence; not a word more had been spoken. He, on his part, seemed to be waiting. She, on hers, bustled about, trying to keep an indifferent countenance. As she made up into a bundle the dirty clothes thrown in the corner behind the trunk, he opened his lips at last, to ask her:

"What are you doing? Where are you going?"

At first she made no answer. Then, when he had repeated his question angrily, she replied:

"Can't you see? I am going to the wash. I can't have the children living in a pig-sty."

She picked up two or three handkerchiefs. Then, after another silence, he went on:

"Have you any money?"

She stood upright, and looked him in the face, still holding the children's dirty shirts in her hand.

"Money? Where do you suppose I have stolen it, then? You know quite well that I raised three francs yesterday on my black skirt. We had dinner on that twice, and fancy cooked meats soon use it up. No, I should think not, I've no money. I have four coppers for the wash-house. I don't earn it like some women do."

He took no notice of the allusion, but got up and looked carefully over the few odds and ends of clothing about the room. He took up the pair of trousers and the shawl, opened the chest of drawers, and took out a night-dress and two chemises; then he tossed the bundle into Gervaise's arms.

"Here, take that; go and pop it."

"Perhaps you would like me to take the children, too? Very handy that would be, if you could raise cash on the children!"

Nevertheless, she took the things to the pawn. She came back after half an hour and put a five-franc coin on the chimney-piece, adding the pawn-ticket to the others between the two candlesticks.

"That's all they would give," she said. "I wanted six francs, but it couldn't be got. They don't mean to ruin themselves. And there are always plenty of people waiting."

Lantier did not take the five-franc piece at once. He would have liked her to have brought some smaller change, so that he might leave her something. But he put the coin in his pocket as soon as he saw on the chest of drawers a bit of ham in a piece of paper, a scrap of bread with it.

'I didn't go for the milk," Gervaise explained, "because

we owe them a week's money. But I shall be back early, and you can fetch some bread and chops while I am out. Get a bottle of wine, too."

He made no objection, and peace seemed to have been restored. The young woman went on picking up the dirty clothes; but when she was about to take Lantier's shirts and socks from the bottom of the trunk, he called to her to leave them.

"Leave them alone, do you hear? I won't have it."

"Won't have what?" she said, looking up. "You surely don't intend to put on those beastly things again? You must have them washed."

And she looked at him uneasily, finding the same hard expression on the fellow's handsome face, the expression of one whose mind is fully made up. He grew angry, tore the things from her hands, and flung them back into the trunk.

"Blast you! will you do what I tell you for once—when I tell you that I won't have it?"

"But why?" she said, growing pale, as a sudden suspicion flashed across her mind. "You don't want your shirts now, you are not going away anywhere. What difference does it make to you if I take them?"

He hesitated for a moment, put out by the fixity of her gaze.

"Why—why?" he stammered. "Confound it! you go about saying that you keep me, that you do washing and mending. Well, I won't stand it—there! You attend to your business, and I'll attend to mine. Washerwomen don't work for dogs."

She entreated him, declaring that she had never made a single complaint; but he banged the trunk, sat down upon it, and shouted in her face, "No!" He was master of his own belongings! Then, to avoid the looks with which she followed him, he went back and lay down once more on the bed, saying that he was sleepy, and she need not make any more row. And this time he seemed to go to sleep.

Gervaise stood for a moment undecided. She was half inclined to kick the bundle of clothes into a corner, and sit down and do some sewing. Lantier's regular breathing at last reassured her. She took the dolly of blue and the bit of soap left over from her last washing; and going over to the children, who were quietly playing with old corks in front of the window, she kissed them, and whispered:

"Be good now, and don't make a noise. Papa is asleep."

When she left the room, nothing was to be heard in the

still silence but the subdued laughter of Claude and Étienne. It was ten o'clock. A ray of sunlight entered through the half open window.

On the boulevard Gervaise turned to the left and followed the Rue Neuve de la Goutte-d'Or. As she passed before Madame Fauconnier's shop, she greeted her with a little nod. The wash-house was situated half-way up the street, at the point where the road began to ascend. Above a flat block of building, three enormous reservoirs, cylinders of zinc strongly clamped with iron, displayed their grey bulk; while behind them rose the drying-room, a very lofty second storey, closed on all sides by shutters with thin laths, through which the air passed freely, and through which one could see the linen hung up to dry on brass wires. To the right of the reservoirs the straight funnel of the steam-boiler puffed out jets of white smoke with a strong and regular respiration. Gervaise, without picking up her skirts, like one accustomed to puddles, made her way through the door blocked with jars of bleach. She knew the overseer of the place, a little delicate woman with sore eyes, who sat, in a compartment framed in with glass, the registers before her, blocks of soap on shelves, cakes of blue in bowls, and pound packets of carbonate of soda; and in passing she asked for her bat and her brush, which she had left there in charge at her last washing. Then, having taken her number, she went in.

It was an immense flat-roofed shed, the beams all showing, with cast iron pillars, and large windows. A wan light from without mingled freely with the hot steam that hung like a milky-coloured fog. Smoke rose from certain corners, and spread in a bluish mist, obscuring the far distance. There was a heavy dampness in the air, smelling of soap, a dull, moist, unchanging smell; and from time to time the stronger odour of the bleach made itself felt. On each side of the passage which ran down the centre there were files of women, their arms bare to the shoulder, their necks bare, their petticoats hitched up, showing coloured stockings and thick laced boots. They pounded away furiously, laughed, leaned back to shout out a word in the general hubbub, bent over their tubs; foul-mouthed, brutal, voluble, dripping with water, their flesh red and steaming. Round them and under them water flowed abundantly, buckets of hot water carried and emptied at one splash, taps of cold water streaming down from high up, soap-suds flying, wrung-up clothes dripping, the pools in which they paddled running off in little rivulets along the sloping tiles. And amidst all the cries, the rhythmical strokes, the murmur of rain, the mutterings of storm choked back under the steaming roof, the steam-boiler on the right, pearled white with dew, panted and snorted unceasingly, with its dancing fly-wheel that seemed to regulate the enormous uproar.

Meanwhile Gervaise made her way slowly down the passage looking to right and left. She carried her bundle of clothes on her arm, her hip a little raised, limping more than ever, in the midst of all this going and coming of women hustling her.

"Hi! this way, my dear!" cried the loud voice of Madame Boche.

When the young woman had made her way up, right at the end on the left-hand side, the *concierge* began to talk in short jerks, while she went on with her work of rubbing a sock with great vehemence.

"Here's your place, I have kept it for you. Oh, mine won't take me long. Boche scarcely dirties his things at all. You won't be long either, will you? It's quite a little bundle. We can get done by twelve, and then we can go and have dinner. I used to give my things to a laundress in the Rue Poulet; but she wore them all to shreds with her washing powder and her brushes. So now I do it myself. You gain every way. There's only the price of the soap. I say, you ought to have put those shirts to soak. Those little brats—my word! they have soot on their backsides."

Gervaise undid her bundle, and spread out the little shirts; and when Madame Boche advised her to get a bucket of lye-wash she answered:

"Oh, no! hot water will do. I'm quite accustomed to the work.'

She picked out the linen, and put the coloured things on one side. Then, having filled her tub with four bucketfuls of cold water from the tap behind her, she plunged into it the heap of white linen; and, raising her skirt and holding it between her legs, she got into a box, standing on end, which reached to her waist.

"You're quite accustomed to it, you say?" repeated Madame Boche. "You used to be a laundress in your home country, didn't you, my dear?"

Gervaise turned up her sleeves, showing her young arms, the arms of a blonde, a little rosy at the elbows, and began to get out the dirt from her linen. She spread out a shirt on the flat washing-board before her, worn and whitened by the action of the water; she soaped it, turned it, rubbed it on the other side. Before answering, she seized the bat, and began to pound away, shouting her words, and punctuating them with heavy, regular strokes.

"Yes—yes—laundress—when I was ten—twelve years ago. We used to go down to the river. Better air than here. You ought to see it; there was a nice corner under the trees—clear running water. You know—at Plassans. Don't you know Plassans, near Marseilles?"

"Well, you are tough all right!" cried Madame Boche, astonished at the vigour of the strokes. "Strong as a horse she is, with her little lady-like arms!"

The conversation went on, in loud tones. Sometimes the *concierge*, obliged to stoop over, did not catch what was said. All the linen was beaten out, and Gervaise replunged it into the tub, taking it out piece by piece, to rub it over with soap for the second time, and scrub it. She held it with one hand on the washing-board; with the other, in which she had the scrubbing-brush, she drew from the linen a dirty froth which fell slobbering to the ground. Then, as the brushes did not make much noise, they drew closer together, and talked over more private affairs.

"No, we are not married," Gervaise went on. "I don't hide the fact. I shouldn't altogether relish the idea of being Lantier's wife. If it were not for the children . . . I was fourteen and he eighteen when we had our first. The other came four years later. It was the usual story, you know. I wasn't happy at home; old Macquart would as soon kick me as look at me. Like that, I tell you, one looks for a bit of fun outside. We might have got married, but I don't know—our parents didn't care about it."

She shook her hands, all red, under the soap-suds.

"The Paris water is damned hard, isn't it?" she said.

Madame Boche went on with her washing very slowly now. She kept stopping and resoaping the things, so as to be able to stay on and find out the whole story, which she had been longing to learn for the last fortnight. Her mouth, in her great fat face, stood half open; her bulging eyes shone with curiosity. She thought, and she was proud of having guessed it:

"The child is too talkative. There has been a squabble."

Then she said aloud:

"He isn't nice to you, then?"

"Don't talk to me about it" replied Gervaise; "he used to be as nice as possible down there, but since we came to Paris I can't make him out. I must tell you that his mother died last year, leaving him something, about seventeen hundred francs. Then he would go to Paris. And as old Macquart still gave me nothing but blows, without rhyme or reason, I agreed to come with him; and we came up with the two children. He was going to set me up as a laundress, and work at his own business as a hatter. We should have been very comfortable. But, you see, Lantier is so uppish, and he's such a spendthrift; never thinks of anything but his own amusement; that's all he's good for! We put up first at the Hôtel Montmartre, Rue Montmartre. And that meant dinners, and cabs, and theatres, a gold watch for him, a silk dress for me; for he's not a bad sort when he has money. You understand, a regular flare-up, and then at the end of two months we were simply cleaned out. Then we had to come and put up at the Hôtel Boncœur, and this cursed existence began."

She stopped, with a choking sensation at her throat, scarcely able to keep back the tears. She had finished scrubbing the clothes.

"I must go and get some hot water," she murmured.

But Madame Boche, very much put out by this break in her confidences, called to the attendant who was passing:

"Charles, be a good fellow and fetch some hot water for this lady; she is in a hurry."

The boy took the bucket, and brought it back full. Gervaise paid; it was a sou the bucket. She poured the hot water into the tub, and gave the clothes a last soaping between her hands, bending over the washing-board in the midst of the steam that left threads of grey smoke in her blonde hair.

"Here, have some soda; I have some left," said the *concierge*, obligingly.

And she emptied into Gervaise's tub what remained at the bottom of a little bag of carbonate of soda, which she had brought with her. She offered her some bleaching solution, but the young woman declined it; it was only good for grease and wine stains.

"I fancied he was a little inclined to be gay," Madame Boche went on, returning to the subject of Lantier, without naming him.

Gervaise, doubled right over, her hands buried and entangled in the clothes, merely shook her head.

"Yes, yes," continued the other, "I noticed several little things . . ."

But she added hastily, as Gervaise raised herself suddenly up, quite pale, and looking straight at her:

"Oh! no, I don't really know anything. He only means it in fun, I know, that is all. The two girls who lodge with us, for instance—Adèle and Virginie, you know them? Well, he fools about with them a bit; but no more than that, I'm sure."

The young woman, rigid before her, her face bathed in sweat, her arms dripping, looked her straight in the face with a fixed and steady stare. Then the *concierge* fired up, and struck her chest with her clenched fist, giving her word of honour. She cried:

"I know nothing—there—I assure you!"

Then calming herself, she added sweetly, speaking as one does to a person from whom it is better to hide the truth:

"For my part, I think he looks quite straightforward. He'll marry you, my dear, I am certain."

Gervaise wiped her forehead with her wet hand. Then she drew another piece of clothes out of the water, shaking her head once more. Both were silent for a few moments. All around them the wash-house had grown quiet. Eleven o'clock struck. The greater part of the washers, crouching on one leg at the edge of their tubs, a small bottle of wine uncorked at their feet, were eating sausages sandwiched into pieces of bread. But those who had to get back to their families hurried on with their work, glancing at the clock suspended above the bureau.

The sound of a bat was heard now and again, at long intervals, amid the subdued laughs, the conversations impeded by the greedy snapping of jaws; whilst the steam boiler, going on without rest or respite, seemed to raise its voice, vibrating, snorting, filling the huge building. But not a single woman noticed it; it was like the very breath of the place itself, an ardent breath drawing up into itself, under the beams of the roof, the eternal cloud of steam. The heat became intolerable; rays of sunlight entered on the left through the high windows, illuminating the steaming mists with coloured streaks, delicately rose-grey and grey-blue. There were loud complaints and Charles the attendant went from window to window, pulling down the coarse canvas blinds; then he crossed to the other side, the shady side, and opened the top of the casements. There was a general applause, a clapping of hands; a gross hilarity reigned. Soon the last strokes of the bat died away. The washers, with their mouths full, made only a motion now and again with the clasp-knives that they held open in their hands. The silence became so profound that the scraping of the stoker's shovel, as it shovelled the coal into the furnace, could be heard distinctly at the other end of the building.

Meanwhile Gervaise went on washing the coloured things in the hot water, thick with soap, which she had not thrown away. When she had finished, she went over to a trestle, and threw the things one after another across it, leaving little bluish pools on the ground. And she began to wring them out. Behind her the cold-water tap ran into a huge tub fastened to the ground, and crossed by two wooden bars on which to place the linen. Above, in the air, there were two other bars on which linen was put to finish dripping.

"There now, that's nearly finished, and a good job too," said Madame Boche. "I'll stop and help you to wring out your things."

"Oh, you needn't, thanks very much," replied the young woman, kneading the coloured things in her hands, and dipping them into the fresh water. "If I had sheets to do, I wouldn't say no."

But after all she had to accept the *concierge's* aid. They were both wringing out a petticoat, one at each end, a drab woollen stuff, badly dyed, out of which ran a yellowish stream, when Madame Boche cried out:

"Hallo, there's big Virginie! What is she coming here to wash for, I wonder, with her two or three rags in a handkerchief?"

Gervaise raised her head sharply. Virginie was a girl of her own age, taller than herself, dark, pretty, despite her rather long face. She had on an old black dress with flounces, a red ribbon at her neck; and her hair was carefully done, the chignon confined in a net of blue chenille. For a moment, as she came down the central aisle, she blinked her eyelids, as if she were looking for someone; then, seeing Gervaise, she came close past her, stiff and insolent, swaying her body as she walked, and installed herself in the same row, five tubs away.

"There's a notion!" Madame Boche went on lowering her voice. "She never soaped a pair of cuffs in her life. A lazy lie-a-bed, I can tell you! A sempstress who can't so much as sew on a button to her boots! She's like her sister, that little scrub of an Adèle, who stays away from the work-room two days out of three. Hasn't father or mother that I know of, lives nobody knows how, and if one liked to tell tales. . . . What is she rubbing? Oh, a petticoat! Frightful; it must have seen something that petticoat!"

Madame Boche evidently wanted to make herself agreeable to Gervaise. The truth was, that she often had a glass with Adèle and Virginie when they had any money. Gervaise made no reply, but went on hurriedly, with feverish hands. She had just been making her blue in a little three-legged tub. She dipped in her linen, stirred it for a minute in the coloured water, which in its reflection had a touch of lake, then, wringing the things tightly, she laid them out on the wooden bars above. While doing this she made a pretence of turning her back on Virginie. But she heard her chuckling, she felt her eyes upon her. Virginie seemed to have come there for the special purpose of annoying her. Presently Gervaise turned; their eyes met, and they looked at each other fixedly.

"Come, come now," murmured Madame Boche. "Don't fly at one another's throats. I assure you it's nothing—nothing. It isn't her!"

At that moment, as Gervaise hung up her last article, there was a roar of laughter at the door of the wash-house.

"Two kids who want mamma," cried Charles.

The women all looked. Gervaise recognized Claude and Étienne. As soon as they saw her they ran towards her through the puddles, the heels of their unlaced shoes clattering on the tiles. Claude, the elder, held his little brother by the hand. The washers, as they passed along, uttered little affectionate cries, seeing the children frightened, yet smiling. And they stood there before their mother, holding one another tight, and lifting their little blonde heads.

"Did papa send you?" asked Gervaise.

But as she stooped to lace up Étienne's shoes she saw on Claude's finger the key of the room, with its metal number.

"What! you have got the key?" she cried, greatly surprised. "Why have you brought it?"

The child, noticing the key, which he had forgotten on his finger, seemed to recollect, and cried in his clear voice:

"Papa is gone away."

"He has gone to get the dinner, you mean; he sent you for me, did he?"

Claude looked at his brother, not knowing what to say. Then he said straight off:

"Papa is gone away. He got out of bed, he put his things in the trunk, he put the trunk in a cab. He is gone away."

Gervaise rose slowly up, her face quite white; she put her hands to her cheeks and her temples, as if her head were splitting. And she could only say over and over again, in a monotonous voice:

"Oh, God! oh, God! oh, God!"

Meanwhile Madame Boche questioned the child in her turn, quite excited at finding herself mixed up with the affair.

"Look here, my child, you must tell us all about it. He locked the door himself, didn't he, and told you to bring the key?"

Then, lowering her voice, she said in Claude's ear:

"Was there a lady in the cab?"

The child was worried for a moment; then began his story over again triumphantly:

"He got out of bed, he put his things in the trunk, he is gone away."

Then, as soon as Madame Boche left off questioning him, he pulled his brother over to the tap, and they both amused themselves by setting the water running.

Gervaise could not cry. She stood choking, leaning up against the tub, her face between her hands. Little shivers ran through her, and now and again she heaved a long sigh, whilst she squeezed her fists harder against her eyes, as if seeking oblivion in the depths of her desolation. She seemed to be falling down, down into a great pit of darkness.

"Well my dear, this *is* a go!" murmured Madame Boche.

"If you only knew—if you only knew!" she said at last in a low voice. "He sent me out this very morning to take my shawl and my chemises to pawn, so that he could pay for that cab."

And she burst out crying. The recollection of that visit to the pawn-shop, bringing out one definite detail of what she had gone through that morning, had set flowing the tears that stuck in her throat. And it seemed to her an abomination, the special drop of gall in her cup of bitterness. The tears ran down her chin, already wet with her hands, and she never even thought of using her handkerchief.

"Hush! hush! be sensible now," said Madame Boche, bustling about her. "People are watching you. To think of making all that fuss for a man! You're still in love with him then, my poor dear? Why, just now you were quite mad with him, and now you're crying your eyes out for the man! Lord! what fools we women are!"

Then she grew quite maternal.

"Such a nice, pretty woman too, if one may say so. You don't mind me telling you everything now, do you? Well, you remember when I saw you at the window, I had my suspicions. What do you think? That very night when Adèle came in I heard a man's footstep with her. So as I was curious I looked up the staircase. The party had got to the second story, but I could recognize Monsieur Lantier's coat. Boche, who was on the look-out this morning, saw him come downstairs quite composedly. He was with Adèle, you understand. Virginie has a gentleman whom she goes home with twice a week. Still, it is not quite decent, all the same, for they have only one room and a recess, and I don't quite see where Virginie could sleep."

She paused for an instant, looked around, and resumed in her big, husky voice:

"She is laughing at you because you are crying, heartless thing! I'd wager her coming here to wash is only a lay. She has packed off the two of them, and come here to tell them how you take the news."

Gervaise lifted her face from her hands, and looked. When she saw Virginie in the midst of two or three women, whispering and staring over at her, she was seized with a sort of mad rage. She made a few steps forward, fumblingly, her arms outstretched, all her limbs a-tremble; and finding a full bucket in her way, she seized it with both hands and emptied it at one splash.

"Get away, you bitch!" cried Virginie, jumping back, so that the water only just wetted her shoes. All the women, consternated at the sight of Gervaise's tears, crowded round to see the fight. Some of them, who were just finishing their meal, mounted on tubs; others ran up, their hands covered with soap-suds. A circle formed.

"Ah, the bitch!" repeated the tall girl. "What's up with her, crack-brain?"

Gervaise, her mouth set, her face working convulsively, made no reply; she had not got into the Paris way of slanging. The other went on:

"Look at her! she served her time in the country, she did.

She was a soldiers' mattress before she was twelve—left a leg behind her at home. It was rotten—that's why."

There was a general laugh. Virginie, seeing her advantage, made two steps forwards, drawing herself up to her full height, and cried louder still:

"Come on then, let's see you and have it out! We don't want you plaguing us here. Don't I know her, the drab! If she had only touched me, I'd have given her a good walloping—you see! What have I done to her? What's the matter, draggle-tail?"

"Don't talk so much," stuttered Gervaise. "You know very well. Where was my husband last night? Be quiet, or I swear I'll strangle you."

"Her husband! oh, that's good! The lady's husband! As if people who waddled like that have husbands! It isn't my fault if he has thrown you over. I haven't stolen him, at any rate. Would you like to search me? Do you want to know the truth? You were simply killing the man. He was much too good for you. But had he got his collar on? Has anyone found the lady's husband? A reward will be given."

There was another laugh. Gervaise simply answered, almost in a whisper:

"You know—all right; you know—all right. It is your sister. I'll strangle her—I will."

"Well, go and lick my sister, then," said Virginie, sniggering. "My sister, if you like! Oh, very likely! my sister cuts a very different figure from you. But what's that to me? Can't I do my washing in peace? Just shut up, do you see; I've had enough of it."

But after having pounded away five or six times with her bat, she returned to the charge, intoxicated with her own abuse. Thrice she finished up, and thrice she began again.

"Well—yes, it was my sister. Will that satisfy you? They're awfully in love with one another. You should see them kissing and cuddling! And so he has thrown you and your bastards over? Nice kids they are, with their snotty faces! You had one off a policeman, didn't you? and you starved three more, so as not to have too much luggage to bring with you. Your Lantier told us all that. Ah, he says nice things of you; he's had quite enough of your old carcase!"

"You slut! you slut! you slut!" shrieked Gervaise, beside herself, and shaking with fury.

She turned, looked down, and finding only the small tub

full of blue, seized it by the legs, and flung the water in Virginie's face.

"The jade! she has spoilt my dress," cried Virginie. One shoulder was simply soaked, and her left hand all over blue. "Wait a minute, you dirty whore!"

And she too seized a bucket, and emptied it over her opponent. Then began a regular battle royal. Both ran to the tubs, seized on the full buckets, and dashed the water at one another, accompanying each deluge with a volley of abuse, in which even Gervaise joined.

"Take that, dirty beast! That got you! That'll cool your arse for you!"

"Ah! the drab! There's for your dirt. That'll wash your face for once in your life."

"Yes, yes, I'll salt you, you kipper!"

"There's another for you! That'll tidy you up for tonight, when you walk the Rue Belhomme!"

Finally they filled the buckets at the taps, and while they waited for them to fill, they still went on hurling abuse at one another. The first few buckets, badly aimed, hardly touched them. But they soon got more expert. Virginie was the first to get one full in the face; the water went in at her neck, streamed down her back and chest, and ran out under her dress. She had not recovered from the shock when another caught her sideways, giving her a sharp slap on the left ear, and soaking her chignon, which unrolled like a cord. Gervaise was hit first in the legs; one bucketful filled her shoes, and squirted half-way up her leg; two others deluged her thighs. And it was soon impossible to tell which strokes took effect. Both were streaming from head to foot, their bodices plastered down on their shoulders, their skirts glued to their waists; they seemed to have shrunk up and stiffened out, they were shivering with cold, and the drops ran out of them on all sides like umbrellas in the rain.

"Don't they look funny!" came one husky voice. All the women were immensely amused. Everyone had drawn back so as not to get splashed; and jokes and applause mingled with the sluicing of water, as the buckets were emptied at random. Great pools formed on the ground, in which the women splashed up to their ankles. Meanwhile Virginie, with a tricky movement, caught up a bucket of boiling water which had been brought for one of her neighbours, and emptied it over Gervaise. There was a cry; everyone thought Gervaise

was scalded. But the boiling water had only slightly caught
her left foot. Frantic with pain, she hurled an empty bucket
with all her force straight at Virginie. It caught her in the
legs and she fell.

All the women cried out together:

"She has broken her leg!"

"Good Lord!—well, but she wanted to scald her alive!"

"She's in the right, after all—if they sneaked away her man."

Madame Boche exclaimed aloud, lifting her hands to
heaven. She had kept at a safe distance, between two tubs;
and the two children, Claude and Étienne, choking with tears
and fright, clung to her dress, with a little ceaseless wail of
"Mamma! Mamma!" half lost in their sobs. When she saw
Virginie on the ground, she rushed forward and caught
Gervaise by the skirt, saying again and again:

"Come now, that's enough. Do give over. My word! you
make my blood run cold. I never saw such a shocking row in
my life."

But she soon drew back, and sought refuge between the two
tubs, with the children. Virginie sprang at the throat of
Gervaise. She squeezed as hard as she could, trying to strangle
her, but Gervaise with a violent effort shook herself free, and
fastened upon the tail of her chignon, as if she would tear it
bodily away. The fight was now in silence, without a word or
cry. They did not wrestle with one another, but aimed straight
for the face, their fingers crooked out, clutching and clawing
at whatever they could seize. The tall girl's red ribbon and
blue chenille hair-net were torn away; her bodice, splitting
at the neck, showed her bare flesh, right along one shoulder;
while the other—one arm, in some unaccountable way, slipped
out of the sleeve of her white bodice—had a rent in her
chemise, which showed a bit of her bare side. Tattered strips
flew in all directions. It was from Gervaise that blood was
first drawn, three long scratches from her mouth along her
chin; and she safeguarded her eyes by shutting them at every
blow, for fear of being blinded. As yet she had drawn no blood
from Virginie. She tried to get at her ears, furious at not being
able to seize them; at last she clutched one of her ear-rings, a
drop of yellow glass; she pulled it clean through the ear;
blood flowed.

"They will kill each other! Separate them—the bitches!"
cried several voices.

The women came closer, some of them urging on the

combatants as if they were bitches fighting; others, more
nervous, turned away their heads, trembling, saying they had
had quite enough, it would certainly make them ill. It was
near coming to a general fight; the two parties declared one
another heartless, not up to anything; bare arms were outstretched; three slaps were heard.

Meanwhile Madame Boche looked about for the attendant.

"Charles! Charles! Where is he?"

She found him in the front row, his arms folded, staring
with all his might. He was a great big bull-necked fellow. He
laughed, chuckling over the bits of bare flesh that he could
see in the two women. The little blonde was as plump as a
quail. It would be a lark if her chemise were torn open.

"See!" he said with a wink, " she has a strawberry under her
arm."

"What! you there!" cried Madame Boche, as she caught
sight of him. "Why don't you help to separate them? You
could do it easily enough."

"No thanks, not for me," he answered composedly. "Get
my eye scratched as I did the other day? That's not what I
come here for; I have plenty else to do. Don't you be frightened.
A little blood-letting will do them good: that'll cool them
down!"

The *concierge* talked of going for the police; but the overseer
of the wash-house, the little delicate woman with sore eyes,
would not hear of it. She repeated several times:

"No, no, I won't have it; it will disgrace the place."

The two women still fought on the ground. Suddenly
Virginie rose to her knees, brandishing in the air a bat that
she had picked up. In a choking voice she screamed:

"I'll give it to you! Bring your dirty things here!"

Gervaise reached out sharply, and seized another bat,
which she held in the air like a club. And she too screamed
hoarsely:

"Ah! you want a good drubbing, do you? I'll make dish-
clouts of you!"

For a moment they remained motionless, crouching
menacingly opposite to one another. Their hair in their eyes,
their chests heaving, covered with dirt and bruises, they
waited their chance, and tried to regain breath. Gervaise
struck the first blow, the bat just touching Virginie's shoulder.
She leant on one side to avoid the return blow, which caught
her lightly on the hip. Then, warming up, they went at it as

if they were beating linen, hard and regularly. When a blow
struck it sounded dully, as if it had fallen in a bucket of water.

By this time no one laughed; some of the women had
moved away, saying the sight made them sick; those who
remained leaned forward, their eyes alight with a cruel glitter,
saying they *were* game—these two lasses. Madame Boche
hurried Claude and Étienne away, and their sobs could be
heard from the other end of the place between the ringing
blows of the bats.

All at once Gervaise uttered a howl. Virginie had caught
her, full force, on her bare arm, just above the elbow; a red
mark appeared, and the flesh swelled up at once. Then she
flung herself on the other, as if she were going to demolish her.

"That's enough! that's enough!" was the cry.

Her face was so awful that no one dared to approach her.
With superhuman strength she seized Virginie by the waist,
doubled her over, and laid her face downwards on the floor;
then, despite her struggles, she tore her skirts sheer off her.
When she came to her drawers, she thrust her hand into the
opening and gave it a great tear, laying bare her naked thighs
and buttocks. Then she raised her bat, and began to pound
away, as she had once done at Plassans, on the banks of the
Viorne, when her mistress was washing the garrison linen. The
wood went thud, with a dull sound, into the white flesh,
leaving a red streak at every blow.

"Oh! oh!" murmured Charles, opening his eyes in blank
amazement.

A few laughs were heard again. But soon the cry "Enough!
enough!" began once more. Gervaise untiring, heard nothing.
She went steadily to work, leaning over, intent on not leaving
a dry inch; set on beating all that flesh through and through,
blasting it with confusion. And in her fierce jollity she
shouted scraps of a washerwoman's song that came into her
mind:

> "Bang! bang! Moll's at the wash,
> Bang! bang! the bat goes squash;
> Bang! bang! get your heart clean,
> Bang! bang! black as a bean."

Then she went on:

"That's for you, and that's for your sister, and that's for
Lantier. When you see them, give them that. Wait a bit; I'm

beginning again. That's for Lantier and that's for your sister, and that's for you.

> "Bang! bang! Moll's at the wash,
> Bang! bang! the bat goes squash."

They tore Virginie bodily out of her hands. The big girl, weeping, shamefaced, and crimson, pulled together her things and took to her heels, utterly conquered. Meanwhile Gervaise slipped her arm back into her sleeve, and fastened up her skirts. Her arm pained her, and she begged Madame Boche to lift her bundle of clothes on her shoulder. The *concierge* told how the fight had gone, how she herself had felt, and wanted to examine her to see if she was all right.

"You must really have something broken. I heard such a blow."

But Gervaise insisted on going. She answered not a word to the condolements, the gushing ovation of the washers who stood all around her in their long, straight aprons. When she had her bundle she made her way to the door, where the children were waiting for her.

"It is two hours, that makes two sous," said the overseer, already re-installed in her glassed compartment.

Why two sous? She could not understand that they were simply asking for the entrance-money. But she put down her two sous. Then, limping badly under the weight of the damp things on her shoulder, herself dripping, her elbow black and blue, her face bleeding, she went her way, dragging at her bare arms Étienne and Claude, who trotted along beside her, their faces still smudged and working with their sobs.

When she had gone, the wash-house returned to its huge monotonous noise, as of a rushing weir. The washers had eaten their bread and drunk their wine, and they pounded away harder than ever, still excited and amused with Gervaise and Virginie's knock-down fight. All along the tubs, over again, there was a furious stir of arms; sharp profiles worked violently up and down like marionettes on hinges, their limbs doubled up, their shoulders awry. There was a general conversation from end to end of the two lines. The sound of voices, of laughter, of broad jokes, struck sharply through the continuous splash of the water. The taps ran over, the buckets spilled at every step, a rivulet made its way underneath the washing-boards. It was the last spurt of the afternoon, the bats went pounding away on the linen. The steam took a reddish tinge in the immense shed, flaked with rays of sunlight, golden motes that the rent in the blinds left a way for. The stifled warmth of soapy odours went up. All at once the shed was filled with a white mist; the huge cover of the boiler went slowly up a toothed rod in the middle, and the gaping aperture of the boiler, embedded in its brick masonry, puffed out clouds of steam, in which one distinguished the sweet savour of potash. Meanwhile, at the sides, the wringing machines worked away; bundles of linen between the cast-iron cylinders were wrung dry with a turn of the wheel, and the great machine, panting and smoking, shook the whole place with the ceaseless activity of its arms of steel.

When Gervaise put foot in the street of the Hôtel Boncœur, tears came into her eyes again. It was a dark and narrow side street, with a gutter along the wall to throw the slops in; and the smell, coming back on her again, recalled the fortnight she had spent with Lantier, a fortnight of misery and squabbling, the remembrance of which at that moment brought a sting of regret. It all seemed to her a piece with her own desolation.

Upstairs she found the room bare, the sunlight striking full in, the window open. And the sunlight, with its sheet of dancing gold, seemed to make the blackened ceiling, the tattered walls, more dismal than ever. There was nothing now on the nail over the chimney-piece but a little kerchief twisted into a knot. The children's bed had been pulled out into the middle of the room, away from the chest of drawers— the drawers all open and empty. Lantier had washed, and had finished up the pomatum, a pennyworth in a playing card; the grease from his hands filled the basin. And he had forgotten nothing. The corner in which the trunk had always stood seemed to Gervaise like a great empty hole. She could not even find the little round looking-glass that hung on the window catch. Then, with a presentiment of what she would find, she looked over the chimney-piece. Lantier had carried off the pawn-tickets; the little packet, delicately pink-coloured, was no longer there, between the two ill-matching candlesticks.

She hung her linen over the back of a chair, and she stood there looking round her, looking at thing after thing, too overcome even to weep. A single sou remained out of the four sous she had put aside for the wash-house. Then, hearing

Étienne and Claude laughing gaily by the window, she crossed over, and put her arms about them, losing sight of the present for a moment as she looked out on the grey road, where, that morning, she had seen the huge awakening of Paris to its toil. At that hour the street flung up a hot and burning shadow above the town behind the city wall. And she was thrown on the street, on that very pavement, with its stifling air, she and her little ones alone; and she looked slowly along the line of the outer boulevards, to right, to left, pausing at each end with a sort of dull terror, feeling as if all her life were to be lived out now there between a slaughter-house and a hospital.

CHAPTER TWO

THREE weeks later, about half-past eleven o'clock on a fine
sunny day, Gervaise and Coupeau were having a glass together at Père Colombe's bar. Coupeau, who was smoking a
cigarette outside, had seen her coming along the street on her
way back from taking home some clothes, and he had insisted
on her coming in. Her big square laundry basket lay on the
ground beside her, behind the little zinc table.

Père Colombe's bar was at the corner of the Rue des
Poissonniers and the Boulevard de Rochechouart. On the
sign was painted, from end to end, in long blue letters, the one
word *Distillery*. At the door, in two half-casks, were planted
some dusty oleanders. The great bar, with its rows of glasses,
its draw-out and its pewter measures, was at the left on
entering; and the big room was decorated all round by great
casks painted bright yellow, varnished, and glittering with
shining hoops and brass taps. Above, on shelves, liqueur and
syrup bottles, all sorts of phials ranged in order, covered the
walls, and in the glass behind the counter one saw reflections
of bright greens, of apple greens, of pale lake. But the curiosity
of the place was further back, on the other side of an oak
barrier, in a covered court, the distilling apparatus, which the
customers could see working; long-necked alembics, "worms"
that sank into the earth, a very witches' brew, at which boozy
workmen were never tired of staring.

At the hour of the midday meal the bar was quite empty.
Père Colombe, a big man of forty, in his shirt-sleeves, was
serving a little girl of twelve, who had asked for four penn'orth
of spirits in a cup. A broad ray of sunlight entered at the door,
warming the floor under foot, always humid with the spittle
of smokers. And, from counter, from cask, from the whole
interior, there rose a liquorish odour, a reek of alcohol, in
which the dancing motes of the sunlight seemed to turn
heavy and grey.

Meanwhile, Coupeau rolled a fresh cigarette. He looked
quite neat, with his working jacket and his little blue canvas cap;
he laughed showing his white teeth. His under lip protruded,

he had rather a snub nose, but his eyes were dark and handsome, and he had a jolly good-humoured expression. His
thick curly hair was brushed right up; his skin, despite his
twenty-six years, had not yet hardened. Over against him,
Gervaise, in her black fustian, and bareheaded, finished
eating her prune, which she held by the stalk with the tips of
her fingers. They were close to the street, at the first of the
four tables ranged along the casks before the counter.

When the tinsmith had lit his cigarette, he put his elbows
on the table, and, leaning forward, looked for a minute,
without speaking, at his neighbour, whose pretty blonde face
had, just then, the milky transparency of fine porcelain. Then,
referring to a matter of which only they two knew, already
much debated, he said quietly, in a low voice:

"Then it is no? You say no?"

"Oh, yes, indeed, Monsieur Coupeau!" replied Gervaise,
composedly, with a smile. "You are surely not going to bring
up that subject here. You said you would behave yourself.
If I had known, I shouldn't have accepted your drink."

He said nothing, merely looked at her, quite close, with a
tender assurance, transported by the corners of her lips, a
pale rose, just moistened, and showing the vivid red of her
mouth when she smiled. She did not draw back, but sat there
quiet and affectionate. After a silence she said:

"You don't really mean it, after all, I am quite old: I have
a big boy of eight. What should we do together?"

"Damn!" murmured Coupeau, with a wink, "what everybody else does!"

She made a gesture of annoyance.

"Ah! if you imagine life's all fun, it is very evident that you
have never had to look after a household. No, Monsieur
Coupeau, I have to look at things seriously. Fooling about is
all very well, but it doesn't mean much after all. How do you
suppose I am to bring up my little ones at that rate? Besides,
you see, my ill luck has been a fine lesson for me. I don't go
in for men again. I'm not easily caught now."

She made the explanation without any air of annoyance,
quite sensibly, quite coldly, as if she had been discussing a
business matter—the reasons why a habit-shirt should not be
starched. She had evidently made up her mind, after long
reflection.

Coupeau repeated tenderly:

"You distress me very much! You distress me very much!"

"Yes, I see it," she replied, "and I am sorry for you, Monsieur Coupeau. You mustn't take it amiss. If I had any inclination that way, it would be with you rather than with anyone else. You seem a good sort, you are always nice with me. We might join together, and get on as best we could. I don't put on any uppish airs; I don't say that that couldn't have happened. Only, what's the use, when I don't feel inclined? I have been at Madame Fauconnier's for the last fortnight. The children are at school, I have work, I am quite content as it is. Well, the best thing seems to be to stay as I am."

And she stooped to take up her basket.

"You make me stop and talk, and they must be waiting for me at Madame's. Come, come, you will find someone else, Monsieur Coupeau, prettier than I am, and without two urchins at her heels."

He looked at the clock set in the mirror, and insisted her sitting down again, saying:

"Wait a bit! it is only thirty-five minutes after eleven. I have five-and-twenty minutes left. You needn't fear I shan't behave: the table is between us! Or do you dislike me so much that you won't have even a little chat with me?"

She put down the basket again, so as not to seem rude, and they had a friendly talk. She had had her meal before taking out the clothes; he had hurried through his soup and beef so as to be on the look-out for her. Gervaise, all the while she answered his questions, quite amiably, looked out of the window, where the lunch hour brought together an extraordinary crush of people.

All along both footpaths, in the narrow squeeze of the street, there was a hurry of steps, a swinging of arms, an elbowing without end. Workmen who had been detained over their work, grim and hungry of aspect, strode across the street to the baker's opposite; then, with their bread under their arms, went three doors higher up to the "Veau à Deux Têtes", to the threepenny ordinary. And close to the baker's there was a fruiterer, who sold fried potatoes and mussels in parsley sauce; a constant relay of work girls in long aprons carried off screws of fried potatoes and mussels in cups; others, pretty, dainty-looking girls with bare heads, bought bundles of radishes. When Gervaise leaned forward she could see also a pork-butcher's, crowded with people, from which streams of children came out, holding in their hands, wrapped up in greasy paper, a little chop, a sausage, or a bit of hot

black-pudding. Meanwhile, along the pavement, slimy with
black mud, even in fine weather, under the trampling of many
feet, a few workmen already made their way out of the eating-
houses, and strolled downwards in little groups, replete with
feeding, slow and composed in the midst of all the hustling
crowd.

A group began to form at the door of the bar.

"I say, Bibi-la-Grillade," cried a husky voice, "are you
going to stand the booze?"

Five workmen came in, and stood up by the bar.

"Robber, that's what old Colombe is. . . . We want matured
liquor, and not . . ." continued the voice. "The good old
stuff for us, you know, and not thimblefuls—proper glasses!"

Père Colombe placidly served everybody. Three more
workmen came in. Little by little a crowd of blouses collected
at the corner of the street, stopped there a short while, and
then pushed in past the two dusty oleanders at the door.

"Don't be silly; you only think of those beastly things,"
said Gervaise to Coupeau. "Of course I was fond of him.
Only, after the horrid way he left me. . . ."

They were talking of Lantier. Gervaise had not seen him
again; she heard that he was living with Virginie's sister at
La Glacière, in the house of that friend of his who was going
to set up a hat factory. Besides, she had no inclination to run
after him. At first it had been a great distress to her, she had
even thought of throwing herself in the river; but by this time she
had come to the conclusion that it was all for the best. Perhaps
if Lantier had stayed on she would never have been able to
bring up the children, so spendthrift was he. He might come
and see Claude and Étienne if he would; she would not turn
him away. Only, as far as she was concerned, she would be
hacked to bits before she would let him touch her with the
tips of his fingers. And she said all this in a quite convinced
manner, as if she had mapped out her life quite clearly, whilst
Coupeau, never losing sight of his desire of getting hold of
her, turned it all into fun, made jokes and very crude questions
on the subject of Lantier, showing his white teeth so gaily that
she could not take offence.

"It was you who used to beat him," he said at last. "Oh!
you are not nice at all. You beat up everybody!"

She interrupted him with a long peal of laughter. It was
true, certainly, she had beaten up that great hulking Virginie.
At that moment she could have strangled anyone quite

readily. And she laughed louder than ever when Coupeau told her that Virginie, distressed at having been made such an exhibition of, had left the neighbourhood. Meanwhile her face maintained a childlike sweetness; she stretched out her plump hands, declaring that she could not brush away a moth; all the blows she knew of were those she had received, pretty well all her life. Then she began to talk of her childhood at Plassans. She had never been one of those who ran after men; that did not amuse her; when Lantier had had her at fourteen, she had liked it because he said she was his little wife, and she wanted to play at housekeeping. It all came, she declared, of being too impressionable, too amiable with everybody, too ready to attach herself to people who only brought misery upon her. Thus, when she loved a man, it was not because she wanted to fool about; she only wanted to live with him always, perfectly happy. And when Coupeau chuckled, and spoke of the two children, whom she had certainly not found in a cabbage, she rapped him over the knuckles, adding that of course she was built on the same lines as other women; only it was a mistake to fancy that women were always thinking of that; they had their household to look after, they were fagged out with housework, and when they got to bed at night they wanted to go to sleep at once. She was like her mother, too, a great worker, who died in childbirth, after having served old man Macquart as beast of burden for more than twenty years. She herself was still quite slim, whilst her mother had had shoulders capable of demolishing the doors she came through; but they were alike in their obstinate attachment to people. Even her limp came to her from the poor woman, whom old Macquart used to beat black and blue. She had heard endless tales of nights when her father, coming home tipsy, had made love to his wife so brutally as to leave her all bruised; doubtless it was on one of those nights that she had been begotten, with her poor lame leg.

"Oh, it's nothing, one scarcely notices it," said Coupeau, to flatter her.

She shook her head, knowing very well that it was quite visible; at forty she would be bent double. Then she said softly, with a little laugh:

"It is so funny of you to like a woman who limps."

At that he leaned closer, his elbows still on the table, paying her still more outspoken compliments, trying to turn her head. But she only said no, inflexibly, though her ears

were tickled by the wheedling voice. She listened, looking out
of the window, as if she were interested in watching the crowd
outside. They were sweeping out the empty shops; the
fruiterer removed his last panful of fried potatoes, whilst the
pork-butcher put in order the disarranged plates on his
counter. Bands of workmen poured out of all the eating-
houses; great bearded chaps slapped one another on the back,
romped like little children, banging their great hob-nailed
boots on the pavement, and scratching it with a slide; others
both hands thrust deep into their pockets, smoked philo-
sophically, staring up at the sunlight, and blinking their eyes.
Pavement, street, the very gutters, were flooded with the
lazy crowd streaming out of open doors, blocked between
passing carts, leaving a trail of blouses, of short jackets, of
old overcoats, pale and colourless under the pale gold light
that filled the street. Further off, factory bells tolled; but the
workmen were in no hurry, lit their pipes again; then, after
going across the road to another wine-shop, they made their
way back to work, with bowed shoulders and dragging feet.
Gervaise was amused by three workmen, one tall and two
little, who turned back every ten yards; finally they got to
the bottom of the street, and came straight over to the bar.

"They do feel Mondayish, those three!" she said, in a low
voice.

"Hallo!" said Coupeau, "I know one of them, the tall one;
it's Mes-Bottes, a pal of mine."

The bar had filled up. Everyone talked loudly, and a
sound of noisy shouts broke sharply through the oily murmur
of hoarse voices. Every now and again the blow of a fist on the
counter made the glasses ring. The drinkers stood about in
little groups, jammed tightly together, their hands behind
their backs or their arms folded; some of them, back by the
casks, had to wait a quarter of an hour before they could get
their drinks from the bar.

"What! it's the swell Cadet-Cassis!" cried Mes-Bottes,
giving Coupeau a hearty whack on the shoulder. "A gent who
smokes cigarettes and wears a white shirt! Wants to show off
before his friends, does he? Must have his little delicacies!"

"No backchat from you," said Coupeau, in a tone of
annoyance.

The other man merely chuckled.

"Enough said. On the high horse, old cock! Turds will be
turds."

And he turned his back, with a horrible leer at Gervaise. She drew back, half frightened. The smoke of pipes, the strong odour of all these men, rose in the air, already charged with alcohol. It gave her a feeling of suffocation, and she began to cough.

"Drinking is horrid!" she said, in a low voice.

And she told how she used at one time to drink anisette with her mother at Plassans. But one day it made her quite ill, and that had disgusted her with drinking; she couldn't look at liquor.

"See," she added, pointing to her glass, "I have eaten my prune, but I shall leave the juice, it would quite upset me."

Coupeau, too, could not understand how one could go on drinking glass after glass of brandy. A prune now and again, that was all right. As for spirits, absinthe, and that sort of mess—no, thanks, he would have none of them. His pals might chaff him as much as they liked, he always stayed outside while those sots went crowding into the pubs. Old Coupeau, who like himself had been a tinsmith, had dashed out his brains on the pavement of the Rue Coquenard, on one of his drunken days, by a fall from the roof of No. 25; and the memory of this kept the family all sober. When he went that way, and saw the place, he felt that he would rather drink out of the gutter than have a free drink at a bar. And he wound up:

"In my business a man wants firm legs."

Gervaise had picked up her basket once more. She did not rise, however, but sat holding it on her lap absent-mindedly, as if the young workman's words had called up all sorts of vague ideas in her mind. And she said slowly, without apparent transition:

"I haven't any extravagant notions, you know; I am easily satisfied. My ideal would be to go on working quietly, to always have bread to eat, and a decent corner to sleep in; you know, a bed, two chairs, and a table—not more. And I should like to bring up my children honest, if I could. I should like, too, if I ever lived with anybody again, not to get knocked about; I don't at all relish the idea of being knocked about any more. But that's all, really, that's all."

She stopped to think, considering what she really wished for; but she could find nothing more of any importance. However, she went on, with a little hesitation:

"Then, too, one would like to end quietly in one's bed. I

have trudged about so much all my life, I should like to die in my own bed."

She got up. Coupeau, who agreed heartily with all her wishes, was already on his feet, looking anxiously at the time. But they did not go out at once; she was curious to go right through, behind the oak barrier, to see the great still of burnished brass working away under the glass roof of the little court; and the tinsmith, who had followed her, explained all its working, pointing out the different pieces of the machine with his finger, showing her the huge retort from which trickled a limpid stream of alcohol. The still, with its oddly-formed receivers, its endless coils of pipes, had a gloomy air; not a breath of steam escaped; one could only just perceive an internal murmur, a subterranean grumbling; it was like some deed of darkness done at midday, by a grim, mighty, and speechless toiler. Meanwhile, Mes-Bottes, with his two companions, had come to lean over the rail, waiting till a corner of the bar was free. He had a laugh like the creaking of a pulley, he shook his head, gazing at the drink-producing machine with watery eyes. It was a damned nice thing to look at! Why, in that big-bellied copper, there was enough to whet one's whistle for a week on end. He would have liked to have the end of that "worm" soldered to the roof of his mouth, so that he might feel the hot liquor trickle down inside him, down to his very heels, endlessly, like a flowing stream. Lord! that would just suit him; how much better it would be than the thimblefuls of that old rogue Colombe! And his pals all laughed, saying that good old Mes-Bottes could jaw! Meanwhile, the still, without a flicker or a sound, went on exuding its stream of alcohol, like a slow, inexhaustible fountain-head, which would gradually flow out over all the place, which would spread over the outer boulevards, which would inundate Paris itself, gaping monstrously down below. Gervaise shivered and drew back, trying to smile, as she murmured:

"I'm silly, but it gives me the creeps; drink always gives me the creeps."

Then, going back to her notion of perfect happiness:

"Don't you think so? Don't you think that is the best that can happen, to get work to do, bread to eat, a hole and corner of one's own, to bring up the children, and to die in one's bed?"

"And not get knocked about," added Coupeau, gaily. "But I shan't beat you, if you don't wish it, Madame Gervaise.

You needn't fear, I never drink, and I'm much too fond of you. Come now, tonight, we'll warm our tootsies together."

He had lowered his voice, whispering in her ear, whilst she made her way through the crowd of men, holding her wash-basket in front of her. But she said, "No, no," shaking her head again and again. Yet she turned and smiled back on him, and seemed pleased to find that he did not drink. She would doubtless have said yes if she had not sworn to keep away from men in future. At last they reached the door, and went out, leaving behind them the crowded bar, which puffed out into the very street its husky murmur of voices and its thick, sweet odour of spirits. Mes-Botfes was telling old Colombe that he was a bad lot, he had only half filled his glass. But he was game, he was, a good sort, not the man to knuckle under. Confound it all! the boss would have to get on as best he could; he wasn't going back to his beat, he had the blues. And he invited his two companions to go with him to the "Petit Bonhomme qui Tousse", a pub at the Barrière Saint-Denis where you get real good stuff.

"Ah! I can breathe again!" said Gervaise, finding herself on the pavement.

"Well, good-bye, and thanks, Monsieur Coupeau, I must get back at once."

And she began to move up the boulevard, but he seized her hand, would not let go, insisting:

"Just come around with me by way of the Rue de la Goutte-d'Or, it's hardly out of your way. I must go and see my sister before I go back to the yard. We can go along together."

She finally consented, and they went slowly up the Rue des Poissonniers, side by side. She did not take his arm. He spoke to her of his family; the mother, an old waistcoat-hand, looked after the house, for her sight was failing. She was sixty-two on the third of làst month. He was the youngest. One of his sisters, Madame Lerat, a young widow of thirty-six, worked at the flowers, and lived in the Rue des Moines, at Batignolles. The other, who was thirty, had married a chain-maker, the sharp-tongued Lorilleux. It was to their house that he was going, in the Rue de la Goutte-d'Or. They lodged in the large house on the right. He had his supper every night with the Lorilleux; it saved something all round. Indeed, he was going there now to tell them not to expect him, because he had been invited out that day by a friend.

Gervaise, who had been attending to what he was saying, suddenly interrupted him to ask smilingly——

"Is your name Cadet-Cassis, Monsieur Coupeau?"

"Oh," he replied, "that's only a nickname the fellows have given me, because I generally take a cassis when they insist on my having a drink. One may as well be called Cadet-Cassis as Mes-Bottes!"

"Indeed, yes, it is not at all bad, Cadet-Cassis," she answered.

And she questioned him about his work. He was always at work now over yonder, outside the city wall, at the new hospital. Oh! there was always plenty of work to be had, he should certainly not leave the place this year. There were yards and yards of gutters to be done.

"You know I can see the Hôtel Boncœur," he said, "when I am up there. You were at the window yesterday, and I waved my arms to you, but you didn't see me."

They had already gone about a hundred yards along the Rue de la Goutte-d'Or, when suddenly he stopped, lifted his eyes, and said:

"This is the house. I was born only just on there, at No. 22. But the house here, all the same, is a jolly bit of masonry. It's as big as a barracks inside."

Gervaise looked up, and examined the front of the house. It had five storeys looking on the street, each with fifteen windows in a line; their black and dilapidated shutters gave an aspect of desolation to the immense frontage. Four shops occupied the ground floor; on the right of the entrance, a great greasy eating-house; on the left, a coal merchant's, a haberdasher's, and an umbrella shop. The house looked all the bigger because it was built between two little low rickety buildings on each side; and, with its square bulk, like a block of mortar roughly thrown together, crumbling and chipping under the rain, it stood out in relief against the sky, high over the neighbouring roofs, with its huge rough cubic mass, its dingy, unplastered sides, stark and interminable as prison walls, in which the rows of dentated ornament seemed like decrepit jaws gaping. But Gervaise noticed particularly the doorway, an immense round door, rising to the second storey, and having a deep porch, at the other end of which could be seen the dim daylight of a large courtyard. Under the porch, in the middle of the paving stones, a gutter carried off a stream of pink-coloured water.

"Come in," said Coupeau, "they won't eat you."

She preferred to wait for him outside. Still, she could not help making her way under the porch, as far as the *concierge's* lodge, and then she looked up once more. Inside, the elevation had six storeys, four regular sides surrounding the huge square of the court-yard. The walls were grey, eaten away with a yellow rot, marked in long streaks by the drippings of the roofs; they rose straight up in the air, from the paving stones to the slates, without a single moulding; only the waste-pipes curved out at the different storeys, where the gaping mouths of the gulleys left a stain of rusty iron. The windows had no shutters, the curtainless glass had the greenish hue of muddy water. Some of them were wide open, with mattresses, patterned in blue squares, hanging out to air; outside, other linen was hung out to dry on lines, the whole washing of the establishment, men's shirts, women's under-bodices, children's knickers; at one, on the third storey, there was a child's mattress, all plastered with dirt. From top to bottom, these narrow lodgements burst their way out, showing the fag-ends of their misery at every crevice. Below, at the corner of each wall, a narrow doorway, without wainscoting, taken sheer out of the plaster, opened on a cracked lobby, at the end of which rose the slimy steps of an iron-railed staircase; one counted four staircases, indicated by the first four letters of the alphabet painted on the wall. The ground floors were laid out in huge workshops, their windows black with dust; one saw through them the flame of a locksmith's forge; further on could be heard the plane of a carpenter; whilst near the lodge from a dyer's workshop, there escaped in big bubbles the runlet of pink-coloured water that ran out under the porch. Messy with puddles of various colours, with shavings and cinders, with a ring of grass growing all round between the stones, the court-yard was lit by the strong sunlight, as if it were divided in two by a line drawn sharply across. In the shade, around the tap that leaked continually, three little hens scratched the ground with their dirty claws, looking for worms. And Gervaise looked slowly up and down, from the sixth storey to the ground, and up again, overwhelmed by the hugeness of the place, feeling as if she were in the midst of a living organism, in the very heart of a city, interested by the house as if it were some great living giant.

"Do you want anyone?" asked the *concierge*, puzzled, coming out to the door of the lodge.

But the young woman explained that she was waiting for

someone. She turned back in the direction of the street; then, as Coupeau still delayed, she returned for another look, as if drawn by some fascination. The house seemed to her by no means ugly. Here and there, among the odds and ends at the windows, were touches of gaiety, a stock in a pot, a cage of canaries all a-twitter, shaving glasses which sparkled like round stars in the depths of shadow. Below, a carpenter was singing to the accompaniment of the regular hiss of his plane; while in the smith's shop a clang of hammers falling in cadence gave out a silvery ring. At almost every open casement, against a background of wretchedness just visible, there were the laughing, tangled heads of children, women sewing, with their calm profiles bent over the work. The midday meal was over, work was beginning again, the men had all gone out to their occupations, and the house returned to its customary tranquillity, broken only by the regular sounds that went on without intermission all day long. The court struck her as a little damp. If she had to live there she would rather be on the sunny side, right at the end. She made five or six steps, breathing the musty odour of poor people's houses, an odour of long-lying dust, of rancid dirt; but as the sharpness of the dyer's washes predominated, she disliked the smell less than that of the Hôtel Boncœur. And she picked out a particular window that she would like, one in the left corner, where there was a little window-box planted with scarlet runners, whose slim tendrils were beginning to twist upwards around a trellis-work of string.

"Have I kept you waiting?" said Coupeau, all at once, behind her. "It is quite a job when I am not going to have dinner with them, especially today, as my sister had bought some veal."

And as she made a little movement of surprise he went on, looking round the place in his turn:

"You are looking at the house. It is all let from top to bottom. There are about three hundred tenants, I believe. If I had any furniture, I should look out for a little room there myself. It is nice here, isn't it?"

"Yes, it is nice here," murmued Gervaise. "At Plassans there were not so many people in all our street. Look, isn't that window pretty, up there on the fifth storey, with the runners?"

At that he returned obstinately to the attack. As soon as they had a bed, they would take that room. But she hurried

out, begging him not to begin it all over again; the house
might crumble to bits, but she certainly wouldn't share a bed
with him. Nevertheless, when Coupeau left her before Madame
Fauconnier's laundry, she let him hold her hand in his for a
moment in the friendliest manner.

These friendly relations between the two went on for a
month. She seemed to him very plucky to go on as she did,
slaving all day looking after the children, finding time in the
evening for all sorts of little sewing jobs. Some women were
anything but tidy, fond of eating and gadding about; but she
was not one of that sort, sure enough, she took things much
too seriously.

At that she laughed, and made modest objections. She had
not always been so steady, worse luck! Had she not slept with
a man at fourteen? Didn't she use to drink anisette with her
mother? She had learnt by experience, that was all. It was
not true that she was strong-minded; on the contrary, she
was very weak; she went wherever she was led, not wanting
to give anyone trouble. She only wanted to keep good company,
for bad company, she declared, bowled you over, did for a
woman in less than no time.

And she shuddered in thinking of the future, comparing
herself to a penny tossed up, heads or tails, as luck fell. What
she had seen already, all the bad examples she had had before
her as a child, had given her a good lesson. But Coupeau
laughed at her gloomy notions, told her to keep up her
courage, and tried to put his arm round her waist. She pushed
him back, rapping his fingers, while he cried, laughing, that
she was not easy to get hold of, for a weak woman. He was
gay and confident, and did not trouble about the future. One
day brought another, and there you were. One would always
have a bit and a crumb somewhere. The neighbourhood
seemed decent enough but for a pack of drunkards, who ought
to be kicked into the gutter. He was not a bad sort of fellow,
could talk at times very sensibly, and was even a bit of a dandy,
with his hair carefully parted at the side, his bright ties, his
shining boots on Sunday. And he was as cheeky as a monkey,
he had the quizzical drollery of a genuine Paris workman, a
regular chatterbox, so charmingly young too.

They both did one another all sorts of little services at the
Hôtel Boncœur. Coupeau got the milk for her, did her errands,
carried her washing bundles; often in the evening, if he came
home first, he would take the children for a walk along the

boulevard. Gervaise in return went up to his little room under the roof, turned over his clothes, and sewed on buttons or mended his canvas jackets. They were now on terms of the utmost familiarity, and she was never bored when he was there, with his street songs, his street jokes, all so new to her. And Coupeau, with a woman always about, became more set on her than ever. He was smitten this time, sure enough; and at last it became quite awkward. He only laughed as before, but he felt so upset that all the fun of the thing was gone. He still fooled about, and could never meet her without crying, "When is it to be?"

She knew what he meant, and she promised it when the moon turned to green cheese. The he tried teasing her, and would come down with his slippers in his hand, as if to take up his abode. She turned it off as a joke, and was not in the least discomposed by the continual spicy allusions amid which he made her live. As long as he was not brutal, she could stand anything. She only got angry once, when, in trying to snatch a kiss from her, he had pulled out some hair from her head.

Towards the end of June, Coupeau lost his spirits, and got quite out of sorts. Troubled by certain looks that he gave her, Gervaise barricaded the door at night. Then, after a tiff which had lasted from Sunday to Tuesday, he came one night about eleven o'clock knocking at her door. She would not open it; but he spoke to her so quietly, and in quite a shaky voice, that at last she drew aside the chest of drawers from before the door. When he had come in she thought he must be ill, he looked so pale, with his haggard face and red eyes. He stood before her, shaking his head, stammering out a few words. No, he was not ill. But he had been up in his room crying, crying like a child, biting the pillow so that his neighbours should not hear. He had not slept now for three nights. He could not go on any longer.

"Look here, Madame Gervaise," he said, chokingly, almost on the point of crying again, "we must put an end to all this. Let's go and get married. I want to; I've made up my mind."

Gervaise looked greatly surprised. She was very grave.

"Oh, Monsieur Coupeau!" she murmured, "what is it you are saying to me? I never have asked you for that, as you know, I couldn't do such a thing. Oh, no, no, this is a serious matter; think it over, I beg you."

But he continued to shake his head with an air of un-alterable resolution. He had thought it all out. He had come down to her so that he might get some sleep that night. She would not surely send him back to his misery like that. If she would only say yes, he would bother her no further; she could go to bed in peace. He merely wanted to hear her say yes. They would talk it over next day.

"Surely, I shall not say yes like that," replied Gervaise. "I wouldn't have you say, later on, that I made you do a foolish thing. Look here, Monsieur Coupeau, you should not be so headstrong. You don't know your own mind about me, really. If you were not to see me for a week I'd wager that it would all pass off. Very often men marry for the sake of one night, the first one, and then night follows night, day after day, a whole lifetime, and they repent bitterly of their bargain. But sit down, we must talk it out straight away."

Then, up to one o'clock in the morning, in the dim room, lit only by a smoky candle that they forgot to snuff, they discussed the project of marriage, in low voices, so as not to disturb the two children, Claude and Étienne, who breathed quietly, both heads on the same pillow. And Gervaise came back again and again to the subject of the children, pointing them out to Coupeau; that was an odd sort of dowry to bring with her, she could not really put such a burden on his shoulders. And then she was ashamed, on his behalf. What would the neighbours say? They knew all about her and her lover; it would not be decent to go and get married two months after. To all these good reasons, Coupeau answered by shrugging his shoulders. Pretty much he cared for the neighbours! He didn't stick his nose into other people's affairs; he preferred not to dirty it, indeed! Well, and if she *had* had Lantier before him, where was the harm? She wasn't living on the loose; she didn't bring men home with her, as lots of women did—ladies! As for the children, they were all right, they would grow up, Never could he find another woman so plucky, so good, so full of all sorts of qualities. Besides, it was not that; she might have rolled in the gutter, she might be ugly, lazy, and odious, she might have a whole series of dirty brats, that would not count in his eyes; he wanted her, and her only.

"Yes, I want *you*," he repeated, hammering his fist on his knee. "You understand, I want *you*. I don't see there is any-thing more to say."

Little by little Gervaise gave way. An abandonment of heart and sense invaded her, before this brutal desire which seemed to envelop her. She hazarded only a few timid objections, her hands crossed on her lap, her face softened. Through the half-opened window the warm June night came in sultry breaths, making the long red wick of the candle gutter; through the heavy silence of the slumbering neighbourhood one could hear only the sobs of a drunkard, who lay on his back in the middle of the road, sobbing like a child; whilst at a distance, in some restaurant, a violin played a vulgar quadrille for some late revellers, a faint crystalline music, clear and thin as the sound of a harmonica. Coupeau, seeing Gervaise at the end of her arguments, silent and vaguely smiling, seized her hands and drew her towards him. She was at one of those moments of abandonment, to which she knew herself so liable, won over at last, and too weak to refuse anything, to disappoint anyone. But Coupeau did not see that she surrendered herself to him; he merely squeezed her wrists tight until he nearly bruised them, taking possession of her so; and they had a long sigh, both of them, at this little pain, given and taken, in which their tenderness found vent.

"It is yes?" he asked.

"How you torment me!" she murmured, "Must I? Well then, yes! Good Lord! I think we are both very foolish."

He got up, seized her by the waist, and gave her a hearty kiss on the face, quite at random. The noise of the kiss startled him, and he looked over at Claude and Étienne, stepping softly, and lowering his voice.

"Hush!" he said, "we mustn't wake the kids. Good-bye till tomorrow."

And he went back to his room. Gervaise, all of a tremble, sat down on the edge of her bed, and stayed there for more than an hour without thinking of undressing. She was deeply moved, she thought it very good of Coupeau, for at one moment she had fancied it was all over—that he would go to bed with her there and then. The drunkard, below in the street, made a harsher noise, like a lost animal. The jigging violin in the distance had ceased.

For the next few days, Coupeau tried to induce Gervaise to come and see his sister, some evening, at the Rue de la Goutte-d'Or. But she was very nervous, and seemed terrified at the idea of going to see the Lorilleux. She saw clearly that he was in terror of the whole family. No doubt it was not his

sister's concern, she was not even the elder. The mother
would give her consent in a minute, for she never contradicted
her son. Only the Lorilleux were supposed, in the family, to
earn ten francs a day; and on that account they wielded a
certain authority. Coupeau would never dare marry her
unless they all agreed to accept his wife.

"I have spoken to them about you," he explained to
Gervaise; "they know all about our plans. What a silly child
you are! Come tonight. You are quite prepared, aren't you?
You will find my sister a little stiff. Lorilleux, too, is not
always quite amiable. At heart they are vexed, because, if I
marry, I shall not take my meals with them any more, and
that won't be so economical for them. But that doesn't matter;
they won't turn you out of doors. Do this much for me; it
is absolutely necessary."

These words frightened Gervaise still more. One Saturday
night, however, she gave in. Coupeau called for her at half-
past nine. She had her things on, a black dress, a shawl of
thin woollen stuff with a pattern of yellow palm leaves, and a
white bonnet trimmed with lace. During the six weeks she
had been at work she had saved up the seven francs for the
shawl, and the two francs fifty for the bonnet; the dress was
an old one cleaned and done up.

"They are expecting you," said Coupeau, as they made
their way through the Rue des Poissonniers. "Oh! they are
beginning to get used to the idea of my marrying. They are
in a very good humour tonight. Then if you have never seen
people making gold chains it will amuse you to see it. They
have just had an urgent order for Monday.

"Have they got gold there?" asked Gervaise.

"I should think so! On the walls, on the ground—everywhere."

Meanwhile they had reached the great porch and crossed
the court. The Lorilleux lived on the sixth storey, staircase B.
Coupeau told her laughingly to hold on to the banister and
not let go. She raised her eyes, blinking her eyelids as she saw
the tall cavity of the staircase, lit with three gas-burners, one
at every two storeys; the furthest, at the very top, looked
like a star flickering in a dark sky, whilst the two others
glared irregularly across the interminable spiral ascent.

"Ha!" said the tinsmith, pausing on the first landing, "a
damn strong smell of onion soup. Somebody has certainly
been having onion soup."

Staircase B, grey and filthy, with its greasy steps and rails, its walls from which the plaster was dropping, was indeed full of the odour of cooking. On each landing there were long corridors, loud and echoing; there was an opening of doors, painted yellow, and blackened at the lock by the dirt of hands; and at the level of the window, the gulleys gave out a fetid odour, which mixed with the sharp smell of boiled onions. From ground floor to sixth storey could be heard the clatter of dishes, of frying-pans moved, of saucepans scraped with spoons to scour them. On the first storey, Gervaise saw, through a half-open door on which the word *Draughtsman* was painted in large letters, two men sitting before a table on which a large prepared canvas was outspread; they were talking excitedly, amidst the smoke of their pipes. The second and third storeys were quieter; one heard only the rocking of a cradle, a child crying, a woman's loud voice mingled with the sound of running water, in which the words were drowned: and Gervaise saw various names on cards nailed to the door: *Madame Gaudron, wool-carder* and further on, *Monsieur Madinier, cardboard-maker.* There was a fight going on at the fourth storey; a trampling which shook the floor, furniture knocked about, a horrible uproar of blows and curses; while the neighbours opposite went on with a game of cards, the door open to let in a breath of air. When Gervaise reached the fifth story she was quite out of breath; she was not accustomed to going up so many stairs, and this turning wall, this series of glimpses into interiors, bewildered her. A whole family blocked up the landing; the father was washing plates on a little stove by the window, whilst the mother, leaning against the banister, was wiping the baby before putting it to bed. Coupeau urged on Gervaise with what encouragement he could, and at last they reached the sixth storey. Coupeau turned to her with a smile; they were at the top. She looked about her to find where a voice was coming from, a voice she had heard all the way, shrill and piercing, above all the other sounds. It was a little old woman in an attic, singing as she dressed her sixpenny dolls. As a tall girl, carrying a pail, re-entered a room near by, Gervaise had a glimpse of a tumbled bed on which a man in his shirt-sleeves was sprawling lazily; on the door a visiting-card, written by hand, announced, *Mademoiselle Clémence, Ironing done.* Then, stiff and panting, she leaned curiously over the banister; now it was the lowest gas-burner which looked like a star, at the foot of the six storeys; and the smells, the rumbling sound of the whole huge place came up all in one breath—a great puff of heat against her anxious face, leaning forward as at the edge of a pit.

"We haven't got there yet," said Coupeau. "Oh! it is a regular journey."

He led the way down a long corridor on the left, turning twice, first to the left, then again to the right. The corridor went on further still, going both ways, cramped, dilapidated, and unplastered, lit at long intervals by a tiny flame of gas; and the doors, all of one pattern, like the doors of a prison or a monastery, and almost all wide open, displayed, one after another, miserable interiors, filled, this hot June evening, with a sort of reddish haze. At last they reached a bit of passage completely dark.

"Here we are," said Coupeau. "Be careful, keep close to the wall; there are three steps."

Gervaise went forward cautiously about a dozen paces stumbling as she came to the three steps. Meanwhile at the end of the passage, Coupeau pushed open a door without knocking. A bright light fell on the floor of the passage. They went in.

It was a narrow, tunnel-like place, which seemed like a continuation of the passage. A faded woollen curtain, caught up by a piece of string, separated the place in two. The first compartment contained a bed, pushed under an angle of the sloping roof, a cast iron stove still warm after the dinner, two chairs, a table, and a cupboard, which had had to to have the cornice sawn off before it could be got between the bed and the door. The second compartment was the work room; at the other end was a little forge with its bellows; on the right, a vice riveted to the wall, under a shelf on which were bits of old iron; on the left, near the window, a tiny bench, littered with microscopic pincers, nippers, and saws, all very dirty and oily.

"Here we are!" cried Coupeau, advancing as far as the curtain.

But at first no one replied. Gervaise, quite confused, especially by the idea that she was coming into a place full of gold, kept behind Coupeau, stammering out something, and nodding at random by way of salutation. The bright light, coming from the lamp on the bench and the brazier of coal in the forge, increased her bewilderment. At last she saw

Madame Lorilleux, short, ruddy, and thick-set, pulling away with all the vigour of her short arms, and with the aid of a pincers, at a black metal wire which she inserted in the holes of a draw-plate attached to the vice. Before the bench, Lorilleux, equally short as his wife, but slighter of build, plied his pincers with a monkey-like vivacity, working on something so minute that it was lost to sight between his bony fingers. It was he who was the first to raise his head, a head partially bald, long, sickly, and yellow as old wax.

"Ah, it's you; all right!" he murmured. "We are awfully busy, you know. Don't come into the work-room, you'll be in our way. Stay where you are."

And he went on with his work again, his face once more in the greenish shadow of a bowl of water, through which the lamp cast a ray of vivid light on his work.

"Sit down, won't you?" cried Madame Lorilleux in her turn. "This is the lady, isn't it? Good, good!"

She had wound the wire, and now she took it over to the forge, where, making the fire burn briskly with a large wooden fan, she put it to heat again before passing it into the last holes of the draw-plate.

Coupeau moved the chairs forward, and made Gervaise sit down by the curtain. The room was so narrow that he could not bestow himself by her side, so he sat down behind, and whispered in her ear, explaining all that was going on. The young woman, taken aback by the strange reception of the Lorilleux, and uneasy under their sidelong glances, had a humming in her ears which hindered her from hearing anything. The wife seemed to her old for her thirty years, surly in her manner and untidy in appearance, with her pigtail of hair hanging down on her unbuttoned under-bodice. The husband, older by a year only, looked to her quite an old man; he had thin malicious lips, was in his shirtsleeves, and his bare feet were thrust into slippers down at heel. And what amazed her the most was the smallness of the work-room, the smeary walls, the tarnished iron of the tools, the dirtiness of everything about, like a scrap-iron merchant's stock. It was frightfully hot. Drops of sweat stood out on the livid forehead of Lorilleux, and Madame Lorilleux pulled off her white bodice, working away with bare arms, her chemise plastered over her pendent breasts.

"But the gold?" whispered Gervaise.

She looked all round the place, peering under all the muck
to find the splendour she had fancied.

Coupeau burst out laughing.

"The gold?" he said; "why there is some, and there, at
your very feet!"

He pointed successively to the thin wire on which his
sister was working, and to another bundle of wire, like a coil
of iron-wire, which hung on the wall near the vice; then,
going down on hands and knees, he picked up, under the
board for chips which lay on the workshop floor, a paring of
gold-leaf, a tiny scrap like the point of a rusty needle. Gervaise
exclaimed that couldn't be gold, that black stuff as ugly as
iron! He bit the paring and showed her the shining notch
left by his teeth. And he went on with his explanation: the
employers provided the gold-wire in its alloy; the workers
first of all passed it through the draw-plate in order to get it
to the required size, taking care to heat it five or six times over
during the operation, so as not to break it. It needed a good
strong wrist, and a knack as well. His sister would not let her
husband touch the draw-plate because he coughed. She had
splendid arms; he had seen her draw the gold-wire as fine as
a hair.

Meanwhile Lorilleux, taken with a turn of coughing,
doubled up on his stool. In the midst of his fit, he said in a
choked voice, without looking at Gervaise, as if he stated the
matter for her benefit:

"I make the links."

Coupeau insisted on Gervaise getting up. If she would go
nearer she could see. The chain-maker consented with a
growl. He twined the wire prepared by his wife round a
mandrel till it formed a winding like a fine coil spring. Then he
drew the saw lightly along, cutting the wire along the whole
length of the mandrel, each ring forming a link. Then he
welded them together. The links were laid on a large piece of
charcoal. He moistened them with a drop of borax, which he
took from the bottom of a broken glass by his side, and rapidly
reddened them at the lamp, under the horizontal flame of the
chimney. Then, when he had a hundred links, he returned to
his delicate work, leaning over on the plug, a little piece of
thin board which his hands had made quite shiny. He twisted
loop after loop with the pincers, pressed it on one side, brought
it through the loop above it, already in its place, re-opened it
with the assistance of a pointed tool; and it was done with an

unintermittent regularity, link succeeding link with such rapidity that the chain began to lengthen out slowly under the very eyes of Gervaise, without her quite understanding how it was done.

"Those are the links," said Coupeau. "There is the small-link, the heavy-curb, the chain-link. But Lorilleux only makes this particular kind."

Lorilleux gave a chuckle of satisfaction. As he went on twisting his curbs, hardly visible between his black nails, he exclaimed:

"I say, Cadet-Cassis! I was making a little calculation this morning. I began when I was twelve—well, do you know what length of curb-chain I must have made, up to now?"

He raised his pale face, blinking his red eyelids.

"Eight thousand yards! do you hear? Nearly five miles! Fancy! a chain five miles long! It is long enough to go round the neck of all the females in the neighbourhood. And you see it is always getting longer. I hope to get from Paris to Versailles."

Gervaise had gone back to her seat quite disillusioned. It all seemed to her very ugly. She smiled, to please the Lorilleux. But what made her feel particularly awkward was the silence in regard to her marriage, the matter of such importance to her, without which she would certainly not have come. The Lorilleux continued to treat her as if she were some inquisitive bore brought in by Coupeau. And when a conversation was at last started, it was confined entirely to the people who lodged in the house. Madame Lorilleux asked her brother if he had heard the people on the fourth floor fighting as he came up. Those Bénards went for each other every day; the husband came in drunk as a pig; the wife too, wasn't entirely without blame, she used the most filthy language. Then they spoke of the draughtsman on the first floor, that sponger Baudequin, who put on airs, but was in debt all round, always smoking, always jawing away with his friends. The card-board business of M. Madinier was on its last legs. The master had turned off two work-girls the day before; it would serve him right if he came to smash, for he spent everything on drink; he left his children without a shirt to their back. Madame Gaudron went on in a funny sort of way; she was going to have another child, which was hardly reasonable at her age. The landlord had just given the sack to the fifth-floor Coquets; they owed for three quarters; besides, they would insist on lighting their stove out on the landing, and only last Saturday, Mademoiselle Remanjou, the old woman who lived on the sixth floor, going downstairs with her dolls, was only just in time to save the little Linguerlot from getting badly burnt. As for Mademoiselle Clémence, who took in ironing, she might carry on as she pleased, but one couldn't complain, she adored animals, she had a real good heart. What a pity a fine girl like that went after all the men! One would see her walking the streets some day or other.

"Here you are, here is another," said Lorilleux to his wife, giving her the chain on which he had been working since dinner. "You can finish it off."

And he added with the insistence of a man who does not easily let go a joke:

"Four feet and a half more. I am getting nearer Versailles."

Meanwhile Madame Lorilleux was finishing off the chain, after having once more heated it by passing it through the regulator draw-plate. Finally she put it in a little brass saucepan with a long handle, filled with lye-wash, and dipped it into the flame of the forge. Gervaise, pushed forward again by Coupeau, had to follow this last operation. When the chain had been passed through the fire it turned a dull red colour. It was finished, ready to send in.

"It is sent in in the rough," Coupeau explained. "The polishers rub it up afterwards."

Gervaise felt that she could endure it no longer. The room became hotter and hotter, and she was stifling. The door had to be kept shut, because the least draught gave Lorilleux a cold. Then, as no allusion was made to the marriage, she was anxious to be gone; and she gave Coupeau's jacket a little pull. He understood what she meant. He, too, was growing embarrassed and annoyed by this affectation of silence.

"Well, we are off," he said. "We'll leave you to your work."

He moved uneasily about for a moment, waiting, hoping for a word, some sort of reference. At last he made up his mind to break into the subject himself.

"I say, Lorilleux, we depend on you. You will be my wife's witness, won't you?"

The chain-maker raised his head, pretending to be surprised, and gave a chuckle; whilst his wife, leaving the draw-plates, planted herself in the middle of the workshop.

"You really mean it then?" he murmured. "One never

knows, with that damned Cadet-Cassis, whether he means a thing or not."

"Ah, yes! so this is the lady," said Madame Lorilleux, looking Gervaise in the face. "Lord! we haven't any advice to give you, as far as we are concerned. It is rather an odd idea to go and get married, all the same. However, if you have quite agreed about that. . . . When it doesn't succeed it is one's own fault, that is all. And it doesn't often succeed; not often, not often."

Her voice lingered over the last words, and she shook her head, looking Gervaise up and down from head to foot, as if she would like to have examined every inch of her body. She evidently found her better than she had expected.

"My brother is quite free," she continued, in a more acid tone. "No doubt his family would have preferred. . . . One always has one's projects. But things fall out so oddly. For my part, I have no wish to raise a dispute. If he had brought to me the lowest of the low, I should have said, 'Marry her by all means, and say no more about it'. Still, he used to get on all right with us here. He looks plump enough; it is evident he hasn't starved. Always had his hot soup, right to the minute. I say, Lorilleux, doesn't it occur to you that the lady is something like Thérèse, you know, the woman opposite, who died of consumption?"

"Yes, there is a sort of resemblance," replied the chain-maker.

"And then there are your two children, madam. Indeed, I remarked to my brother, 'I don't understand, for my part, how you can marry a woman with two children'. You mustn't mind, if I look at it from his side; it is quite natural. And you don't look very strong either. Isn't it so, Lorilleux, the lady doesn't look strong?"

"No, no, she isn't strong."

They said nothing about her limp. But Gervaise understood, by their sidelong glances, and the movement of their lips, that they were alluding to it. She stood up before them, drawing her little palm-leaf shawl tightly about her, and replying in monosyllables as if she were before a judge. Coupeau, seeing her distress, cried at last:

"That's not the last word on the subject. Whatever you like to say, it won't make any difference. The wedding will take place on Saturday, the 29th of July. I looked it up in the almanac. You understand, then? that will suit you?"

"Oh yes, of course, that will suit us," said his sister. "You really need not have consulted us. I shall not hinder Lorilleux from acting as witness. I only want to keep friends."

Gervaise bent her head, not knowing what to do with herself, and catching her foot in one of the squares of wood with which the work-room was covered, she stooped down, fumbling with her hand, fearing she had displaced something. Lorilleux moved the lamp sharply over. He looked suspiciously at her hands.

"You must be careful," he said, "little bits of gold stick on to one's feet, and one carries it away without knowing."

It was quite a job. The employers would not allow you so much as a grain of waste. And he displayed the hare's foot with which he brushed off the filaments of gold that remained behind on the plug and the leather on his knees, put there to catch them. The work-room was carefully swept out twice a week; all the dust and dirt was collected and burned, and the ashes searched, in which there was generally five-and-twenty or thirty francs' worth of gold a month.

Madame Lorilleux could not take her eyes off Gervaise's shoes.

"There is no harm meant," she said, with an amiable smile, "but perhaps the lady wouldn't mind looking at her shoes."

Gervaise, blushing deeply, sat down and turned up her shoes, to show that there was nothing there. Coupeau had opened the door, calling out sharply, "Good-night!" He called her from outside, and she followed, after having stammered out some polite phrase: she hoped to see them again, and that they would be on good terms with one another. But the Lorilleux had already returned to their work at the dark end of the work-room, where the little forge shone like the last coal turning white in the fierce heat of a furnace. The wife, her chemise slipping down over one shoulder, her skin reddened by the glow from the brazier, pulled away at another wire, the muscles in her neck swelling out at each effort like great cords. The husband, bending under the green light of the bowl of water, set to work once more on a chain, bent the link with the pincers, pressed it on one side, drew it through the link above, opened it again with the assistance of a sharp-pointed tool, mechanically, unintermittently, without even stopping to wipe the sweat from his face.

When Gervaise came out on the landing, she could not help saying, with tears in her eyes:

"That is not very promising for us."

Coupeau shook his head furiously. He would pay out Lorrilleux for the way he had treated them that evening. Did one ever see such an old screw! to think they were going to rob him of three grains of his gold-dust! All their talk, it was nothing but sheer greed. Did his sister think he was never going to marry, so as to save her twopence on her *pot-au-feu?* Anyway, it should be the 29th of July, all the same. Much he cared for them.

But Gervaise was heavy at heart, seized with a sort of fear, as she picked her way downstairs in the shadow of the banisters. At that hour the staircase was deserted, lit only by the burner on the second floor, which, with its shrunken flame, down in those depths of darkness, looked like a night-light. Behind the closed doors there was a heavy silence, the dead sleep of workmen who had gone to bed the moment they got up from the table. Only a hushed laugh came from the room of the girl who took in ironing, whilst a streak of light shone through the keyhole of Mademoiselle Remanjou, still at work with her scissors at the gauze dresses of her sixpenny dolls. Further down, at Madame Gaudron's, a child was crying. And the gulleys stank worse than ever in their deep quietude, black and silent.

Then, in the courtyard, as Coupeau sang out to the *concierge* to open the door, Gervaise turned and gave a last look at the house. It looked larger than ever under the moonless sky. The grey walls, as if cleansed of decay and whitewashed with shadow, broadened and lengthened; and they were barer and flatter than ever, without their day's dress of rags a-drying. The closed windows slept, only one here and there, brightly lit up, opened its eyes, seeming to squint out of certain corners. Over each vestibule, one above another, from top to bottom, the six windows on the landing, white and pallid, rose like a narrow tower of light. A ray of lamplight, coming from the bookbinder's on the second floor, left a yellow streak on the pavement of the court, striking through the dark shadows which enveloped the shops on the ground floor. And in their depths of shadow, in the damp corner, drops of water dripped one by one, loudly in the midst of the silence, from the leaky tap. And it seemed to Gervaise that the house was upon her, about to crush her, striking a chill to her shoulders. It was that foolish fear of hers again, a childishness which made her smile a moment after.

"Take care!" cried Coupeau.

And, in order to get out, she had to jump over a great puddle, which had trickled out of the dyer's. That day it was blue, the deep azure of a summer sky, which the little night-lamp of the *concierge* lit with stars.

CHAPTER THREE

GERVAISE did not wish to have any wedding-party. Why spend the money? Besides she was a little ashamed: it seemed needless to parade the wedding before all the neighbours. But Coupeau cried out on her; it was impossible to get married like that, without a bit of a feast. He didn't care a straw for the neighbours. Oh! something quite simple: a little outing in the afternoon, then they would just pick a bone at the first eating-house they came to. And no music at dessert, for certain, nothing to set the ladies bums a-jigging; they would simply have a glass together and then everybody should go quietly back to bed.

The tinsmith laughed and joked away, and Gervaise gave in when he had sworn there should be no larking. He would keep his eye on the glasses, and see that nobody got top-heavy. Thereupon he organized a feed at five francs a head at Auguste's, at the "Moulin-d'Argent", Boulevard de la Chapelle. It was a cheap wine-shop, with a dancing-hall at the back of the bar, under the three acacias of the courtyard. They would be all right on the first floor. For the next ten days he looked up guests in his sister's house, Rue de la Goutte-d'Or: M. Madinier, Mademoiselle Remanjou, Madame Gaudron and her husband. He even induced Gervaise to let him bring two of his fellow-workmen, Bibi-la-Grillade and Mes-Bottes. No doubt Mes-Bottes usually got fuddled, but he had such a deuce of an appetite that they always invited him to a little dinner for the sake of the long face that was always pulled by the landlord when he saw what the blooming guzzler could stow away. Gervaise, for her part, promised to bring Madame Fauconnier, for whom she worked, and the Boches, very good people. That would make fifteen altogether; quiet enough, for with too many people it always ends in a dispute.

Meanwhile, Coupeau had absolutely no money. Without having a showy affair, he wished to do everything decently. He borrowed fifty francs from his employer. Out of that be bought the wedding-ring, a twelve-franc gold ring, which

Lorilleux got for him at wholesale price for nine francs. Then he ordered a frock coat, a waistcoat and a pair of trousers, from a tailor on the Rue Myrrha, to whom he gave twenty-five francs in part payment; his patent leathers and his tile might still pass muster. When he had put aside his ten francs for the feed, his own score and that of Gervaise (the children could be thrown into the bargain), there remained just six francs, the price of a mass at the Altar of the Poor. He didn't care much about the crows, certainly; it went to his heart to give his six francs to those greedy grabs, who didn't want all that to clear their throats. But a marriage without a mass (the saying went) was no marriage at all. He went to the church himself in order to make a bargain, and for an hour he slanged away with a little old priest in a dirty cassock, as grasping as a Jew. He felt inclined to box his ears for him. Then, by way of chaffing him, he asked if he hadn't about him a second-hand mass, not in too bad repair, on which a decent couple might gain something. The little old priest, grumbling out that God would not be pleased to bless his union, finished up by letting him have his mass for five francs. That was a franc saved. He had now just a franc left.

Gervaise, too, was anxious to look her best. As soon as the marriage was decided upon, she pulled herself together, worked on late in the evening, and scraped together thirty francs. She was greatly set on having a little silk mantle, marked at thirteen francs in the Rue du Faubourg-Poisonnière. She bought it, then gave ten francs to the husband of a washer-woman who had died at Madame Fauconnier's for a dress of thick blue woollen stuff, which she altered to fit herself. Out of the seven francs over, she had a pair of cotton gloves, a rose for her bonnet, and shoes for her eldest, Claude. Luckily the children had passable blouses. She spent four night in cleaning up everything, not overlooking the smallest holes in her chemise and stockings.

Finally, on Friday night, the day before the great day, Gervaise and Coupeau, after returning from their work, had to trudge about till eleven o'clock. Then, before they separated for the night they spent an hour together in the room of Gervaise, well pleased to have got things at last into order. Despite their resolution of not bestirring themselves on account of the neighbours, they had taken the thing to heart after all, and regularly tired themselves out. When they said good-night, they were ready

to drop with fatigue. But, all the same, they were well
satisfied with things as they were. Now everything was
arranged. Coupeau had as witnesses M. Madinier and
Bibi-la-Grillade; Gervaise counted on Lorilleux and Boche.
They were to go quietly to the mayoralty and the church, the
six of them, without taking a whole bevy of people along with
them. The two sisters of the bridegroom had said that they
would remain at home, their presence not being necessary.
Only old Madame Coupeau had begun to weep, declaring
that she would sooner go beforehand and hide away in a
corner; so they had promised to let her come too. The hour
of meeting was fixed for everybody at one o'clock, at the
"Moulin-d'Argent". Then they were to go and get an appetite
in the Plaine Saint-Denis; going by railway, and coming back
on foot along the main road. The party promised well, not
a regular tuck-in, but a bit of a spree, a nice quiet affair.

Saturday morning, as he was dressing, Coupeau began to
feel anxious about his solitary franc. It had just occurred to
him that he was bound to offer a bite and a sup to the witnesses
before dinner. Then there would very likely be some unlooked-
for expenses. It would really never do to have only a franc. So
after having taken Claude and Étienne across to Madame
Boche, who had promised to bring them on to dinner, he
ran to the Rue de la Goutte-d'Or and went up boldly to
borrow ten francs from the Lorilleux. It went very much
against the grain, for he anticipated the grimace his brother-
in-law would make. And indeed he grumbled, gave a nasty
chuckle, but finally produced the two five-franc pieces, while
his wife muttered between her teeth that "that was a good
beginning".

The marriage was fixed at the mayoralty for half-past ten.
It was a splendid morning, the sun pouring down like a furnace,
scorching the streets. So as not to attract attention, the bride
and bridegroom, the mother, and the two witnesses split into
two parties. Gervaise walked in front on the arm of Lorilleux,
whilst M. Madinier escorted Madame Coupeau; then, a little
way behind, on the other side of the street, came Coupeau,
Boche, and Bibi-la-Grillade. They all had black tail-coats;
Boche wore yellow trousers, Bibi-la-Grillade, buttoned to the
throat, without a waistcoat, displayed only a bit of a knotted
tie. M. Madinier alone had a dress-coat, a big coat cut
square; and the passers-by all turned to see the gentleman
escorting fat Madame Coupeau in her green shawl and

black bonnet with red ribbons. Gervaise, gay and charming
in her dark blue dress and tight-fitting little mantle, listened
indulgently to the sneers of Lorilleux, buried in an immense
overcoat in spite of the heat; and from time to time, at the
corner of the streets, she turned her head a little, and smiled
back at Coupeau, ill at ease in his shiny new clothes.

Slowly as they walked, they reached the mayoralty a good
half-hour before the time; and as the mayor was late their
turn did not come till eleven. They sat down and waited in a
corner of the room, staring at the high ceiling and the bare
walls, and speaking in low voices, drawing back their chairs
in their excess of politeness every time that an office boy went
by. Nevertheless they whispered to one another that the
mayor was a dawdler; he was sure to be paying a visit to his
best girl, for the benefit of his gout; perhaps he had had too
much, and swallowed his scarf. But when the magistrate
appeared, they rose respectfully. They had to sit down again,
and look on at three weddings, weddings of respectable folk,
with brides in white, little girls with curled hair, young ladies
in pink sashes, interminable trains of gentlemen and ladies
in their best togs, looking quite stylish. Then, when their
turn came, the marriage was near not coming off, Bibi-la-
Grillade having disappeared. Boche discovered him downstairs in the square, smoking his pipe. Nice sort of people they
were too, in this establishment, giving one the go-by, simply
because one hadn't brand new gloves to sport! And the
formalities, the reading of the Code, the questions, the
signatures, were hurried through so quickly, that they looked
at one another in amazement, imagining that they had been
cheated out of a good half of the ceremony. Gervaise, agitated
and overcome, pressed her handkerchief to her lips. Madame
Coupeau wept copiously. All bent over the register, writing
their names in great shaky letters, with the exception of the
bridegroom, who made his mark, as he could not write.
Each gave twopence to the poor-box, and Coupeau, at a
nudge from Gervaise, gave the office-boy five sous in addition,
when he brought him the marriage certificate.

It was a good step from the mayoralty to the church. On
the way the men had some beer, Madame Coupeau and
Gervaise, cassis with water. And they had to make their way
through a long street, on which the sun poured straight down,
without an inch of shade. The beadle was waiting for them in
the empty church; he hurried them towards a little chapel,

demanding angrily if they wished to make a mock of religion
by coming in so late. A priest came striding up with a surly
air his face pale with hunger, a clerk in a dirty surplice
trotting before him. He hurried through the mass, swallowing
his Latin words, turning, bowing, spreading out his arms in
great haste, with side glances on the married couple and the
witnesses. The married couple before the altar, very much
embarrassed, not knowing when to kneel, to stand up, or to
sit down, waited for the clerk to motion to them. The witnesses,
wishing to behave in a dignified manner, stood up all the
time; while Madame Coupeau, once more overcome by her
tears, wept into the prayer-book she had borrowed from a
neighbour. Twelve o'clock had struck, the last mass had been
said, the steps of the sacristans sounded out in the church,
and there was a noise of chairs being put back into their
places. The high altar was evidently being prepared for some
fête, for the hammers of upholsterers could be heard nailing
up hangings. And in the little dim chapel, in the midst of the
dust raised by the beadle as he swept up the place, the surly-
faced priest laid his withered hands rapidly on the bowed
heads of Gervaise and Coupeau, seeming to join them in
wedlock in the midst of a sort of house-moving, during an
absence of God, between two real masses. When the wedding-
party had once more signed the register, and found itself out
of doors again, it stood there for an instant, struck all of a heap,
out of breath with its rapid transit.

"Here we are!" said Coupeau, with an embarrassed laugh.

He wriggled himself about, finding it anything but a lark.
Then he added:

"Well, there's no time wasted. You get there in four steps.
It is just like the dentists; one hasn't time to cry oh! they
marry you 'without pain'."

"Yes, yes, fine work," sneered Lorilleux. "You get spliced
in five minutes, and it holds all your life. Poor old Cadet-
Cassis!"

And the four witnesses slapped the tinsmith between the
shoulders, for all his airs of importance. Meanwhile Gervaise
kissed Madame Coupeau, smiling and crying, answering the
old woman's broken words:

"Never fear, I will do my best. If it turns out badly, it will
not be my fault. No, indeed; I am too anxious to be happy.
Well, it is done now, anyway. It rests with him and me to do
our best to get on together."

After that they went straight to the "Moulin d'Argent". Coupeau had taken his wife's arm; they walked fast, laughing and excited, two hundred yards before the others, without seeing the houses, or the people, or the vehicles. The deafening noises of the faubourg rang in their ears. When they reached the wine-shop, Coupeau immediately ordered two bottles, and some bread and ham, in the little parlour on the ground floor, just to have a bite. Then, as Boche and Bibi-la-Grillade manifested a hearty appetite, he sent for another bottle and a little cheese. Madame Coupeau was not hungry, she was too overcome to eat. Gervaise, dying of thirst, drained great glasses of water just tinged with wine.

"This's my party," said Coupeau, going to the bar, where he paid four francs five sous.

By this time it was one o'clock, and the guests were arriving. Madame Fauconnier, a plump, good-looking woman, was the first comer. She had a frock of printed Holland, a pink silk scarf, and a bonnet covered with flowers. Next came Mademoiselle Remanjou, lean and spare in her invariable black dress, which she was supposed never to take off, even when she went to bed; and the Gaudrons, the husband with his huge bulk packed into a brown jacket, which creaked at every movement, the great fat wife, big with child, and showing up larger than ever in her staring violet skirt. Coupeau explained that they were not to wait for Mes-Bottes; he would join them on the way to Saint-Denis.

"Well, well!" cried Madame Lerat, as she came in, "we shall have a nice downpour. It *is* going to be nice!"

And she called everybody out to the door to see the clouds, black as ink, which rose rapidly to the south of Paris. Madame Lerat, the eldest of the Coupeaus, was a tall, skinny, mannish-looking woman, who talked through her nose. She looked a fright in her ill-fitting puce dress, which, with its long streamers, made her look like a little lean cur coming out of the water. She brandished her umbrella like a walking stick. When she had kissed Gervaise she went on:

"You have no idea; one is simply scorched in the street. It is like a flame beating right in your face."

At that everyone declared that they had felt the storm coming on. When they came out of the church Monsieur Madinier had seen how it was going to turn out. Lorilleux told him his corns had kept him awake till three in the morning. Besides, it was bound to come sooner or later; the last three days had been too hot for anything.

"I think we are going to have a downpour," said Coupeau at the door, looking anxiously at the sky. "There is only my sister to come, and then we can start at once."

Madame Lorilleux was behind the time. Madame Lerat had looked in for her on the way, but, as she was only then putting on her corset, they had both come to words. And the lanky widow added in her brother's ear:

"I gave her the slip. She is in a fine temper. You'll see presently."

The wedding-party had to wait a quarter of an hour longer, loitering about the wine-shop, elbowed about by men coming in to drain a glass at the bar. Every few minutes Boche, or Madame Fauconnier, or Bibi-la-Grillade would leave the others, and go to the edge of the pavement, turning up their faces. Not a drop of rain; the light grew darker, puffs of wind swept the streets, raising little clouds of dust. At the first stroke of thunder Mademoiselle Remanjou crossed herself. All eyes were turned in the direction of the clock over the mirror; it was already twenty to two.

"Look!" cried Coupeau. "It's raining cats and dogs."

A downpour of rain swept the streets, and women ran helter-skelter, holding up their skirts with both hands. And it was in the midst of this deluge that Madame Lorilleux arrived, panting and furious, struggling on the threshold with her umbrella, which refused to shut.

"Did you ever see!" she spluttered, "I got caught in it at the very door. I was half inclined to go back and take off my things again. And I jolly well wish I had. A nice wedding, this is! I told you so, I wanted to put it off to next Saturday. And it's raining now, because you wouldn't listen to me. All right, all right; let it come down!"

Coupeau tried to calm her. But she told him to go about his business. He wouldn't have to pay for her dress if it were spoilt. She had on a black silk dress, in which she could hardly breathe; the bodice was too tight, it dragged at the button-holes, and cut into her shoulders; and the skirt, cut very narrow, squeezed her so tight at the hips that she had to take tiny steps. Nevertheless, the other ladies looked at her with pursed lips, quite overcome by her toilette. She took no notice of Gervaise, and seated herself by the side of Madame Coupeau. She called over Lorilleux, asked for his handkerchief, and then, going into a corner, carefully wiped one after another the drops of rain that had fallen on her silk dress.

Meanwhile, the downpour had suddenly ceased. It grew darker and darker, almost like night, a livid darkness lit up by great sheets of lightning. Bibi-la-Grillade said jocosely that it was black enough to rain monks and friars. Then the storm burst out with extreme violence. For a good half hour the rain fell in buckets, the thunder rumbled without intermission. The men, standing at the door, gazed out at the grey veil of rain, the swollen gutters, the spray rising from the splash of the puddles. The women all remained in their seats, terrified, covering their faces witht their hands. There was no more conversation, and a joke about the thunder, ventured on by Boche—that St. Peter was snoring up above—did not gain a single smile. But when the thunder grew more distant, and at longer intervals, the company began to get impatient, furious against the storm, swearing and shaking their fists at the clouds. A fine, incessant rain fell from the ashen sky.

"It is past two," cried Madame Lorilleux. "We can't stay here all night."

Mademoiselle Remanjou suggested going into the country all the same, even if one had to take shelter in the fosse of the fortifications; but there was a general outcry; the roads would be anything but pleasant, one couldn't even sit down on the grass; then, too, it wasn't over yet, perhaps there would be another storm. Coupeau, following with his eyes a workman soaked through, who went his way tranquilly under the rain, murmured:

"If that ass, Mes-Bottes, is waiting for us on the way to Saint-Denis, he certainly won't get a sunstroke."

At that everybody laughed. But the general ill-temper went on increasing. It was really intolerable; one must decide on something. There was not much fun staring at one another like that till dinner-time. Then for a quarter of an hour they racked their brains, while the downpour continued obstinately. Bibi-la-Grillade proposed a game of cards; Boche slyly suggested a nice little game, the game of father-confessor; Madame Gaudron spoke of going to have an onion pie at the Chaussée Clignancourt; Madame Lerat wanted everybody to tell stories; Gaudron was quite comfortable as he was, but thought they might sit up to table at once. At every proposition there was a discussion, a dispute; it was silly, it would send them all to sleep, they would look like a pack of children.

Then, when Lorilleux, wanting to say his say, suggested something quite simple, a stroll along the outer boulevards as far as Père-Lachaise, where they could go in and see the tomb of Héloïse and Abélard, if they had the time, Madame Lorilleux, unable to contain herself any longer, exploded. She was simply going about her own business! A nice thing to propose! Perhaps they wanted to make game of her! Did they think she had dressed, and then got wet through, simply to go and stick in a wine-shop! Not a bit of it; she had had quite enough of their wedding. she preferred her own home. Coupeau and Lorilleux had to bar the way.

"Get out of the way!" she cried, "I tell you I am going!"

At last her husband succeeded in calming her, and Coupeau went up to Gervaise, who sat quietly in her corner, chatting with her mother-in-law and Madame Fauconnier.

"You don't suggest anything," he said, not yet venturing to address her in the second person.

"Oh! anything you like," she replied, with a smile. "I am not hard to please. We can go out or stay here, it's the same thing to me. I am quite comfortable; I don't ask for anything more."

And, indeed, her face shone with a quiet content. She addressed each of the guests in a low, slightly trembling voice, taking everything simply, and not mixing herself up in the disputes. While the storm had been raging, she had sat there with her eyes fixed on the clouds, as if she were looking into the future, seeing distant things, of grave import, in the vivid flashes of lightning.

M. Madinier had not yet made any suggestion. He leant against the bar, his coat-tails spread out with an air of importance, feeling himself the master. He spat deliberately, rolled his eyes, and then remarked:

"Why shouldn't we go to the museum?"

And he stroked his chin, looking round at the company and blinking his eyes.

"There are curiosities, heaps of things. It is most instructive. Perhaps you have never been there. It is a thing one ought to see once, at all events."

The wedding party looked at one another hesitatingly. No, Gervaise had never been there; nor had Madame Fauconnier, nor Boche, nor any of them. Coupeau fancied he had looked in one Sunday, but he was not quite clear about it. There was still, however, some hesitation, until Madame Lorilleux, on

whom M. Madinier's consequential air produced a great
impression, declared that the proposal was excellent, the
very thing. Since it was a day lost, anyway, and they were all
dressed, it was just as well to see something instructive.
Everyone agreed. Then, as there was still a little rain, they
borrowed some umbrellas, old umbrellas left behind by
customers, blue, green, and brown, and started for the
gallery.

The wedding party turned to the left, and set out for the
city by the Faubourg Saint-Denis. Coupeau and Gervaise
once more walked ahead, hurrying along, outstripping the
others. M. Madinier now escorted Madame Lorilleux,
Madame Coupeau having remained behind on account of
her legs. Then came Lorilleux and Madame Lerat, Boche and
Madame Fauconnier, Bibi-la-Grillade and Mademoiselle
Remanjou, the Gaudrons at the end. They were twelve in
number. That made a good string on the pavement.

"Oh! we are not here for nothing, I assure you," explained
Madame Lorilleux to M. Madinier. "We don't know where
he picked her up, or rather we know only too well; but then
it is not for us to speak about it My husband had to buy the
wedding ring. And this morning, when he was getting up, he
had to lend them ten francs, without which nothing would
have come off. A bride who doesn't bring a single relation to
the wedding! She is said to have a sister in Paris, who is in
the pork-butcher's line. Why wasn't she invited, I wonder?"

She broke off, to point out Gervaise, who limped badly
over the descent of the road.

"Look at her! if one may! Oh! Clop-clop!"

And this epithet, Clop-clop, went from mouth to mouth.
Lorilleux, in his sneering way, said they ought to call her that.
But Madame Fauconnier stood up for Gervaise; they had no
right to laugh at her, she was as trim as a new penny, and got
through a famous amount of work when it was wanted.
Madame Lerat, always full of dubious allusions, said her leg
was "a lover's pin"; and, she added that lots of men liked
that, without explaining herself further.

The party turned out of the Rue Saint-Denis and crossed
the boulevard. They had to wait a moment before the crowd
of carriages; then they ventured upon the roadway, which
was now streaming with mud. It was pouring again, and they
had to open their umbrellas; and, with their wretched gamps
held over them by the men, the women gathered up their

skirts, and picked their way across, one after another reaching from side to side of the street. Two street urchins yelled out; the passers-by stopped; shop-keepers looked out amused from behind their windows. Among all the swarm of people, against the grey, wet background of the boulevard, the procession of couples came with a violent contrast, Gervaise with her dark blue dress, Madame Fauconnier in her flowered Holland, Boche in his canary-yellow trousers; while the constrained air of people out in their Sunday best gave a fantastic look to Coupeau's shining tail-coat and the square dress-coat of M. Madinier; whilst the fine get-up of Madame Lorilleux, the streamers of Madame Lerat, the rumpled skirts of Mademoiselle Remanjou, made a mixed medley, trailing all the hand-me-downs of poor people's fashions. But it was the men's hats in particular that amused the folk—old hats, long laid away, dimmed with the dirt of cupboards, with conical tops, tall, broad, and pointed, extraordinary brims, curled and flat, too wide and too narrow. And the smiles increased, when, right at the very end, as if to finish up the show. Madame Gaudron, the wool-carder, in her staring violet dress, advanced with her bulging belly borne proudly before her. The wedding-party did not hasten, taking it all good-naturedly, pleased to be stared at, amused with the jokes.

"Hallo! there's the bride!" cried one of the street urchins. "Oh dear! she's swallowed a big pip!"

All the party burst out laughing. Bibi-la-Grillade, looking round, swore that the kid had had a good one that time. The wool-carder laughed the loudest of all, showing herself off all the more; there was no disgrace in that, quite the contrary; more than one of the ladies who looked askance at her in passing would have been only too glad to change places with her.

They took the Rue Cléry by mistake; then the Rue du Mail. On the Place des Victoires there was a stoppage. The bride's left shoe-lace had come undone; and as she tied it up at the foot of the statue of Louis XIV, the couples came close up behind her, joking, as they waited, on the bit of ankle that she showed. At last, after passing through the Rue Croix-des-Petits-Champs, they reached the Louvre.

M. Madinier politely asked leave to lead the way.

It was a large place, they might easily lose themselves; and he knew the best parts, too, because he had often come there with an artist, a very intelligent fellow, who did designs for a large firm of cardboard makers, to put on boxes. The wedding-party wandered into the Assyrian Gallery, where they were somewhat taken aback. It was deucedly cold there; just the thing for a wine-cellar. The couples advanced slowly, their chins in the air, blinking their lids between the stone colossi, the black marble gods, mute in their hieratic rigidity, the monstrous beasts, half-cat and half-woman, with the faces of the dead, noses shrunken and lips swollen. They thought them very ugly. One knew a jolly lot better than that now-a-days how to carve stone. An inscription in Phœnician characters stupefied them. It was not possible, no one could ever have read that scrawl. But M. Madinier, who had already reached the first landing with Madame Lorilleux, shouted out to them:

"Come along, that's nothing, those objects. What you have to see is up here."

The bareness and severity of the staircase solemnized them. A superb door-keeper, in red waistcoat and gold-braided livery, who seemed to await them on the landing, redoubled their terror. It was with great respect, walking as softly as they could, that they entered the French Gallery.

Then, without pausing, their eyes dazzled by the gold of the frames, they went through the string of rooms, seeing picture after picture go by, too many of them to be properly seen. They would have to spend an hour before each, if they were to take it in. What a heap of pictures, damn it all! it would never finish. They must have cost a pretty lot. Then, at the very end, M. Madinier stopped them suddenly before the "Raft of the Medusa"; and he explained the subject to them. All stood silent and transfixed. As they moved on, Boche summed up the general feeling: it was ripping.

In the Apollo Gallery it was the floor that specially amazed them, a floor shining like a mirror, in which the legs of the benches were reflected. Mademoiselle Remanjou closed her eyes, for it seemed to her that she was walking on water. They called to Madame Gaudron to plant her feet firmly, on account of her condition. M. Madinier wanted them to look at the gilding and frescoes of the ceiling; but they strained their necks, and made out very little. Then, before entering the Salon Carré, he pointed to a window, saying:

"That is where Charles IX fired on the people."

He looked around to see that everybody was following,

then he called for a halt in the middle of the Salon Carré. "There are only masterpieces here," he murmured under his breath, as if he were in church. They all went round the room. Gervaise asked the subject of the "Marriage at Cana"; it was so stupid not to write the names on the frames. Coupeau stopped before "La Gioconda", which seemed to him to resemble one of his aunts. Boche and Bibi-la-Grillade tittered, pointing out the naked women to one another out of the corner of their eye; they were specially impressed by the thighs of the "Antiope". And, at the very end, the Gaudrons, the husband open-mouthed, the wife with her hands folded across her stomach, stood and gaped blankly, before the "Virgin" of Murillo.

When they had gone all round, M. Madinier suggested that they should go round again; it was quite worth the trouble. He was very attentive to Madame Lorilleux, on account of her silk dress; and every time that she asked him a question, he answered gravely, with the greatest confidence. As she was taken with "Titian's Mistress", whose hair seemed to her something like her own, he told her that it was "la belle Ferronnière", a mistress of Henri IV, on whom there had been a play given at the Ambigu.

Then the wedding-party struck into the long gallery containing the Italian and Flemish schools. Pictures, and yet again pictures, saints, men and women with faces that one could not make out, landscapes gone black, beasts turned yellow, a jumble of people and things in glaring colours, which began to give them a headache. M. Madinier no longer talked, he went slowly at the head of the procession, which followed in order, every neck twisted and every head uplifted. Centuries of art passed before their bewildered ignorance, the fine rigidity of the early Italians, the splendour of the Venetians, the sleek and sunny life of the Dutchmen. But what interested them the most were the copyists, with their easels set up in the midst of the people, painting away undisturbed; and an old lady mounted on a long ladder, washing a pale sky in an immense picture with stone-colour, struck them particularly. Little by little the news had spread that there was a wedding-party at the Louvre; painters came running up with broad grins, curious onlookers planted themselves beforehand on the benches in the way, whilst the attendants bit their lips to keep back the jokes that came into their minds. And the wedding-party, tired out and losing their respect for things, dragged their hob-nailed shoes along, clattering over the sounding floor with the noise of a herd in confusion, let loose in the midst of the bare and composed neatness of the place.

M. Madinier kept silence, in order to lead up to an effect. He went straight to the "Kermesse" of Rubens. He said nothing, but merely indicated the canvas with a knowing wink. The women, after looking closely at the picture, gave little screams and turned away, blushing red. The men held them back, laughing and looking out the dirty details.

"Well, here now!" said Boche, "that's worth the money. Look! there's somebody spewing, and somebody watering the dandelions! And look at that one! oh, look at that one! Clean lot, aren't they?"

"Come along," said M. Madinier, enchanted with his success, there is nothing more to see this way."

The wedding-party went back the way they had come, through the Salon Carré and the Apollo Gallery. Madame Lerat and Mademoiselle Remanjou complained that their legs were giving way under them. But the cardboard-maker wanted to show Lorilleux the ancient jewels. It was at the side, in a little room which he could find with his eyes shut. Nevertheless, he lost his way, and led them through seven or eight rooms, cold and deserted, containing nothing but glass cases, in which were innumerable quantities of broken pots and hideous little objects. The party was cold, and bored to death. Then, fumbling at a door, they found themselves among the drawings. It was a fresh tramp; the drawings seemed never ending. Room after room with nothing amusing, only bits of paper covered with scribbles, under glass cases and against the walls. M. Madinier had quite lost his head, which, however, he would not admit; and he took them upstairs to the floor above. This time they found themselves in the marine gallery, among the models of instruments and cannons, raised plans, and ships like big toys. After a quarter of an hour's walk they came at last to another staircase. Having reached the bottom they found themselves once more among the drawings. Then, giving it up in despair, they went forward at random, two and two, following M. Madinier, who mopped his brow, quite beside himself, raging against the management, which he accused of having altered the position of the doors. The door-keepers and visitors gazed at the cavalcade in amazement. In less than twenty minutes it was to be seen in the Salon Carré, in the French Gallery, and beside the cases in which sleep the little gods of the East. Never would they find the way out. Dragging their tired legs after them as best they could, the wedding-party clattered along, leaving Madame Gaudron's big belly far behind.

"Closing time!" cried the loud voices of the door-keepers.

They were very nearly locked in; a door-keeper had to take them in charge and show them the way to one of the doors. Once in the courtyard of the Louvre, the umbrellas recovered from the cloakroom, they breathed again. M. Madinier recovered his self-possession; he had made a mistake in not turning to the left; he remembered now that the jewels were to the left. And all the party affected to be very much pleased to have seen it all.

Four o'clock was striking. There were still two hours before dinner-time. They decided on a little walk, in order to kill time. The women, who were very tired, would have preferred to sit down; but as no one offered any refreshments, they set forth again along the embankment. Here they were caught in another shower, so heavy, that, despite the umbrellas, the dresses got quite in a mess. Madame Lorilleux, her heart sinking at every drop that fell on her dress, proposed that they should take refuge under the Pont-Royal; indeed, if they would not accompany her, she threatened to go down by herself. They all went down under the Pont-Royal. There it was all right. Wasn't that really a stunning idea! The women spread out their handkerchiefs on the stones, and sat down, their knees wide apart, plucking with both hands the blades of grass that grew between the stones, gazing at the dark water as it flowed by, as if they were in the country. The men amused themselves with shouting loudly, so as to arouse the echo of the arch opposite; Boche and Bibi-la-Grillade, one after the other insulted vacancy by howling "Cochon!" and roared with laughter as the echo flung back the word in their faces; then, getting hoarse, they picked up flat stones, and played at ducks and drakes. The shower was over, but they were all so comfortable that they felt no inclination to move on. The Seine drifted past them greasily, bearing along with it old corks, parings of vegetables, a heap of filth that whirled round for an instant in the gloomy water under the heavy shadow of the arch; whilst on the bridge above them there was a rumbling of omnibuses and cabs, the mob of Paris, of which they could only see the roofs to the right and left, as from the bottom of a pit. Mademoiselle Remanjou sighed; if there had only been any trees, she said, it would have recalled a little corner of the Marne, where she went in 1817, with a young man whose loss she still mourned.

However, M. Madinier gave the signal to move on. They crossed the garden of the Tuileries, through a whole throng of children, whose hoops and balls disturbed the regular order of the couples. Then, as they reached the Place Vendôme, and stopped to look at the column, M. Madinier proposed to the ladies that they should go up and see the view of Paris. The idea seemed a capital one. Yes, yes, they must go up; it would be a great joke. Besides, it was very interesting for those who had never left the plain soil.

"You don't fancy Clop-clop will risk her precious pins on that staircase!" muttered Madame Lorilleux.

"I don't mind going up," said Madame Lerat, "but I don't care about having a man just behind me."

The party began the ascent. The twelve mounted, one after another, in the narrow spiral of the staircase, stumbling against the worn steps, holding on to the walls. Then, when they plunged into utter darkness, there was a roar of laughter. The women uttered little shrieks; the men tickled them and pinched their legs. But it wasn't worth while saying anything; it was better to pretend that it was the mice. Besides, they knew when to stop, they wouldn't go too far. Then Boche hit on a joke which everybody caught up. They called out to Madame Gaudron, as if she had stuck on the way, asking if she could pull herself through. Only fancy! if her time were to come where she was, without being able to get either up or down, she would block up the way, and no one would be able to get past her. And they laughed over the big-bellied woman with shouts of laughter that seemed to shake the column. Then Boche, now set going, declared that they would grow old in this blessed flue; was it never coming to an end? were they going right up to heaven? Meanwhile Coupeau said nothing; he came after Gervaise, his arms around her, feeling her abandon herself to him; and when they suddenly came into the full light he was in the act of imprinting a kiss on her neck.

"Well! that's all right; pray don't disturb yourselves, you two!" said Madame Lorilleux, with a scandalized air.

Bibi-la-Grillade was furious. He muttered between his teeth:

"What a noise they make! I couldn't even count the stairs."

M. Madinier, on the leads, was already pointing out the monuments. Madame Fauconnier and Mademoiselle Reman-jou could never go farther than the staircase; the mere thought of the pavement down below turned their heads; they would do no more than venture a few glances through the open door. Madame Lerat, more daring, walked all round the narrow space, keeping close against the bronze of the dome. But it was all the same pretty stiff, when you remembered that you only need slip your foot. Good God! what a tumble! The men, rather pale, looked down at the square below. One seemed to be in mid air, away from everything. It positively made one's blood run cold. Meanwhile, M. Madinier advised them to look up, and in front of them, as far as they could; that took the giddiness off. And he went on pointing out the Invalides, the Panthéon, Notre-Dame, the Tour Saint-Jacques, the Buttes Montmartre. Then Madame Lorilleux asked if one could see the wine-shop where they were going to dine, the "Moulin-d'Argent", on the Boulevard de la Chapelle. For ten minutes they looked for it and disputed over it; each placed it in a different spot. Paris all around them stretched out in its grey immensity, with its blue distances, its deep valleys, with their rolling waves of roofs; on the right of the Seine, all lay in shadow, beneath a great sheet of copper-coloured cloud; and from the edge of this cloud, with its fringe of gold, a great ray of sunlight shot out, lighting up thousands of window panes, to the left of the river, with sparkling flashes, blocking out this corner of the city in a flood of light against the clear sky, swept clear by the storm.

"It wasn't worth while coming up here to fly at one another's throats," said Boche, angrily, making his way downstairs.

The wedding-party descended in gloomy silence, without a sound save the clatter of their shoes on the stairs. When they reached the bottom M. Madinier offered to pay, but Coupeau would not hear of it, and thrust twenty-five sous into the attendant's hand, two sous each. It was nearly half-past five, that gave them just the time to get back. They went back along the boulevards and by way of the Faubourg Poissonnière. Coupeau, however, declared that the outing could not be allowed to end like that, and he hurried everybody into a wine-shop, where they took vermouth.

Dinner had been ordered for six. The party had been due at the "Moulin-d'Argent" for the last twenty minutes. Madame Boche, who had left her *concierge's* lodge in the care of someone in the house, was chatting with old Madame Coupeau on the first-floor dining-room, opposite the spread table; and the two children, Claude and Étienne, whom she had brought along, amused themselves by running under the table in the midst of a medley of chairs. When Gervaise saw the children, whom she had not seen all day, she lifted them on her knees, and began to kiss and fondle them.

"Have they behaved themselves?" she asked Madame Boche. "They haven't given you too much bother, I hope?"

And as Madame Boche related the droll things the little rascals had said during the afternoon, she caught them up again, and clasped them to her in a very passion of tenderness.

"It is rather funny for Coupeau, all the same," said Madame Lorilleux to the other women at the far end of the room.

Gervaise still kept the quietly-smiling air she had had in the morning. Since the outing, however, she became pensive from time to time, considering her husband and the Lorilleux in her thoughtful way. Coupeau seemed to her afraid of his sister. The night before, he had sworn that he would soon put them in their places with their backbiting tongues, if need were. But, once before them, she saw well, he crouched like a beaten cur, waited on all their words, and was on pins and needles when he thought they were put out. And all that disturbed her a little for the future.

Meanwhile there was only Mes-Bottes to wait for.

"Oh! hang it all!" said Coupeau, "let's sit down to table. You'll soon see him crop up; he has a sharp nose, he can sniff the grub a long way off. I say, he's having a jolly time if he has been cooling his heels all this while on the road to Saint-Denis!"

Thereupon the wedding-party, much diverted, drew up to table with a great scraping of chairs. Gervaise was between Lorilleux and M. Madinier, and Coupeau between Madame Fauconnier and Madame Lorilleux. The other guests seated themselves where they pleased, because there were always grumblings and jealousies when the places were arranged beforehand. Boche slipped into the seat by Madame Lerat. Bibi-la-Grillade had for neighbours Mademoiselle Remanjou and Madame Gaudron. As for Madame Boche and old Madame Coupeau, right at the end, they looked after the children, and promised to cut up their meat, and give them something to drink; above all, not much wine.

"Doesn't anyone say grace?" asked Boche, whilst the ladies were arranging their skirts under the table, for fear of staining them.

But Madame Lorilleux did not approve of such jokes. The vermicelli soup, almost cold, was eaten very quickly, with lips hissing in the spoons. Two waiters were in attendance, dressed in little greasy jackets and aprons of dubious whiteness. Through the four windows, opening on the acacias of the court, the air entered freely, a calm evening after storm, still with a lingering heat. The reflection of the dripping trees cast a greenish light over the smoky room, making the shadows of the leaves flicker over the table-cloth, smelling faintly of mouldiness. There were two fly-spotted mirrors, one at each end, seeming to lengthen out the table indefinitely, with its dingy plate turning yellow, the grease of the sink clotted black in the scratches of the knives. Every time that a waiter came up from the kitchen, a door at the end banged, letting through a strong smell of burning fat.

"Now don't speak all at once," said Boche, in the midst of a general silence, as they bent over their plates.

The first glass of wine was being drunk, and two force-meat pies were being served by the waiters, when Mes-Bottes entered.

"Well! you are a nice lot, you people!" he cried. "Here have I been kicking my heels on the road these three hours, till a gendarme actually came and asked for my papers. Is that the dirty way you serve your friends? You might at least have sent a cab for me. No, joking apart, it's a bit thick. Why it rained so hard my pockets were filled with water; there's still some small fry for the fishing in them."

The company went into fits of laughter. Mes-Bottes was quite screwed; he had already had his two bottles, merely as a sort of counter-blast to the dose of Adam's ale which the storm had soused him with.

"Now, daddy-long-legs!" said Coupeau, "go and sit down at the end by Madame Gaudron. You see, we waited for you!"

Oh, that was all the same to him, he would soon catch them up; and he called three times for soup, helpings of vermicelli, in which he cut up huge chunks of bread. When they attacked the pies, he became the wonderment of the whole table. How he did guzzle! The astonished waiters took turns in passing him the bread. little neat bits which he swallowed at one mouthful. At last he lost his temper, and demanded a whole length of bread to himself. The landlord looked in anxiously for a moment at the door, and the company, who were expecting his advent, went into fresh fits of laughter. And that fetched him, the poor old boss! And wasn't he a stunner, Mes-Bottes! One day he had eaten twelve hard-boiled eggs and drunk twelve glasses of wine, while it was striking twelve! There were not many like that! And Mademoiselle Remanjou, quite moved by his prowess, watched his jaws going, whilst M. Madinier, casting about for a word to express his astonishment, which amounted almost to respect, declared that such a capacity was extraordinary.

There was a silence. A waiter had just placed on the table a ragout of rabbit in a huge dish as deep as a salad-bowl. Thereupon Coupeau played off a famous bit of spoof.

"I say waiter, you've brought us a nice sort of rabbit. I should call it a gutter-rabbit. Why, it still mews."

And, indeed, a faint mew, perfectly imitated, seemed to issue from the plate. It was Coupeau who did it in his throat, without moving his lips; a show accomplishment which never failed of success, so that he never ordered a meal without including rabbit. After that he purred. The women hid their faces in their handkerchiefs; they could not stop laughing.

Madame Fauconnier asked for the head; she only cared for the head. Mademoiselle Remanjou adored the fat. And when Boche said that he preferred the little onions when they were well done, Madame Lerat pursed up her lips and muttered:

"I can quite understand that."

She was as thin as a lath, lived a hard-working, cloistral existence, and had scarcely seen a man since her husband died, but she had a perfect mania for indecent allusions, so very obscure that only she herself could understand them. Boche bent over and asked her in a whisper to explain her meaning, but she only repeated:

"Oh, yes, the little onions. I fancy that will just do."

But the conversation became serious. Everyone talked shop. M. Madinier bragged about his cardboard making; there were genuine artists employed in it; and he referred to the fancy boxes, of which he knew the models, perfect wonders. Meanwhile Lorilleux sneered; he was very proud of working in gold, he seemed to see the glitter of it on his fingers, from head to foot. "Well," said he, "goldsmiths once upon a time used to wear swords," and he referred at random to Bernard Palissy. Coupeau told of a weathercock that one of his fellow workmen had made; it was composed of a column, then of a sheaf, then of a basket of fruit, then of a flag, all copied to the life, and made merely out of bits of galvanized cut out and soldered together. Madame Lerat explained to Bibi-la-Grillade how the stalk of a rose was turned, making the handle of her knife revolve between her bony fingers. Meanwhile voices grew louder, and spoke all at once. In the midst of the noise Madame Fauconnier was heard complaining of one of her work-girls, a bit of trash, who had caught fire to a pair of her sheets only last night.

"You may say as you like," cried Lorilleux, bringing down his fist on the table, "gold is gold."

And, in the silence caused by this truism, nothing was heard but the thin voice of Mademoiselle Remanjou continuing:

"Then I pull up their skirts, I stitch inside, I stick a pin into the head to keep on the bonnet, and it is finished. They are sold at sixpence."

She was explaining her dolls to Mes-Bottes, whose jaws worked on slowly and steadily, like millstones. He paid no attention, but wagged his head, and kept an eye on the waiters, so that they should not change the plates before they were well scraped out. They had had a *fricandeau au jus* and French beans. Now the roast was brought in, two meagre fowls laid out on cress, faded and frizzled by the heat. Outside, the sun was fading behind the high branches of the acacias. In the room, the greenish reflection grew darker in the steam that rose from the table, stained with wine and sauce, and encumbered with all the dishes. And along the wall, the dirty plates and empty bottles, placed there by the waiters, seemed the sweepings of the feast. It was very hot. The men took off their coats, and went on eating in their shirt-sleeves.

"Madame Boche, please don't let the children stuff so much," said Gervaise, who had spoken little, keeping an eye on Claude and Étienne from a distance.

She got up, and went round behind their chairs to speak to them for a moment. The children, you may be sure, would eat all day long without refusing anything; and she gave them herself some fowl, a bit of the white. But old Madame Coupeau declared that they might have an indigestion if they would, for once. Madame Boche, in a low voice, accused Boche of pinching Madame Lerat's knee. He was a sly dog; he was easily worked up. She saw his hand go out of sight. If he did it again she had a good mind to fling a decanter at his head; she had indeed.

In the midst of the general silence M. Madinier talked politics.

"Their law of the 31st of May is an abomination. Now you are obliged to have been a householder for two years. Three thousand citizens are struck off the lists. They say that Bonaparte is really at heart much put out about it, for he loves the people, he has shown it."

For his part he was a Republican, but he admired the prince on account of his uncle, a man the like of whom would never be seen again. Bibi-la-Grillade grew wroth. He had worked at the Élysée; he had seen Bonaparte as well as he saw Mes-Bottes there opposite to him. Well, as for the president, the bounder looked for all the world like a nark! It was reported that he was going on a tour Lyons way: it would be a good riddance if he were to break his neck in a ditch. And as the discussion grew heated, Coupeau had to interfere.

"Well, you are bookies to quarrel over politics! There's a nice business, politics! What have we to do with politics, I should like to know? They can have what they like, a king, an emperor, or nothing, but will that hinder me from earning my five francs, from eating and sleeping, eh? It's too ridiculous!"

Lorilleux shook his head. He was born the same day as the Compte de Chambord, the 29th of September, 1820. This coincidence impressed him deeply; and he had vague dreams, in which there was a certain connection between the return of the king and his own luck. He did not say exactly what he hoped for, but he gave out that it would be something uncommonly pleasant. So, whenever he hoped for anything that was not likely to be realized, he put it off till later, "when the king comes back".

"Besides," he went on, "I saw the Comte de Chambord one day. . . ."

Every face turned in his direction.

"Certainly. A big good-natured looking man in a greatcoat. I was at Péquignot's, a friend of mine who sells furniture, Grande-Rue de la Chapelle. The Comte de Chambord had left his umbrella there the day before. Well, he came in, he said, 'Would you kindly give me my umbrella?' just like that, quite simply. Fact! it was he himself, Péquignot gave me his word."

None of the guests threw any doubt on the story. By this time they had come to the dessert. The waiters cleared the table with a great clatter of dishes. And Madame Lorilleux, who till then had behaved in the most genteel and ladylike manner, screamed out "Damn your butter fingers!" as one of the waiters, in removing a dish, dropped something wet on the back of her neck. Her silk dress must surely be stained. M. Madinier had to look up and down her back, but he swore there was nothing to be seen. Meanwhile some *œufs à la neige* were laid out in a salad bowl in the middle of the table, with two plates of cheese on one side and two plates of fruit on the other. The *œufs à la neige*, the over-done white crumbling into the yellow cream, caused quite a sensation; they were something unexpected, quite stylish. Mes-Bottes continued to eat. He had asked for another roll of bread. He finished up both sorts of cheese; then, finding some cream left, he had the salad bowl passed to him, and proceeded to ladle out huge pieces, as if it were soup.

"The gentleman is really very remarkable," said M. Madinier, once more lost in admiration.

Then the men rose to fill their pipes. They stopped for a moment behind Mes-Bottes, slapping him on the shoulder; and asking him if he felt better now. Bibi-la-Grillade lifted him, chair and all; but God damn it, the fellow was twice as heavy as he was before. Coupeau declared jokingly that he was only just getting under way; that he would go on eating bread at that rate all night. The terrified waiters disappeared. Boche who had gone downstairs just before, came up declaring that the landlord was sitting pallid inside the bar, while his wife, all in a flurry ,had sent out to see if the bakers were still open; the very cat went about looking the picture of misery. It was really absurd; it was worth the price of the dinner; it was impossible to have a proper feed without that great guzzler Mes-Bottes. And the men, as they smoked their pipes, looked at him enviously; for a man must be solidly built to be able to eat all that.

"I shouldn't like to have to look after your keep," said Madame Gaudron. "No, indeed!"

"I say, mother, none of that," replied Mes-Bottes, with a

side-glance at the big belly of his neighbour. "You've swallowed more than I have."

Everyone applauded, and cried "Bravo!" It was a good hit. The light had now quite gone, and three gas-burners flickered in the room, giving a wavering light in the midst of the smoke of pipes. The waiters, after having served the coffee and cognac, had cleared away the last piles of dirty plates. Below, under the three acacias, the dancing had begun, a cornet and two violins playing loudly, the women's laughter sounding shrill in the warm night.

"Now for a good stiff drink!" cried Mes-Bottes. "Two bottles of rare old stuff, plenty of lemons, and not too much sugar!"

But Coupeau, seeing Gervaise look anxious, got up and declared that there was to be no more drink served. They had disposed of five-and-twenty bottles, each his bottle and a-half, counting the children; that was quite enough. They had had a mouthful together in a friendly way, without making any great to-do, because they were all good friends, and wished to celebrate a family-rejoicing together. All had gone off merrily and well; it wouldn't do now to go and get beastly tight if they had any respect for the ladies. In a word, and this was the last he should say, they had met together to drink to their splicing, and not to get sozzled. This little speech, delivered in a determined voice by the tinsmith, who laid his hand on his heart at the close of each phrase, was received with warm approbation by Lorilleux and M. Madinier. But the others, Boche, Gaudron, Bibi-la-Grillade, Mes-Bottes in particular, all four very screwed, merely sneered, declaring they felt damned inclined to wet their whistle.

"Those who are thirsty are thirsty, and those who are not thirsty are not thirsty," observed Mes-Bottes, "consequently we are going to have our drink. We don't prig nothing from nobody. Swells can have sugar and water if they like."

And as the tinsmith was beginning to speak again, the other got up, smacked his thigh, exclaiming:

"You be hanged! Waiter! two bottles of old."

At that Coupeau said that it was all very well, only they had better settle up the amount of the meal at once, and so have things clear. There was no reason why decent folk should pay for boozers. And it turned out that Mes-Bottes, after great fumbling, could only find three francs seven sous. Why had they left him in the lurch on the road to Saint-Denis? He couldn't stay there and be drowned, so he had split his five franc piece; it was their own fault. Finally, he handed over three francs, keeping the seven sous for his next day's tobacco. Coupeau was furious, and would have kicked at it, had not Gervaise pulled him by the sleeve, frightened and supplicating. He decided to borrow two francs from Lorilleux, who, after having refused, slipped them into his hand, for his wife would certainly never have allowed it.

Meanwhile, M. Madinier had taken a plate. The unaccompanied ladies, Madame Lerat, Madame Fauconnier, Mademoiselle Remanjou, put down their five franc piece first, discreetly. Then the men went to the other end of the room, and went over the accounts. They were fifteen; that should be seventy-five francs. When the seventy-five francs were in the plate, every man added five sous for the waiters. It took a quarter of an hour's hard work before it was all settled to everyone's satisfaction.

But when M. Madinier, who wished to settle up with the landlord, had sent to summon him, the whole company was struck with amazement on hearing him declare with a smile that that was not all. There were certain extras. And as this word of "extras" was received with frantic exclamations, he gave the details: twenty-five bottles instead of twenty, the number agreed upon beforehand; the œufs à la neige, which he had added, he said, on seeing the dessert rather meagre; finally, a carafe of rum, served with the coffee, in case anyone preferred rum. Then a formidable battle began. Coupeau, brought to bay, held out firmly; he had never said a word about twenty bottles; as for the œufs à la neige, they were a part of the dessert, so much the worse for him if he had added them on his own hook; as for the carafe of rum, that was a mere trick, done to swell out the bill by putting liqueurs on the table which one helped oneself to without noticing.

"It was on the tray with the coffee," he cried; 'well, it ought to be included with the coffee. Just clear off, take your money along with you, and be damned to you if ever we set foot in this hole again!"

"It is six francs extra," repeated the landlord. "Give me my six francs. And I don't include that gentleman's three loaves either!"

The whole party crowded round him, buffeting him with a very fury of gesticulation, a scream of voices half strangled with rage. The women especially, coming out of their reserve,

refused to add a cent. A nice sort of wedding this was, indeed!
It was not Mademoiselle Remanjou who would ever poke
herself into one of those dinners again! Madame Fauconnier
had had an extremely bad dinner; at home, for forty sous,
she could have had quite a tasty little meal. Madame Gaudron
complained bitterly of having been shoved away at the far
end of the table by the side of Mes-Bottes, who had not paid
the slightest attention to her. These arrangements always
turned out badly. When one wanted people to come to a
wedding dinner—Heavens!—they might be decently invited!
And Gervaise seeking refuge beside old Madame Coupeau by
one of the windows, said nothing, feeling horribly ashamed,
as if all these outcries were directed against herself.

M. Madinier finally went downstairs with the landlord.
They could be heard discussing the matter. In half an hour's
time the cardboard-maker reappeared; he had settled the
account by paying three francs. But the company was still
vexed and exasperated, going back again and again to the
question of extras. And the confusion was increased by a
vigorous act of Madame Boche. She kept an eye constantly
on Boche, and spied him, in a corner, putting his arm round
the waist of Madame Lerat. Thereupon she flung a decanter
at his head, smashing it in pieces against the wall.

"It is evident that your husband is a tailor, madame,"
said the tall widow, with her much-meaning purse of the lips.
"He is an A1 for the petticoats. I kept kicking him under the
table, all the same."

The harmony of the evening was spoilt; a note of bitterness
crept in. M. Madinier proposed some singing, but Bibi-la-
Grillade, who had a good voice, was nowhere to be found;
at last Mademoiselle Remanjou saw him from the window,
whirling round a fat, bare-headed girl under the acacias. The
cornet and the two violins played "*Le Marchand de Moutarde*",
a quadrille, in which one clapped hands, *à la pastourelle*.
Thereupon there was a rush; Mes-Bottes and the Gaudrons
went down, Boche himself followed. From the windows, the
couples could be seen turning, between the leaves, to which
the coloured lanterns, suspended from the branches, gave the
crude, painted green of stage scenery. The night was still and
breathless after the great heat. Upstairs, a serious conversation
had arisen between Lorilleux and M. Madinier, whilst the
ladies, unable to give vent to their rage, examined their
dresses, to see if they had got in a mess.

Madame Lerat's streamers appeared to have been dipped into the coffee. Madame Fauconnier's Holland dress was covered with sauce. Old Madame Coupeau's green shawl, which had fallen off the back of a chair, had just been discovered in a corner, crumpled and stepped upon. But it was Madame Lorilleux in particular who worked herself up into a fury. Her dress was spotted at the back. Everybody might swear to the contrary, but she could feel it. And after wriggling about before the glass, she finally discovered the stain.

"What did I say?" she cried. "It is gravy off the fowl. The waiter shall pay for my dress; I will summons him. That is the finishing touch! I had better have stayed in bed all day. I shall go directly; I have had quite enough of their blessed wedding!"

She set off in a fury, making the staircase tremble under her. Lorilleux ran after her, but all he could do was to induce her to wait five minutes on the pavement, in case they would all start together. She would have done better to have gone right back after the storm, as she had wished to do. She would serve out Coupeau for that day! When Coupeau heard the state she was in, he seemed quite overcome; and Gervaise, to smooth the way for him, agreed to come home at once. Thereupon the women hastily kissed one another. M. Madinier undertook to see old Madame Coupeau home. Madame Boche was going to take Claude and Étienne home with her for the first night; their mother need have no fear, the little ones were already asleep on chairs, stupefied with an indigestion of œufs à la neige. At last the bride and bridegroom made their escape with Lorilleux, leaving the rest of the party at the wine-shop, where a squabble had arisen in the dancing hall between their set and another; Boche and Mes-Bottes, who had embraced a certain lady, being unwilling to give her back to two soldiers whom she was with, threatening to knock over the whole apple-cart, while the cornet and the two violins went on beating out the polka of the Perles.

It was not yet quite eleven. On the Boulevard de la Chapelle and all around the Goutte-d'Or, the fortnight's pay-day, which fell on that Saturday, brought out a noisy swarm of tipplers. Madame Lorilleux waited twenty yards away from the "Moulin-d'Argent", motionless under the gas-lamp. She took Lorilleux's arm, and marched ahead without turning, at such a rate that Gervaise and Coupeau got quite out of breath in trying to keep up with them. Sometimes they had to move off the footpath in order to get past a drunkard who had fallen there, and lay sprawling on his back. Lorilleux turned his head, trying to patch up the peace.

"We will see you to your door," he said.

But Madame Lorilleux, raising her voice, said it seemed to her odd to pass one's wedding-night in such a beastly hole as the Hôtel Boncœur. Wouldn't they have done better to put off the marriage, save a few pence, and buy some furniture, so as to be in their own home for the first night? Very comfortable they would be up under the roof, packed away in a ten-franc room, where there was not room to breathe.

"I have given notice, we shan't stay up there," objected Coupeau, timidly. "We shall keep Gervaise's room; it is larger."

At that Madame Lorilleux forgot herself, and turned round sharply.

"That is too much!" she cried, "to sleep in Clop-clop's room!"

Gervaise turned quite pale. The nickname, which she heard flung in her face for the first time, struck her like a blow. Then, too, she quite understood the meaning of her sister-in-law's exclamation: Clop-clop's room, that meant the room where she had lived a month with Lantier, where there was still the trail of her past life. Coupeau saw nothing of it, was only wounded by the nickname.

"You make a mistake in calling other people names," he replied angrily. "You don't know that they call you Cow-tail all about here, because of your hair. There, you don't much care about that, do you? Why shouldn't we keep the room on the first floor? The children are not sleeping there tonight, we shall be all right."

Madame Lorilleux made no reply; she was on her dignity. for she had been horribly vexed at being called Cow-tail. Coupeau, to console Gervaise, squeezed her arm in his, and he succeeded even in making her smile as he whispered in her ear that they were setting up house on the sum of seven sous all told, three big sous and one little sou, which he jingled in his trousers pocket. When they reached the Hôtel Boncœur, they said good night in a constrained manner. And as Coupeau thrust the two women into one another's arms, calling them two sillies, a drunkard, who seemed to be going to pass on the right, gave a sudden stagger to the left, and came just between them.

"Hallo! it's old Bazouge!" said Lorilleux. "He's on his beam's-end tonight,"

Gervaise, in a fright, retreated against the door of the Hôtel Boncœur. Old Bazouge, an undertaker's man of about fifty, had stained his black trousers with mud, his black cloak was slipping off his shoulders, his black hat squashed and battered by a fall.

"Don't be frightened, he's all right," continued Lorilleux. "He is a neighbour of ours, the third room in the corridor, before you get to us. It would look nice if his employers saw him like that."

Meanwhile old Bazouge had taken offence at the young woman's fright.

"Well, well!" he stuttered out, "we ain't going to eat nobody. I'm as good as anyone else, eh! my dear? Of course, I have had a glass. When you've got plenty of work you must grease the wheels. It isn't you nor the others who would have brought down the party of forty stone that we had to bring down between us from the fourth storey to the ground, and wthout letting him drop. I like jolly folk."

But Gervaise drew back closer into the angle of the door, ready to burst into tears, feeling as if all her day's happiness were spoilt. She forgot all about embracing her sister-in-law, she only begged Coupeau to send away the drunken man. Thereupon Bazouge, staggering, made a gesture of philosophic disdain.

"Your turn will come one day, my dear, all the same. Perhaps you'll be only too glad for your turn to come, one day. Yes, I know women who would say thank you if one came to fetch them.".

And as the Lorilleux made up their minds to take him along with them, he turned, stuttering out a last word between two hiccups.

"When you're dead . . . look you here . . . when you're dead, you're dead for a long time."

CHAPTER FOUR

THEN came four years of hard work. In the neighbourhood Gervaise and Coupeau had a good reputation, they kept themselves to themselves, had no squabbles, and went out regularly for a walk on Sundays, Saint-Ouen way. The wife worked twelve hours a day at Madame Fauconnier's, and managed to keep everything at home as bright as a new penny, and to have something to eat for her people morning and evening. The husband lived soberly, brought home his fortnight's wages, and smoked his pipe at the window before going to bed, by way of taking a breath of air. They were held up for their good behaviour. And as they earned between them nearly nine francs a day, it was thought that they must be putting aside a tidy lot of money.

But, especially to begin with, they had to work with all their might to make both ends meet. Their marriage had involved them in a debt of two hundred francs. Then they were very much discontented with the Hôtel Boncœur; it seemed to them horrible, with its dirty people coming and going; and they longed to have a house of their own, where they could have their own furniture, and look after it themselves. Twenty times over, they reckoned up how much it would cost; in round figures, it came to three hundred and fifty francs, if they were to have things comfortable at once, and be able to lay their hands on a saucepan or a frying-pan when they wanted it. They were in despair of being able to save such a large sum in less than two years, when a stroke of luck befell them: an old gentleman of Plassans offered to put Claude, the eldest of the children, to school there; the generous whim of an eccentric character, a great lover of pictures, who had been greatly struck by some little daubs that the child had done. Claude was already a heavy drag upon them. With only the younger, Étienne, they got together the three hundred and fifty francs in seven months and a half. The day when they bought their furniture at a second-hand shop in the Rue Belhomme, they were in such a state of delight that they had to take a little walk along the outer boulevards before going home. There was a bed, a night-table, a marble-topped chest of drawers, a cupboard, a round table covered with oilcloth, six chairs, all in old mahogany; besides bedclothes, linen, and kitchen utensils, almost new. It was for them a serious and considerable step in life, something which gave them, as householders, a certain importance among the poorer people of the neighbourhood.

For the past two months they had been looking out for a place to live in. They tried first of all to rent a room in the big house of the Rue de la Goutte-d'Or. But there was not a single room free, and they had to give up their old idea. To tell the truth, Gervaise was not sorry at bottom; the neighbourhood of the Lorilleux at such close quarters quite frightened her. Thereupon they looked elsewhere. Coupeau very properly wished not to be far from Madame Fauconnier's, so that Gervaise could be at home in one step, any hour of the day. And they made quite a find, a large room with a small room attached, and a kitchen, Rue Neuve de la Goutte-d'Or, almost opposite to the laundry. It was a little one-storey house with a narrow staircase, at the top of which there were only two sets of rooms, one on the right hand, the other on the left; the lower part was taken up by a man who let out carriages, whose stock filled the sheds in the great court-yard level with the street. Gervaise was delighted; she seemed to be in the country again; no neighbours, no uproars to dread, a little quiet corner which reminded her of a Plassans alley near the ramparts, and to put the finishing touch to their luck she could see her own window from the ironing-board by merely stretching forward her head.

The house-moving took place in the April term. Gervaise was then eight months gone with child. But she kept up a good show of courage, saying with a laugh that the child helped her while she was working; she felt its little fists move within her, giving her strength to labour. She gave Coupeau a pretty warm reception when he suggested that she should take to bed, and look after herself a bit. She would do that when the pains took her; it would be quite time enough, and now, with another mouth to feed, they would have to stick at it harder than ever. And she cleaned out the new rooms herself, before helping her husband to put the furniture in its place. She simply worshipped this furniture of hers, wiping it all down with a sort of maternal care, seized with dismay at the slightest scratch. She drew back in fright, as if she had knocked herself, when her broom came against it in sweeping up. The chest of drawers was specially dear to her, it seemed to her so fine and solid and respectable-looking. It was a dream of hers, of which she dared not speak, to have an ornamental clock which she could put in the centre of the marble-top, where it would have a superb effect. But for the baby she was expecting, she would perhaps have run the risk of buying it. However, she put it off for the future, with a sigh.

They lived in a state of enchantment over their new dwelling. Étienne's bed occupied the little room, where there was also space for another child's cot. The kitchen was a mere hand's breadth, and as dark as pitch; but by leaving the door open, one could see all right; besides, Gervaise had not got to cook for twenty people, she only wanted somewhere to put her *pot-au-feu*. As for the large room, it was their great pride. In the morning they drew the curtains of the alcove, white calico curtains; and at once the room was transformed into a dining-room, with the table in the middle, the cupboard and the chest of drawers, one at each end. As the chimney used up fifteen sous' worth of coal a day, they stopped it up; a little iron stove on the hearth gave them warmth enough during the cold weather for seven sous. Then Coupeau did his best to ornament the walls, hoping for better things by and by; a large engraving representing a marshal of France, prancing on horseback, baton in hand, between a cannon and a heap of cannon balls, took the place of a mirror; over the chest of drawers some family photographs were arranged in two rows, to right and left of an old holy-water basin of gilt china, in which they kept matches; on the top of the cupboard a bust of Pascal stood side by side with a bust of Béranger, the one grave, the other smiling, near the tall clock whose ticking they seemed to be listening. It was really a beautiful room.

"Guess how much we pay here?" Gervaise would ask each visitor.

And when they guessed too much she was quite triumphant, and she would cry in an ecstacy at being so well off for so little money:

"A hundred and fifty francs, not a penny more! It is like getting it for nothing!"

The Rue Neuve de la Goutte-d'Or had itself not a little to do with their satisfaction. Gervaise spent her whole time in it, going to and fro constantly between her own house and

Madame Fauconnier's. Coupeau now went down in the evening, and smoked his pipe on the doorstep. The street was a steep incline, it had no footpath, and the road was very irregular. At the top, in the direction of the Rue de la Goutte-d'Or, there were gloomy shops, with dusty windows, shoe-makers', coopers', a grocer's, very dingy, and a wine-shop, which had gone bankrupt, and had been shut up for some weeks, the shutters all covered with announcements. At the other end, citywards, four-storey houses blocked the sky, their ground floors occupied by laundries, a whole crowd of them all together; only a single provincial hair-dresser's shop, painted green, full of delicate coloured bottles, lightened up the dark corner with the glitter of its brass sign, always brightly burnished. But the bright part of the street was in the middle, at the point where the buildings, lower and fewer in number, left a space for the sun and air. The carriage-sheds, the neighbouring soda-water manufactory, the wash-house opposite, left free a large and silent space, in which the stifled voices of the washerwomen and the regular respiration of the steam-boiler seemed to heighten the quietness of the place. Large open paces, and little lanes leading up between dark walls, gave it the air of a village. And Coupeau, amused by the rare passers-by, who had to be always jumping over streams of soapy water, said it reminded him of a place where one of his uncles had taken him when he was five. The delight of Gervaise was in a tree planted in the court, to the left of her window, an acacia, which spread out a single branch, a thin patch of green, which was enough to brighten the whole street.

It was on the last of April that Gervaise was confined. The pains came upon her in the afternoon about four, as she was ironing a pair of curtains at Madame Fau-connier's. She would not go at once, and remained there rocking to and fro on a chair, passing the iron over the curtains when she felt a little easier; the curtains were urgent, she *would* finish them. Then, after all, it was perhaps only a colic, it was not worth paying too much heed to a mere stomach-ache. But, as she was speaking of beginning some shirts, she turned white, and had to leave the shop, and hasten across the street, bent in two, holding on to the walls. One of the work-girls offered to go with her. She refused, only asking her to go and call the midwife near by, Rue de la Charbonnière. Her time was not come yet, she would have all the day and night before her. It would not hinder her from getting Coupeau's dinner ready; after that she would lie down a bit, without undressing. On the stairs she was taken with such an agony that she had to sit down right in the middle of the staircase; and she held both her hands over her mouth, so that she should not scream, for she could not bear the idea of some man coming up, and finding her there. The pain passed over, she could open her door, feeling easier, fancying she had made a mistake. She was preparing that evening a mutton stew with trimmings of chops. All seemed well as she peeled the potatoes. The bits of chop were in the saucepan when the sweats and throes took her again. She stirred her sauce, shifting from foot to foot before the stove, her eyes blinded with great tears. If she were going to be confined, that was no reason for letting Coupeau go without his dinner. At last the stew simmered away over a fire covered with ashes. She returned to the room, thinking she had time to lay one end of the table. She nearly dropped the bottle of wine; she had not strength enough to reach the bed, and she fell on the ground, and gave birth there on the matting. When the midwife arrived, a quarter of an hour too late, it was there that she attended to her.

The tinsmith was still employed at the hospital. Gervaise would not have him summoned. When he came in at seven o'clock he found her in bed, well wrapped up, looking very pale against the pillow. The baby was crying, swaddled in a shawl, at its mother's feet.

"Oh, my poor wife!" said Coupeau, embracing her. "And to think I was laughing and joking only an hour ago when you were yelling away as hard as you could. I say, you're quick enough about it; it's all over before one has time to sneeze."

She smiled feebly; then she murmured:

"It's a girl."

"Good," cried Coupeau, taking it jokingly in order to cheer her up; "just what I ordered. The order is already attended to. You get me whatever I want."

And taking up the baby he went on:

"Let's see a bit of you, little miss slut. You have a very black little phiz. But that'll get whiter, never fear. Now you must be good, you mustn't be a naughty girl; you must grow up sensible, like papa and mamma."

Gervaise looked solemnly at the baby with wide-open eyes

in which there was a touch of sadness. She shook her head; she would rather have had a boy, because boys can look out for themselves, and don't run such risks in Paris. The midwife had to take the little creature out of Coupeau's hands. She declared that Gervaise must not talk; it was bad enough to be making such a noise all around her. Thereupon the tinsmith said that he must go and tell the news to his mother and the Lorilleux but he was dying of hunger, he must have some dinner first. It was very painful to Gervaise to lie there and see him waiting on himself, running to the kitchen to fetch the stew, eating out of a cracked plate, not able to find the bread. Despite her orders, she lamented, and turned uneasily between the sheets. It was so silly not to have been able to lay the table; the colic had knocked her over like a blow of a stick. Her poor man mustn't be angry, to see her there cockering herself in bed, while he had such a poor meal. Were the potatoes cooked enough, anyway? She did not remember if she had put in the salt.

"Now be quiet!" cried the midwife.

"Ah! if you could only cure her of worrying herself!" said Coupeau, with his mouth full. "If you were not here, I wager she'd be up to cut my bread for me. Lie still and be easy, you great silly! You must take care of yourself, or you'll have a fortnight's job of it before you're on your legs again. Your stew is awfully good. Perhaps Madame will have some with me. Won't you, Madame?"

The midwife declined, but she would take a glass of wine with pleasure; it had given her quite a turn, she said, to find the poor woman and the baby on the matting. At last Coupeau departed to tell the news to his family. In half an hour, he had returned with them all, old Madame Coupeau, the Lorilleux, Madame Lerat, whom he had found at the house of the latter. The Lorilleux, now that things were going so prosperously, had become quite amiable, and always praised Gervaise to the skies, with little gestures of reservation, little nods, little winks, as if to put off their own verdict in the matter. They knew what they knew; only they had no desire to go contrary to the received opinion of the neighbourhood.

"Here's the whole lot of them!" cried Coupeau. "I told them not to, but they would come. Don't you open your mouth, you're not allowed to. They will keep quiet, and have a look at you; without offence, eh? I'm going to make some coffee, real fine!"

He disappeared into the kitchen. Old Madame Coupeau, after embracing Gervaise, exclaimed at the heaviness of the child. The two other women also printed big kisses on the confined woman's cheeks. And all three, standing around the bed, went over all the details of lyings-in: not so much after all, just like having out a tooth. Madame Lerat examined the infant all over, and declared it well formed, adding with much meaning, that it would make a fine woman; and as its head seemed to her too pointed, she gently pressed it in, despite its cries, so as to round it out properly. Madame Lorilleux tore the baby angrily from her: it was enough to spoil the creature to pull it about like that when its skull was so tender. Then they tried to find likenesses, and nearly quarrelled over them. Lorilleux, who was peering over the women's shoulder's, declared that the little object hadn't anything of Coupeau; the nose a little, perhaps, but that was all. It was just like its mother, with eyes different from either; certainly those eyes didn't come out of their family.

Meanwhile, Coupeau did not return; he could be heard in the kitchen, clattering about with the stove and the coffee-pot. Gervaise was quite uneasy: it was not a man's work making coffee, and she called to him what he ought to do, without heeding the energetic "hush"! of the midwife.

"Here, take this bucketful!" cried Coupeau, coming in with the coffee-pot in his hand. "It is a bore! It is a beastly nuisance! We must drink out of glasses, if you don't mind; because you see, the cups are still at the shop-keeper's."

They sat down to the table, and Coupeau insisted on pouring out the coffee himself. It was jolly strong, not dish-water this time! When the midwife had sipped her coffee, she departed: things were going all right, she was no longer wanted; if the patient had a bad night, send for her in the morning. She was still on the stairs when Madame Lorilleux began to abuse her as a lick-fingers and good for nothing. She put four knobs of sugar in her coffee, and she charged fifteen francs for merely letting you be confined all by yourself. But Coupeau stood up for her; he would willingly have given her more than fifteen francs; after all, those women had spent a lifetime in studying, they did rightly to charge dear. Then Lorilleux began to dispute with Madame Lerat; he declaring that, in order to have a boy, you ought to turn the head of your bed to the north; she, shrugging her shoulders, and declaring that it was all nonsense; but that an infallible recipe was to hide under the mattress, without letting your wife know, a handful of fresh nettles, picked in the open air. The table had been moved up by the side of the bed. Till ten o'clock, Gervaise, gradually sinking into an immense fatigue, lay smiling and vacant, her head turned over on the pillow; she saw and heard, but she had no strength to move or speak; it seemed to her that she was dead, very sweetly dead, and happy, a great way off, in seeing other people live. From time to time the baby gave a little wail, which came to her ears amongst the sound of loud voices, making interminable reflections on a murder that had been committed in the Rue du Bon-Puits, at the other end of La Chapelle.

Then, when everybody was ready to go, there was some talk of the baptism. The Lorilleux had consented to be godfather and godmother; they grumbled a bit, but they would have been greatly offended if they had not been asked. Coupeau did not at all see the necessity of baptizing the child; it certainly wouldn't bring him in ten thousand a year, and it would perhaps give the child a cold. The less one had to do with the priests the better. But old Madame Coupeau declared that he was a heathen; and the Lorilleux, without thinking it necessary to go and take the sacrament in church, prided themselves on having religion.

"Let it be Sunday, if you will," said the chainmaker.

And Gervaise having agreed with a little motion of her head, everybody kissed her and told her to take care of herself. They they said good-bye to the baby. One after another they leant over the poor little quivering body, with little chirrups and tender words, as if it could understand them. They called it Nana, the pet name of Anna, its godmother's name.

"Good-night, Nana. Now, Nana, be good girl."

When they had all gone, Coupeau drew up his chair against the bed, and finished his pipe, holding the hand of Gervaise in his. He smoked slowly, speaking between two whiffs; he was deeply moved.

"Well, old girl, have they given you a headache? You know I couldn't hinder them from coming after it, it shows they are friendly. But we're better all by ourselves, aren't we? I wanted to have you all to myself for a bit. All the evening did seem long! Poor little thing; she did have a time of it! Those precious kids, when they come into the world, they don't know what trouble they give. Sure, it must be like having your loins laid open. Let me kiss the place and make it well."

He had slipped one of his great hands delicately under her, and he drew her towards him; he kissed her body through the bed-clothes, with a rough man's tenderness for the still aching child-bearer. He asked her if it hurt her; he would have liked to heal her in a breath. And Gervaise was very happy. She declared that she was not suffering at all. She only wanted to get up again as soon as possible; because it would never do to fold one's arms now. But he reassured her. Wouldn't he make it his business to provide for the little one? He would be a great blackguard if he ever left the urchin in want. It didn't seem to him a great thing to know how to beget a child; the credit, surely, was in bringing it up.

That night Coupeau never slept. He had covered in the fire in the stove, and every hour he had to get up to give the baby a teaspoonful of sugar and water just tepid. In the morning he went off to his work, nevertheless, just as usual. He even took advantage of the dinner-hour to go and make his declaration at the mayoralty, Meanwhile, Madame Boche, having heard the news, came to pass the day with Gervaise. But Gervaise, after ten hours of sound sleep, complained that she already felt quite stiff from keeping her bed so long. She would get quite ill if she were not allowed to get up. That night, when Coupeau returned, she told him all her troubles; of course she had perfect confidence in Madame Boche, only it made her quite mad to see a stranger take up her abode in the room, opening her drawers, handling her things. Next day the *concierge*, who had been sent out on an errand, found her up and dressed, sweeping up the place, and getting her husband's dinner. And she refused to go to bed again. Were they joking? It was all very well for rich ladies to pretend to be knocked up. Poor people hadn't the time. Three days after her confinement she was back ironing at Madame Fauconnier's, working and sweating in the fierce heat of the furnace.

On Saturday night, Madame Lorilleux brought her christening gifts: a little thirty-five sous bonnet, and a christening robe, flounced and trimmed with a little lace, which she had had for six francs because it had been standing by. Next day Lorilleux, as godfather, gave six pounds of sugar. They knew how to do things decently. On the evening too, at the feast which took place at old Madame Coupeau's, they did not come empty-handed. The husband arrived with a bottle of wine, all sealed, under each arm, whilst the wife carried a large custard bought at a famous pastry-cook's in the Chaussée Clignancourt. Only, the Lorilleux went about telling everybody about their handsome presents; they had spent close upon twenty francs. Gervaise, when she heard of their tattling, was furious, and had no more sense of obligation to them for their generosity.

It was at the christening dinner that the Coupeaus made friends with their neighbours on the same landing. The other set of rooms in the little house was occupied by two people, a mother and son, called Goujet. Till then they had merely bowed on the staircase and in the street, without going any further; the neighbours seemed rather crusty. But the mother having carried up a can of water for Gervaise the day after her confinement, Gervaise thought it only decent to invite them to the feast, all the more so as they seemed to her quite nice people. And thereupon, naturally, they had got friendly.

The Goujets were from the Département du Nord. The mother mended lace, the son, a blacksmith by trade, worked in a manufactory of bolts. They had lived in the rooms on that landing for the last five years. Behind the silent quietude of their life lay buried a great sorrow: the father, in a moment of drunken madness, had killed a fellow-workman at Lille with a crow-bar, and had then hanged himself in his cell with a pocket-handkerchief. The widow and her child, coming to Paris after their great misfortune, always seemed to feel this horror weighing upon them, and did their best to redeem it by a strict uprightness, an unalterable calmness and courage. They put, indeed, a certain amount of pride into it, for they came to look upon themselves as better than their neighbours. Madame Goujet, always dressed in black, her forehead framed in by a sort of nun's coif, had a matron's white, still face, as if the whiteness of the lace, the delicate work of her fingers, had cast upon her a shadow of serenity. Goujet was a superb giant of twenty-three, with rosy cheeks and blue eyes, and the strength of a Hercules. In the workshop he was known as Gueule-d'Or, on account of his yellow beard.

Gervaise felt at once a great liking for these people. When she paid them her first visit, she was astonished at the neatness of the place. It was incredible; you could not find a speck of dust anywhere, and the floor shone like glass. Madame Goujet took her into her son's room to have a look. It was white and sweet as a girl's room; a little iron bed with white muslin curtains, a table, a toilet-stand, some narrow shelves hung on the wall, with pictures from top to bottom of the walls, pictures cut out from the illustrated papers, coloured prints fixed up with four nails, portraits of all sorts of people. Madame Goujet said with a smile that her son was a great child. He got tired of reading in the evenings; then he liked looking at his pictures. Gervaise spent nearly an hour at her neighbour's, who had returned to her frame by the window. She was absorbed in the hundreds of pins fastening on the lace, and she felt happy at being there, breathing the good, cleanly odour of the place, into which the delicate work brought a sort of meditative silence.

The Goujets grew on acquaintance. They worked hard all day, and put more than a quarter of their fortnight's money in the savings' bank. The neighbours treated them with respect, and spoke of their economies. Goujet never had a hole in his things, and always went out with spotless jackets. He was very polite, indeed rather timid, despite his great shoulders. The washerwomen at the end of the street laughed to see him look down as he went by. He did not like their coarse language, thought it disgusting that women should always have dirty words in their mouths. One day, however, he came in drunk. Thereupon, Madame Goujet, without a word, placed before him a portrait of his father, a wretched painting, piously laid away at the bottom of the chest of drawers. Since that lesson Goujet drank only very moderately, without however taking a dislike to wine, for a workman needs wine. On Sunday he went out with his mother on his arm, generally in the direction of Vincennes, sometimes he took her to the theatre. He simply idolized his mother, to whom he still spoke as if he were a child. With his square head, his heavy frame, torpid after the hard work at the anvil, he was like a great animal, dull of intellect and good of heart.

For a little while Gervaise put him out considerably. Then, after a few weeks, he got quite accustomed to her. He was on the look-out for her, to show her his parcels, treating her just like a sister, with blunt familiarity, and cutting out his figures under her direction. One morning, however, having turned the key without knocking, he surprised her half undressed, washing her neck; and for a week afterwards he dared not look her in the face, so that finally he made her blush herself.

Cadet-Cassis, with his Parisian jabber, thought him a blockhead. It was all very well not to swill, not to be after the girls, but, all the same, a man must be a man, or he may as well wear petticoats at once. He ragged him before Gervaise, accusing him of making eyes at all the women in the neighbourhood; and the big baby defended himself violently. In spite of all, the two workmen were good friends. They called one another in the morning, started together, and sometimes had a glass of beer together before coming in. Since the christening feast they spoke to one another in the second person, because using the third was so much more to say. They had got to that point, and no further, when Gueule-d'Or rendered Cadet-Cassis a great service, one of those signal services which can never be forgotten. It was the 2nd of December. The tinsmith, just for fun, had gone out to see the disturbance; he didn't care two pins for Bonaparte, the Republic, or the whole blooming lot, only he loved the smell of powder, and it seemed amusing to see people shooting one another; and he came very near being nabbed behind a barricade, only the blacksmith, turning up at the right moment, had thrown himself in the way, and helped him to cut and run. Goujet, as they returned up the Rue du Faubourg-Poissonnière, walked fast, looking very serious. He interested himself in politics, and was a serious Republican, in the name of justice and the general good. Only he had not taken part in the fighting, and he gave his reasons; the people were tired of burning their fingers for the middle classes in pulling their chestnuts out of the fire for them; February and June had taught them a good lesson, and now in future the suburbs would leave it to the city to fight its own battles. Then, as they reached the top of the Rue des Poissonniers, he turned and looked back over Paris; they were bungling up a fine piece of business down there, all the same, and perhaps some day the people would repent of having crossed its arms and done nothing. But Coupeau merely sneered, and declared that people were too idiotic to risk their skins just in order to keep the damned lazy-bones of the House going, on their twenty-five francs. In the evening the Coupeaus invited the Goujets to dinner. At dessert Cadet-Cassis and Gueule-d'Or solemnly kissed one another on each cheek; now they were sworn friends through thick and thin.

For three years the life of the two households on each side of the landing went on without an incident. Gervaise had nursed her child without losing, at the outside, more than two days' work a week. And she had now got to be a good work-

woman, and earned as much as three francs. So she was able
to put Étienne, who was soon going on for eight, in a little
boarding school in the Rue de Chartres, where she had to
pay five francs. Despite the expenses connected with the two
children, they now put aside twenty or thirty francs every
month in the savings' bank. When their savings had reached
the sum of six hundred francs, Gervaise could hardly sleep for
thinking of plans for the future; she would like to set up for
herself, take a little shop, and to have work-women of her
own. She had worked it all out. At the end of twenty years,
if they had plenty of work, they would have a regular income
of their own, which they could retire upon somewhere in the
country. Nevertheless, she dared not run the risk. She said
she was looking out for a shop, in order to give herself time to
think it well over. The money lost nothing in the savings'
bank; on the contrary, it added to its stock. In three years she
had indulged herself with one of her great desires, she had
bought a clock; though for this clock, which was made of
coloured marble, with twisted columns and a gilded brass
pendulum, she had to pay out instalments of twenty sous
every Monday during the whole year. She was quite vexed
when Coupeau spoke of winding it up; she would allow no
one but herself to take off the glass dome, and she wiped down
the columns reverentially, as if the marble of her chest of
drawers were transformed into a church. Under the shade,
behind the pendulum, she hid away the savings' bank book.
And often, when she dreamed of her shop, she went into a
brown study in front of the clock, staring fixedly at the hands
as they turned, as if she were waiting for some particular and
solemn moment in which to decide.

The Coupeaus went out almost every Sunday with the
Goujets. They were pleasant little excursions; some fried fish
at Saint-Ouen, some rabbit at Vincennes, eaten anyhow,
under the arbour of an eating-house. The men had something
to drink when they felt thirsty, and came home as sober as
could be, giving their arm to the ladies. At night, before
going to bed, both households made up their accounts, and
shared the expenses equally; never was there a dispute as to
a penny more or less. The Lorilleux were jealous of the
Goujets. It seemed strange, surely, for Cadet-Cassis and
Clop-clop to be always going about with strangers when they
had relations of their own. Oh, no doubt, they only looked
upon their relations as an encumbrance! As soon as they had

put aside four sous they were nice and independent. Madame Lorilleux, greatly vexed to see her brother getting away from her influence, began to talk no end of abuse against Gervaise. Madame Lerat, on the other hand, took the young woman's part, and related extraordinary tales, attempts upon her honour on the boulevard at night, from which she came out melodramatically, boxing the ears of her cowardly pursuers. As for old Madame Coupeau, she did her best to settle up the differences all round, to make herself agreeable to all her children; her sight was giving way more and more; she had a roof over her, but that was all, and she was glad of a few francs now and again from one and another.

On Nana's third birthday, when Coupeau came home at night, he found Gervaise in a great state of excitement. She would not say what it was about; it was nothing, she said. But when she began to lay the table all topsy-turvy, stopping to think with the plates in her hands, her husband insisted on knowing what was up.

"Well, it's this," she admitted at last, "the little haberdasher's shop in the Rue de la Goutte-d'Or is to be let. I saw it only an hour ago, when I went out to get some thread. It gave me quite a turn."

It was a neat little shop, and in the very house where they had formerly wanted to live. There was the shop, a back parlour, and two other rooms, to right and left; in short, all they needed, rather small rooms, but well laid out. Only it seemed to her too dear; the landlord spoke of five hundred francs.

"You went in then, and asked the price?" said Coupeau.

"Oh, just as a matter of curiosity, you know," she replied, trying to put on an air of indifference. "One looks about, one goes in wherever there is a poster: that binds you to nothing. But it is too dear; there's no doubt about it. Then it would be silly, I dare say, to set up for myself."

However, after dinner, she returned to the subject of the haberdasher's shop. She drew the plan of the house on the margin of a newspaper, and, little by little, she talked about it, measured all the corners, arranged all the order of the rooms, as if she were going to put her furniture into them tomorrow. Thereupon, Coupeau, seeing how she longed after it, urged her to take it; it was certain, she would find nothing decent under five hundred francs; besides, she might, perhaps get something taken off. The only tedious part of the business was to go and live in the same house with the Lorilleux, whom she couldn't abide. But she fired up, declared she hated nobody; and, in the heat of her desire, she even stood up for the Lorilleux; they were not bad at heart. She would get on with them all right. When they had gone to bed, Coupeau went off to sleep, while she still continued making arrangements for the fitting up of the place before she had even definitely agreed to take it.

Next day, as soon as she was alone, she could not resist taking off the shade of the clock, and looking at the savings' bank book. To think that her shop was there, in those soiled leaves with their smudgy handwriting! Before going out to work, she asked the advice of Madame Goujet, who greatly approved of her project of setting up for herself; with a husband like hers, a decent fellow, who didn't drink, she was certain to make a good thing of it, and not get in arrears. At the dinner hour she even went up to see the Lorilleux, so as to have their opinion; she did not wish to seem to be doing anything without consulting her relations. Madame Lorilleux was quite overwhelmed. What! Clop-clop was going to set up shop now, was she? And, disgusted as she was, she tried to appear very pleased: no doubt the shop was just the thing, Gervaise was right in taking it. However, when she had recovered herself, she and her husband spoke of the dampness of the court, the darkness of the rooms on the ground floor. Oh! it was quite the place to get rheumatism. However, if she had made up her mind to take it, their objection, most assuredly, would not hinder her from taking it.

That evening Gervaise frankly confessed, laughing, that it would have made her quite ill if she could not have had the shop. However, before saying "Done!" she wanted Coupeau to come and see the place, and try and get something taken off from the rent.

"Well then, tomorrow, if you like," said her husband, "You can call for me just before six at the house where I am working, Rue de la Nation, and we will look in at the Rue de la Goutte-d'Or on our way home."

Coupeau was just finishing the roofing of a new three-storey house. That day, in fact, he had to put on the last sheets of galvanized. As the roof was almost flat, he had set up his bench there, a large plank on two trestles. It was a beautiful May sunset, which touched the chimneys with gold. And, high up against the clear sky, the workman quietly cut

out his galvanized with shears, leaning over his bench like a
tailor cutting out a pair of trousers in his shop. Against the
wall of the neighbouring house his assistant, a blond slim
youth of seventeen, kept the fire burning in the brazier by
working a pair of bellows, which at every puff blew out a
cloud of sparks.

"Hi, Zidore, put in the irons!" cried Coupeau.

The assistant thrust the soldering-irons into the flame,
which looked, in the open air, a pale rose colour. Then he
began to blow the bellows again. Coupeau held the last sheet
of galvanized. It had to be fixed at the edge of the roof, near
the gutter; just there, there was a sharp descent, and below
gaped the open mouth of the street. The tinsmith, quite at
home in his list slippers, advanced in a leisurely manner,
whistling the air, "Ohé! les p'tits agneaux!" Arrived at the
spot, he let himself slide, propped his knee against the brickwork of a chimney, and remained half-way out over the
street, one of his legs hanging over. When he turned to call
out to that lumpish Zidore, he caught hold of a corner of the
brickwork, on account of the pavement down below.

"Come now, you infernal dawdler! Give me the irons!
What are you staring at, you skinny bugger? Do you think the
sky is going to fall?"

Zidore did not hurry himself. He was interested in some
roofs near, in a great column of smoke that rose at the other
end of Paris, Grenelle way; it was very likely a fire. However,
he laid himself down on his stomach on the roof above and
handed the irons to Coupeau. Then Coupeau began to solder
the sheet. He squatted down, reached out, always managing
to keep his balance, half sitting, perched on the point of his
foot, holding on by a mere finger. He had an infernal assurance,
a devil of a lot of confidence, he was quite free and comfortable
in the face of danger. He was so accustomed to it. If anyone
came to grief, it would be the street, not he. As he still went
on smoking his pipe, he turned his head from time to time,
and quietly spat into the street.

"Hallo, Madame Boche!" he cried, suddenly. "Hi! Madame
Boche!"

He had seen the *concierge* crossing the street below. She
raised her head and recognized him. Then they began to talk
from roof to pavement. She covered her hands with her apron,
and stood looking up. He was now standing, his left arm
round a pipe, leaning over.

"You haven't seen my wife?" he asked.

"No, indeed," replied the *concierge*. "Is she about here?"

"She is going to call for me. All well your way?"

"Oh! yes, thanks; I'm the worst of the lot! I'm just going to the Chaussée Clignancourt for a small leg of mutton. The butcher by the 'Moulin Rouge' charges sixteen sous for it."

They had to raise their voices, a cart was passing, in the Rue de la Nation, along the broad deserted street; and their words, shouted out at the top of their voices, brought a little old woman to a window. And the old woman remained there leaning out, indulging in the luxury of a painful sensation, staring at the man on the roof opposite, as if she hoped every minute to see him fall.

"Well, good-night," cried Madame Boche, presently, "I won't hinder you."

Coupeau turned, and took the iron that Zidore handed him. But at the moment when the *concierge* was turning away, she saw Gervaise on the other side of the road, holding Nana by the hand. She had raised her head again to tell the tinsmith, when Gervaise stopped her by an energetic movement, and in a low voice, fearing to be heard from above, she said what it was that frightened her. She was afraid if she let him see her all at once that it would give him a start, and he would fall over. In all these four years she had only once gone to call for him when he was at work. Today was the second time. She could not look on at it, it simply turned her head to see her man between heaven and earth, in places where even the sparrows did not venture.

"Yes, indeed, it isn't pleasant," murmured Madame Boche. "My husband is a tailor; I have no course to be afraid."

"If you only knew, at first," went on Gervaise, "I was in a fright from morning to night. I kept seeing him all the time with his head crushed, carried on a shutter. Now, I think no more about it. One gets used to everything. And one must earn one's living. All the same, it is a hard way to earn it, for one risks one's bones more than is needful."

She stopped, hiding Nana with her skirts, fearing the child would cry out. Despite herself, she could not help looking up; she went quite pale. Coupeau was just then soldering the extreme edge of the sheet of galvanized by the gutter; he slid down as well as he could, unable to get into the proper position. Then he ventured along with a workman's slow movements, so easy and heavy. For a moment he hung right

out over the road, not holding on at all, going on quietly
with his work, and from below could be seen the little white
crisp flame of the solder under the iron, worked carefully to
and fro. Gervaise clasped her hands in silent agony, lifting
them upward with a mechanical gesture of supplication. But
she breathed again, Coupeau had made his way up the roof
once more, deliberately spitting down into the street again.

"Ah! there you are spying on me!" he cried gaily, catching
sight of her. "She was in a funk, wasn't she, Madame Boche?
and wouldn't let you call to me. Wait for me, I have just ten
minutes more work."

He had to fix a chimney-pot, a mere nothing. The washerwoman and the *concierge* stood in the street talking over the
gossip of the neighbourhood, and keeping an eye on Nana, so
that she would not dabble in the gutter, where she was looking
for little fish; and the two women looked back now and again
to the roof with smiles and nods, as if to say that they were not
impatient. The little old woman opposite had not left her
window, watching the man, and waiting.

"What is she spying after, the old mare?" said Madame
Boche. "What a horrid phiz!"

From above they heard the loud voice of the tinsmith
singing, "Ah! qu'il fait donc bon cueillir la fraise!" Now,
bending over his bench, he worked away at his zinc like an
artist. He traced a line with the compass, and then cut out a
large fan-shaped slice by means of a pair of circular cutters;
then, lightly with his hammer, he beat the piece into the
shape of a toadstool. Zidore went on, blowing at the brazier.
The sun set behind the house in a bright rose-colour, slowly
paling into a faint lilac. And against the sky, at this peaceful
hour of the day, the silhouettes of the two workmen, increased
to an enormous size, stood out in the limpid air, with the
dark outline of the bench and the profile of the bellows.

When the chimney-pot was cut out, Coupeau called
out:

"Zidore, the irons!"

But Zidore had disappeared. The tinsmith cursed and
stared all round, and shouted down the sky-light of the
garret, which had been left open. Finally he discovered him
on a neighbouring roof, two houses off. The young rascal was
exploring all round about, his scrimpy blond hair blown
about by the gusts of wind, blinking his eyes at the immensity
of Paris.

"I say, dawdler, do you think you are in the country?" said Coupeau, angrily. "You are like Monsieur Béranger, you compose verses, I suppose! Will you give me the irons? Did you ever! taking a little stroll on the roofs! Wouldn't you like to bring your woman here, right off, and give her a serenade? Will you give me the irons, you damned bungler you?"

He did his soldering, calling out to Gervaise:

"There, it's all done. I am coming down."

The flue to which he had to fit the chimney-pot was just in the middle of the roof. Gervaise, at ease now, smiled as she followed his movements. Nana, delighted at suddenly catching sight of her father, clapped her little hands. She was sitting on the pavement, so as to see him better at that distance.

"Papa! papa!" she cried, as loud as she could; "papa! look!"

The tinsmith tried to lean over, but his foot slipped. Then, all at once, clumsily, like a cat that has got its feet caught, he rolled over and over, down the slight incline of the roof, without being able to save himself.

"Damnation!" he cried, in a choked voice.

And he fell. His body described a slack curve, turned twice on itself, and crashed down in the middle of the street with a thud like a bundle of linen dropped from a great height.

Gervaise, stupefied, gave one scream, and flung her arms into the air.

Passers-by ran up, a crowd formed. Madame Boche, quite overcome, her legs trembling under her, took Nana in her arms, so as to cover her face and prevent her from seeing. Meanwhile, the little old woman opposite, as if satisfied, calmly closed her window.

Four men carried Coupeau into a chemist's, at the corner of the Rue des Poissonniers, and he lay there nearly an hour, in the middle of the shop, on a quilt, whilst someone went for a stretcher to the Hôpital Lariboisière. He still breathed, but the chemist shook his head gravely. Gervaise crouched on the ground, sobbing without intermission, her face drenched with tears, blinded and dazed. With a mechanical movement, she stretched out her hands, and felt over the limbs of her husband, very gently. Then she drew back, catching sight of the chemist who had forbidden her to touch him; and a few seconds after she began again, unable to refrain from assuring herself that he was warm, fancying she was doing him good. When the

stretcher at last arrived, and there was some talk of taking
him to the hospital, she got up, saying violently:

"No, no, not to the hospital! We live in the Rue Neuve de
la Goutte-d'Or."

It was useless to explain to her that it would cost a lot
of money if she took her husband home. She reiterated
obstinately:

"Rue Neuve de la Goutte-d'Or, I will show you the door.
What has it got to do with you? I have money. Isn't he my
husband? He is coming home; I will have it."

So Coupeau was taken home. When the stretcher was
carried through the crowd that had formed outside the
chemist's shop, the women in the neighbourhood spoke of
Gervaise with animation; she limped, it was true, but she was
a plucky creature all the same; she would bring her husband
round, to a certainty, whilst at the hospital the doctors
simply let you kick the bucket if you were too badly hurt, so
as not to have the bore of curing you. Madame Boche, after
having taken Nana home with her, had come back again,
and she told the story of the accident with interminable
details, still agitated with her fright.

"I was going to get a leg of mutton—I was there—I saw
him fall," she repeated. "It was all through the child, he
wanted to see her, and then—slap bang! Oh! Lord, Lord! I
wouldn't like to see another fall. I must go and get my leg of
mutton all the same."

For a week Coupeau was very bad. The relations, the
neighbours, everyone, in short, expected at every moment to
see him turn his toes up. The doctor—a very expensive
doctor, who charged five francs for every visit—feared an
internal lesion; and the word frightened everybody greatly;
it was reported in the neighbourhood that the tinsmith's heart
had been displaced by the shock. Only Gervaise, pale with
all her sleepless nights, serious and collected, shrugged her
shoulders. Her man had his right leg broken, that everybody
knew; he would get over that. As for the rest, as for the
displaced heart, it was all nonsense. She would soon put his
heart into its right place again. She knew how to put a heart
back into its right place, with care, cleanliness, good looking
after. And she showed a superb conviction, certain of curing
him if only by staying by him and touching him with her
hands in his hours of fever. She did not give way to doubt for
an instant. She was on her feet for a whole week, spea king

little, absorbed by her resolve to save him, forgetting the children, the street, the whole city. On the ninth day, when the doctor at last declared the patient out of danger, she sank on a chair, her legs giving way under her, all her strength gone, in a flood of tears. That night she consented to sleep for two hours, her head on the end of the bed.

Coupeau's accident had brought out all the family. Old Madame Coupeau passed her nights with Gervaise; only, after nine o'clock, she went to sleep in her chair. Every night, on her way home from work, Madame Lerat went a long way out of her road in order to have the latest news. The Lorilleux at first came two or three times a day, offering to share in staying up, even bringing an arm-chair for Gervaise. But quarrels soon arose as to the best way of looking after sick folk. Madame Lorilleux declared she had cured enough people in her life to know the proper way to set about it. She accused Gervaise of hustling her out of the way, of driving her from her brother's bedside. Of course Clop-clop was quite right in wishing to cure Coupeau herself; for, if she had not disturbed him at his work, he would never have fallen. Only, by the way in which she was treating him, she was certain to finish the job.

When Coupeau was out of danger Gervaise ceased to keep watch over his bed with such jealous vigilance. No one could kill him now, and she let people come near him without suspicion. Then the family took possession of the room. It was going to be a long convalescence; the doctor had spoken of four months. Then, during the tinsmith's long hours of sleep, the Lorilleux pointed out to Gervaise how silly she was. Much good it did anybody, her having her husband in the house. At the hospital he would have been on his legs again in half the time. Lorilleux would just like to be ill, some trifle or other, to show whether he would hesitate a second in entering Lariboisière. Madame Lorilleux knew a lady who had just come out; well, she had had a chicken morning and evening. And both, for the twentieth time, made the calculation of what all these four months of convalescence were going to cost. First the working days lost, then the doctor, the medicines, and afterwards the good wine, the underdone meat. If the Coupeaus only used up their bit of savings they ought to be jolly well glad; but they would certainly run into debt. Oh! that was their affair; only they must not count on their relations, who were not rich enough to support an invalid at home. So much the worse for Clop-clop, of course. She might just as well have done like everybody else, and let her man be taken to the hospital. That was the last touch; she was stuck up.

One day Madame Lorilleux was malicious enough to ask her suddenly:

"Well, what of your shop? When are you going to take it?"

"Yes," sneered Lorilleux, "the *concierge* is still expecting you."

Gervaise was quite taken aback. She had completely forgotten the shop. But she saw the malicious delight they had in the thought that all her projects for the shop had gone to pot. And in fact, from that time onwards, they were on the lookout for occasions to joke on her vanished dream. When everyone spoke of an unrealizable hope, they put it off to the day when she would have a shop of her own with a street front. And behind her back they laughed at her still worse. She did not like to think anything so dreadful; but, really, the Lorilleux seemed quite pleased with Coupeau's accident, seeing that it had hindered her from setting up a laundry in the Rue de la Goutte-d'Or.

Thereupon she joined in the laugh herself, and took a pride in showing how willingly she gave up the money for her husband's recovery. Every time she took out the savings' bank book in their presence, from under the shade of the clock, she said laughingly:

"I am going out; I am going to take my shop."

She would not withdraw the money all at once. She asked for it a hundred francs at a time, so as not to keep such a lot of gold in her chest of drawers; besides, she had vague dreams of some miracle, a sudden rallying, which would not force her to take out the whole amount. Every time she came in after her visit to the savings' bank she added up on a piece of paper how much they had left. It was merely an orderly habit. However much she was obliged to pick into her little stock, she still made up the accounts of this inroad into their savings. Wasn't it some sort of consolation to put the money to such good use, to have it to draw upon in their misfortune? And without a regret she put the book carefully back behind the clock, under the glass case.

The Goujets were extremely nice to Gervaise during Coupeau's illness. Madame Goujet was at her beck and call the whole time; she never went out without looking in to know if she was in want of sugar, or butter, or salt; she always sent over to her the first drop of broth when she had a *pot-au-feu*; she even looked after the kitchen for her if she was too busy, and gave her a hand with the plates and dishes. Goujet carried her cans to the tap in the Rue des Poissonniers, and filled them for her every morning; that was a saving of two sous. Then after dinner, when the relations were not about, the Goujets would come into the Coupeaus' and keep them company. For two hours, until ten o'clock, the blacksmith smoked his pipe, and watched Gervaise moving about the sick man. He did not say ten words in the course of the evening. His great blond head sunk between his huge shoulders, he was absorbed in watching her preparing the invalid's gruel, stirring up the sugar without making a noise with the spoon. When she tucked up the bed, and cheered up Coupeau with her soft voice, he was quite overcome. Never had he come across such a real good woman. It was all the more credit to her to limp, seeing how she was on the move all day about her husband. It was incredible; she never sat down for a minute, hardly even to take her meals. She was constantly running over to the chemist's, she had to mess about with all sorts of things, she worked like a nigger to keep the room in order, the room in which everything had to be done; and for all this, not a complaint, always amiable, even in the evening, when she was so tired that she could hardly keep her eyes open. And the blacksmith, watching her and wondering at her devotion, in the midst of all the medicine bottles strewed about the place, took a great affection for Gervaise, seeing how she put her whole soul into the task of looking after her husband.

"I say old chap," he said one day to the convalescent, "you'll soon be patched up again; I never doubted it. I declare your wife is God Almighty!"

He himself was thinking about getting married; at least, his mother had found a very suitable girl, a lace-maker like herself, whom she was very anxious for him to marry. To please her he said yes; and the marriage was fixed for the beginning of September. The money for setting up house had long been laid by in the savings' bank. But he shook his head when Gervaise spoke to him of his marriage, and he murmured in his slow voice:

"All women are not like you, Madame Gervaise. If women were all like you, one would marry any amount of them."

Meanwhile Coupeau, at the end of two months, could get up a little. He could not walk many steps, only from the bed to the window, and supported by Gervaise. There he sat himself down in the Lorilleux's arm-chair, his right leg stretched out on a hassock. He had always laughed at broken bones, and he was greatly annoyed by his accident. He could not get over his annoyance. The whole two months he had spent in bed he had cursed and stormed at everybody. A pretty sort of existence this was, to lie on your back with your leg tied up stiff as a sausage. He would soon get to know the ceiling at any rate; there was a crevice in the corner of the recess which he could draw with his eyes shut. Then, when he could sit out in the chair, it was another story. Was he going to stay there all his life, nailed to the chair, like a mummy? The street wasn't so very amusing to look at, nobody ever passed; it stank all day long of bleaching water. It was too tedious, he would give ten years of his life to be able merely to go and see how the fortifications were getting on. And he returned again and again to his violent accusations against fate. His accident was not fair; it oughtn't to have happened to him, a good workman like him, neither a dawdler nor a drunkard. He might have understood in the case of others.

"Old Coupeau," he said, "broke his neck because he was tight. I don't say that ought to have happened, but at all events it explains itself. But for my part, I hadn't taken a drop, and over I go merely in turning to wave my hand to Nana. I call that a little too strong! If there's any God Almighty at all, He arranges things very queerly. I can't quite swallow it."

When he was able to get about again, he still kept a deep aversion against his work. It was a luckless trade, crawling about all day long like a cat on the house roof. Not bad of people to send you out to get killed, and too much cowards themselves to venture upon a ladder, sticking at home by their fires, and not caring two pins for the rest of the world. And he went so far as to say that everyone should put on his flashings for himself. Hang it all! it was only justice; that was the general rule—if you don't want to be wet, get under cover. Then he regretted that he had not learnt another trade, pleasanter and not so risky, a cabinet-maker's, for instance. It was old Coupeau's fault again; fathers were so silly, to always want their children to do as they had done.

For two months longer Coupeau had to walk on crutches.

First he was able to go down below, and smoke his pipe on the doorstep. Then he went as far as the outer boulevard, crawling along in the sun, remaining for whole hours sitting on a bench. His cheerfulness returned, his deuce of a tongue came back to him once more in his long strolls. And, in his delight at merely being alive, he loved to lounge about doing nothing, his muscles relaxed into a peaceful slumber; it was like the slow inroad of idleness, which profited by his convalescence to soak into him, drowning him delightfully. His health returned, and his life seemed to him perfectly comfortable; why should it ever change? When he could get on without his crutches he took longer walks, and went the round of the workshops to see his old pals. He stood with his arms folded in front of houses that were building, sneering and shaking his head; and he ragged the workmen who were bustling about, holding out his leg to show what you got by doing more than your fair share of work. Making fun of others while they worked satisfied his grudge against the work itself. Of course he would go back to it again, he must; but not before he could help it. Oh! he was paid out for his want of enthusiasm. Then it seemed so nice to dawdle about a bit!

In the afternoons, when Coupeau had nothing to do, he went in to see the Lorilleux. They condoled with him, and won him back by all sorts of nice little ways. For the first few years after his marriage he had got away from their influence, thanks to Gervaise. Now they got hold of him again, joking him about the fright he was in in regard to his wife. Let him be a man! Nevertheless, the Lorilleux were extremely discreet, and heaped up the most extravagant praises of Gervaise, and all her good qualities. Coupeau did not dispute them, but he assured his wife that his sister adored her, and told her she ought not to be so unfriendly herself. The first quarrel fell out one evening on the subject of Étienne. The tinsmith had been spending the afternoon with the Lorilleux, and on coming in, finding the dinner not ready and the children crying after the soup, he suddenly went for Étienne, and gave him two good boxes on the ear. And for an hour he muttered between his teeth: the brat wasn't his, he didn't know why he tolerated him in the house; he would send him about his business one of these days. Up to then he had accepted the child without any fuss. The next day he spoke of his dignity. Three days after, he took to kicking him from morning to night, so that when the child heard his steps on the stairs, he would take refuge in at the Goujets', where the old lace-worker always kept a corner for him at the table.

Gervaise had now been back at her work for a long time. She had no need now to take on and off the shade of the clock; all the savings were gone, and it was necessary to buckle-to right hard, and do the work of four, for there were now four mouths to feed. She supported them all by herself. When people condoled with her, she quickly took off all the blame from Coupeau. Just think what he had suffered! it was not surprising if it had soured him a bit. But that would pass off when he was strong again. And if anyone intimated that Coupeau was strong enough now to go back to the yard, she protested vigorously. No, no, not yet. She didn't want to have him in bed again. She knew what the doctor had ordered. And it was she herself who kept him from work, telling him every morning to take his time, not to over-exert himself. She even slipped a franc now and again into his waistcoat pocket. Coupeau took it as the most natural thing in the world, he complained of all sorts of pains and aches in order to be petted up. At the end of six months he was still convalescent. And now, when he did not go to look on at the others working, he was quite ready to have a glass with his pals. One really wasn't badly off in a wine-shop; it was jolly enough, and one only stayed five minutes. It was no disgrace to anybody. Only hypocrites pretended to drink because they were dying of thirst. It was quite right of people to have joked him about it before now: a glass of wine never killed a man. But he tapped his chest, and took a pride in drinking nothing but wine; always wine, never spirits; wine lengthened your life, didn't knock you up, and didn't make you tipsy. Nevertheless, several times, after days of idleness, spent in workshop after workshop, tavern after tavern, he came in slightly elevated. On those days Gervaise shut her door, pretending that she herself had a bad headache, in order to keep the Goujets from seeing the state Coupeau was in.

Little by little, however, Gervaise grew melancholy. Morning and evening she went to the Rue de la Goutte-d'Or to have another look at the shop, which was still to let; and she did not like to be seen, as if it were a childish whim that she indulged in, unworthy of serious people. This shop began to absorb all her thoughts; and at night, when the light was turned out, she found all the charm of forbidden fruit in still dreaming over it with her eyes open. She made her calculations over again: two hundred and fifty francs of rent, one hundred and fifty francs for the fixings, a hundred francs in hand, on which to live for a fortnight; altogether five hundred francs at the lowest reckoning. If she did not talk much on the subject, it was for fear of seeming to be hankering after the savings swallowed up by Coupeau's illness. Sometimes she turned quite pale, finding she had let slip something about it, catching back her words in confusion, as if she had given utterance to some enormity. Now it would take four or five years of work before being able to put aside such a large sum. What distressed her was that she could not set up for herself at once; she would have kept the entire house going without counting upon Coupeau, allowing him a few months more to pick up inclination for work again; she would have been quite comfortable, certain of the future, disembarrassed of the secret fears that sometimes arose in her mind when he returned in a state of great jollity, singing and relating some fresh absurdity of that creature Mes-Bottes, to whom he had stood a bottle.

One evening, as Gervaise was alone, Goujet came in; he did not rush off as he was accustomed to do, but sat down and went on smoking, looking at her. He had evidently something important to communicate; he turned it over in his mind without being able to get it into proper order. At length, after a painful silence, he summoned up his courage, took his pipe out of his mouth, and said right off:

"Madame Gervaise, will you allow me to lend you some money?"

She was leaning over a drawer of the chest of drawers looking for some dusters. She looked up, very red. He must have seen her that morning, standing transfixed before the outside of the shop for nearly ten minutes. He smiled with an embarrassed air, as if he had made an unpalatable suggestion. But she declined sharply; never would she accept money without knowing when she would be able to return it. Then it was really too large an amount. And as he pressed it upon her, she finally cried in amazement:

"But your marriage? I certainly can't take the money for your marriage!"

"Oh! don't trouble about that," he said, going red in turn. "I am not going to get married. A whim, you know. . . . Really, I would rather lend you the money."

At that they both looked down. There was something tender in the air, to which neither of them gave voice. And Gervaise accepted. Goujet had forewarned his mother. They crossed the landing, to go and find her at once. The old lace-worker was grave, a little sad, her calm face bent over her frame. She would not go against the wish of her son, but she did not even approve of Gervaise's project, and she said why, quite definitely. Coupeau was going to the bad; he would squander the whole business. She had never forgiven the tinsmith for refusing to learn to read during his convalescence. The blacksmith had offered to teach him, but the other had told him to mind his own business, declaring that learning only made people thin. The two workmen had almost come to variance over it; each went his own way. However, Madame Goujet, seeing the looks of entreaty of her big boy, was very kind to Gervaise. It was agreed that they should lend their neighbours five hundred francs, to be paid back in instalments of twenty francs a month until it was all made up.

"Good! The blacksmith is making eyes at you," cried Coupeau, merrily, when he heard the story. "Oh! I am quite easy; he is too simple for anything. We will pay him back all his money. But, all the same, if he had to do with rogues, he would be nicely rooked, he would."

On the very next day the Coupeaus took the shop. Gervaise was running to and fro all the day from the Rue Neuve to the Rue de la Goutte-d'Or. The neighbours, seeing her darting lightly to and fro, so excited that she never limped at all, declared that she must have undergone an operation.

CHAPTER FIVE

It happened that the Boches, since the April quarter-day, had left the Rue des Poissonniers, and had the *concierge's* lodge in the large house of the Rue de la Goutte-d'Or. How oddly things turned out sometimes! One of the things that Gervaise dreaded, after having got on so well with the *concierge* of the Rue Neuve, was to fall under the power of some disagreeable creature, with whom one would get into trouble if one spilt a little water, or shut the door too loudly at night. *Concierges* are such a bad lot! But with the Boches it would be a pleasure. They were old friends; they were sure to get on together. It was like being in one's own family.

On the day of allotment, when the Coupeaus had to sign the lease, Gervaise felt a strange feeling come over her as she passed under the lofty entrance. She was really going to live in this big house, as big as a city, with its interminable streets stretching and twisting in staircase and corridor. The grey walls, with their rags drying at the windows, the dingy courtyard, with its pavement worn like the pavement of a public square, the dull rumbling of labour that sounded from within its walls, made a great impression on her: half joy, to be at last near the goal of her ambition; half fear, lest after all she should not succeed, should be beaten down in the enormous fight against starvation which she heard going on around her. It seemed to her quite a daring thing to fling herself into the very midst of a machine in motion, while the hammers of the locksmiths and the planes of the cabinetmakers clattered and hissed from the workshops on the ground floor. That day the stream running out under the porch from the dyer's was a pale apple-green. She stepped across it gaily; the colour seemed to her a good omen.

They were to meet the landlord in the Boches' lodge. M. Marescot, a large cutler of the Rue de la Paix, had once turned a grindstone in the streets. He was now said to be worth several millions. He was a man of fifty-five, large, bony, decorated with the huge hands of an old workman; and one of his delights was to carry off the knives and scissors of his lodgers, which he sharpened himself for his own amusement. He was looked upon as not at all proud, because he spent hours in the lodges of his *concierges* making out all his accounts. He transacted all his business there. When the Coupeaus arrived, they found him at Madame Boche's greasy table, listening to the tale of how the sempstress of the second floor, staircase A, had refused to pay, with a disgusting epithet. Then, when they had signed the lease, he shook hands with the tinsmith. He loved workers. He had himself had a pretty hard time of it. But there was no point you couldn't reach with work. And, having counted out the two hundred and fifty francs of the first half-year, which he thrust into his huge pocket, he talked about his career and exhibited his decoration.

Meanwhile Gervaise was a little put out by the attitude of the Boches. They affected not to know her. They cringed before the landlord, hanging on his words, confirming him with nods. Madame Boche rushed out to drive away a band of children who had turned on the tap in the court, and were paddling about in the stream of water; and as she made her way back in her loftiest manner, looking along at the windows as if to assure herself that the house was all in order, she pursed up her lips, as much as to say that she was a person of considerable importance now that she had three hundred lodgers to look after. Boche went back to the subject of the sempstress on the second floor; he recommended turning her out, and he added up the terms in arrears, with the importance of a steward whose administration is in danger of being compromised. M. Marescot approved of the expulsion; but he would wait till the half-quarter. It was hard on people to throw them right out on the street, all the more so as it didn't put a farthing into the landlord's pocket. And Gervaise, with a little shiver, asked herself if they would throw her, too, on the street, if a day came when bad luck were to prevent her from paying. The lodge, smoky, and filled with dingy furniture, was as damp and dismal as a cellar; all the light from the window fell on the tailor's working board, on which was spread an old frock-coat sent in to be turned; whilst Pauline, the Boche's child, a red-haired little child of four, sat on the ground staring solemnly at a piece of veal over the fire, absorbed and enchanted with the strong smell of cooking that came from the stove.

M. Marescot was again holding out his hand to the tinsmith,

when the latter spoke of repairs, and reminded him of his verbal promise of seeing about that later. But the landlord grew angry; he had promised nothing; besides, it was never customary to make repairs in a shop. However, he agreed to go and see the place, together with the Coupeaus and Boche. The little haberdasher had carried off the whole lot of his shelves and counters; the shop was perfectly bare, with its blackened ceiling, its unsightly walls, from which hung strips of an old yellow paper. There, in the echoing emptiness of the place, a furious discussion went on. M. Marescot declared that it was the business of shop-keepers to tidy up their shops, for a shop-keeper might want gold everywhere, and he as a landlord could not supply the gold; then he related his own experience in the Rue de la Paix, where he had spent more than twenty thousand francs. Gervaise, with her woman's obstinacy, stated over and over again an argument which seemed to her irrefutable; when you rent rooms, the landlord papers the walls; why should not a shop be the same as a room? She asked for nothing more; merely that he should whitewash the ceiling, and put on fresh paper.

Boche, meanwhile, remained solemn and impenetrable; he turned his head, looked in the air, giving no opinion. Coupeau winked at him in vain, he affected not to wish to abuse his great influence with the landlord. Finally, however, he made a movement with his face, a little faint smile accompanied by a shake of the head. Just then, M. Marescot, in a state of exasperation, putting on an air of misery, and spreading out all his fingers with a cramped gesture like a miser, gave in to Gervaise, and promised the white-washing and papering, on condition that she paid half the cost of the paper. And he hurried away, refusing to listen to another word.

As soon as Boche was alone with the Coupeaus, he slapped them on the shoulder in the most exuberant manner. Well, that's done! But for him they would never have had their paper and their ceiling. Had they noticed how the landlord had consulted him out of the corner of his eye, and had decided at once on seeing him smile? Then, in confidence, he declared that he was the real master of the house. He decided who were to be given notice, let out rooms to those who seemed to him suitable, received the quarter's rent, which he had had for the last fortnight in his chest of drawers. That evening the Coupeaus, by way of thanking the Boches, thought they could do no better than send them two bottles of wine. They deserved a present.

On the following Monday the workmen began on the shop. The purchase of the paper was a very serious affair. Gervaise wanted a grey paper with blue flowers, so as to liven up the walls. Boche offered to take her with him; then she could choose. But he had strict orders from the landlord not to go beyond fifteen sous a roll. They spent an hour in the shop. Gervaise returned again and again to a very pretty chintz at eighteen sous. She was in despair; all the other papers seemed to her hideous. At last the *concierge* gave way; he would square it up by counting in an additional roll if necessary. And Gervaise, on the way back, bought some little cakes for Pauline. She did not wish to be behindhand; it was quite to her advantage to be on good terms.

The shop ought to have been ready in four days. The work dragged on three weeks. First, there had been talk of simply washing the paint. But the paint, which had formerly been a reddish-brown, was so dirty and dingy that Gervaise resolved on having all the shop-front re-done in blue, with bands of gold. Then the repairs seemed never to come to an end. Coupeau, who was still doing no work, arrived early in the morning, to see how the work went. Boche left the frock-coat and trousers, of which he was mending the button-holes, and joined him in looking after the men. Both stood in front of the workmen, their hands behind their back, smoking and spitting, and spending the whole day in judging the effect of every stroke of the brush. There were interminable reflections, profound reveries, before a nail that had to be pulled out. The painters, two great jolly chaps, came down from their ladders every moment, and stood about in the middle of the shop, joining in the discussion, wagging their heads for hours before the work which they had scarcely begun. The ceiling was soon whitewashed, it was the paint that never seemed to be any further forward. It would not dry. About nine o'clock the painters turned up with their paint-pots, laid them in a corner, gave a look round, and disappeared; they were not seen again for the day. They had gone to get their dinner, or they had had a small job to finish near by, in the Rue Myrha. Other times Coupeau took out the whole lot to have a drink, Boche, the painters, and any fellow-workman who might be passing; there was another afternoon wasted. Gervaise was beside herself. Suddenly, in two days, everything was finished,

the paint varnished, the paper put on, the refuse carted away.
The workmen had worked it off as if in sport; whistling
on their ladders, and singing until they deafened all the
community.

The house-moving took place at once. Gervaise, for the
first few days, was as happy as a child when she crossed the
street on her way home from an errand. She paused, and
smiled across at her home. From a distance, in the midst of
the black file of the other shops, her shop looked quite bright,
with a new gaiety in its pale blue sign, on which the words,
Hand Laundry, were painted in large gilt letters. In the window,
closed at the back with little muslin curtains, and papered in
blue so as to show off the whiteness of the linen, men's shirts
were laid out, and women's caps were hung up, the strings
tied to brass wires. And her shop looked to her beautiful, all
azure like the sky. It was blue inside as well as outside; the
paper, an imitation of Pompadour chintz, represented a trellis
covered with creepers; the ironing-board, an immense table
taking up two-thirds of the place, was covered with a heavy
ironing-blanket, and draped with a piece of cretonne with
large blue flowers, to hide the trestles. Gervaise seated herself
on a stool, overpowered with satisfaction, enchanted with the
pretty neatness of things, tenderly regarding all her new
apparatus, But her first glance always went to her ironing-
stove, a stove of cast-iron, on which ten irons could be heated
at once, ranged all round on slanting slabs. She would kneel
down and look inside, always frightened lest her silly little
apprentice would burst the stove by stuffing it too full of coke.

The rooms behind the shop were very comfortable. The
Coupeaus slept in the first room, at once kitchen and dining-
room; a door at the back opened on the court-yard. Nana's
bed was in a little room on the right, which got its light from
a round window near the ceiling. As for Étienne, he shared
the room on the left with the dirty clothes, always lying about
the ground in great heaps. Nevertheless, there was one
inconvenience, though at first they scarcely like to admit it,
but the walls ran with water, and there was hardly any light
after three o'clock.

The new shop made a great sensation in the neighbourhood.
The Coupeaus were going ahead at too great a rate, said
the neighbours, and would get into difficulties. They had, in
fact, spent the whole of the five hundred francs of the Goujets
setting up the place, without keeping enough for the fortnight's

expenses on which they had counted. The day when Gervaise took down her shutters for the first time, she had just six francs in her purse. But she had no uneasiness in the matter, business flowed in, the enterprise looked quite promising. A week afterwards, before going to bed, she spent two hours in making out her calculations on a scrap of paper; and she woke up Coupeau, her face all aglow, to tell him that there was money to be gained, by the hundred and thousand, if they were sensible.

"Well, well!" cried Madame Lorilleux to everybody, "my idiot of a brother has a droll way of going on! Very nice of Clop-clop to set up on her own account! It looks well, doesn't it?"

The Lorilleux were now at deadly enmity with Gervaise. From the very first, while the repairs were going on, they were bursting with rage; they went by on the other side of the street, so as not even to look at the painters; they passed upstairs with set teeth. This good-for-nothing with her blue shop, it was enough to drive decent people frantic. And on the very second day, as the apprentice was emptying out a bowl of starch, just as Madame Lorilleux came out, she had raised the street with her outcries against her sister-in-law for putting her work-people to insult her. All friendly relations were entirely broken off, they glared at one another whenever they met.

"Yes, nice goings on!" declared Madame Lorilleux. "We know very well where the money comes from, the money for her shop. She earned that off the blacksmith. Nice people they are, too, on that side! Didn't the father cut off his head with a knife, so as to escape the guillotine? At any rate, some dirty story of the kind!"

She flatly accused Gervaise of going to bed with the blacksmith. She invented a story as to having surprised them together one evening on a seat on the outer boulevard. The thought of this *liaison*, and the pleasure her sister-in-law must get out of it, exasperated her all the more from her own propriety, the propriety of an ugly woman. Every day the cry of her heart came to her lips:

"What is there in her, then, this cripple, to set men after her? Does anyone come after me?"

Then she spread interminable scandals among the neighbours. She told the whole story. Why, on the wedding-day she had had a very queer look about her. As for herself, she

E

had a sharp nose; she felt at once how it was going to turn out. Then, afterwards, Clop-clop had made herself out so sweet, so artful, that she and her husband, out of regard for Coupeau, had consented to be godfather and godmother for Nana; though it was a pretty experience, that christening. But now Clop-clop might be in the very article of death, and in need of a glass of water, it certainly wouldn't be she who would give it to her. She didn't favour saucy people, nor sluts, nor strumpets. As for Nana, she would always be welcome if she came to see her godfather and godmother; the child was not responsible for the sins of her father and mother. Coupeau had no need of advice; anyone else, in his place, would have let out with his fist at his wife, and soused her backside in a bucket; however, that was his own look-out; they only asked him to have a little respect for the feelings of his family. Good God! if she, Madame Lorilleux, had caught Lorilleux in the act, she would not have let it pass so quietly; she would have planted her scissors in his belly.

Meanwhile the Boches, who passed severe judgment on all the quarrels in the house, found the Lorilleux in the wrong. No doubt the Lorilleux were quite quiet respectable people, working all the blessed day, punctual with their rent; but, in truth, they were madly jealous. Besides, they were regular skinflints, shabby creatures who covered up their bottles of wine as they went up, so as not to be obliged to offer them a glass; really, they were too bad. One day, as Gervaise was standing the Boches some blackcurrant and soda-water, and they were drinking it in the lodge, Madame Lorilleux went by stiffly, affecting to spit before the *concierge's* door. Since that time, when Madame Boche swept out the staircase and the passages, she left the dust-heap outside the Lorilleux's door.

"Ah!" cried Madame Lorilleux, "Clop-clop stuffs them, the gluttons! Nice people they are, indeed! They'd better look out! I'll complain to the landlord. Only yesterday I saw that artful old Boche making up to Madame Gaudron. To go for a woman of that age, a woman who has had half a dozen children, I call that sheer beastliness! Let them serve me another dirty trick like that, and I'll just go and tell Mother Boche; won't she give her man a nice dressing! Lord! it would be quite a joke!"

Old Madame Coupeau saw both households continually, agreeing with everybody all round, getting invited to dinner

all the oftener because she listened indulgently to her daughter
and her daughter-in-law, one, one evening, one another.
Madame Lerat for the moment did not go near the Coupeaus
because she had had a quarrel with Clop-clop on the subject
of a Zouave who had cut off his mother's nose with a razor.
She defended the Zouave; the razor-cut seemed to her very
loving indeed, she would not say why. And she had added
yet more to the wrath of Madame Lorilleux by declaring
that Clop-clop, in conversation, before everybody, spoke of
her quite naturally as Cow-tail. All the people, the Boches,
the neighbours, now called her Cow-tail.

In the midst of all these disturbances Gervaise would come
to the door of her shop, quiet and composed, with a little
friendly nod for her friends as they went by. It delighted her
to go out there for just a minute, in the midst of her work, and
look down the street with all the pride and vanity of a woman ·
of business who has a bit of the pavement to herself. The Rue
de la Goutte-d'Or was all hers, and the streets near by, and
the whole neighbourhood. When she leaned out in her white
bodice, with her bare arms, her blonde hair ruffled with the
work, she could look from end to end of the street, right and
left, taking in at a glance people and houses, street and sky.
On the left the Rue de la Goutte-d'Or dwindled away,
peaceful and deserted, into quite a bit of country, where the
women chatted to one another on their doorsteps; on the
right, a few yards distant, the Rue des Poissonniers was
noisy with vehicles and the tramp of men, making this end
of the street a general meeting-place for all the streets round
about. Gervaise loved the street, with its trucks jolting over
the ups and downs of the road, its cram of people along the
narrow pavements, interrupted by the sharp descent of
the irregular pavement. Her three inches of gutter before the
shop took an immense importance in her eyes, a very river,
which she wished to keep clean and tidy, a strange and
living river, to which the dyer's colours gave all sorts of
delicate variations in the midst of the mud of the street. She
took an interest, too, in the other shops; a big grocer's, with
its spread of dried fruits hung up with string; a cheap draper's,
where jackets and blue blouses, their arms standing out stiff,
swayed at the least puff of wind. Inside the fruiterer's and the
tripe-seller's, she could see just a bit of the counter, with their
fine peaceful cats stretched out at length. Her neighbour,
Madame Vigouroux, the coal dealer, was on nodding

acquaintance with her; she was a little plump, dark, bright-
eyed woman, always dawdling about with men in front of her
shop, which was ornamented with a complicated design of a
rustic châlet, painted on logs of reddish-brown colour.
Mesdames Cudorge, mother and daughter, her other neighbours, at the umbrella-shop, never showed themselves outside
their gloomy window, their closed door, embellished with
two little tin parasols coated with a thick layer of bright
vermilion. But Gervaise, before going in again, always gave
a glance across the road opposite, to a great white wall,
without a window, with only a huge doorway, through which
could be seen the blaze of a forge, inside a court strewed with
carts and waggons, their shafts in the air. On the wall the word
Farrier was painted in large letters, surrounded by a fan of
horse-shoes. All day long the hammers rang on the anvils,
and a shower of sparks lit up the shade of the court. And at
the end of this wall, up a passage not bigger than a cupboard,
between a seller of old iron and a vendor of fried potatoes,
there was a watchmaker, a spruce frock-coated gentleman,
who fumbled away at watches all his time with little tiny
tools, before a shop-board with dainty things under glass
cases; whilst, behind him, the pendulums of two or three
dozen little clocks ticked all at once, in the dirt and squalor
of the street and the rhythmical clatter of the smithy.

The neighbours found Gervaise very pleasant. No doubt
there was some talk against her, but they were all of one account
in admitting that she had large eyes, a mouth no bigger than
that, with very white teeth. She was certainly a pretty blonde,
and would have been extremely pretty but for her limp.
She was in her twenty-eighth year; she had grown stouter.
Her sharp features rounded out; her movements were somewhat more deliberate. She would sometimes sit absent-
mindedly on the edge of a chair, while she was waiting for
her iron to heat, her face drowned in a sort of animal delight.
She was getting fond of good things to eat; in that everybody
agreed, but it was not a bad fault, quite the contrary. When
you have the income to pay for delicacies, it would be silly
indeed to eat potato-peel. All the more so, as she always
worked hard, slaving at her business, and going on late into
the night, with closed shutters, when there was anything
urgent. As the neighbours said, she had luck; everything
succeeded in her hands. She washed for the house, for M.
Madinier, Mademoiselle Remanjou, the Boches; she even

carried away some customers from her former mistress, Madame Fauconnier, town ladies, living in the Rue du Faubourg-Poissonnière. At the end of the second fortnight she was obliged to take in two work-women, Madame Putois, and the tall Clemence, the girl who lived on the sixth floor; that made three people about, besides her apprentice, that little cross-eyed slip of an Augustine, who was as ugly as sin. Some people would have had their heads quite turned by such luck. It was very excusable if she let the work slide a bit on Monday, after slaving away all the week. Indeed, she was bound to; it would have made her quite silly to go on doing nothing but look at shirts being ironed, if she were not to go in for something good now and then when her mouth watered for it.

Never had Gervaise shown herself so amiable to everybody. She was as meek as a lamb, as sweet as sugar. Apart from Madame Lorilleux, whom she called Cow-tail in order to pay her out, she hated no one; she was indulgent to everybody. Letting herself go a bit, after she had had a good meal and her coffee, she professed a vague, general benevolence. Her saying was, "Oughtn't we to put up with one another, if we are not to live like savages?" When anyone said, "How good you are!" she only laughed. She might just as well have been unamiable. She denied that there was any merit in her good-nature. Had not all her dreams been realized? Had she anything to wish for? She recalled her old ideal when she was in destitution: to get work, have bread to eat, a hole and corner of her own, bring up her children, not get knocked about, and die in her bed. Now her ideal was already surpassed; she had all she had wished for, and more. As for dying in her bed, she said laughingly she quite counted on that, but not just yet, you may be sure.

Gervaise was specially good to Coupeau. Never an unkind word, never a complaint behind his back. The tinsmith had finally gone back to his work, and as his workshop was now at the other end of Paris, she gave him every morning forty sous for his dinner, his drop of drink, and his tobacco. Only, two days out off six, Coupeau stopped on the way, drank his forty sous with a friend, and came home for dinner with some tale or other. On one occasion he did not get far; he treated himself, Mes-Bottes, and three other friends, to a fine spread— snails, a joint, and good wine, at the "Capucin", Barrière de la Chapelle. Then, as his forty sous was not enough, he sent the bill to his wife by the waiter, saying that he was stony-broke. She laughed and shrugged her shoulders. What was the harm if her man amused himself a bit? You must give men their run, if you want to get on happily together. From one thing to another one might soon come to blows. Good Lord! it was easy enough to understand. Coupeau still suffered in his leg; he had let himself be persuaded; he had to do as others did, if he were not to pass for a muff. Besides, it was nothing very serious; if he came in a bit screwed he lay down, and was all right two hours after.

By this time they had come to the heat of the summer. One June afternoon, a Saturday when they were extra busy, Gervaise herself stuffed the coke into the stove, around which the ten irons were set to heat, while the flue was roaring above. At this hour the sun poured down on the front of the shop; the pavement cast up a very blaze of light and heat, setting great motes a-dancing on the ceiling; and this flood of light, a little blue in the shadow of the paper on shelves and window, threw a blinding brightness on the shop-board, like a cloud of gold-dust sifted all over the fine linen. The heat was intolerable. The door was wide open, but not a breath of air entered; the things hung up on wires to dry, steamed, and were as dry as shavings in less than three-quarters of an hour. For a little while, in this furnace-like heat, there had been a heavy silence, in which the irons sounded bluntly, dulled by the thick ironing-blanket covered with calico.

"Well!" said Gervaise, "if we don't melt today! One could take off one's chemise!"

She was kneeling on the ground before an earthenware pan, dipping the linen in the starch. She was in her white petticoat, with her bodice turned up at the sleeves and open at the neck, her arms and neck bare, all over rosy, and so covered with sweat that her little blonde fluffs of hair stuck to the skin. She carefully dipped caps, shirt-fronts, petticoats, and the embroidery on the drawers, into the milky water. Then she rolled them up, one after another, and laid them at the bottom of a square basket, after having sprinkled water with her hand over the parts of the shirts and drawers that had not been starched.

"This basket is for you, Madame Putois," she went on. "Be quick please. It will dry at once; you must do it over again in an hour's time."

Madame Putois, a little, lean woman of forty-five, ironed

away without a drop of sweat, buttoned up in an old brown dress. She had not even taken off her bonnet, a black bonnet trimmed with green ribbons, turning yellow. She stood upright before the shop-board, which was too tall for her, her elbows raised, moving her irons with the jerky movement of a marionette. All at once she cried:

"Now, now. Mademoiselle Clémence, put on your bodice. It's indecent. While you are about it, you might as well show all your wares. There are three men stopping opposite to look."

The big Clémence called her an old silly, between her teeth. She was suffocating; she only wanted to be as comfortable as she could; everybody hadn't the skin of a rhinoceros. Besides, what did it matter if people saw anything? And she threw up her arms, her fine, firm bust nearly coming out of her chemise, her shoulders dragging at the short sleeves. Clémence was going on at such a rate that she threatened to use herself up before she was thirty; the day after she had been out on the loose she was always on the move; she seemed to work in her sleep, as if her head were stuffed with sawdust. But she kept on all the same; there was not a single workwoman who could iron a man's shirt-front with such skill. That was her speciality, men's shirts.

"It's all my own," she declared, slapping her bosom. "And it don't bite, it don't harm anybody."

"Clémence, put on your bodice," said Gervaise. "Madame Putois is right; it is not decent. People will take my house for what it is not."

Clémence grumblingly obeyed. Fiddlesticks! as if nobody had ever seen titties before! And she vented her wrath on the apprentice, the cross-eyed slip of an Augustine, who stood beside her, ironing the plain part of the linen, the stockings and handkerchiefs; she hustled her, and jogged her with her elbow. But Augustine, with the sly and peevish malevolence of a laughing-stock and an abortion, spat on her dress behind, without anyone's seeing it, to pay her out.

Gervaise was just beginning a cap belonging to Madame Boche, which she wanted to be particular about. She had made fresh starch so as to freshen it up again. And she was gently working the *polonais*, a little iron rounded at both ends, to and fro in the cap, when a woman entered, a meagre woman with great red spots in her cheeks, her skirts sopping. It was a washerwoman who employed three work-women at the wash-house in the Rue de la Goutte-d'Or.

"You have come too soon, Madame Bijard," cried Gervaise. "I told you this evening. It is very tiresome of you to come at this hour of the day."

But as the washerwoman lamented, declaring she was afraid she couldn't set the wash going that day, Gervaise promised to give her the dirty clothes at once. They went for the bundles into the room on the left, Étienne's room, and came back with great armfuls, which they heaped up on the floor at the back of the shop. The sorting took a good half-hour. Gervaise made heaps all round her, putting together the shirts, the chemises, the handkerchiefs, the socks, the dusters. When she came upon anything belonging to a new customer, she marked it with a cross in red thread, so as to recognize it. A dull stench rose into the hot air out of all this dirty linen.

"Oh, I say, that does hum!" said Clémence, stopping up her nose.

"Well, if it was clean, would they send it to us?" said Gervaise, composedly. "All the better for us! We said fourteen chemises, didn't we, Madame Bijard?—fifteen, sixteen, seventeen——"

She went on counting out aloud. She felt no disgust; she was quite used to it; and she thrust her bare, rosy arms into the heaps of underwear yellowed with dirt, dusters stiffened with the grease of dishwashing, socks eaten away with sweat. Nevertheless, the strong odour that mounted to her nostrils from the pile of clothes before her gave her a feeling of drowsiness. She sat down on the edge of a stool, half doubled up, reaching out her hands mechanically to right and left, slowly, as if intoxicated by this odour of humanity, a vague smile on her face, her eyelids drooping ; and an incipient laziness seemed to come over her so, in this asphyxia of old clothes that poisoned the air about her.

Just as she was shaking out a child's diaper, so messed up that she could not recognize it, Coupeau entered.

"This blasted sun!" he stuttered. "It bowls you clean over."

The tinsmith held on to the ironing-board to keep himself from falling. It was the first time that he had brought home quite such a heavy load. Up till then he had only been a bit boozed, nothing more. But this time he had his eye blacked, a chance blow in a friendly scuffle. His curly head, in which the white hairs were already beginning to show, seemed to have been propping up the wall in some low wine-shop, for a cobweb hung from a lock of hair at the back of the neck. He was still as jolly as ever, his features a little bit drawn and worn, but always good-tempered, as he said, and his complexion still enough to put a duchess to shame.

"I must explain," he said, addressing Gervaise. "It was Pied-de-Céleri; you know him, the chap with a wooden leg. Well, he is just leaving to go home, and he wanted to have a bust-up. Oh, it finished us up, that beastly sun! The whole street is sick. Lord! they're staggering all over the place."

And as Clémence began to laugh at the idea of all the street being tipsy, he was seized with a hilarity which nearly choked him. He cried:

"Ha! ha! the damned sots! Isn't it funny? But it isn't their fault; it's the sun."

The whole laundry was convulsed with laughter, even Madame Putois, who disapproved of drink. The cross-eyed Augustine crowed like a cock, her mouth wide open, in convulsions. Gervaise had an idea that Coupeau had not come straight home, but had been spending an hour at the Lorilleux's where they put all sorts of bad notions into his head. He swore that he had not been there, and she, too, laughed indulgently, not even scolding him for having lost another day's work.

"What things he says! Lord! Lord!" she murmured, "how can one say such things?"

Then, in a motherly tone:

"Better go and lie down. You see we are busy; you are in the way. That makes thirty-two handkerchiefs, Madame Bijard; and two more, thirty-four."

But Coupeau was not sleepy. He stood there, swaying to and fro like a pendulum, sniggering in a persistent, teasing sort of way. Gervaise, wanting to get rid of Madame Bijard, called Clémence over to count the clothes while she made the list. Thereupon the cheeky beggar had her say, some dirty word or other, over each article; she laid bare all the misfortunes and all the misconduct of the customers, joking over all the holes and all the stains that passed through her hands. Augustine pretended not to understand, opening her ears to their widest, with a premature taste for vice. Madame Putois pursed up her lips; it did not seem to her the thing to say all that before Coupeau; a man has no business to see the dirty clothes; proper sort of people never do that sort of thing. As for Gervaise, absorbed in her work, she seemed not to hear. As

she made out the list, she looked at each article carefully, to
see who it belonged to; and she never made a mistake,
assigning each to its proper owner, from its look, its colour.
Those towels belonged to the Goujets; it was evident that they
had not been used to wipe out the casseroles. There was a
pillow-case which certainly came from the Boche's, on account
of the pomade with which Madame Boche plastered all her
linen. One need not look closely, either, at M. Madinier's
flannel vests; he turned the colour of the stuff, his skin was so
greasy. And she knew other particularities, all about the
cleanliness of everyone, the under-garments of the neighbours
who sported their silk dresses in the streets, and how many
stockings, handkerchiefs, and chemises they dirtied in a week,
and the rents that some people got in certain things, always
in the same spot. She was full of anecdotes. Mademoiselle
Remanjou's chemises, for instance, gave rise to endless
comments; they wore out at the top, the old maid must have
very sharp shoulder-blades; and they were never soiled, not
if she had worn them for a fortnight, which proved that at
her age one is as dry as a faggot. So, at every sorting, the whole
neighbourhood of the Goutte-d'Or was taken to pieces in
the shop.

"Here are some goody-goodies!" cried Clémence, opening
a fresh bundle.

Gervaise, suddenly seized with a great repugnance, drew
back.

"Madame Gaudron's bundle," she said, "I won't wash it
any more; I only want to find an excuse. No, I am not more
particular than other people. I have turned over very nasty
linen in my life; but as for that—no, I really can't. It nearly
makes me sick. What does the woman do, to get her linen in
such a state?"

And she begged Clémence to hurry on. But the work-
woman continued her remarks, stuck her finger into the holes,
referring to every article, which she flourished in the air like
banners of triumphant filth. Meanwhile, the pile increased all
round Gervaise. Now, still sitting on the stool, she was almost
lost to sight in the midst of all the shirts and petticoats; before
her were sheets, drawers, table-cloths, a very confusion of
dirtiness; and there, in the midst of this rising flood, she sat
with her bare arms and neck, her fluffs of blonde hair sticking
to her temples, rosier and drowsier than ever. She had
recovered her air of composure, her careful and attentive

smile, forgetting Madame Gaudron's linen, not smelling it any more, turning over the heap with one hand to see if there was any mistake. That little hussy Augustine, who loved shovelling coke into the works, had piled it up so that the tiles were glowing red. The sun slanted through the doorway; the shop was a blaze of heat. Coupeau, the heat of the place getting more and more into his head, was seized with a sudden tenderness. He came towards Gervaise with open arms, very moved.

"You're a good wife," he stuttered. "I must give you a kiss."

But he caught his feet in the petticoats which were in the way, and nearly fell.

"What a nuisance you are," said Gervaise, without showing any annoyance. "Be quiet, we have finished now."

No; he must give her a kiss, he must, he loved her dearly. As he stammered out these phrases, he made his way round the heap of petticoats, stumbled against the heap of shirts, and then, still pushing his way on, his foot caught, and he fell flat on the heap of dusters. Gervaise, beginning to get angry, pushed him away, declaring he would get everything mixed up. But Clémence, and even Madame Putois, found fault with her. After all, it was nice of him to want to give her a kiss. She might as well have let him do it.

"You are lucky, Madame Coupeau," said Madame Bijard, whom her husband, a locksmith, was accustomed to batter about whenever he came home. "If mine was like that when he has had a drop too much, it would be a blessed thing!"

Gervaise, recovering herself, was already sorry for her impatience. She helped Coupeau up again, and held out her cheek to him with a smile. But the tinsmith, without minding the people about, took hold of her breasts.

"I don't want to say it," he murmured, "but your linen is nifty, isn't it? But I love you all the same, you know."

"Let me go, you are tickling me!" she cried, laughing more than ever. "You silly thing! How can you be so silly?"

He had seized hold of her, and would not let her go. She gave way, overcome with a sort of dizziness that came to her from the pile of clothes, without minding the liquorish breath of Coupeau. And the great kiss that they exchanged, mouth to mouth, in the midst of the dirty things, was like a first step in the slow, downward course of their life.

Meanwhile Madame Bijard tied up the clothes in bundles. She spoke of her little girl, Eulalie, now two years old, who was already as wise as a little woman. One could leave her all by herself; she never cried, or played with matches. Finally she carried off the bundles one after another, stooping under the heavy weight, her face growing purple with the exertion.

"It is unbearable; we are simply roasting," said Gervaise, wiping her face before returning to work on Madame Boche's cap.

And she had a good mind to box Augustine's ears when she saw that the stove was red-hot, and the very irons as well. She was a little devil; if you merely turned your back, she was up to some mischief. Now they would have to wait a quarter of an hour before it was possible to use them. Gervaise damped down the fire with two shovelfuls of ashes. It also occurred to her to hang a pair of sheets on the wires along the ceiling like blinds, so as to take off some of the sun. Then it was quite tolerable inside. The temperature was still pretty strong; but it was like being in an alcove, with a white light, all by one's self; for all that, the footsteps outside could still be heard, on the other side of the sheets; and now one could do just as one pleased. Clémence took off her bodice. As Coupeau refused to go and lie down, he was allowed to remain; but he had to promise to keep quiet in the corner, for they couldn't afford to rest on their oars just then.

"What has that little wretch done with the *polonais*?" muttered Gervaise, referring to Augustine.

They were always looking for the little iron, which they found in all sorts of odd places, where the apprentice was supposed to have hidden it away maliciously. Gervaise was at last finishing Madame Boche's cap. She had roughed out the lace, drawing it apart with her hand, setting it up with a little touch of the iron. It was a cap with very elaborate puffs, separated by insertions of embroidery. She stuck at the work, silent and attentive, ironing the puffs and insertions with the cock, an egg-shaped tool fitted into a wooden holder.

Silence reigned in the place. Nothing was heard but the dull thud of irons, deadened by the ironing blanket. On both sides of the great square table, the mistress, the two work-women, and the apprentice, all leaned over their work, their shoulders rounded, their arms working to and fro incessantly. Each had a flat brick on her right, burnt by the hot irons. In the middle of the table, on the edge of a deep plate filled with cold water, was a rag and a little brush. A bunch of great lilies stood in an old cherry brandy bottle, bringing a sumptuous bit of garden into the place, with its large snowy clusters. Madame Putois had set to work on the basket of linen prepared by Gervaise, towels, drawers, bodices, and cuffs. Augustine dawdled over her stockings and towels, gazing into the air, absorbed by a big moth that was fluttering about. As for Clémence, she was just doing her thirty-fifth shirt since the morning.

"Always wine, never spirits!" said the tinsmith suddenly, as if he were obliged to make the declaration. "Spirits knock me up, no mistake."

Clémence took an iron from the stove with her leather holder, and put it up to her face to see if it was hot enough. She rubbed it on a brick, wiped it on a cloth attached to her waist, and attacked her thirty-fifth shirt, first ironing the body and the two sleeves.

"Bah! Monsieur Coupeau," she said, after a minute, "a little glass of French cream isn't so bad. It suits me jolly well. Then, you know, the sooner one kicks the bucket the better. I know very well I shan't make old bones."

"How horrid you are with your graveyard notions!" broke in Madame Putois, who disliked gloomy conversations.

Coupeau got up angrily, fancying that he was being accused of having drunk brandy. He swore on his life, on the life of his wife and child, that he had not a drop of brandy in his body. And he went up to Clémence, breathing in her face so that she could verify it. Then, with her bare shoulders right under his nose, he began to snigger. He wanted a look. Clémence, after having folded the back of the shirt and ironed over the two sides, was at work on the wrists and collar. But as he shoved up against her he made her make a wrinkle, and she had to take the brush from the plate in order to smooth out the starch.

"Madame!" said she, "keep him off me, will you!"

"Leave her alone; you can't behave," said Gervaise composedly. "We are busy, can't you see?"

Well, what if they were busy? it wasn't his fault. He wasn't doing any harm. He didn't touch; he only looked. Wasn't one to be allowed to look at the nice things that God Almighty had made? She had damned good arms, any way, this rip of a Clémence. She might show herself for two sous, and let people feel her; no one would regret his money. The workwoman meanwhile made no objections, only laughing at his boozy compliments. And she began to joke with him. He bantered her about her men's shirts. She was always at men's shirts. Why, yes! she lived with them, damn it all! She knew them jolly well. She knew how they were made. They had passed through her hands in hundred and hundreds. All the fellows in the neighbourhood carried about her work on them. And she went on shaking her shoulders with laughter; she had marked five large folds down the length of the back, inserting the iron through the opening of the front; then she turned down the front flap and worked it into large folds in the same way.

"That's the banner!" she said, laughing louder than ever.

Augustine broke into a splutter of laughter, so funny did the word strike her. She got a scolding: brats like her had no business to laugh at what they shouldn't understand. Clémence handed her her iron; the apprentice finished off the irons on her dusters and stockings, when they were not hot enough for the starched things. But she took hold of it so clumsily that she burnt herself all down the wrist. She began to sob, accusing Clémence of having burnt her on purpose. The workwoman, who had just fetched a very hot iron for the shirt-front, consoled her by threatening to iron her two ears for her, if she said any more. Meanwhile, she had stuck a cloth under the shirt-front, and she moved the iron slowly over it, leaving time for the starch to soak out and dry. The shirt-front came out as stiff and shining as a sheet of thick paper.

"Damnation!" cried Coupeau, shifting from foot to foot behind her, with a drunkard's obstinacy.

He raised himself on tip-toe laughing like a creaking pulley. Clémence leaning heavily on the board, her wrists bent, her elbows in the air and wide apart, bent her neck in a great effort; and all her bare flesh swelled out, her shoulders heaved up, the tension of the muscles setting the fine skin palpitating, her bosom rose, pearled with perspiration, in the rosy shadow of the half-open chemise. He put out his hands, trying to touch.

"Madame, Madame," cried Clémence, "make him leave off, do! I shall go if you don't stop him. I won't be insulted."

Gervaise had just placed Madame Boche's cap on a head-block covered with a cloth, and was working out the lace minutely with the small iron. She raised her eyes just as the tinsmith reached out his hands fumbling at the chemise.

"Really, Coupeau, you can't behave yourself," she said with

a bored air, as if she were scolding a child who would insist on eating jam without bread. "You just come to bed."

"Yes, you be off to bed, Monsieur Coupeau. You'll be much better off there," said Madame Putois.

"All right," he stammered, still sniggering away; "you're as cracked as the rest of them. Can't one have a little joke, then? Women, I know all about women; I've never done any harm. One fools about a bit, but one doesn't go any further; it is simply a compliment to the sex. And then, when you put out all your goods, why shouldn't one take his choice? Why does the creature show all she's got? No, it's not fair."

Then, turning to Clémence:

"You know, ducky, you needn't be spiteful. If it is because there are people about——"

He got no further. Gervaise, without violence, took hold of him with one hand and laid the other over his mouth. He struggled, by way of joke, while she pushed him through the shop into the bedroom. He got his mouth free, and declared that he was quite ready to go to bed, but that the girl was to come and warm his tootsies. Then Gervaise could be heard taking off his shoes. She undressed him, scolding him a bit in a maternal way. When she pulled at his trousers he roared with laughter, sprawling out on the bed; and he kicked, declaring she was tickling him. At last she covered him up carefully like a child. Was he all right now? He did not reply; he called out to Clémence:

"I say, ducky, here I am; I'm waiting for you."

As Gervaise returned to the shop, the cross-eyed Augustine was just having her ears boxed by Clémence. It was on account of a dirty iron, which Madame Putois had taken off the stove; not suspecting anything, she had smutted a whole shirt; and as Clémence, in order to redeem herself from the charge of not having cleaned her iron, swore loudly that the iron was not hers, despite the patch of burnt starch underneath it, the apprentice had spat on her dress openly, before her, furious at the injustice. This brought on her a good sounding smack. The cross-eyed chit kept back her tears, cleaned the iron, scratching it, then wiping it, after having rubbed it over with a candle-end; but every time that she passed behind Clémence she kept her saliva, and spat it out, laughing inwardly as it slobbered down over the skirt.

Gervaise returned to her task of goffering the lace of the cap. And in the sudden calm one could hear the thick voice of Coupeau from the back of the shop. He was still good-tempered, laughed all by himself, letting some disconnected phrases escape him.

"My wife is silly! Isn't she silly to send me to bed? Eh, it's too silly, in the middle of the day, when one isn't even sleepy-eyed."

Then all at once he began to snore. At that Gervaise heaved a sigh of relief, happy to know he was at last quiet, sleeping off his befuddledness, safe in bed. And she spoke in the silence with a slow, continuous voice, without taking her eyes off the little goffering-iron which she was manipulating briskly.

"What would you have? He doesn't know what he is doing; it's no use being angry. If I were to be always blowing him up, it would do no good. I prefer to say as he says, and get him off to bed; then it's all done with, and I'm in peace and quiet. Then he means no harm, he's very fond of me. You saw, just now, he would have gone through fire and water to give me a kiss. It's very nice of him, for there are a pretty lot of them who go off after women as soon as they've drunk a drop. He comes straight back home. He fools about a bit with the work-women, but it doesn't go further than that. You understand, Clémence, you mustn't be offended. You know what a man is when he is tipsy; if he were to kill his father and mother, he wouldn't remember anything about it. Oh! I forgive him with all my heart. He is only like the rest of them, sure enough."

She said it all composedly, without anger or revolt, already quite used to Coupeau's boozy exploits; still making excuses for him, but already seeing no harm in his fooling about with the girls in her presence. When she had ended there was again silence, which remained unbroken. Madame Putois, as she took each article, pulled out the basket from under the cretonne with which the table was draped. Then, when it was ironed, she lifted up her short arms and laid it on a shelf. Clémence was finishing off her thirty-fifth shirt. They were crowded with work; they had calculated that it would be needful to go on till eleven, working as hard as ever they could. All the workshop, now undistracted, went at it like grim death. Bare arms went and came, lighting up the whiteness of the linen with their rosy shadows. The stove was again filled with coke, and as the sun striking through an opening between the sheets, fell right upon it, the intense heat could be seen rising in the air on the ray of sunlight, an invisible flame which seemed to shiver in the air.

It grew so stifling, with all those petticoats and table-cloths drying on the lines, that the cross-eyed Augustine, unable to find any more saliva, stuck the end of her tongue out between her lips. There was an odour of furnace, of starch, of burnt iron, the insipid odour of a bath-room, to which the four work-women added the sharper savour of their sopping necks and chignons, whilst the bunch of great lilies, in the green water of its bottle, withered away, exhaling a pure, strong perfume. And, from time to time, in the midst of the noise of irons and of the poker stirring the fire, a snore of Coupeau sounded out, with the regularity of a loud clock ticking, keeping time with the women's unceasing labour.

After a day's hard drinking, the tinsmith always had a headache, a terrible headache which put his hair out of curl, his nose out of joint, and his mouth out of taste, for the whole of the next day. He rose late, slept till eight o'clock; and he dawdled about the shop, unable to make up his mind to set out for the yard. The day was by this time lost. In the morning he complained that his pins felt like cotton-wool, declared that it was too idiotic to go on the booze like that; it simply did for you. It was merely that one came across a set of sots, who wouldn't let you be; one swilled a bit, without intending to; one got into one sort of affair or another, and finally one got a bit elevated, and there you were! The devil! it wouldn't occur again; he didn't mean to leave his boots at the bar, in the flower of his age. But after dinner he put on his tidy things, and began to hum and haw, to show he was in good voice. He began to deny that he had been drunk the night before, a bit "on", perhaps. There weren't many of his make, sound as a bell, with a wrist like iron, drinking as hard as he liked without being any the worse for it. Then he mooned about the street all the afternoon. When he had worried the work-women beyond endurance, his wife gave him twenty sous, to rid the place of him.

He set off at once, and went to buy his tobacco at the "Petite Civette", Rue des Poissonniers, where he generally had a prune, if he chanced to meet anybody that he knew. Then he used up the rest of the change at François', at the corner of the Rue de la Goutte-d'Or, where there was a delightful wine, a young wine, that tickled your palate. It was an old-fashioned pot-house, dark, low-ceilinged, with a smoky room at the right, in which soup was sold. And he stayed on there till the evening, drinking glass after glass; he had tick there, and the landlord had solemnly promised not to send in the bill to his good woman. One had to rinse out one's mouth a bit, obviously, to get rid of the bad taste of the day before. One glass of wine leads to another. He was all right, he was; didn't run after girls, though he liked a bit of a joke now and then, certainly; got a bit top-heavy now and then, but decently, not like those beastly chaps who were always in liquor. And he went home gay as a lark.

"Has your sweetheart been in?" he would sometimes ask Gervaise, banteringly. "We never see him now; I must go and fetch him."

The sweetheart was Goujet. He was careful, indeed, not to come too often, for fear of being in the way, and causing talk. Nevertheless, he seized on all sorts of pretexts, brought the linen, passed twenty times a day. There was a particular corner in the laundry, at the back, where he liked to sit for hours without moving, smoking his short pipe. In the evening after dinner, once every ten days or so, he ventured in and installed himself; and he never talked, sat with his mouth sealed, his eyes fixed on Gervaise, only taking his pipe from his lips to laugh when she said anything. When the laundry was at work late on Saturdays, he sat there absorbed, seeming to find it as amusing as the theatre. Sometimes they went on till three o'clock in the morning. A lamp was suspended from the ceiling by a wire; the shade cast a great circle of light, in which the linen took the soft whiteness of snow. The apprentice put up the shutters; but as the July nights were broiling, the street-door was left open. As the hours went by, the women undid button after button of their dresses, to get a little air. Their fine skin turned golden under the light of the lamp, that of Gervaise in particular. She was plump now, her shoulders blonde, shining as silk, with a little wrinkle like a baby's at the neck; he could have drawn that dimple from memory, so well he knew it. Gradually he was overcome by the heat of the stove, the smell of the linen steaming under the irons; and he half dozed in a sort of vague dream as he watched the women pushing on with their work, moving their bare arms to and fro, working deep into the night, that the neighbours might have their Sunday things. All round the laundry the houses slept; a deep and slumbrous silence fell heavily on all around. Twelve struck, then one, then two. In the black deserted street the doorway cast a single streak of light, like a roll of yellow cloth on the ground. From time to time a distant footstep was heard, a man approached, and as he crossed the streak of light he turned, surprised by the sound of the irons, getting a glimpse of bare-necked women in a reddish mist.

Goujet, seeing that Gervaise did not know what to do with Étienne, and wishing to get him out of the way of Coupeau had taken him to blow the bellows at his forge in the bolt factory. The bolt-making trade—if it was not very grand in itself, what with the dirt of the forges, and the tediousness of always hammering away at the same piece of iron—was a trade which brought in money, ten or twelve francs a day. The youngster, who was now twelve, could soon get into it if the work suited him. And Étienne was now another link between the laundress and the blacksmith. He would bring the boy home, telling how well he had been getting on. Everybody joked Gervaise about Goujet, declaring he was quite mashed on her. She was well aware of it, she blushed like a child, and her cheeks went as red as a biffin apple. Poor dear fellow, he was never in the way. Never had he said anything to her; never a smutty word or a familiarity. There were not many men like that. And, without ever confessing it, she was filled with joy at being loved like this, like a holy virgin. When she had any serious trouble, she thought of the blacksmith; and that consoled her. When they were alone together, they were quite at their ease; they smiled contentedly in one another's faces, without putting their feelings into words. It was a sober sort of affection, without a thought of anything wrong, since it was better far to live in peace and quietness when one could be happy that way, simply by living so.

Meanwhile, Nana, towards the end of the summer, began to put things in the house upside down. She was six, and a regular little terror. Her mother took her every morning, so as not to have her always in the way, to a little school in the Rue Polonceau, Mademoiselle Josse's. She pinned her schoolfellows' dresses together at the back; she filled the schoolmistress's snuff-box with ashes; she was up to other tricks, dirtier still, which were not to be repeated. Twice had Mademoiselle Josse turned her away, and twice had she taken her back, so as not to lose the six francs a month. After school hours, Nana made up for having been shut up so long by kicking up an infernal row under the porch and in the court, where the work-women, half-deafened with her noise, sent her to play. There she found Pauline, the Boche's little girl, and Victor, a great lout of ten, the child of Gervaise's old mistress, who loved to trot about with quite little girls. Madame Fauconnier, who had remained on good terms with the Coupeaus, sent the child herself. Besides, there was an extraordinary swarm of children in the house, a bevy of urchins rushing up and down the long staircases all day long, like flocks of noisy, pilfering sparrows. Madame Gaudron alone was responsible for nine, some light, some dark, all with uncombed hair and unwashed faces, their trousers up to their eyes, their socks rolling down over their shoes, their jackets in rags, bits of white skin showing through all the filth. Another woman, a bread-carrier on the fifth floor, had seven. There were lots in every room. And in all this crowd of rosy-cheeked urchins, whose faces were washed, at all events, whenever it rained, there were big ones, tricky, some of them, some of them fat as little old men; little ones, quite tiny, only just out of the cradle, hardly able to use their legs, going on all fours if they wanted to run. Nana reigned over all the kids, ruling with a rod of iron over girls twice as big as herself, only delegating a little of her authority to Pauline and Victor, who were her sworn allies, and did whatever she told them. The little devil was for ever playing at mother, undressing the smallest ones and dressing them again, wanting to examine the others all over, pulling them about, and exercising the fantastic despotism of a vicious grown-up person. Under her leadership they were always up to mischief. The band paddled in the dyer's stream, and came out blue or red to the knees; then rushed off to the blacksmith's where it prigged nails and iron-filings; and then went on to sprawl on the carpenter's shavings, huge heaps of shavings, full of fun, in which one could roll over and over, petticoats in the air. The court, too, belonged to it; it resounded with the clatter of little shoes going hurry-skurry, the shrieks which went up every time the flock took flight. On certain days the court was not sufficient. Then the band made for the cellars, then up again, up one staircase, along a passage, down another staircase, then along another passage, without ever getting tired, for hours together, yelling all the time, shaking the great house with the rush of wild beasts let loose from every corner.

"They are a nuisance, those little wretches," cried Madame

Boche. "Really, people must have very little to do to have so many children. And yet they are always complaining of being hard up."

Boche declared that children sprang from poverty like toadstools from a dunghill. The *concierge* was after them all day, threatening them with her broom. At last she fastened up the doors leading to the cellars, for she found out from Pauline, to whom she gave a good box on the ears, that Nana had taken it into her head to play at doctor, down below in the dark; the vicious little rascal gave the others enemas with sticks.

One afternoon there was an awful scene; it was bound to come sooner or later. Nana had hit on a very amusing game. She had stolen away one of Madame Boche's sabots from before the lodge, tied on a string to it, and set to dragging it about like a carriage. On his part, Victor had filled the sabot with apple parings. Then a procession was formed. Nana walked at the head, dragging the sabot. Pauline and Victor supported her to right and left. Then the whole string of urchins followed in order, the big ones first, the little ones after, all shoving one another about; a baby in petticoats no bigger than a doll, with a bonnet all over one ear, came last. And the procession chanted something melancholy, with "ohs" and "ahs". Nana had said they were going to play at funeral; the apple-parings were the dead person. When they had been once round the court they began again. They found it highly amusing.

"What are they up to?" murmured Madame Boche, coming out of her lodge to have a look, always suspicious of some fresh mischief.

When she saw what it was: "Why, it's my sabot!" she cried furiously. "Oh, the little blackguards!"

She slapped their heads right and left, boxed Nana's both ears, and gave Pauline a kick, the great goose, letting her mother's sabot be knocked about. Gervaise was just then filling a pail at the tap. When she saw Nana bleeding at the nose, sobbing loudly, she nearly flew in the *concierge's* face. Did she think children were to be banged about as if they were oxen? One must be hard-hearted to do that—oh! the lowest of the low. Naturally, Madame Boche answered her back. When one had such a disgrace of a child as that, one ought to keep her under lock and key. At last Boche himself came to the door of the lodge, and called to his wife to come in, and not stand discussing things with low people. It was a regular downright quarrel.

As a matter of fact, the Boches and the Coupeaus had not been getting on very well together for the last month. Gervaise, naturally of a very liberal disposition, was always giving away bottles of wine, cups of broth, oranges, and pieces of cake. One evening, she left at the lodge the remains of a salad of beetroot and dandelion, knowing that the *concierge* would have sold herself for salad. The next day she went quite white on hearing from Mademoiselle Remanjou that Madame Boche had thrown it away before a lot of people, with an air of disgust, declaring that she was not yet reduced, thank God! to living off other people's leavings. From that time Gervaise put an end to her presents. No more bottles of wine, no more cups of broth, no more oranges, no more pieces of cake—nothing. The Boches pulled a very long face; it seemed to them like a sort of theft on the part of the Coupeaus. Gervaise saw the mistake she had made; for if she had not been foolish enough to cram them with good things, they would never have disagreed at all. Now the *concierge* said all manner of bad things about her. At the October term she kicked up no end of a row with the landlord, M. Marescot, because the laundress had been eating up house and home with her gluttony, and was a day behindhand with her rent; whereupon M. Marescot, not too polite either, came into the shop without taking off his hat, and asked for his money down, which was given him at once. Naturally the Boches had now joined hands with the Lorilleux. It was now the Lorilleux who fêted them in their lodge, with all the effusiveness of a reconciliation. If it had not been for Clop-clop they would never have fallen out; she was enough to make the very stones fight with one another. Ah! now the Boches knew what she really was, now they knew what the Lorilleux had had to put up with. And, when she passed, they all pretended to make fun of her behind the door.

One day, however, Gervaise went up to the Lorilleux. It was on account of old Madame Coupeau, who was then sixty-seven. Her sight had now quite given way; and her legs were giving way as well. She had been forced to give up her last lodgings, and she was in danger of starving to death if someone did not look after her. It seemed to Gervaise shameful that a woman of that age, with three chldren, should be so utterly abandoned and without help. And as Coupeau

refused to speak to the Lorilleux, telling Gervaise that she
could go up and see them if she liked, she went straight up in
a whirl of indignation, which completely possessed her.

Once there, she entered without knocking, a very tempest.
Nothing was changed since the evening when she had seen the
Lorilleux for the first time, and when they had given her such
a far from agreeable reception. The same piece of faded stuff
separated the work-room from the living-room, an elongated
dwelling place which seemed made from an eel. At the other
end, Lorilleux, leaning over his bench, twisted together his
chain-links one after another, while Madame Lorilleux drew
a piece of gold-wire through the draw-plate, standing in
front of the vice. The little forge, in full daylight, cast a rosy
shadow.

"Yes, it's me!" said Gervaise. "You're surprised, I suppose,
since we're at daggers drawn? But I don't come on my account,
nor on yours, as you may be quite sure. It's about old Madame
Coupeau that I've come. Yes, I want to know if we are going
to let her wait on the charity of others for a mouthful of
bread."

"Well, well! there's a nice way to come in!" murmured
Madame Lorilleux. "I call that cheek."

And she turned her back, going on pulling at her gold-wire
as if her sister-in-law were not there. But Lorilleux raised his
pallid face, crying:

"What do you say?"

Then, as he had heard everything perfectly well, he went on:

"More rows still, I suppose! It is very nice of old Madame
Coupeau to go about everywhere complaining of her poverty,
yet the day before yesterday she had a meal here. We do
what we can, for our part; we haven't got all Peru. Only, if
it pleases her to gossip at other people's houses she can stay
there. We don't want anyone spying about here."

He took up his chain once more, and turned his back also,
adding, with a certain reluctance:

"If everyone else likes to give a hundred sous a month, we
will give a hundred sous."

Gervaise had calmed down, her rage cooled somewhat by
the stony faces of the Lorilleux. She never put a foot in their
place without a feeling of uneasiness. She looked down on the
ground, on the squares of wood put to catch the gold dust
and explained how matters stood, with more moderation.
Old Madame Coupeau had three children; if each gave a

hundred sous, that would only make fifteen francs, and really that wasn't enough, she couldn't live on that; it must be at least three times as much as that.

Lorilleux, aghast, demanded where he was to raise fifteen francs every month? People were very much mistaken if they supposed he was rich, because he had gold about. Then he began to grumble at old Madame Coupeau; she would have her coffee in the morning, she took brandy, she made as many demands as if she had a fortune. Good Lord! everybody liked to take it easy, but if you had never put aside a sou in your life, you had simply to tighten your belt and go without. Besides, old Madame Coupeau was not too old to work; she could still see jolly clear when she wanted to pick a good morsel out of a dish; in fact, she was a tricky old person, who wanted to be cockered up all her time. Even if he had the means, he should have disapproved of supporting anybody in idleness like that.

Meanwhile Gervaise remained conciliatory, discussing peaceably all these objections. She tried to soften the Lorilleux. But at length the husband gave over answering her. The wife was now before the forge, finishing off a bit of chain in the long-handled copper saucepan filled with lye-water. She still turned her back ostentatiously, as if she were a hundred leagues away. And Gervaise still went on speaking, watching them at work, in the black dust of the workroom, their bodies bent, their clothes patched and stained, and themselves hardened and blunted as old tools, in their constrained, mechanical labour. Then her anger boiled up in her again, and she cried:

"All right, that's just what I want; keep your money! I shall take in Old Madame Coupeau, do you understand? I picked up a stray cat the other day; I can very well pick up your mother. And she shall want for nothing, and she shall have her coffee, and she shall have her brandy. Good God! what a filthy set!"

Madame Lorilleux faced about all of a sudden. She brandished the saucepan as if she were going to throw the lye-water in her sister-in-law's face. She stuttered out:

"You sling your hook, or I shall do you a mischief! And don't you count on the hundred sous, because I shall not give a brass farthing; no, not a brass farthing! A hundred sous, indeed! Mother would simply be your servant, and you would stuff yourself with my hundred sous! If she goes to you,

you just tell her I wouldn't send her a glass of water; no, not if she were dying! Out you go—quick! Rid the blessed place of you!"

"Oh you monster!" said Gervaise, banging the door behind her.

Next day she took old Madame Coupeau into her house. She put her bed in the little room where Nana slept, and which got its light from a little round window near the ceiling. The house-moving was not a lengthy one, for old Madame Coupeau's only pieces of furniture were a bed, an old mahogany cupboard, which was put in the dirty clothes' room, a table, and two chairs; the table was sold, the chairs new seated. And the old woman, the very night she came, gave the place a sweeping up and washed up the dishes; in short, made herself quite useful, very pleased at getting out of a difficulty. The Lorilleux were simply frantic; the more so as Madame Lerat had made friends again with the Coupeaus. One day the two sisters had exchanged words on the subject of Gervaise. The former had ventured to approve of her conduct in regard to their mother; then, seeing the other exasperated, she had gone on teasingly to praise the laundress's eyes, magnificent eyes, at which you could light a candle; and after slapping one another's faces, they swore never to speak to one another again. Now Madame Lerat spent her evenings in the laundry, where she was finely tickled by Clémence and her naughty sayings.

Three years passed. There were quarrels, and quarrels were made up again. Gervaise cared very little for the Lorilleux, the Boches, and all who chose to have differences with her. If they were not satisfied, they could go about their own business. She earned as much money as she liked, which was the main thing. In the neighbourhood she had come to be a good deal looked up to, for there were not many customers so good, so prompt in payment, so little difficult to deal with. She had her bread from Madame Coudeloup, Rue des Poissonniers; her meat from fat Charles, a butcher in the Rue Polonceau, her groceries from Lehongre, Rue de la Goutte-d'Or, almost opposite the laundry. François, from the wine-shop at the corner of the street, served her with wine, fifty bottles at a time. Her neighbour Vigouroux, whose wife must be black and blue, one would think, with all the pinching and pulling about that she got, sold her coke at the gas company's rates. And it must be said they all did their best for her, knowing it was to their advantage to be on good terms with her. So when she came outside, bareheaded and in her slippers, she was greeted on all sides; she was still in her own domain, the streets nearby being like natural dependencies of her business-place, planted there squarely on the pavement. Sometimes, now, she would leave an order a little in the lurch in her pleasure at being out of doors in the midst of her friends. When she had no time to cook anything, she went out and got something ready cooked, and she would stop and gossip with the eating-house keeper who had the opposite side of the house, a great place with immense dusty windows, through which the dim light of the courtyard made its way. Or she would stop and chat, her hands full of plates and dishes, before one of the ground-floor windows, looking in at the interior of the cobbler's, the bed not made, the ground strewn with things, two lop-sided cradles, and an earthenware pot full of black water. But the neighbour that she respected the most was still the one opposite to her, the watchmaker, the spruce frock-coated gentleman always fumbling away at his watches with little tiny tools; and she often crossed the street to nod to him, laughing with pleasure as she looked into the little shop, no bigger than a cupboard, and saw all the clocks ticking gaily away, striking the wrong hours all together.

CHAPTER SIX

ONE autumn afternoon, Gervaise, on her way back from the Rue des Portes-Blanches, where she had been taking some clothes to a customer, found herself at the bottom of the Rue des Poissonniers just as the light was fading. It had rained that morning, the air was soft, an odour rose from the damp pavement; and the laundress, hampered by her big basket breathed heavily, dragging her feet a little, her body drooping, making her way up the street with a sort of vaguely sensual desire, bred of her lassitude. She would have liked to have something nice to eat. Then, as she raised her eyes, she saw the name of the Rue Marcadet on the corner of the street, and the idea suddenly occurred to her to go and see Goujet at his forge. Twenty times he had asked her to step over some day when she would like to see how iron was worked. Besides, before the other workmen, she would ask for Étienne, she would seem to have come merely to see her son.

The manufactory of bolts and rivets must be in that direction at the end of the Rue Marcadet, she did not quite know where; especially as the numbers were often wanting, along the buildings, separated by open spaces. It was a street in which she would not have lived for worlds, a big, dirty street, black with coal dust from the manufactories all round, with dilapidated pavements, and ruts in which the water lay in puddles. At each end was a row of sheds, great workshops with glass windows, grey elevations, unfinished-looking, their bricks and timbers bare, a confusion of tumble-down masonry with great gaps between, with dubious lodging-houses and low taverns on either side. She only remembered that the manufactory was near an old rag and iron store, a sort of open sewer, in which slept hundreds of thousands of francs' worth of merchandise, Goujet had told her. And she tried to find her way in the midst of the roar of factories: thin chimneys on the roof poured out great clouds of steam; a steam-saw sounded out with a continuous screech, like the sharp tearing of a piece of calico; button manufactories shook the soil with the roll and tic-tac of their machines. As she gazed towards Montmartre, undecided, not knowing whether to go on further, a puff of wind blew down the soot from a tall chimney, filling the street with stench; and she closed her eyes, half suffocated, when she heard a ryhthmical sound of hammers; without knowing it, she was right opposite the manufactory, which she recognized by the hole at the side, full of old rags.

Nevertheless she still hesitated, not knowing where to find an entrance. A broken-down fencing opened up a passage that seemed to lose itself in the rubbish of a house that was being pulled down. As a pool of muddy water barred the way two planks had been laid across. At last she ventured upon the planks, turned to the left, and found herself lost in a strange forest of old carts, lying with their shafts in the air—ruined hovels whose beams still remained standing. At the end, like a bit of day in the midst of this dark and dismal night, a red light burned. The noise of hammers had ceased. She advanced cautiously towards the light, when a workman passed her close by, his face blackened with coal and covered with a bristling beard; he gave her a sidelong glance out of his pale eyes as he passed.

"Monsieur," she asked, "it is here, isn't it, that a boy called Étienne works? It is my boy."

"Étienne, Étienne," said the workman, huskily, swaying to and fro. "Étienne—no, don't know him."

When he opened his mouth, he exhaled an odour of alcohol like that which comes from a newly-opened cask of brandy. And as he was beginning to be rather familiar, meeting a woman like that in a dark corner, Gervaise recoiled, murmuring:

"It is here, though, that Monsieur Goujet works?"

"Ah! Goujet, yes!" said the workman; "I know Goujet. If it is Goujet you want to see, go right to the end."

And turning he shouted with his voice, that sounded like cracked brass:

"I say, Gueule-d'Or, a lady for you!"

But the shout was lost in a clatter of iron. Gervaise went right to the end. She reached a great door, and looked in. It was a huge building in which she could at first distinguish nothing. The forge, as if extinct, shone in a corner with the pale brilliancy of a star, beating back the darkness about it. Great shadows floated round; and from moment to moment black masses were to be seen passing in front of the fire blocking up this last patch of light—men of incredible size, whose huge proportions one guessed at. Gervaise dared not venture in; she called out softly from the door:

"Monsieur Goujet! Monsieur Goujet!"

Suddenly the place was all lit up. The bellows had begun to work, and a jet of white flame issued. The shed was now visible, closed in by great planks, with holes roughly plastered and corners consolidated with brickwork. The coal dust, flying in every direction, covered the place with a sort of greyish soot. Cobwebs hung from the beams, like rags hung out to dry, heavy with years of accumulated dirt. About the walls, lying on shelves, hung on nails, or thrown in dark corners, a pell-mell of old irons and implements, huge tools, were strewn about, standing out in sharp, hard outline. And the white flame still rose dazzlingly, falling like a ray of sunlight on the beaten soil, where the polished steel of four anvils, fixed in their blocks, looked like silver dotted with gold.

Then Gervaise recognized Goujet beside the forge, by his yellow beard. Étienne was blowing the bellows, and there were two other workmen there. She only saw Goujet, and she went forward and stood in front of him.

"What! Madame Gervaise!" he cried, his face beaming, "what a good surprise!"

But, as his fellow-workmen looked very quizzical, he drew Étienne over to his mother, and went on:

"You have come to see the boy. He gets on very well; he is getting a famous wrist of his own."

"Well, well!" she said, "it isn't easy to get here. I thought I had got to the end of the world."

And she told him how she had come. Then she asked why the name of Étienne was not known there. Goujet laughed; he explained to her that everyone called him little Zouzou, because his hair was cropped close like that of a Zouave. While they were talking, Étienne stopped blowing the bellows, and the flame of the forge went down, the rosy light dwindled away into the darkness of the shed. The blacksmith looked tenderly at Gervaise, who stood there smiling, bringing so fresh an aspect into that artificial light. Then, as neither of them spoke, standing there together in the darkness, he seemed to recollect himself, and broke the silence:

"Excuse me, Madame Gervaise, I have something to finish. Stay there; you are not in anybody's way."

She stood there. Étienne had returned to the bellows. The forge flamed, sending up rockets of sparks; especially as the boy, wanting to show off his strength before his mother, let loose a perfect whirlwind. Goujet stood watching a bar of iron which he was heating; he waited, pincers in hand. He was in the full blaze of the light. His shirt sleeves were rolled up, his collar was open at the neck, leaving bare his arms and his chest, a rosy skin like that of a girl, on which curled little blonde hairs; and, with his head bowed on his huge shoulders, on which the muscles stood out in knots, his face attentive, his pale eyes fixed steadily on the flame, he looked like a giant in repose, tranquil in his strength. When the bar was white-hot he seized it with the pincers, and with his hammer cut it off into regular sections on the anvil, as if he had been breaking bits of glass, with little taps. Then he put the bits back in the fire, taking them out again one by one, to work them into shape. He was forging hexagonal rivets. He put the ends in a heading frame, hammered down the iron at the top, flattened the six sides, and then threw the finished rivets, still red-hot, on the ground, where they went out in darkness; and he hammered away without a pause, swinging in his right hand a hammer weighing five pounds, finishing off some detail at every blow, turning and manipulating his iron so deftly, that he could go on talking and looking about all the time. The anvil rang out its silvery chime, and the blacksmith, without a drop of sweat, quite at his ease, hammered away as composedly, and apparently with as little effort, as when he was cutting out his figures at home in the evening.

"Oh, that—it's only a small rivet, twenty millimètres," he said, in answer to Gervaise's questions. "One could do three hundred a day. But it needs practice, because one's arm soon get tired."

When she asked him if his wrist was not stiff by night, he had a good laugh. Did she think he was a young lady? His wrist had seen some hard work since he was fifteen; it had turned to iron with pulling about so many tools. However, she was right enough; a gentleman who had never forged a rivet or a bolt, and who tried to play with his five-pound hammer, would get a pretty stroke of lumbago at the end of two hours, It looked nothing at all, but it often cleaned out a good solid chap in a few years. Meanwhile the other workmen went on hammering away, all together. Their huge shadows danced in the light, the red gleam of the iron as it was taken out of the fire flashed into the darkness, a splutter of sparks flew out under the blows of the hammers, shining like suns, almost on the level of the anvils. And Gervaise seemed to be caught up into the wind of the forge, happy to be there, without a wish to be going. She made a large détour in order to get near Étienne without risk of getting her hands burnt, when she saw the dirty-bearded workman, whom she had spoken to outside, come in.

"So you found him, Madame?" said he, with his bantering, drunken air. "Gueule-d'Or, you know it was I who told the lady where to find you."

He was called Bec-Salé, otherwise Boit-sans-Soif, a bolt-maker of great dash, as strong as a horse, who rinsed his irons in a pint of brandy a day. He had gone out for a drop then, unable to wait till six o'clock. When he found out that Zouzou was called Étienne, he thought it very droll; and he laughed, showing his discoloured teeth. Then he recognized Gervaise. Only the day before, he had had a glass with Coupeau. You might mention Bec-Salé, otherwise Boit-sans-Soif, to Coupeau; he would say at once, he's a good fellow! That chap Coupeau was a good sort, he stood treat oftener than his turn.

"I am very glad to know you are his wife," he went on. "He deserves a pretty wife. I say, Gueule-d'Or, she is pretty, isn't she?"

He came close to her with a gallant air, and she had to take up her basket, and hold it in front of her, in order to keep him at a distance. Goujet was vexed, knowing that his fellow-workman wanted to tease him on account of his friendly relations with Gervaise, and he shouted:

"I say, lazy-bones! when are we to do the forty millimetres? Are you game now, now that you've got your belly full, you damned bibber?"

The blacksmith referred to an order for big bolts, which needed two strikers at the anvil.

"Right away, if you will, big baby!" replied Bec-Salé, otherwise Boit-sans-Soif. "Sucks its thumb, it does, and thinks itself a man! I've eaten others as big as you?"

"All right, straight away! Come along, us two!"

"Right you are, old joker!"

The presence of Gervaise had put them both on their metal. Goujet put the pieces of iron, ready cut, into the fire; then he fixed on the anvil a large sized heading-frame. The other workman had taken from against the wall two huge sledge-hammers of twenty pounds, the two big sisters, Fifine and Dédèle. And he bragged away, telling of a half-gross of rivets that he had forged for the Dunkerque lighthouse, regular jewels, things to be put in a museum, so prettily he had worked them. What the blazes! he wasn't the man to fear competition; you might hunt all over the city without finding another like him. Oh, it was going to be a joke; now we shall see what we shall see.

"The lady shall decide," he said, turning to Gervaise.

"Enough chatter!" cried Goujet. "At it, Zouzou. There's no heat there, my lad!"

But Bec-Salé, otherwise Boit-sans-Soif, asked again:

"Do we strike together?"

"No, one each."

The proposition caused a sensation, and the other workman, despite his cheek, felt his mouth turn dry. Forty-millimetre bolts made by one man? such a thing had never been heard of, especially as the bolts had to be rounded at the top—a deuce of a piece of work, a regular poser. The three other workmen had left their work to look on; a big lean fellow wagered a bottle of wine that Goujet would be beaten. Meanwhile the two blacksmiths each took a sledge-hammer choosing them with eyes closed, for Fifine weighed half a pound more than Dédèle. Bec-Salé, otherwise Boit-sans-Soif, had the good luck to lay hands on Dédèle; Gueule-d'Or took Fifine. And the former, as he waited for the iron to get white hot, stood before the anvil, throwing tender glances in the direction of Gervaise; then he put himself in position, tapping his foot like one who is ready for the fight, already swaying Dédèle lightly in the air. Damn it all! he was all there; he'd make a cake of the Vendôme Column!

"Now, at it!" said Goujet, placing in the heading-frame one of the bits of iron, as big as a girl's wrist.

Bec-Salé, otherwise Boit-sans-Soif, leant back, and whirled Dédèle into the air with both hands. Small and lean, with his stubbly beard, and his wolfish eyes shining under his matted crop of hair, he made a tremendous exertion at every blow of the hammer, leaping off the ground as if carried away by his own fury. He went at it desperately, fighting with his iron, wroth with it for being so hard; and he gave a grunt when he had given it a good sound box. Brandy might weaken the arms of others, but he had need of it in his veins instead of blood; the last drop he had drunk warmed his carcase like a boiler, he felt as damned strong as a steam-hammer. And the iron feared him that day; he beat it flatter than a quid of tobacco. And didn't Dédèle waltz! She cut capers, heels in the air, like a little baggage at the Elysée-Montmartre showing off her under-things; for it is no good dawdling, iron is such a brute, it cools in no time, with one hammer. In thirty strokes Bec-Salé, otherwise Boit-sans-Soif, had formed the head of his bolt. But he was panting, his eyes starting out of their sockets; and he was seized with a furious anger when he heard his joints crack. Then, dancing and grimacing, he delivered two more blows, simply to revenge himself for his discomfort. When he took it out of the heading-frame, the bolt was deformed, the head on one side like a hunch-back's.

"Well, does that look neat?" said he, with his usual self-confidence, presenting his work to Gervaise.

"I am not well up in it, monsieur," she answered, with an air of reserve.

But she saw clearly enough on the head of the bolt the mark of Dédèle's last two kicks, and she was awfully pleased. She put her lips together so as not to laugh, for Goujet now had all the chances on his side.

It was Gueule-d'Or's turn. Before beginning, he threw Gervaise a look of full confidence and of tenderness. Then, without hurrying, he measured his distance and brought down the hammer in steady, downward, regular strokes. His stroke was classic, correct, measured, supple. Fifine, in his hands, danced no low high-kick, her legs outside her petticoat; she rose and fell rhythmically, like a noble lady leading a grave and ancient minuet. Fifine's heels beat the measure solemnly, sinking into the red-hot iron on the head of the bolt with a deliberate skill, first flattening the metal in the middle, then modelling it with a series of strokes, each delivered with perfect precision. Sure enough, it was not brandy that Gueule-d'Or had in his veins; it was blood, pure blood, whose mighty beats made themselves felt in the very hammer, marking time. What a splendid fellow he was for work! He stood full in face of the whole heat of the forge. His short hair, curling over his low forehead, his fine golden beard, with its close ringlets, were lit up, they shone all golden, a very head of gold, in truth. And he had a neck like a pillar, white as the neck of a child; an immense breadth of chest, wide enough for a woman to lie across it; shoulders and arms that seemed to belong to some sculptured giant in a museum. When he put forth all his strength, his muscles swelled, mountains of flesh rolling and hardening under the skin; his shoulders, neck, and chest distended, he cast a light all around him, he was strong and mighty as a god. Twenty times already he had brought down Fifine, his eyes fixed on the iron, drawing in his breath at each stroke, with only two large drops of sweat trickling over his forehead. He counted; twenty-one, twenty-two, twenty-three. Fifine continued tranquilly her lordly reverences.

"What showing off!" muttered sneeringly Bec-Salé, otherwise Boit-sans-Soif.

And Gervaise, standing opposite to Gueule-d'Or, gazed at him with an affectionate smile. Good Lord! what fools men were! Were not those two hammering away on their bolts in order to pay court to her? Oh, she saw well enough that they were disputing over her, they and their hammers; they were like two great crested cocks showing off before a little white hen. It was an odd contrivance, wasn't it? Still, people sometimes make love in a very strange manner. Yes, it was for her, this thunder of Dédèle and Fifine on the anvil; it was for her, all this battering of iron; it was for her, this forge in motion, flaming like a conflagration, sending out showers of sparks. They were fashioning their love for her, and it was for that they disputed with each other, seeing who could fashion it the best. And, truly, she was glad at heart; for what woman does not love compliments? The hammering of Gueule-d'Or, in particular, spoke to her heart; it rang out a clear music on the anvil, as if in accompaniment to the beating of her own blood. Folly as it seems, she felt as if that drove something home in her, something solid, like bolt-iron. That evening, on her way home, along the damp pavement, she had had a vague desire, a longing after something good to eat; now she was satisfied, as if the strokes of Gueule-d'Or's hammer had sufficed her. Oh! she had no doubt of his success. It was to him that she was destined to fall. Bec-Salé, otherwise Boit-sans-Soif, was too hideous in his dirty workman's things, skipping about like an escaped monkey. And she waited, flushed and yet happy in the intense heat, delighting to be shaken from head to foot by the last strokes of Fifine.

Goujet still went on counting.

"And twenty-eight," he said at last, resting the hammer on the ground. "It is finished; you can look at it."

The head of the bolt was smooth, flawless, without a crease, a regular bit of jeweller's work, round as a billiard ball made in a mould. The workmen gazed at it, wagging their heads; there was not a word to be said, one might go on one's knees to it. Bec-Salé, otherwise Boit-sans-Soif, tried to turn if off as a joke; but he found nothing to say, and he went back to his anvil with his tail between his legs. Meanwhile, Gervaise pressed against Goujet, as if to see better. Étienne had left the bellows, the forge was once more sunk in shadow, like a red sunset falling all at once into the sheer darkness of night. And to the blacksmith and the laundress it seemed delicious to be there, with this night about them, in the shed black with soot and iron filings, full of the smell of old iron; they would have seemed more alone in the Bois de Vincennes, if they had had a rendezvous in mid-forest. He took her hand as if he had won her.

But outside, they had not a word to say. He could think of nothing; except that she might have taken Étienne along with her if he had not another half-hour's work to do. She was on the point of going, when he called her back again, trying to keep her with him a few minutes longer.

"Come, you haven't seen everything. Really it is very interesting."

He took her to the right, into another shed, where there was a machine-manufactory belonging. On the threshold she hesitated, taken with an instinctive fear. The great building, shaken by all these machines, trembled; and huge shadows waved in the air, streaked with vivid fire. But he reassured her, smiling, swearing that there was nothing to fear; she must only be careful not to let her skirts go too near the cog-wheels. He went first, she following, in a deafening din where all sorts of noises hissed and rumbled, in the midst of smoke peopled with vague beings, black hurrying men, machines with waving arms, which she could not distinguish from one another. The passages were very narrow, one had to step over obstacles. get out of the way of holes, step aside to make way for a cart. They could not hear each other speak. As yet she saw nothing; all danced before her eyes. Then, as she felt a sensation above her like a great flutter of wings, she looked up, and stood still to watch the belting running along the ceiling like a gigantic spider's web, every thread going in a different direction; the steam-engine was hidden away in a corner, behind a little brick wall; and the driving-belts seemed to run of their own accord, coming swiftly out of the shadowy distance, with a regular, soft, continuous, gliding motion, like a bird of the night. But she nearly fell, striking her foot against one of the ventilating pipes, which crossed in all directions on the beaten soil, sending out their little sharp breath of wind on all the little forges beside the machines. And first of all he showed her that: he let loose the air on one of the furnaces; large sheets of fan-shaped flames spread from all four sides, a circle of indentated flames, dazzlingly, turning to a deep red; the light was so strong that the workman's small lamps looked like spots of shadow on the sun. Then he raised his voice to explain things to her, he showed her the machines, mechanical scissors which cut up bars of iron, severing a piece at each bite, spitting out the ends at the back, one by one; bolt and rivet machines, big and complicated, forging the heads with a single pressure of their powerful screw; the shearing machines with cast-iron fly-wheels, an iron ball which struck the air furiously at every piece they trimmed; the screw-cutting lathes, manipulated by women, threading the bolts with their bolts, with the tic-tac of their wheelwork of steel, shining under the grease with which they had been oiled. She could thus follow the whole series, from the wrought-iron leaning against the walls, to the finished bolts and rivets, heaped up in cases in every corner. She understood it all now, and she smiled and nodded; but she was a little nervous all the same, nervous at being so small and frail among all these rugged metal-workers; turning, now and again, her blood curdling, at the dull noise of a shearing-machine. She grew accustomed to the dim light, could see into the recesses where men, standing motionless, regulated the panting dance of fly-wheels, when a furnace suddenly let loose the vivid illumination of its circle of flame. And, in spite of herself, it was constantly to the ceiling that she turned back, to the very life-blood of the machines, the flexile flight of leather belting above her, with its huge and silent force passing in the vague night of the rafters.

Meanwhile Goujet had stopped before one of the riveting machines. He stood there, looking down with fixed eyes, absorbed in a reverie. The machine forged rivets of forty millimetres with the tranquil ease of a giant. And nothing, indeed, could be more simple. The stoker took the piece of iron from the furnace; the striker placed it in the heading-frame, on which a stream of water was constantly running in order to preserve the temper of the steel; and it was done the screw came down, the bolt fell to the ground with its head as round as if it had been placed in a mould. In twelve hours this infernal machine turned out hundreds of kilogrammes. Goujet, little disposed as he was to malevolence, felt at certain moments as if he would gladly have brought down Fifine on all that apparatus of iron, whose arms were so far more powerful than his own. It caused him a huge annoyance, even when he reasoned that flesh and blood could not fight against iron. One day, for certain, the machine would put an end to the workman; already their day's wages had fallen from twelve to nine francs, and there was talk of reducing them yet further; and they were not pretty at all, those great beasts that made rivets and bolts as if they were making sausages. He gazed at the machines for three good minutes without speaking; he frowned, and his golden beard bristled threateningly. Then a resigned and composed air came slowly back to his features. He turned towards Gervaise, who pressed up against him, and said with a sad smile:

"Well, it takes us down a peg! But perhaps one day it will be for the general good."

Gervaise laughed at the "general good". The machine-made bolts seem to her badly made.

"You know what I mean!" she cried, excitedly, "they are too well made. I like yours better. There one feels the artist's hand."

It was a great joy to him to hear her say that, for he was wondering if she would despise him after having seen the machines. Lord! if he were stronger than Bec-Salé, otherwise Boit-sans-Soif, the machines were stronger than he. When at last he left her in the court-yard, he squeezed her hands nearly hard enough to break them, in his delight.

The laundress went every Saturday to the Goujets' to fetch the clothes. They still lived in the little house of the Rue Neuve de la Goutte-d'Or. The first year she had paid them regularly twenty francs a month, on the five hundred francs, so as to keep the accounts straight. The book was made up at the month, and she added the amount necessary to make up the twenty francs, for the Goujets' washing was never more than seven or eight francs a month. She had paid off about half the amount, when, one quarter-day, not knowing how to pay the rent, her customers having failed to settle up, she had had to run and borrow the money from the Goujets. Two other times, in order to pay her work-people, she had

had to come to them, so that the debt had gone up again to
four hundred and twenty-five francs. Now she paid out nothing;
she acquitted herself simply by the washing. It was not that
she was working less, or her business less flourishing, quite
the contrary; but money with her had a way of melting, and
she was only too thankful when she could make both ends
meet. Goodness knows, if one can just get along, there is not
too much to complain of. She took on flesh, and she gave way
to all the little idle inclinations that came with it, not having
the strength of mind to look the future fairly in the face. So
much the worse, the money would come in somehow: it only
rusted by being put aside. Madame Goujet, meanwhile, still
kept a maternal eye on Gervaise. She sometimes lectured her
kindly, not on account of her money, but because she liked
her, and feared to see her get on a wrong tack. She never so
much as referred to her money. She treated her, in short, with
the most delicate consideration.

The day after the visit of Gervaise to the forge was the last
Saturday of the month. When she reached the Goujets',
where she always went herself, she was quite out of breath for
a few minutes, so hard had the basket been pulling at her
arms. You would never think how heavy linen is, especially
when there are sheets.

"You have brought it all?" asked Madame Goujet.

She was very strict on the subject. She insisted on having her
linen brought back to her in good order, without an article
missing. And she was particular, too, that the laundress
should come exactly on the same day, and at exactly the same
hour; in that way there was no time lost.

"Oh yes, there is everything there," replied Gervaise, with
a smile. "You know that I am never behindhand."

"True," Madame Goujet admitted, "you are acquiring
some faults, but you have not yet got that one."

And while the laundress took the things out of her basket
and placed them on the bed, the old woman praised up her
good qualities; she did not burn the things, she did not tear
them as so many others did, did not pull off the buttons with
the iron; only she used too much blue, and starched the
shirt fronts too much.

"Look here, it is like cardboard," she went on, making one
of the shirt fronts crack. "My son never complains, but it
cuts into his neck. His neck will be all red tomorrow when we
come back from Vincennes."

"No, don't say that!" cried Gervaise, in distress. "White shirts ought to be rather stiff, if one is not to carry about rags on one. See how gentlemen wear them. I do all your linen myself. The work-people never touch it, and I look after it very carefully, I assure you; I would go over it ten times, because it is yours, you know."

She blushed a little as she said the last words. She was afraid she had shown too clearly the pleasure she took in ironing Goujet's shirts herself. Indeed she had no improper thoughts in that connection, but she was none the less a little ashamed of herself.

"Oh, I don't complain of your work; you do it to perfection, I know," said Madame Goujet. "Here, for instance, is a cap which is exquisite. Nobody brings out the embroidery like you do. And the goffering is beautifully done, too. Oh, I know your hand in a minute. If you only give a duster to one of the work-people, one sees it. Only, please put a little less starch, that's all. Goujet isn't so anxious to pass for a gentleman."

Meanwhile, she had taken the book and struck out the list of articles with her pen. It was all right. When they made out the account she saw that Gervaise had charged her six sous for a cap; she protested, but she had to admit that it was not dear, as things went; no, shirts, five sous, women's drawers, four sous, pillow-cases, one sou and a half, aprons, one sou, it was not dear, considering that many laundresses charged half a sou or a whole one extra for all these articles. Then, when Gervaise had called over the dirty linen, which the old woman wrote down, she stowed it away in her basket; but still she did not move, looking embarrassed, as she if had something on her lips which it irked her to bring out.

"Madame Goujet," she said at length, "if you don't mind, I'll take the money for the washing this month."

The month was rather a dear one, the account they had just made out came to ten francs seven sous. Madame Goujet considered her seriously for a moment. Then she replied:

"My child it shall be as you like. I don't wish to refuse you the money, if you are in need of it. Only, it is not the way to pay off your debts. I say that for your sake, you understand. Really, you ought to be careful."

Gervaise looked down, and took her lesson with some confusion. The ten francs were to make out the amount of a note that she had given her coke dealer. But Madame Goujet was more severe than ever at the word note. She mentioned what she herself was doing, she was reducing her expenses, now that Goujet's wages had gone down from twelve to nine francs. When you were not wise in your youth you had to suffer for it when you were old. However, she restrained herself from telling Gervaise that she gave her the clothes to wash, simply in order that she might be able to pay off her debt; formerly she had done all the washing herself, and she meant to do so again, if the washing were going to put her out of pocket to that extent. As soon as Gervaise had the ten francs seven sous, she thanked her and hurried off. When she got outside on the landing she was ready to dance, for she was already used to the evils and worries of money, and she only thought now of the luck of getting through them until next time.

It was on this very same Saturday that Gervaise had a strange encounter on the stairs, as she was coming down from the Goujets. She had to squeeze herself and her basket against the wall to make room for a tall woman, without a bonnet, who was coming upstairs with a very fresh mackerel, its gills still bleeding, in a piece of paper. It was Virginie, the girl to whom she had given such a trouncing at the wash-house. They both stared at one another, and Gervaise instinctively shut her eyes, expecting to have the mackerel flung in her face. Not at all; Virginie gave a faint smile. Thereupon the laundress, whose basket blocked up the staircase, said politely:

"I beg your pardon."

"It is granted," replied the other.

And they stopped in the middle of the staircase, chatting as if they were on perfectly good terms, without a single allusion to the past. Virginie, who was then twenty-nine, had turned out a fine strapping woman, her face rather long between the two jet-black coils of hair that framed in her forehead. She told her whole story at once, in order to show off: she was married now, since the spring; her husband had been a cabinet-maker; he had just served his time as a soldier, and was trying to get a place as policeman, because a place is more certain and more respectable. She had just been out to get a mackerel for him.

"He simply dotes on it," she said. "We have to spoil them, these wretched men, don't we? But come up. Come in and see our place. We are in a draught here."

When Gervaise, after having in turn told her of her marriage, mentioned that she herself had lived there, and even had a child there, Virginie pressed her more urgently to come in. It is always pleasant to see the places where one has been happy. She, for the last five years, had been living across the water, at the Gros-Caillou. It was there that she had met her husband, when he was still in the army. But she found it tedious there, she longed to come back to the Goutte-d'Or quarter, where she knew everybody. Oh! all her things were in disorder; they would get straight little by little.

Then, on the landing, they told one another their names.

"Madame Coupeau."

"Madame Poisson."

And from that time they called one another Madame Poisson and Madame Coupeau, out in full, simply for the pleasure of being married ladies, after having known one another under less orthodox circumstances. However, Gervaise retained a certain amount of mistrust. It might be that Virginie was patching up matters in order to have her revenge for the thrashing at the wash-house; it might be she was meditating some hypocritical little scheme. Gervaise said to herself that she would be on her guard. For the moment Virginie was so amiable that one must needs be amiable as well.

Upstairs in the room, Poisson, the husband, a man of five-and-thirty, with an ashy face and red moustache and imperial, was sitting working at a table by the window, making little boxes. His only tools were a penknife, a little saw as big as a nail-file, and a glue-pot. The wood that he used came from old cigar-boxes, thin slips of unpolished mahogany, which he cut and carved with extraordinary delicacy. All day long, from year's end to year's end, he went on making the same box, eight centimetres by six; only, he inlaid it, invented new kinds of lid, put in compartments. It was merely for his own amusement, a way of killing time until he should get his nomination as policeman. Out of his old trade as cabinet-maker the passion for little boxes had stuck to him. He did not sell his work; he gave it away to his acquaintances.

Poisson rose and bowed politely to Gervaise, whom his wife introduced as an old friend. But he was not much of a talker, and he soon went back to his little saw; only from time to time he glanced at the mackerel lying on the edge of the dresser. Gervaise was very much interested to see her old place again. She pointed out where the furniture had been placed, and she showed the spot where she had given birth to her child on the ground. How oddly things turned out! After having lost sight of one another for so long, who would have thought that they would meet again like that, both having lived in the same room? Virginie added further details about herself and her husband; he had had some money left him by an aunt; he would get settled later on, no doubt; for the moment, she still went on with her sempstress work, she patched up a dress now and again. After a good half hour's talk, the laundress got up to go. Poisson barely turned his head, but Virginie, accompanying her out, promised to return her visit; besides she would send her her things to wash; that was understood. And as she still kept her talking on the landing, Gervaise fancied that she wanted to talk to her of Lantier and her sister Adèle, the metal-polisher. She felt, inwardly, quite alarmed at the idea. But not a word was said in regard to these old annoyances, and they said good-bye in the most amiable manner.

"*Au revoir*, Madame Coupeau."

"*Au revoir*, Madame Poisson."

This was the beginning of a close acquaintance. Within a week, Virginie could not pass the laundry without dropping in, and she stayed gossiping for two and three hours together, so that Poisson, fearing she had been run over, would come to look for her, with his silent, corpse-like face. Gervaise, seeing the sempstress coming in every day, gradually grew absorbed in one idea: whenever she heard her begin a phrase, she expected it was going to be about Lantier; her mind turned inevitably to Lantier the whole time Virginie was there. It was silly enough, in all conscience, for she cared precious little for Lantier and Adèle, and what had become of them; she never asked a question about them; she did not even feel curious to have news of them. No, it was a feeling she had, quite apart from her own will. The notion of them rang in her head like the refrain of a stupid song, which one cannot get rid of. Besides, she bore no grudge against Virginie; it was not her fault by any means. She got on very well with her, and she called her back again and again before she would let her go.

Meanwhile the winter had come, the fourth winter which the Coupeaus had spent in the Rue de la Goutte-d'Or. The

December and January of that year were particularly cold. It froze hard enough to split a stone, and after New Year's Day the snow lay in the streets for three weeks without melting. It was good for work all the same, for winter is much the pleasantest time of the year when you have to work in the laundry. How pleasant it was in the shop! There were no icicles to be seen on the windows, as there were across the road, at the grocer's and the fancy shop. The stove, packed with coke, kept the place as hot as a bath-room; the linen steamed as if it were midsummer, and it was quite nice inside with the doors shut, warmed throughout, so warm, indeed, that one might drop asleep without knowing it. Gervaise would say, laughingly, that she could fancy herself in the country. And, indeed, the sound of wheels outside was lost in the snow; one could scarcely hear the sound of footsteps; only the voices of children rose into the chill silence, the uproar of a band of urchins who had made a long slide in the gutter outside the farrier's. Gervaise went sometimes to the door, and, rubbing away the steam from the glass, looked out to see how the neighbours were getting on in this infernal weather; but not a nose was put outside the door, the whole quarter seemed to have gone to sleep; and she merely nodded to the coal-dealer's wife near by, who marched about bare-headed, grinning from ear to ear, ever since the frost set in.

What was specially pleasant in this abominable weather was to have one's coffee in the middle of the day nice and hot. The work-women had nothing to complain of; the coffee was always strong, without a grain of chicory in it; not at all like the coffee at Madame Fauconnier's, which was mere slops. Only, when old Madame Coupeau looked after the boiling, it was always behindhand, because she would go to sleep while it was over the fire. So, after dinner, the women went on with their ironing for a bit, until the coffee was ready.

The day after Twelfth Night, half-past twelve had struck, and the coffee was not ready. It would not filter out properly. Old Madame Coupeau tapped on the filter with a spoon, and the drops could be heard falling one by one, without hurrying themselves.

'Let it alone,' said Clémence. 'You will make it muddy. We shall have plenty to eat and drink today.''

Clémence was working over a shirt a second time, smoothing out the creases with her nail. She had a frightful cold, her eyes swollen, her chest racked with paroxysms of coughing which

simply shook her to pieces. For all that, she had not even a
scarf about her neck; she was dressed merely in a little cheap
woollen dress, in which she shivered. By her side Madame
Putois, enveloped in flannel, wrapped up to the ears, was
ironing out a petticoat, which she turned round and round the
dress-board, one end of which was fixed on the back of a chair,
while a cloth laid on the ground kept the petticoat from getting
soiled by touching the floor. Gervaise had got a good half of
the ironing-board to herself; she was doing embroidered muslin
curtains, over which she ran her iron straight along, reaching
out her arms, so as to avoid wrinkles. All at once the coffee
began to run loudly, and she looked up. It was the cross-eyed
Augustine, who had made a hole in the middle of the grounds,
by sticking a spoon into the filter.

"Will you be quiet?" cried Gervaise. "What is the matter
with you? Now we shall have to drink mud."

Old Madame Coupeau had laid out five glasses in a row on
a free corner of the ironing-board. The women left their work,
and Gervaise herself poured out the coffee, after putting two
lumps of sugar in each glass. It was the long-looked-for hour of
the day. As each took her glass and sat down on a little stool
before the stove, the street door opened, and Virginie entered,
shivering with the cold.

"My dear friends," she said, "it simply cuts you in two. I
can't feel my ears. What beastly cold!"

"Hallo, it's Madame Poisson!" cried Gervaise. "Good! you
come just at the right moment. Have some coffee with us."

"Gracious! it isn't an offer to refuse. Merely to cross the
street, you get the winter in your bones."

Luckily there was some coffee left. Old Madame Coupeau
brought a sixth glass, and Gervaise let Virginie help herself to
sugar, out of politeness. The women spread out a bit, so as to
leave a little room for her near the stove. She shivered a
moment, her nose red with cold, and she clasped her fingers
tightly round the glass so as to warm them. She had just come
from the grocer's, where you simply froze while you were
waiting for a quarter of Gruyère. And she exclaimed at the
heat of the laundry; you would fancy yourself in an oven; it was
enough to arouse the dead; it tickled your skin nicely. Then,
the numbness going off, she stretched out her long legs. All six
sipped their coffee slowly in this momentary interruption of
work, with the steam of the linen drying all around them. Only
old Madame Coupeau and Virginie were sitting on chairs; the

others, on their little foot-stools, seemed as if they were sitting on the ground; the cross-eyed Augustine had even pulled out a corner of the cloth under the petticoat to sit down on. At first not a word was spoken; they all had their noses in the glasses, draining out the coffee.

"After all, it is good," declared Clémence.

Then she nearly choked in a paroxysm of coughing, leaning her head against the wall to cough louder.

"You've got an awfully bad cold," said Virginie. "Where did you pick that up?"

"How should I know?" replied Clémence, wiping her face with her sleeve. "I suppose it was the other evening. There were two people flying at each other's throats on the way out from the 'Grand-Balcon'. I wanted to see; I stopped there, in the snow. Oh! what a tussle! I nearly died of laughing. One of them had a bloody nose, it was all running down on the ground. When the other saw the blood—a great spindle-shanks like me —she took to her heels. That night I began to cough. Then, too, I must say men are clumsy when they sleep with a woman; they keep pulling the clothes off all the night."

"Pretty conduct!" murmured Madame Putois. "You'll kill yourself, my dear."

"Well, and if it amuses me to kill myself! A nice thing life is! Scramble the whole blessed day to earn fifty-five sous, poison your blood from morning to night in front of the stove—no, no, that isn't my idea of things! However, this cold won't do me the service of finishing me up; it will go as it came."

There was a silence. That scamp of a Clémence, who led the *chahut* in the dancing halls with shrieks of gaiety, was as doleful as could be in the work-shop, with her funereal notions. Gervaise knew her of old, and merely remarked:

"You are always dismal when you've been out on the loose."

The fact was that Gervaise would have preferred that she should talk on any subject rather than that of women fighting. It made her feel awkward, on account of the thrashing at the wash-house, when anyone spoke before her and Virginie of a box on the ears, or a kick in the shins. And Virginie looked across at her with a smile.

"Oh!" she murmured, "I saw a nice clawing of chignons yesterday. They were starting right and left. . . ."

"Who?" asked Madame Putois.

"The midwife at the bottom of the street, and her servant— you know, a little fair girl. She is a little bitch, that girl! She shouted out to the other: 'Yes, yes, you made the fruiterer's wife have a miscarriage, and I'll go and tell the police if you don't pay me!' And she jawed away at her like anything. Whereupon the midwife landed her one right on the jaws. At that the little drab jumped at her mistress's eyes, and nabbed her and clawed her—oh, Lord, like a good 'un! The pork-butcher had to drag her away by force."

The work-women laughed, as in duty bound, then all sipped away at their coffee with an air of satisfaction.

"Do you believe that, that she brought about a miscarriage?" asked Clémence.

"Gracious! why everybody says so," replied Virginie. "I wasn't there, you know. But it's all in the way of trade. They all do it."

"Indeed, yes!" said Madame Putois, "but it's too silly to put confidence in them. A nice thing to be maimed for life! But there's one infallible recipe. You swallow a glass of holy water every night, making three signs of the cross on your stomach with your thumb. It goes off like a bit of flatulence."

Old Madame Coupeau, who seemed to be asleep, shook her head in protestation. She knew another recipe, also infallible. You must eat a hard-boiled egg every two hours, and apply spinach-leaves to your loins. The four women listened gravely. But the cross-eyed Augustine, who always roared with laughter all by herself without anyone knowing why, gave all at once the cackle which was her way of laughing. They had forgotten all about her. Gervaise lifted up the petticoat, and discovered her on the cloth, rolling about like a pig, her legs in the air. She pulled her out, and made her get up with a box on the ears. What was there to laugh at, great goose? What business had she to listen to what her elders were saying? First of all she was to take back the linen belonging to a friend of Madame Lerat, at Batignolles. While she spoke, her mistress placed the basket on her arm, and pushed her towards the door. Augustine, sulking and sobbing, went off, dragging her feet after her in the snow.

Meanwhile, old Madame Coupeau, Madame Putois, and Clémence discussed the efficacy of hard-boiled eggs and spinach leaves. Virginie, who seemed to be pondering, her glass of coffee in her hand, said in a low voice:

"Lord! one fights and one makes it up; that's always the way when one has a good heart of one's own."

And turning towards Gervaise she added, with a smile:

"No, I assure you I don't bear any grudge against you. The little affair at the wash-house, you remember."

The laundress was somewhat taken aback. That was just what she had been fearing. Now she felt sure the subject of Lantier and Adèle would come up. The stove roared, the heat was fiercer than ever. Almost overcome with it, the work-women lingered over their coffee, so as not to get back to work sooner than they were obliged, and gazed out at the snow in the street with languid airs of animal satisfaction. They began to make confidences to one another as to what they would do if they had ten thousand francs a year. They would do nothing at all, they would sit like that the whole afternoon, warming themselves, and cursing work from afar. Virginie had come closer to Gervaise, so as not to be heard by the others. And Gervaise for the moment felt quite helpless, on account of the too great heat, no doubt, so limp and helpless, that she had not the strength of will to change the conversation; she even waited for what was coming, with an emotion which she would not admit even to herself.

"You don't mind talking about it, do you?" said Virginie. "Twenty times already it has been on the tip of my tongue. However, as we are on the subject. . . . It is something to talk about, isn't it?' Oh, no, indeed! I don't bear you any grudge on account of the past. Honour bright! I don't keep that much ill-will against you."

She stirred the remains of her coffee in the glass to get all at the sugar; then she drank three drops with a little sound of her lips. Gervaise, somewhat agitated, still said nothing, wondering if Virginie had really forgiven her for the drubbing she had given her, for she saw little yellow sparks light up in the depths of her dark eyes. The she-devil had pocketed her affront, apparently; and she had put her handkerchief on top of it!

"You had some excuse," she continued; "they had served you a dirty trick—an abomination! Oh! you will admit I am just. If I had been in your place I should have drawn my knife."

She drank three drops more, sucking it up on the side of the glass; and abandoning her drawl, she went on rapidly, without stopping:

"Besides, it didn't bring them much luck; damnation! anything but. They went off to live at some horrible place by La Glacière, in a filthy street, where you are always knee-deep in mud. Two days afterwards I went to have dinner with them, a precious distance by omnibus, I assure you; well, my dear, if they weren't bickering already! On my word, as I entered, they had actually got to blows. Nice sort of lovers! You know that Adèle really isn't worth the cord to hang her. She is my sister, but that won't hinder me from saying that she's a downright little slut. She did me no end of dirty tricks; it would be too long to tell you the whole story; besides, that is for us to settle between ourselves. As for Lantier—good Lord! you know him, he isn't sweet tempered either. A little chap, isn't he? But he's at you for a yes or a no. And he clenches his fist too, when he hits out. Well, they raised hell, those two, I assure you. You could hear them at it as you went upstairs. One day it went so far that the police came in. Lantier wanted an oil soup, some nastiness they eat in the south; and as Adèle declared it was beastly, they threw the bottle of oil in each other's faces, the saucepan, and the soup-tureen, and the whole blooming lot; it was enough to set the neighbourhood upside down."

She told of other pitched battles; she had endless details in regard to the household; she knew of things that would make your hair stand on end. Gervaise heard the whole story without a word; her face was pale, and she had a nervous movement at the corner of her lips which was like a little smile. It was seven years since she had heard of Lantier. She would never have believed that the name Lantier, murmured thus in her ear, would have given her such a sensation of heat in the pit of the stomach. No, she could not understand how she was still so curious in regard to this vagabond, who had behaved to her so badly. It was impossible for her to be jealous of Adèle now, but she laughed all the same, in her heart, at hearing of the squabblings of the couple; she saw the girl's body all black and blue, and it avenged her, it amused her. She could have listened to Virginie all night. She asked no questions, for she did not wish to seem so much interested. It was as if a gap in her existence were suddenly filled up; now her life in the past seemed to run right on, without a break, to her life of today.

Meanwhile, Virginie had returned to her glass, still trying to suck out a little more sugar. At that, Gervaise, feeling that she ought to say something, put on an air of indifference and asked:

"Are they still living at La Glacière?"

"Why no!" replied the other, "didn't I tell you? They are

not together now, this last week. One fine day Adèle carried off her togs, and Lantier, I can assure you, didn't run after her."

The laundress gave a little cry, repeating aloud:

"They are not together now!"

"Who?" asked Clémence, interrupting her conversation with old Madame Coupeau and Madame Putois.

"Nobody," said Virginie; "people you don't know."

But she looked at Gervaise, and it seemed to her that she was pretty much affected by the news. She came closer, seeming to take malicious pleasure in going over her story again. Then all at once she asked what she would do if Lantier came prowling round her again; for men are so odd, Lantier was quite capable of going back to the old love. Gervaise drew herself up, sharply enough, on her dignity. She was a married woman; she would simply send Lantier packing that was all. There could be nothing more between them, not even a hand-shake. She would be inexcusable indeed if she ever looked that man in the face again.

"I know of course," she said, "that Étienne is his, and that is a link between us that can never be broken. If Lantier wants to see Étienne I will send him to him, because it is impossible to keep a child from loving his father. But as for me, Madame Poisson, I would be cut into bits rather than let him touch me with the tip of his finger. It is all over."

As she said these last words, she made the sign of the cross in the air, as if to seal her oath for ever. And anxious to put an end to the conversation, she gave a sudden start, and cried to the work-women:

"I say, you people! do you think the clothes are going to iron themselves? What lazy-bones you are! Come, to work!"

The women were in no hurry to move; overcome with torpor and idleness, they sat with their arms hanging lazily, one hand still holding the empty glasses, a little of the dregs still remaining at the bottom. They continued their conversation.

"It was little Célestine," said Clémence. "I knew her. She went cracked about cat's fur. You know, she saw cat's fur everywhere; she was always moving her tongue like that, because she thought her mouth was full of cat's fur."

"And I," said Madame Putois, "had a friend who had a worm. Oh! they have their little fancies, those beasts. He screwed up her insides when she didn't provide him with chicken. Only fancy, the husband earned seven francs, and it all went in little delicacies for the worm!"

"I could have cured her in a minute," broke in old Madame Coupeau. "You only have to swallow a grilled mouse; that poisons the worm right away."

Gervaise herself had slipped back into a state of dreamy idleness, but she shook herself and got up. There was another afternoon spent in dawdling. She was the first to go back to her curtains, but she found them soiled with coffee, and, before going on with the ironing, she had to remove the stain with a damp cloth. The women stretched themselves before the stove, and went back sulkily to their work. As soon as Clémence began to move she had a fresh access of coughing, enough to spit out her tongue; then she finished her shirt, and pinned the cuffs and collar. Madame Putois had gone back to her petticoat.

"Well, *au revoir*!" said Virginie. "I was just going to get a quarter of Gruyère. Poisson must imagine that I have frozen on the way."

She had only made three steps on the pavement when she came back to say that Augustine was at the other end of the street, making a slide with the boys. The little scrub had been gone two good hours. She rushed in flushed and out of breath, her basket on her arm, her black hair plastered up with a snowball, and she pretended to grumble, in her sly way, declaring that she could scarcely walk, the ground was frozen so slippery. Some young rascal had apparently stuffed her pockets with lumps of ice, for, a quarter of an hour after, her pockets began to water the laundry floor like a hose.

Just now most afternoons passed pretty much in this manner. The laundry became the resort of all the chilly people in the neighbourhood. All the Rue de la Goutte-d'Or knew where there was some warmth to be found. There were always some gossiping women in front of the stove, their skirts pulled up to their knees, warming themselves up. Gervaise was proud of her warm hearth, and she liked people to come in; she held her receptions, as the Lorilleux and the Boches said maliciously. The truth was that she was always obliging and ready to help, and would even bring in the poor people when she saw them shivering outside. She was particularly good to an old house-painter, seventy years old, who had a garret in the house, where he was starved with cold and hunger; he had lost his three sons in the Crimea, and he lived on what he could pick up, now that for two years past he could hold a brush no longer. Whenever Gervaise saw old Bru trudging about in the snow to warm himself, she called him in, and found a place for him near the stove; and she would often insist on his eating a piece of bread and cheese. Old Bru, with his round back, his white beard, his wrinkled face, as wrinkled as an old apple, would sit for hours without saying a word, listening to the crackling of the coke. Perhaps he was thinking over his fifty years of work on the ladders, half a century passed in painting the doors and whitening the ceilings from end to end of Paris.

"Well, old Bru," the laundress would sometimes ask him, "what are you thinking about?"

"Nothing, all sorts of things," he would answer, in a dazed way.

The work-women joked him, and declared he must be in love. But he, not hearing them, fell back into his silence, his gloomy, meditative attitude.

From this time Virginie often talked to Gervaise about Lantier. She seemed to take a delight in putting her in mind of her old lover, for the pleasure of embarrassing her by all sorts of suppositions. One day she mentioned that she had met him, and as the laundress remained silent, she said no more; but next day she let slip that he talked of her a good deal, very affectionately. These conversations, carried on in low voices in a corner of the laundry, always agitated Gervaise. She always felt, at the name of Lantier, a burning sensation at the pit of the stomach, as if the man had left there, under the skin, something of himself. Certainly she was confident of herself, she had resolved to live an honest woman, because honesty is half of happiness. And she did not think of Coupeau in this matter, having nothng to reproach herself with in his regard, not even in thought. She thought of the blacksmith, with a certain hesitation and uneasiness of heart. It seemed to her that the return of the memory of Lantier, slowly taking hold of her again, made her untrue to Goujet, to their unspoken love, with its sweet friendship. She was sad at heart when it seemed to her that she was wronging this good friend. She would have had no affection for anyone but him, outside her own household. It was a sort of ideal of hers, quite apart from all the low thoughts that Virginie seemed to be watching and waiting for.

When the spring was come, Gervaise went for refuge to

Goujet. She could no longer sit quietly thinking, without her
thoughts turning back to her first lover; she saw him leaving
Adèle, putting his linen back into their old trunk, coming
back to her, with the trunk in the cab. When she went out, she
was seized all at once with foolish fears, in the street; she seemed
to hear the footsteps of Lantier behind her; she dared not
turn, she trembled, fancying that she felt his hands taking
her by the waist. He was sure to be spying on her; he would
come upon her some day; and the thought gave her a cold
sweat, for he would certainly kiss her on the ear as he used
to do, to tease her, in the old days. It was this kiss that terrified
her; merely to think of it made her deaf, filled her ears with
a ringing in which she could only distinguish the beating of
her heart, beating loudly. When these fears came over her,
the forge was her sole refuge; she breathed again under
Goujet's protection; the ringing strokes of his hammer set
all her bad dreams to flight.

It was her moment of happiness. She took special trouble
with her washing at the Rue des Portes-Blanches, and always
took it there herself, because the journey gave her a pretext
every Friday, for coming back by way of the Rue Marcadet,
and looking in at the forge. The moment she turned the corner
of the street she was as light and gay as if she were in the
country, there in the midst of those empty spaces framed in
with grey factories; the road black with coal, the plumes of
steam on the roofs, amused her like a mossy way in a suburban
wood, lost in clusters of greenery; and she loved the dim
horizon, streaked by the high chimneys of the manufactories,
Montmartre blocking the sky with its chalky houses, pierced
with regular rows of windows. As she came near she slackened
pace, jumping across puddles, finding a pleasure in picking
her way through the deserted corners, heaped up with all the
rubbish of a house being pulled down. At the end she could
see the glow of the forge, even at midday. Her heart leapt to
the dance of hammers. When she got there she was all flushed,
the little blonde hairs at the back of her neck flying out, like
a woman who is coming to a rendezvous. Goujet awaited her,
his arms and chest bare, hammering away louder than usual
on the anvil those days, so that she could hear him from a
distance. He saw her coming, he welcomed her with his good
silent laugh in his golden beard. But she would not have him
leave his work, she begged him to go back to his hammer, for
she liked him all the more when he brandished his great

arms, knotted with muscles. She went over to Étienne, who was pulling away at the bellows, and gave him a little tap on the cheek, and she stayed there for an hour, looking at the bolts. They did not exchange ten words, but they felt as if their affection for one another could not have expressed itself better in a room by themselves, locked and double-locked. The sneers of Bec-Salé, otherwise Boit-sans-Soif, troubled them not at all; they did not so much as hear them. After a quarter of an hour she began to feel the stifling atmosphere, the heat, the strong odour, the smoke that went up while the dull blows shook her from head to foot. She wished no otherwise; it was her delight. If Goujet had clasped her in his arms, it would not have given her such a keen emotion. She came near him, to feel the wind of his hammer on her cheek, to feel herself in every blow he struck. When the sparks pricked her sensitive hands, she did not draw them back, she gloated over the rain of fire that lashed her skin. And he realized all her happiness in it; he kept for Friday the most difficult pieces of work, so as to do her homage with all his strength and all his skill; he abandoned himself to the work, as if he would shiver the anvil in two, panting, his veins vibrating with the joy that he gave her. For a whole spring, the love of these two set the forge in motion with a very tempest of toil. It was an idyll in the midst of this immense labour, in the midst of this flaring of oil, this great building that rocked to its foundations, its soot-blackened frame crackling and splitting. And all this iron, moulded like red wax, seemed to bear the rude imprint of their affection. When the laundress left Gueule-d'Or on these Fridays, she went slowly up the Rue des Poissonniers, happy and at ease, tranquil in mind and body.

Little by little her fear of Lantier diminished; she became herself again. At this period she would have been quite happy but for Coupeau, who was going regularly to the bad. One day, on her way back from the forge, she thought she saw him in old Colombe's bar, standing drinks with Mes-Bottes, Bibi-la-Grillade, and Bec-Salé, otherwise Boit-sans-Soif. She went by quickly, not wanting to look as if she were spying on them. But she looked back; it was Coupeau, and he was tossing off his little glass of schnapps, with already the movement of one accustomed to it. He had lied to her, then; he had got to brandy by this time. She went home in despair; all her horror of brandy had come back to her. She forgave him for drinking wine, for wine makes the workman strong, spirits, on the other hand, were dreadful things, poisons, taking away from the workman his taste for bread. Ah! the government ought not to allow these horrible things to be made!

When she reached the Rue de la Goutte-d'Or, she found the whole place in a stir. Her women had left the ironing-board, and were out in the court gazing up in the air. She questioned Clémence.

"It's old Bijard, knocking his wife about," said the girl. "He was waiting in the porch, as drunk as a lord, waiting till she came from the wash-house. He made her go upstairs, hitting her all the time, and now he's doing for her, up in the room. There! do you hear her shrieking?"

Gervaise hurried upstairs. She liked Madame Bijard, her washerwoman; she was a very persevering woman. She hoped to be able to put a stop to things. Upstairs, on the sixth floor, the door of the room was wide open, and some of the lodgers were standing outside, exclaiming aloud, while Madame Boche, in the doorway, shouted:

"Will you give over? I'll send for the policeman, do you hear?"

No one dared go into the room, for they knew Bijard only too well, a regular brute when he was drunk. For that matter, he was never anything but drunk. On the very few days when he went to work, he placed a bottle of brandy by the side of his locksmith's vice, and took a swig at it every half hour. He simply lived on it; he would have taken fire like a torch if one had put a match to his mouth.

"But one can't let her be killed!" said Gervaise, trembling all over.

And she went into the room. It was an attic, very neat, but cold and bare; the man had stripped it of everything, taking the very sheets to get money for his drink. In the scuffle the table had rolled over by the window, the two chairs had been knocked over, and lay upside down on the floor, in the middle of the room, Madame Bijard, her skirts still sopping from the wash, clinging tightly to her sides, her hair torn out, her face bleeding, groaned heavily, with a long oh! oh! at every kick. Bijard had first of all battered her with his fists; now he trampled upon her.

"Ah, you whore! ah, you whore! ah, you whore!" he growled huskily, accompanying every kick with this word, maddened with the repetition, striking harder as his voice grew more incoherent.

Then his voice failed him altogether and he went on kicking out stupidly, furiously, rigid in his workman's tattered jacket and trousers, his face bluish under his matted beard, his bald forehead spotted with great red streaks. The neighbours outside said that he was beating her because she had refused to give him twenty sous, that morning. Boche's voice was heard at the bottom of the staircase calling to Madame Boche:

"Come here; let them kill each other; it will be a good riddance to bad rubbish."

Old Bru had followed Gervaise into the room. The two of them tried to argue with the locksmith, to get him out of the room. But he turned on them silently, his mouth foaming; the alcohol flamed in his eyes, a flame of murder. The laundress had her wrist half sprained, the old workman was flung back against the table. On the ground Madame Bijard breathed more heavily, her mouth wide open, her eyes closed. For the moment Bijard's kicks were not reaching her. He went back to it frantically, striking wide, blinded with fury, hitting himself with his own aimless blows. And through all this uproar, Gervaise saw little four-year-old Lalie, in a corner of the room, watching her father beating her mother to death. The child, as if to protect her, held in her arms her sister Henriette, a little thing just weaned. She stood there, her head wrapped in a piece of calico, very pale, very serious. And she gazed out of her big black eyes, with a thoughtful fixity, without a tear.

At last Bijard caught his foot against a chair, and fell sprawling on the ground, where he lay and snored. Old Bru helped Gervaise to lift up Madame Bijard, who was now sobbing violently, and Lalie, who had come near, watched her weep, accustomed to it, and resigned already. As the laundress went downstairs, through the house in which quiet had now been restored, she still saw before her the child's look, the look of this child of four, grave and fearless as the look of a woman.

"Monsieur Coupeau is on the pavement opposite," cried Clémence, as soon as she saw her. "He looks jolly boozed!"

Coupeau was just then crossing the street. He stumbled against the door, and nearly sent his shoulder through one of the panels. He was white with drink, his

teeth set, his muscles contracted. And Gervaise recognized
the brandy of the bar in the poison which filtered through
his veins and blanched his skin. She was going to laugh and
put him to bed, as she was accustomed to do when he was
drunk and jolly. But he pushed her away, without opening
his lips; and, as he went by, making his way straight to his
bed himself, he raised his fist against her. He was like the
other, the drunkard who snored upstairs, worn out with his
own blows. And she turned cold, thinking of men, her husband,
Goujet, Lantier; feeling her heart sink, feeling that she would
never be happy any more.

CHAPTER SEVEN

THE birthday of Gervaise fell on the 19th of June. The Coupeaus, on their great occasions, piled up the dishes, the small ones
in the large ones; you came away from the feast as round as
a ball, stuffed for the whole week. There was a general
clearing out of all the small change. As soon as the household
could scrape together four sous, away they went in something
good to eat. Saints' day were always turning up, real or imaginary, always a good excuse for a feed. Virginie approved
loudly of Gervaise in her fancy for good things to eat. When a
man drinks all you have, it is fools' labour to let everything
run away in drink, and not fill your own stomach. Since the
money was safe to go, in any case, it was as well to let the
butcher have some of it as well as the publican. And Gervaise,
with her growing tendency to gormandizing, seized on this
as her excuse. It was all Coupeau's fault if they didn't save
a brass farthing. She had grown stouter, and she limped
more, for her leg, in taking on fat, seemed to have grown
shorter in proportion.

That year, the birthday party was talked of a month
beforehand. Dishes were thought out, and lips were licked
over them. The whole establishment looked forward to a
regular good orgy, something stunning, something quite out
of the common; one didn't get the chance every day. The
laundress's great anxiety was to know who she should invite;
she wished to have twelve guests, neither more nor less. She,
her husband, old Madame Coupeau, Madame Lerat, that
made four people belonging to the family. Then she would
have the Goujets and the Poissons. At first she had decided
not to invite the work-women, Madame Putois and Clémence,
so as not to make them too familiar; but as there was constant
talk about the party before them, and they began to look
very glum, she ended by saying that they could come. Four
and four, eight, and two, ten. Then, in order to make out
the number of twelve, she made friends with the Lorilleux,
who had been hovering about her for some time; at least, it
was agreed that the Lorilleux were to come down to dinner,

and they would all make peace, glass in hand. One really
couldn't keep up a quarrel in one's own family. Then, too,
the thought of the party was of a nature to soften all hearts;
it was impossible to refuse on such an occasion. Only, when
the Boches heard that peace was to be patched up, they too
made up to Gervaise with smiles and polite attentions; and
they, too, had to be asked to come. So there would be fourteen,
without counting the children. Never had she given such a
dinner; she was both proud and scared at the thought of it.

The birthday fell on a Monday. It was a stroke of good
luck. Gervaise counted on Sunday afternoon for beginning
the cooking. On Saturday, as the work-women slaved away
at their work, there was a long discussion as to what they should
have to eat. A single item had been agreed upon for the last
three weeks, a roast goose. They talked it over with greedy
eyes, and now the goose had been duly bought. Old Madame
Coupeau fetched it for Clémence and Madame Putois to
feel the weight of it. There were exclamations, so enormous
did the creature look with its rough skin, its flaps of yellow
fat.

"Before that a good potage, of course," said Gervaise.
"The soup and a little boiled beef; that's always good. Then
there must be a dish with sauce."

Clémence proposed rabbit; but that was what one always
had; everybody had had their fill of it. Gervaise wanted to
think of something more out of the common. Madame
Putois having suggested a *blanquette de veau*, they all looked at
one another with a communicative smile. It was a fine idea;
nothing would be so good as a *blanquette de veau*.

"Then," continued Gervaise, "there must be another dish
with sauce."

Old Madame Coupeau suggested fish. But the others made
a wry face, and tapped more vigorously than ever with their
irons. No one cared for fish; it wasn't digestible, and it was
full of bones. The cross-eyed Augustine having ventured to
say that she liked skate, Clémence shut her up with a smack
on the jaw. Then Gervaise hit upon crackling with potatoes,
which had once more lighted up all faces, when Virginie
entered like a whirlwind, her face aflame.

"You have come just at the right moment," cried Gervaise
"She must see the animal."

And old Madame Coupeau had to fetch the goose a second
time, for Virginie to take in her hands. The devil! it was

heavy! But she put it down at once on the ironing-board between a petticoat and a heap of chemises. She had something else in her head, and she took Gervaise into the next room.

"I say, my child," she whispered hurriedly, "I'll give you warning. You'll never guess who I met at the bottom of the street. Lantier, my dear! He is there prowling about; so I ran to tell you. I was frightened on your account, you know."

The laundress went very pale. What did the wretched man want of her? And just now, when she was in the midst of the preparations for the party. That was always her luck; she couldn't even have a little pleasure in peace. But Virginie replied that she needn't take on in that way. Hang it all! if Lantier had the cheek to follow her, she would simply call a policeman, and have him locked up. Since her husband had got his appointment, she was always taking on lordly airs, and talking of having everybody arrested. As she raised her voice, declaring she wished he would come up to her in the street, merely that she could have the pleasure of taking him to the police-station herself and handing him over to Poisson, Gervaise made a sign to her to be quiet, because the work-women could hear. She went back into the laundry, and continued, with an affectation of calm:

"Now we must have a vegetable."

"Why not peas with bacon?" said Virginie. "For my part, I should like to eat nothing else."

"Yes, yes, peas with bacon!" cried all the others in approval, whilst Augustine, in her enthusiasm, poked the fire more vigorously than ever.

Next day, Sunday, by three o'clock, old Madame Coupeau had lit the two ovens in the house, as well as a third one, in earthenware, borrowed from the Boches. By half-past three, the *pot-au-feu* was boiling in a huge saucepan lent by the restaurant near by, the family saucepan not being big enough. They had decided to cook the *blanquette de veau* and the crackling the day before, because those dishes are all the better for being warmed up; only they would leave the sauce for the *blanquette* to the last moment. There would still be quite enough to do on Monday, the soup, the peas, the roast goose. The room at the back was all illuminated by the three fires; the brown sauce could be smelt in the ovens, with a strong smoke of burnt flour, whilst the big saucepan puffed out clouds of smoke like a boiler, its sides shaken by deep and solemn gurglings. Old Madame Coupeau and Gervaise, each with a white apron on, were all over the place in their haste to chop the parsley, to fetch the salt and pepper, to turn the meat with a wooden skewer. They had turned Coupeau out of doors in order to clear the carpet. But they had plenty of people, all the same, that afternoon. The smell of cooking had spread over the house to such an extent that the neighbours came down, one after the other, on some excuse, simply to find out what was cooking; and they planted themselves there, waiting till the laundress was obliged to lift the lids of the saucepans. Then, about five, Virginie appeared; she had seen Lantier again; one couldn't put foot in the street now without seeing him. Madame Boche, too, had seen him at the edge of the pavement looking warily round the corner. Thereupon Gervaise, who was just going out for a halfpenny-worth of cooked onions for the *pot-au-feu*, was seized with a fit of trembling, and could not go out, especially as the *concierge* and the sempstress added to her fright by telling her awful stories of men waiting for women with knives and pistols concealed under their coats.

Lord! yes, one read about that in the papers every day; when a blackguard of that kind gets roused by finding an old friend in luck, he is capable of anything. Virginie obligingly offered to run out for the onions. Women must look after one another; the poor dear couldn't be left to be massacred. When she returned, she said that Lantier was nowhere about; he must have cut and run as soon as he saw that he was discovered. However, the conversation around the stoves ran on the subject of Lantier till evening. Madame Boche advised Gervaise to tell Coupeau, but she was terribly frightened, and begged her not to let out a word. A nice situation that would be! Her husband seemed already to have some inkling of it, for these last few days he had cursed and struck the wall with his fists when he went to bed. Her hands trembled at the mere thought of two men getting to blows on her account; she knew Coupeau, he was jealous enough to fall on Lantier with his shears. And all the while, as the four of them talked over the situation, the sauces simmered gently on the top of the stoves, covered down with ashes; the *blanquette* and the crackling, when Old Madame Coupeau took off the cover, made a little noise, a discreet murmur; the *pot-au-feu* still snored like a sleeping chorister basking in the sun. Finally, each had a cupful of bread, sopped in the soup, to taste it.

At last Monday arrived. Now that Gervaise was going to have fourteen people to dinner, she was afraid she would never be able to seat so many people. She resolved to lay the table in the laundry; and, early in the morning, she measured out the space with a yard measure, to see which way she should place the table. Then the linen had to be cleared away into another room, and the ironing-board taken down; it was the ironing-board, on other trestles, which was to serve as table. Just in the middle of this upset, a customer appeared, and made a scene, because she had been waiting for her linen since Friday; she was not properly treated, she must have her linen at once. Thereupon, Gervaise excused herself, and told a very neat lie; it was not her fault, she was cleaning out the place, the work-people were not coming back till the next day; and she calmed down her customer, and sent her away, promising to attend to her the very first thing. As soon as she had gone, Gervaise burst out into abusive language. If you listened to your customers, sure enough, you would never have time to eat a mouthful; you would slave out your very life for their precious sakes! One wasn't a dog on a leash, was one? If the Grand Turk in person were to come to her with a collar, if she were to gain a hundred thousand francs by it, she wouldn't do a stroke of ironing that Monday; it was about time she enjoyed herself a bit.

All the morning was spent in completing the purchases. Gervaise went out three times, coming back each time laden like a mule. But, at the moment when she was going out to fetch the wine, she discovered that she had not enough money left. She could get the wine all right on credit, only the house couldn't be left without a penny, on account of the thousand little expenses that are sure to crop up. And, in the back room, old Madame Coupeau and she were in despair, calculating that they needed at least twenty francs. Where were they to raise them? Old Madame Coupeau, who had formerly worked for a little actress at the Théâtre des Batignolles, was the first to suggest the pawn-shop. Gervaise gave a sigh of relief. How stupid of her! She had never thought of it. She hastily wrapped up her black silk dress inside a towel, which she pinned up. Then she herself hid away the bundle under old Madame Coupeau's apron, adjuring her to keep it flat out on account of the neighbours, who had no business to know anything about it; and she went out to the door, and gave a look round, to see that no one followed the old woman. But she had only got as far as the coal-dealers', when Gervaise called her back.

"Mother! mother!"

And she made her come back into the shop, and took off her wedding ring, saying:

"Here, take that too. It will bring in more."

When old Madame Coupeau came back with twenty-five francs, she danced for joy. She would order six bottles of better wine, to drink with the roast. Wouldn't the Lorilleux be taken down a peg!

To take the Lorilleux down a peg had been the dream of the Coupeaus for the last fortnight. Didn't those mean objects, the husband and wife—a nice couple they were—shut themselves up whenever they had anything nice to eat, as if they had stolen it? Why, they blocked up the window with a quilt, to hide the light, and look as if they had gone to bed. Naturally, that kept people from coming up; and they stuffed as hard as ever they could, talking under their breath so as not to be heard. Then, the next day, they took care not to throw the bones on the dust-heap, for fear people would see what they had been eating; Madame Lorilleux went to the other end of the street, and threw them down a drain. One morning Gervaise had come upon her as she was emptying out a basketful of oyster-shells. No, indeed, these close-fisted creatures were as narrow as narrow could be, and they resorted to all these manœuvres in order to make out that they were poor. Well, they should have a good lesson, they should see that other people were not the mere dirt beneath their feet. Gervaise would like to have laid her table in the street, and invited all the passers-by. Money wasn't made to get musty: it is a nice thing to see it brand-new and shining. She was so little like them that if she had only twenty sous, she wanted people to think she had forty.

Old Madame Coupeau and Gervaise talked of the Lorilleux from the time they began to lay the table at three o'clock. They had hung up great curtains over the windows, but, as it was hot, they left the door open, and the whole street could watch the proceedings. The two woman could not place a decanter, a bottle, a salt-cellar, without endeavouring to make it somehow annoying to the Lorilleux. They had arranged their seats so that they could best see the superb array of the spread; and they gave them the best plate, knowing that their china would quite overwhelm them.

"No, no, mother!" cried Gervaise, "don't give them those serviettes! I have two damask ones."

"Good!" murmured the old woman. "They will die of envy!"

And they smiled at each other as they stood at each end of the table, where they gazed with pride at the covers laid for fourteen. It was like a little chapel in the middle of the shop.

"And the thieves they are, too!" continued Gervaise. "Do you remember what a lie they told last month, when the wife told everybody that she had lost a bit of chain on her way back with the work? As if they ever lost anything! It was simply a way to pretend they were in straits, and so not give you your hundred sous."

"I never saw my hundred sous but twice," said old Madame Coupeau.

"I'll bet you anything, next month they'll invent a similar story. That explains why they stop up the window when they eat rabbit. Don't you see, people might say: 'Since you can afford to eat rabbit, you can well afford to give a hundred sous to your mother.' Oh, they are a bad lot! What would have become of you, I wonder, if I had not taken you in?"

Old Madame Coupeau shook her head. Just then she was dead against the Lorilleux, on account of the great feast that the Coupeaus were giving. She was fond of cooking, of gossiping over saucepans, of the general stir about the house when there is a party in the air. Besides, she usually got on well enough with Gervaise. At other times, when they came to words, as will always happen sometimes, the old woman sulked, and declared she was very badly off indeed to be at the mercy of her daughter-in-law. And no doubt she had still a certain affection for Madame Lorilleux; after all, she was her daughter.

"Well!" went on Gervaise, "you wouldn't be so well fed with them, eh? No coffee, no snuff, no dainties at all! I say! do you think they would have put two mattresses on your bed?"

"No indeed," replied old Madame Coupeau. "When they are coming in, I'll go opposite to the door to see what a face they'll make."

The face the Lorilleux were going to make tickled them only to think of. But it would never do to stand there gazing at the table. The Coupeaus had their midday meal very late, about one; just something brought in from the pork-butcher's; for the three ovens were already in use, and they did not want to soil the knives and forks that were ready for the evening. By four o'clock the cooking was at its height. The goose roasted before a roasting-stove placed on the ground by the wall near the open window; and the creature was so big that it had to be thrust into the roaster by main force. The cross-eyed Augustine sat on a little footstool in the full blaze of the fire, and solemnly basted the goose with a long-handled spoon. Gervaise was busy over the peas. Old Madame Coupeau, quite losing her head amidst all these dishes, waited to put the crackling and the *blanquette* to warm. About five o'clock the guests began to arrive. First came the two work-women, Clémence and Madame Putois, both in their Sunday best; the former in blue, the latter in black. Clémence was carrying a geranium, Madame Putois a heliotrope, and Gervaise, who had just then her hands all white with flour, had to give them two big kisses each, her hands behind her back. Then, on their heels, came Virginie, quite the lady in her flowered muslin; she had put on her scarf and hat, though she had only had to come the distance of the street. She brought with her a pot of carnations. She seized the laundress in her great arms, and gave her a good squeeze. Finally, Boche made his appearance with a pot of pansies, Madame Boche with a pot of mignonette, Madame Lerat, with a pot of garden mint, the earth of which had soiled her dress of violet merino. They all kissed one another, crowding into the room with its three fires and the roasting-stove which gave out a perfectly stifling heat, the noise of the frying almost drowning the voices. Somebody's dress caught in the roaster, and gave everybody quite a turn. The smell of the goose came out so strongly that it made all their mouths water. And Gervaise was as amiable as could be, thanking everyone for their bouquet, without ceasing to prepare the sauce for the *blanquette* at the bottom of a soup plate. She had put the flower-pots in the laundry, at the end of the table, without taking off the white paper in which they were wrapped up. A sweet perfume of flowers mingled with the smell of cooking.

"Shall I help you?" said Virginie. "To think that you have been working away at all this food for the last three days, and that we are going to clear it all up in less than no time!"

"Gracious!" replied Gervaise, "one couldn't do that all

by one's self. No, you will soil your hands. You see, everything is ready. There is only the soup.''

At that they began to take off their things. They put their shawls and bonnets on the bed, then pinned up their skirts, so as not to soil them. Boche, who had sent his wife to look after the lodge till dinner-time, sent Clémence almost into the stove by asking her if she was ticklish; and Clémence writhed and doubled herself up till her stays cracked, for the mere idea of tickling sent little shivers all over her. The other women, so as not to be in the way of the cooks, had also gone into the laundry, where they stood about by the walls, over against the table, but as the conversation still continued through the open door, and sometimes they could not hear one another, they were for ever going into the back room, filling the place with the echoes of their voices, crowding about Gervaise, who forgot to answer them, her spoon steaming away in her hand. They laughed and joked, pretty pungent jokes some of them. Virginie having said that she had eaten nothing for the last two days in order to leave room, the outrageous Clémence related a stiffer tale than that; she had cleaned herself out with an enema, like the English. Thereupon Boche gave a recipe for helping you to digest at once; that is, to squeeze yourself in a door after each course; that, too, was used by the English; it allowed you to go on eating for twelve hours running, without your stomach getting out of order. And one is bound to eat, in common politeness, when one is asked out to dinner. You don't set veal, and pork, and goose before dogs. Oh! the lady of the house might set her mind at rest; they were going to clean out her plates so thoroughly that she wouldn't need to wash them in the morning. And the whole company seemed to be whetting their appetite by sniffing at the stoves and the roaster. The women were like young things; they played at touch, and ran from one room to the other, making the boards shake under them, stirring and spreading the smell of cooking with the wind of their petticoats, in a very uproar, the sound of their laughter joining in the noise of old Madame Coupeau's chopper chopping up the bacon.

Goujet made his appearance just at the moment when they were all jumping and shouting for fun. He was afraid to come in; and he stood there, timidly, holding a great white rose-tree in his arms, a magnificent plant, which came up to his eyes, and twined flowers in his yellow beard. Gervaise ran to him with her flaming cheeks, all on fire with the heat of the stoves. But he could not get rid of his flower-pot; and when she had taken it out of his hands, he stammered, not daring to give her a kiss. She had to go on tiptoe, and put her cheek up to his lips; and even then he was so agitated that he kissed her on the eye, and nearly put out her eye with his kiss. Both stood trembling.

"Oh! Monsieur Goujet, it is too lovely!" she said, putting the rose-tree by the side of the other flowers, which it over-topped with its whole feathery cluster of foliage.

"Not at all, not at all," he said, not knowing what to say.

Then, heaving a great sigh, he became more composed, and announced that it was no use expecting his mother; she had the sciatica again. Gervaise was quite distressed; she talked of putting aside a piece of goose, for Madame Goujet absolutely must eat some of the creature. Meanwhile, all the guests had come. Coupeau was probably about somewhere, near by, with Poisson, whom he had called for after lunch; they were sure not to be late, they had promised to be back by six sharp. Then, as the soup was nearly ready, Gervaise called to Madame Lerat, telling her it was time to go and fetch the Lorilleux. Madame Lerat immediately looked very serious; it was she who had conducted all negotiations, and agreed with both parties as to how things were to go. She put on her shawl and bonnet, and went upstairs, holding herself erect, with an air of great importance. Down below, the laundress went on stirring the soup with its *pâtes d'Italie*, without saying a word. The whole company, sobered all at once, waited solemnly.

Madame Lerat was the first to reappear. She had gone round by way of the street, so as to give more ceremony to the reconciliation. She held the laundry-door wide open whilst Madame Lorilleux, in her silk dress, stopped on the threshold. All the guests had risen, and Gervaise came forward and kissed her sister-in-law as they had agreed, saying:

"Come in then. It's all over now, isn't it? We are both going to be nice to one another."

To which Madame Lorilleux replied:

"I only hope things will continue so for always."

When she had come in, Lorilleux also paused on the threshold, and waited to be embraced before coming inside. Neither had brought a bouquet; they had decided not to, considering that it would look too subservient to Clop-clop if they arrived with flowers the very first time. Meanwhile Gervaise called to Augustine to bring out two bottles. Then, on the end of the table, she poured out glasses and summoned everybody. Each took a glass, and they drank to the good friendship of the family. There was a silence as the whole company drank, and the women raised their elbows and drained the glass at one draught.

"There is nothing better before soup," said Boche, clicking his tongue. "It is better than a kick in the backside."

Old Madame Coupeau had placed herself opposite to the door, in order to see what sort of face the Lorilleux would pull. She pulled at Gervaise's skirt, and led her into the back room. And the two of them, bending above the soup, talked rapidly in low voices.

"Well, what a face!" said the old woman. "You couldn't see them, of course, but I could! When she caught sight of the table, look here! her face went like that; the corners of her mouth went up to her very eyes; and as for him, he was so taken aback, it set him off coughing. Look at them now; their mouths are so dry, they're eating their lips."

"It is really painful to see people so envious as all that," murmured Gervaise.

And indeed the Lorilleux looked very queer. No one, certainly, likes to be taken down a peg; and in a family especially, when one succeeds, the others are furious, it is natural enough. Only one keeps it in; one doesn't display it for everyone to see. But the Lorilleux couldn't keep it in. It was more than they could do; they looked askance and thoroughly put out. Indeed, it was so visible, that the other guests looked at them, and asked if they were quite well. Never could they stomach that table laid for fourteen, the white tablecloth, the bread ready cut. It really had the air of a first-class restaurant. Madame Lorilleux went all round the room, looking aside so as not to see the flowers; and she stealthily fingered the great tablecloth, tormented by the idea that it must be new.

"Here we are!" cried Gervaise, reappearing, her face all smiles, her sleeves turned up, her hair in little blonde fluffs around her forehead.

The guests drew near the table. They were all hungry, and they yawned a little, and looked bored.

"If the master were here," said the laundress, "we might begin."

"Well, well," said Madame Lorilleux, "the soup has time to cool. Coupeau is always late. You mustn't let him give us the slip."

It was already half-past six. The things were beginning to burn; the goose would be too much done. Thereupon, Gervaise, in distress, spoke of sending someone out to look for Coupeau in the neighbouring wine-shops. Then, as Goujet offered, she said she would go too; Virginie, anxious on her husband's account, accompanied them. The three of them, all bare-headed, took up the whole pavement. The black-smith, in his frock-coat, had Gervaise on his left arm and Virginie on his right; he was nicely sandwiched, he said, and the idea seemed to them so droll that they stopped to laugh, their legs shaking under them. They looked at them-selves in the pork-butcher's glass, and laughed all the more. By the side of Goujet, all in black, the two women looked like gay girls tricked out in all their finery, the sempstress with her pink-flowered muslin, the laundress with her white cotton cambric with blue spots, her wrists bare, a little grey silk scarf around her neck. Everybody turned to see them pass, so gay and fresh and Sundayish on a week-day, making their way through the crowd which blocked up the Rue des Poissonniers this warm fine evening. But it was no joking business. They went up to the door of every wine-shop, and craned their necks to look in, and see who was inside. Was the creature gone to get his drop of drink at the Arc-de-Triomphe? They had already gone all along the upper part of the street, looking at every likely corner; the "Petite Civette", renowned for its prunes; at old Madame Baquet's who sold Orléans wine at eight sous; at the "Papillon", favourite place for cabmen, who are hard to please. No Coupeau. Then, as they went down towards the boulevard, Gervaise, on passing François', the eating-house at the corner, gave a little cry.

"What is it?" asked Goujet.

The laundress no longer laughed. She had gone quite white and she was so overcome that she nearly fell. Virginie understood in an instant, when she saw, inside Francois', Lantier sitting at one of the tables, quietly having his dinner. The two women hurried on the blacksmith.

"I turned my ankle," said Gervaise, as soon as she could speak.

At the bottom of the street they discovered Coupeau and

Poisson in Colombe's bar. They were standing inside, in the midst of a crowd of men; Coupeau, in a grey blouse, was shouting out, with furious gesticulations, bringing down his fist on the counter; Poisson, who was not on duty that night, buttoned up in an old brown overcoat, was listening with his grim and silent aspect, ruffling his red moustache and imperial. Goujet, leaving the women outside, went in and put his hand on the tinsmith's shoulder. But when the latter saw Gervaise and Virginie outside, he lost his temper. What did he want with women like that coming after him? Always petticoats after him! All right, he wasn't going to budge; they could eat their beastly dinner by themselves. Goujet, to quiet him, had to have a drink with him, and even after that he insisted on dawdling five minutes longer by the bar. When at length he came out, he said to his wife:

"None of that, now. I can look after my own business, do you understand?"

She said nothing. She was trembling all over. Evidently she had been talking of Lantier with Virginie, for the latter pushed her husband towards Goujet, and told them to walk first. The two women put themselves on each side of the tinsmith, to distract his attention, and keep him from seeing. He was scarcely the worse for drink, intoxicated by the sound of his own voice rather than by what he had drunk. As they seemed to wish to keep on the left side of the pavement, he jostled them, out of mere obstinacy, and insisted on crossing to the other side. They followed him in a great fright, and tried to prevent him from seeing into François'. But Coupeau seemed to be aware that Lantier was there, and Gervaise was simply stupefied when he began to growl:

"Yes, yes, my ducky, there's a chap there we know, don't we? Do you take me for a sap? Just let me catch you at it again, with your eyes in your elbows!"

And he began calling her names. It wasn't him she was looking for, with her fly-away get-up and her powdered cheeks; it was that old pimp of hers. Then, all of a sudden, he was seized with a mad rage against Lantier. Sot and scoundrel! one of the two had better clear out the other, and pretty soon, too! Lantier seemed to take no notice, and went on quietly eating his *veau à l'oseille*. People began to collect, and Virginie finally dragged Coupeau away; he calmed down the minute he had turned the corner. All the same, the party returned less gaily than it had set out.

The guests were waiting all round the table, drawing long faces. The tinsmith shook hands with everybody, putting on airs and graces before the ladies. Gervaise, with a certain constraint, told the guests where to sit, in a low voice. All at once she noticed that, as Madame Goujet was not coming, there would be one vacant seat, next to Madame Lorilleux.

"We shall be thirteen at table!" she said, in consternation, finding a new omen of the misfortune which for some time past had seemed to be approaching.

The women, who had already taken their places, rose in some confusion. Madame Putois offered to leave the company, for, to her thinking, it was not right to trifle with such matters; besides, she could eat nothing, every mouthful would stick in her throat. As for Boche, he declared with a laugh that it was better to be thirteen than fourteen; they would all get bigger helpings; that was all.

"Wait a minute!" said Gervaise, "I'll soon put that to rights."

And she went outside and called to old Bru, who was just then crossing the street. The old workman came in, stiff and bowed with age, saying not a word.

"Sit you down, my good man," said the laundress. "You'll take some dinner with us, won't you?"

He simply nodded. He was quite willing; it was all the same to him.

"He'll do as well as anybody else," she continued, lowering her voice. "He doesn't often have a good meal. He shall have a treat for once in his life. Now we shall have no scruples in stuffing!"

Goujet's eyes filled with tears; he was deeply touched. The others all gave their approval, declaring that it would bring them all good luck. However, Madame Lorilleux did not seem to relish being so near the old man; she drew herself away, casting looks of disgust on his horny hands, his patched and faded blouse. Old Bru sat with bowed head, much exercised by the serviette which lay on his plate. At last he took it up and laid it carefully on the edge of the table, without thinking of putting it on his knees.

Meanwhile Gervaise served the soup, the *pâtes d'Italie*, and the guests had taken up their spoons, when Virginie cried out that Coupeau had disappeared. Very likely he had gone back to old Colombe's. There was a general murmur of disapproval. This time, anyway, no one was going to run after him, he could stay in the street if he wasn't hungry. And as the spoons were scraping up the last drops of the soup, Coupeau reappeared, with two flower-pots, one under each arm, a stock and balsamine. The whole table applauded. He placed the pots one on each side of Gervaise's glass with a flourish; then he bent down and kissed her.

"I had forgotten you, ducky. No matter, we love each other just the same, especially on a day like this!"

"Monsieur Coupeau's in good form tonight," whispered Clémence in Boche's ear. "He has had just enough to put him in a good temper."

The master's agreeable way had restored the good spirits of the company, which, but just before, had been endangered. Gervaise, now herself again, was as smiling as ever. The guests had finished their soup, and the bottles were passed round; the first glass of wine was drunk, a thimbleful of neat wine, to settle the *pâtes d'Italie*. In the next room the children were heard quarrelling. There was Étienne, Nana, Pauline, and little Victor Fauconnier. A table had been put there for the four of them, and they had been told they must be very good. The cross-eyed Augustine, who was looking after the fires, had to hold her plate on her knees.

"Mamma! mamma!" cried Nana, all of a sudden, "Augustine is dropping her bread in the roaster."

The laundress rushed in, and surprised her swallowing a piece of bread and butter dipped in the boiling fat, nearly scalding her throat in her hurry. She boxed her ears, for the mischievous imp declared she was doing nothing of the sort.

After the beef came the *blanquette*, in a salad-bowl, the household not having a dish big enough; and it was received with a shout of laughter.

"This is becoming serious," said Poisson, who rarely spoke.

It was half-past seven. They had closed the door of the shop, so as not to have all the neighbours spying upon them; the little watchmaker opposite stared at them with eyes like saucers, watching every mouthful with so greedy a look that they couldn't go on eating. The curtains hung over the windows gave a clear white light without a shadow, bathing the white table, with its knives and forks still in neat order, its flower-pots in their paper frills; and this pale, lingering twilight gave to the company a sort of air of distinction. Virginie found the right word. She looked all round the room,

closed in and hung with muslin, and declared that it was
quite cosy. When a cart passed in the street, the glasses
clattered on the table, and the women had to shout as loud
as the men. But there was not much talking, everyone was on
his best behaviour, a little formal. Coupeau alone wore his
blouse, "because", said he, "one doesn't mind with friends,
and besides the blouse is the workman's garb of honour".
The women were all tightly laced, and their hair was plastered
down with pomade so that it shone like mirrors, whilst the
men, sitting well out from the table, held themselves erect,
and kept their elbows square, for fear of soiling their frock-
coats.

Heavens! what a hole they made in the *blanquette*! If there
was not much talking, there was plenty of eating. The salad
bowl was emptying; it had a spoon planted in the midst of
the thick sauce, a fine yellow sauce which quivered like jelly.
Everyone fished out bits of veal, and the salad-bowl went
travelling continuously from hand to hand, all eyes bent
over it, looking for mushrooms. The great rolls of bread
standing against the wall behind the guests seemed to melt
away. Between the mouthfuls one could hear the sound of
glasses as they were put down on the table. The sauce was a
little too salt, it required four bottles to drown the blessed
blanquette, which melted in your mouth like cream, and felt
like a fire in your insides. And there was no breathing-space,
for the crackling, laid out on a soup-plate, and surrounded
by potatoes, arrived in a cloud of steam. There was a shout.
The devil! it was the very thing! It was just what everybody
liked. Now for a good appetite; and all followed the dish
with longing eyes, wiping their knives on their bread in order
to be ready. When they were served, they jogged one another's
elbows, talking with their mouths full. Eh! isn't the crackling
just nobby? it's soft and it's solid all at once, and it trickles
down your inside, down to your very heels. The potatoes
were stunning. No, not at all too salt, though, on their account
one did have to rinse out one's mouth every minute or
so. So they had to wet their whistles with four more bottles.
The plates were so thoroughly cleaned that they did not
need to be changed for the peas with bacon. Oh! vegetables
were a mere nothing; one could swallow them by the spoonful,
without thinking anything of it. It was a delicacy, certainly,
the sort of thing, in short, "that pleases the ladies". What
was best in the peas were the bits of bacon, which were done

to a turn, till they stank like a horse's hoof. This time two
bottles were enough.

"Mamma! mamma!" cried Nana suddenly, "Augustine is
putting her hands in my plate."

"Don't bother me; give her a slap!" replied Gervaise,
gobbling down her peas.

At the children's table in the next room, Nana was acting
as the lady of the house. She was sitting beside Victor, and
she had put her brother Étienne to sit by little Pauline; they
played at keeping house; they were like newly-married people
on a pleasure party. At first Nana had served her guests
quite prettily, with the little airs and graces of a grown-up
person; but now she had given way to her fondness for bacon,
and kept all the bits for herself. The cross-eyed Augustine,
who prowled about the children's table, seized the excuse for
taking them away from her bodily, under the pretext of
dividing them round more fairly. Nana was furious, and bit
her wrist.

"All right!" muttered Augustine, "I'll tell your mother
that after the *blanquette* you told Victor to give you a kiss."

But quiet was restored as Gervaise and old Madame
Coupeau made their appearance to get out the goose. The
guests at the large table, took deep breaths, lying back in
their chairs. The men unbuttoned their waistcoats, the women
wiped their faces with their serviettes. The feast was momen-
tarily interrupted; but a few of them, their jaws working
unconsciously, went on swallowing great mouthfuls of bread.
They waited, letting the food settle. Night had gradually
come on; a dull ashen light now made its way through the
curtains. When Augustine placed two lamps on the table,
one at each end, the disorder of things was plainly visible,
the greasy plates and knives, the table-cloth stained with
wine and covered with bread-crumbs. A stifling odour rose
all around. However, at certain hot whiffs, all sniffed in the
direction of the kitchen.

"Shall I help you?" cried Virginie.

She left her seat and went into the next room. All the women
followed her, one by one. They stood around the roaster,
gazing with profound curiosity at Gervaise and old Madame
Coupeau, who were extricating the goose. Then a general
shout arose, through which pierced the shrill voices of the
children, jumping for joy. And there was a triumphal entry:
Gervaise carried the goose with outstretched arms, her face

covered with sweat and beaming with smiles; the women
followed her, smiling as well; whilst Nana, at the very end,
her eyes staring thier widest, stood on tip-toe to have a look.
When the goose was on the table, huge and golden and running
with gravy, it was not begun upon all at once. A sort of
respectful wonderment had silenced every tongue. There
were winks and nods, as everybody pointed it out to everybody. What a devilish fine fat beast it was! what legs! what a
breast!

"That didn't fatten itself by licking the walls, I should
say," said Boche.

Thereupon there were endless details about the creature.
Gervaise stated the facts; it was the best that was to be found
at the poulterer's in the Faubourg Poissonnière; it weighed
twelve pounds and a half by the coal-dealer's scales; it had
taken a bushel of coals to cook; and it had made three bowl-
fuls of dripping.

Virginie interrupted her to boast of having seen the creature
before it was cooked.

"You could have eaten it as it was," she said; "it's skin was
so fine and white, a regular blonde's skin."

All the men laughed, and smacked their lips with a knowing
air. Meanwhile, Lorilleux and his wife drew a long face,
filled with envy at seeing such a goose on Clop-clop's table.

"Well, come now!" said the laundress at last, "we can't
eat it as it is. Who is going to carve? No, no, not me! It is
too big; it frightens me."

Coupeau offered. Lord! it was simple enough; you take it
limb by limb, you pull, it turns out all right. But they cried
out, and took the carving-knife out of his hands by force;
when he carved, he turned the dish into a perfect cemetery. For
a moment they looked round to see who would be willing.
Then Madame Lerat said in an amiable tone:

"It is Monsieur Poisson's job, certainly, Monsieur Poisson's."

And as the company did not seem to see the point, she
added, more conciliatory than ever:

"Monsieur Poisson, of course; he is accustomed to the use
of weapons."

And she passed him the carving-knife which she held in
her hands. The whole company laughed approvingly, and
Poisson bowed with military stiffness, and set the goose
before him. His neighbours, Gervaise and Madame Boche,
moved away a little, so as to leave him elbow-room. He

carved deliberately, with great sweeping movements, his
eyes fixed on the creature as if to nail it to the bottom of the
dish. When he stuck his knife into the carcase, which crackled,
Lorilleux was seized with an access of patriotism. He cried:

"Ah! if it were only a Cossack!"

"Have you ever fought with Cossacks, Monsieur Poisson?"
asked Madame Boche.

"No, with Bedouins," replied the policeman, as he separated
a wing. "There are no more Cossacks."

Then there was a profound silence. Necks were craned
out, all eyes following the movements of the knife. Poisson
was preparing a little surprise. Suddenly he gave a last
stroke; the hind-quarters split open and stood erect, the
rump in the air; it was "the parson's nose". There was a
burst of admiration. It was only old soldiers who could make
themselves so agreeable in company. Meanwhile the goose
had let a flood of gravy run out of the gaping orifice; and Boche
began to laugh.

"I'll stand in," he murmured, "if anyone'll do it into my
mouth like that."

"Oh! the dirty beast!" cried the women. "He is a dirty
beast!"

"I never met such a disgusting man!" said Madame
Boche, more furious than the rest. "Will you be quiet! You
would make a trooper blush. You know he sticks at nothing."

At this moment Clémence was heard crying out emphatically:

Monsieur Poisson, listen! Monsieur Poisson, you will keep
the rump for me, won't you?"

"My dear, the rump is yours by right," said Madame
Lerat, in her discreetly venturesome manner.

Meanwhile the goose was all carved. The policeman, after
having allowed the company to admire the parson's nose for
several minutes, had cut up the bits, and ranged them all
round the dish. Now they could help themselves. But the
women, beginning to unbutton their bodices, complained of
the heat. Coupeau declared that his house was his own, and
he didn't care a damn for the neighbours; and he threw the
door wide open. The feast went on to the accompaniment of
the rumbling of vehicles and the trampling of feet on the
pavements. Now their jaws were rested, they had more room
inside, and they set-to once more on the dinner, falling
furiously to work on the goose. Merely to see the creature

being carved, said that inveterate joker Boche, all the *blan-quette* and crackling had gone down into his calves.

And now there was a fine set-to indeed; and no one of all the company remembered to have ever had such an indigestion on his conscience. Gervaise stuffed mightily, eating great chunks of the white meat, not saying a word for fear of losing a mouthful; she was a little ashamed for Goujet to see her like that, as greedy as a cat. Goujet, however, was too busy eating away on his own account to notice that she was getting redder and redder with cramming. Then, *gourmande* as she was, she was so nice and good all the same! She never spoke a word, but she interrupted herself at every moment to look after old Bru, and to put something dainty on his plate. It was quite touching to see her pick out a bit of the wing, halfway to her mouth, and give it to the old man, who seemed unable to distinguish between one piece and another, and who swallowed everything, his head bowed, dazed with so much eating, he whose palate had lost the taste of food. The Lorilleux vented all their rage on the roast; they ate enough to last three days; they would have swallowed up dish and plate and laundry if they could, to have ruined Clop-clop straight away. All the women wanted some of the breast; it was the ladies' part. Madame Lerat, Madame Boche, and Madame Putois scraped the bones, whilst old Madame Coupeau, who adored the neck, picked at the meat with her two last teeth. Virginie loved the skin when it was brown, and all the men passed her their skin in the most gallant manner, till Poisson cast severe looks at her, telling her to give over, that was quite enough; once already she had eaten too much roast goose, and was laid up in bed for a fortnight, her stomach all in disorder. But Coupeau was quite angry and passed Virginie a part of the leg, crying out that if she didn't scrape it clean—blast it all!—she wasn't worth her salt. As if goose had ever hurt anyone! On the contrary, goose was good for the liver. You could eat it by itself, like dessert. He could stuff all night, without being a penny the worse; and by way of boast, he thrust a whole chunk into his mouth. Meanwhile Clémence finished her rump, sucking it with a gurgle of the lips, and screwing about on her chair in a paroxysm of laughter at the smutty stories that Boche whispered in her ear. Oh Lord! it was a tightener, sure enough! When you're at it, you're at it, eh? and if you only get a good tuck-in now and again, you would

be a sap not to stuff yourself up to the ears when you got a
chance. Why, you could see the corporations getting larger
every minute! The women were big enough to burst—
damned lot of gluttons that they were!—with their open
mouths, their chins bedabbled with grease; they had faces
for all the world like backsides, and so red too, that you
would say they were rich people's belongings, rich people
bursting with prosperity.

And the wine too, my friends, the wine flowed round
about the table as the water flows in the Seine. It was like a
stream after the rain, when the soil is athirst. Coupeau lifted
the bottle up when he poured it out, to see the red stream
foam; and when a bottle was empty, he would wring its
neck, for a joke, with the movement of a woman who is
milking a cow. They had cracked another black girl's neck!
And in a corner of the laundry the heap of black girls grew
larger and larger, a very cemetery of bottles, on the top of
which they threw the leavings on the cloth. Madame Putois,
having asked for some water, the tinsmith indignantly got
up and removed the water bottles from the table. Right-
minded people didn't drink water! No Adam's ale to be had
there! And the glasses were drained at a gulp; one heard the
sound of the liquid as it was gulped down, like the noise of
rain water down a water-pipe on a pouring day. It rained
wine, a thin wine which tasted a bit of the cask at first; but
you soon get jolly well used to it, and then you found it
nutty enough. Devil take it all! the Jesuits might say what
they like, the fruit of the wine was a famous find all the same!
The company laughed approval; for the workman, sure
enough, could never have lived without wine, and Father
Noah, without a doubt, planted the vine on purpose for
tinsmiths, tailors, and blacksmiths. Wine brightened you up,
and rested you after your work; it stirred you up if you
weren't inclined to work; and if the joker did you now and
then, well, Lord! the king wasn't your uncle, you had all
Paris before you. As if, too, the workman, penniless and
downtrodden and despised as he was, had so much fun in his
life that anyone had a right to complain if he got a bit boozed
now and again, and all just for the sake of seeing things look
rosy for once in a while. Why, now, for example, who cared
a twopenny damn for the Emperor? Very likely the Emperor
himself was tight; that was all very well. Who cared a twopenny damn for the Emperor? Let him get more tight still,

and he'd have more of a spree. *That* for the swells! Coupeau
sent everybody to the deuce. Women for him, he said; and
he slapped his pocket, in which three sous jingled, laughing
as if he had five-franc pieces in his purse. Goujet himself,
usually so sober, was a bit screwed. Boche's eyes seemed to
shrink up, and Lorilleux's went paler than ever, whilst
Poisson's bronzed soldierly face looked more and more severe
every moment. They were all perfectly drunk. And the women,
too, were a trifle elevated; oh! a mere bit of breeziness, cheeks
flushed, and a sort of necessity of taking off things; only
Clémence began to be not quite decent. All at once Gervaise
remembered the six bottles of better wine; she had forgotten
to serve them with the goose. She went and fetched them, and
the glasses were filled. Then Poisson rose, glass in hand, and
said:

"I drink to the health of the lady of the house."

There was a scraping of chairs, and the whole company rose
to their feet; they clinked glasses in the midst of a regular uproar.

"Fifty years from now," cried Virginie.

"No, no," cried Gervaise, smiling, and half overcome,
"I should be too old. A time is sure to come when one is
glad enough to be taken."

Meanwhile, through the open door, the whole neighbourhood gazed at the feast, shared in it almost. Passers-by stopped
as the light from the open door came across their path, and
laughed good-naturedly, to see these people eat so heartily.
The cabmen bowed on their seats, whipping up their nags,
looked in and made jokes: "I say, how much do you pay?
Mother, shall I fetch the midwife?" And the smell of the
goose was a delight to the whole street; the grocer's boys
opposite felt that they were actually eating it; the fruiterer and
the tripe-seller, every other minute, came and stood outside the
shop, sniffing and licking their lips. The whole street was
positively in a state of indigestion. Madame Cudorge and her
daughter, the umbrella-sellers near by, who were never
seen outside, crossed the road, one behind the other, looking
out of the corners of their eyes, as red as if they had been
making pancakes. The little watchmaker, sitting at his
work-board, could work no longer, drunk with the bottles he
had counted, quite off his head in the midst of all his gay
clocks. "The neighbours are full of it!" cried Coupeau. What
was the good of hiding out of sight? The company were no
longer ashamed to be seen at table; on the contrary, they

gloated over all this greedy crowd which had gathered in their honour; they would gladly have taken down the shop-front, and shoved the table out into the street, and so had their dessert out there, under the very nose of the public, in the very crush of the pavement. They weren't such a sight, eh? Besides, they needn't be selfish enough to shut themselves away. Coupeau, taking pity on the poor thirsting watchmaker across the way, held up to him a bottle from a distance; and as the other nodded vigorously, he took him the bottle and a glass. They were all on friendly terms now, the street and they. They drank to the health of the passers-by. They called out to those who seemed good fellows. The feasting spread and spread, till the whole quarter of the Goutte-d'Or scented the grub, and held their sides in a very hell of a racket.

For a minute or two Madame Vigouroux, the coal-dealer, had been passing and repassing before the door.

"Hi! Madame Vigouroux! Madame Vigouroux!" howled the company.

She entered, with a silly laugh, her face shining with soap; she was plump enough to burst her stays. The men liked to pinch her, for they could pinch her all over without ever finding a bone. Boche made her sit down beside him; and immediately, in his sly way, took hold of her knee under the table. But she was quite used to it, and she placidly drank her glass of wine, telling how the neighbours were all at their windows, and the people of the house were getting quite cross about it.

"Oh, as for that, that is our affair," said Madame Boche. "We are the *concierges*, and we can answer for things being in good order. Let them complain to us; we'll give them a nice reception."

In the back room a furious quarrel had broken out between Nana and Augustine, apropos of the roaster, which both wanted to scrape out. For a quarter of an hour it had been banged backwards and forwards on the floor, sounding out like an old saucepan. Now Nana was attending to little Victor, who had a bone stuck in his throat; she stuck her fingers under his chin, and made him swallow big lumps of sugar as medicine. All the same she kept her eye on the large table, and came at every moment to ask for wine, bread, or meat, for Étienne and Pauline.

"Here, take it and have done with it!" cried her mother. "Will you leave me in peace?"

The children could eat no more, but they stuffed all the same, banging their forks to a hymn-tune so as to rouse themselves.

In the midst of the uproar a conversation had started between old Bru and old Madame Coupeau. The old man, livid white with eating and drinking, talked of his sons who were killed in the Crimea. Ah! if they had only lived he wouldn't be in want of his daily bread. But old Madame Coupeau, speaking a little thick, and nodding her head on one side, answered:

"Ah! but children give a deal of trouble. Look at me now, you might think I was happy enough here; well, I have had cause to weep more than once. No, no, don't wish for children.

Old Bru shook his head.

"They won't have me to work anywhere," he murmured, "I am too old. When I go to a workshop the young people laugh at me, and ask me if I used to black boots for Henri IV. Last year I did earn thirty sous a day, painting a bridge; you had to lie on your back with the river under you. I have had a cough ever since. But now it's all over, I'm turned out of door everywhere."

He looked down at his poor stiff hands, and added:

"It's natural enough, for I am good for nothing. They are right enough; I should do the same in their place. What's wrong is, that I'm not dead. Yes, it's my own fault. One ought to lie down and die when one is past work."

"On my word," said Lorilleux, who was listening, "I can't understand why the Government doesn't give some help to the veterans of toil. I read that the other day in a paper."

But Poisson felt bound to stand up for the Government.

"Workmen are not soldiers," he declared, 'The *Invalides* are for soldiers. It's no use asking impossibilities."

Dessert was now served. In the middle there was a Savoy cake in the form of a temple, with a dome composed of slices of melon; and above the dome was planted an artificial rose, near which a butterfly of silver paper balanced itself on the end of a wire. Two drops of gum in the heart of the flower imitated two drops of dew. On the left there was a piece of cream-cheese on a dish, whilst in another dish on the right there were piles of strawberries, rather squashed, the juice all running out of them. However, there was still some salad left, large lettuce leaves soaked in oil.

"Come, Madame Boche," said Gervaise, in her most amiable manner, "a little more salad. I know you dote upon it."

"No, thanks; no, thanks. I am up to here," replied the *concierge*.

The laundress turned to Virginie, but Virginie stuck her finger into her mouth as if to touch the food.

"I am full up," she said. "There's no more room. I couldn't eat another mouthful."

"Oh! yes, you can with a little pressing," said Gervaise, with a smile. "There's always a little room somewhere. You can eat salad even when you're not hungry. You aren't going to let the lettuce be wasted."

"You can eat it tomorrow pickled," said Madame Lerat. "It is better pickled."

The women sighed, and gazed longingly at the salad. Clémence declared that one day she had eaten three bundles of watercress with her lunch. Madame Putois was more valiant still; she took the lettuce tops without picking them, and munched them straight away like that. They could all live on salad; eat bucketfuls. And with the aid of conversation they finished the salad-bowl.

"I could go on all fours in a field," declared the *concierge*, with her mouth full.

As for the dessert, it was a mere joke that scarcely counted. It came a little late, but that didn't matter; they would nibble at it all the same. Even if you were to burst like bombs, you couldn't but be equal to a few strawberries and a bit of cake. Besides there was no hurry, they had time enough, the whole night, if need be. Meanwhile the plates were heaped with strawberries and cream-cheese. The men lit their pipes, and as the better wine was done they went back to the ordinary, drinking as they smoked. But Gervaise had to cut the Savoy cake. Poisson, in his most gallant manner, got up and took the rose, which he handed to her in the midst of general applause. She pinned it on the left side of her bodice, the heart side. At every movement she made, the butterfly fluttered.

"I say!" cried Lorilleux, who had just made a discovery, "why, we are eating on your ironing-board. I wonder if so much work was ever done on it before!"

This wicked joke had an immense success. Witty remarks became the order of the day. Clémence could not swallow a spoonful of strawberries without saying that she was working the irons; Madame Lerat pretended that the cream-cheese had a taste of starch; whilst Madame Lorilleux mumbled between her teeth that that was just it; squander your money so fast on the very boards where you have taken such a time to earn them. There was a perfect storm of shouts and laughter.

Suddenly a loud voice imposed silence on the whole assembly. It was Boche, who had risen to his feet, and had started singing "Le Volcan d'amour, ou le Troupier seduisant", in his most comical and cheeky way.

"C'est moi, Blavin, que je séduis les belles.

A thunder of applause greeted the first verse. Yes, yes, they would have singing. Everyone should sing something. It was awful fun. And they put their elbows on the table, they leaned back in their chairs, nodding their heads at anything specially good, taking a drink with the refrain. The speciality of the creature Boche was his comic songs. He would have sent the water bottle into fits by the way he imitated a Johnny in the army, his fingers stuck out stiff, his cap on the side of his head. After the "Volcan d'amour", he gave the "Baronne de Follebiche", one of his great successes. When he came to the third verse he turned to Clémence, and murmured in a slow, voluptuous voice:

"La baronne avait du monde,
  Mais c'étaient ses quatre sœurs,
  Dont trois brunes l'autre blonde,
  Qu'avaient huit-z-yeux ravisseurs."

The whole company rose and joined in the refrain, the men beating time with their heels, the women tapping with their knives on their glasses. They all shouted:

"Sapristi! qu'est-ce qui paiera
  La goutte à la pa—à la pa—pa?
  Sapristi! qu'est-ce qui paiera
  La goutte à la pa—à la patrou—ou—ouille?"

The glass of the windows rattled, the breath of the singers made the muslin curtains quiver. Meanwhile Virginie had slipped out twice, and on coming back had leant over Gervaise

to whisper something in her ear. The third time, as she came
back in the midst of all the uproar, she said to her:

"My dear, he is still at François', pretending to read the
papers. You may be sure he is up to some mischief."

She spoke of Lantier. It was for him that she was keeping
a look-out. At each new tidings Gervaise looked very serious.

"Is he drunk?" she asked Virginie.

"No," she replied. "He is quite sober. That is just the
worst part of the business. Why should he stay so long in at
the wine-shop if he is sober? Oh Lord! oh Lord! if only
something dreadful doesn't happen!"

The laundress, in great agitation, begged her to be quiet.
A deep silence had all at once been made. Madame Putois
had risen to her feet, and begun to sing "A l'Abordage!" All
the guests, silent and attentive, gazed at her; Poisson had even
put down his pipe on the edge of the table, so as to hear her
better. She stood there stiff and tiny and impassioned, her
face pallid under her black cap; she shook her left fist in the
air with proud assurance, as she sang in a voice bigger than
herself:

> "Qu' un forban téméraire
> Nous chasse vent arrière!
> Malheur au flibustier!
> Pour lui point de quartier!
> Enfants, aux caronades!
> Rhum à pleines rasades!
> Pirates et forbans
> Sont gibiers de haubans!"

This was something quite serious. But, damn it all! it
gave a good idea of the real thing. Poisson had been to sea,
and he wagged his head in approval of the details. All felt,
too, that the song was quite in Madame Putois's line. Coupeau
leant over to whisper how, one night, in the Rue Poulet,
Madame Putois had put to flight four men who had tried to
outrage her.

Meanwhile Gervaise, with the aid of old Madame Coupeau,
poured out the coffee, though they had not finished eating
the Savoy cake. They would not let her sit down; they all
declared that it was her turn. She protested, looking so white
and uncomfortable, that they asked her if the goose hadn't
agreed with her. Thereupon she sang "Ah! laissez-moi

dormir!" in a sweet but feeble voice; when she came to the refrain, the longing after slumber peopled with fair dreams, her eyes half closed, and she gazed vaguely into the dark of the street. Immediately afterwards, Poisson, with a stiff inclination of the head, addressed to the ladies, broke into a drinking song, the "Vins de France"; but he sang vilely out of tune, and only the last verse, a patriotic one, went well; speaking of the tricolour flag, he raised his glass on high, held it for a moment, and emptied it at one gulp into his open mouth. Then came the sentimental songs; with something about Venice and gondoliers in the *barcarolle* of Madame Boche, of Seville and the Andalusians in the *bolero* of Madame Lorilleux, whilst Lorilleux went so far as to refer to the perfumes of Araby, apropos of the loves of Fatima, the dancing-girl. Around the heaped table, in the heavy atmosphere, a very atmosphere of indigestion, there was a glimpse of golden horizons, of necks of ivory, tresses of ebony, kisses beneath the moonlight to the sound of guitars, houris showering a rain of pearls and jewels about their feet as they danced; and the men smoked their pipes meditatively, the women had on their lips a half-unconscious smile of animal ecstasy: all felt themselves transported far away into a perfumed land. When Clémence began to warble "Faites un nid", with a tremolo in her throat, it delighted everybody; it recalled the country, the birds on the wing, the dancing on the green, the flowers with their honeyed breath; in short, it was just like the Bois de Vincennes on a picnic. But Virginie brought back the fun with "Mon petit Riquiqui"; she imitated the *vivandière*, hand on hip, elbow in the air; she pretended to pour out the wine with the other hand, with a turn of the wrist. And this went so well that the whole company begged old Madame Coupeau to sing "La Souris". The old woman refused, swearing she had forgotten the naughty thing. However, she began to sing in her little cracked voice; and her wrinkled face, with its sharp little eyes, brought out all the points, the terrors of Mademoiselle Lise pulling up her petticoats about her at the sight of the mouse. There was a general roar of laughter; the women simply could not keep serious, and they glanced laughingly at their neighbours; it wasn't smutty, after all, there were no naughty words. Boche, to tell the truth, was playing mouse up and down *Madame* the coal-dealer's calves. Things were in danger of going a little too far, when Goujet, at a glance from Gervaise, brought back

silence and order with the "Adieux d'Abd-el-Kader", which
he thundered out in his deep bass voice. It came out of his
spreading golden beard as if out of a brass trumpet. When he
cried, "O ma noble compagne!" referring to the warrior's
sable steed, all hearts beat, and the applause broke out before
the song was ended, so sonorously had he uttered the words.

"Now it's your turn, old Bru!" said old Madame Coupeau.
"You must sing your song. The older the better, you know."

And they all turned in the direction of the old man, urging
and encouraging him. He sat there as if benumbed, looking
at them, as if he understood nothing, out of the expressionless
mask of his tanned skin. They asked him if he knew the
"Cinq voyelles". His head sank lower: he seemed to remember
nothing; all the old songs were jumbled together in his old
pate. But, as they were giving up in despair, his memory
seemed to come to him, and he faltered out in a cavernous
voice:

> "Trou la la, trou la la,
> Trou la, trou la, trou la la!"

His face lit up, as if the refrain called up in him the recollection of old gaieties, which he gloated over all by himself,
listening to the sound of his own voice, now duller and duller,
with a sort of childish ecstasy.

> "Trou la la, trou la la,
> Trou la, trou la, trou la la!"

"I say, my dear," whispered Virginie in the ear of Gervaise,
"you know I've been having a look again. Well, Lantier has
gone from François'."

"Did you meet him outside?" asked the laundress.

"No, I walked quickly; I didn't pretend to see him."

But as Virginie raised her eyes, she stopped suddenly, and
gave a stifled sigh.

"Oh Lord! there he is, right opposite; he is looking across."

Gervaise, greatly agitated, ventured a glance in that
direction. A crowd of people had got together in the street to
listen to the singing. The grocer's boys, the tripe-seller, the
little watch-maker, formed a group, as if they were looking on
at a play. There were some soldiers, men in frock-coats, three
little girls of five or six, hand in hand, with an air of solemnity

par14 214

and wonderment. And there in the front rank stood Lantier, looking and listening composedly. Under the circumstances, it was cheek! Gervaise felt a chill strike through her, mounting from her legs to her heart, and she dared not move, while old Bru still went on:

> "Trou la la, trou la la,
> Trou la, trou la, trou la la!"

"Come now old chap, that's enough," said Coupeau. "Do you know the rest of it? You shall sing it to us some other day, when we feel too lively."

There was a laugh, and the old man stopped short, looked all round the table with his pale eyes, and relapsed into his former inanimate condition. The coffee was drunk, and the tinsmith had called for more wine. Clémence had started again on the strawberries. For a few moments the singing had ceased; they talked of a woman who had been found hanged that morning in the house adjoining. It was Madame Lerat's turn, but she required many preparations. She dipped the corner of her serviette in a glass of water, and applied it to her forehead because she was too hot. Then she asked for a drop of brandy, drank it, and wiped her lips slowly.

"L'Enfant du bon Dieu, eh?" she murmured, "L'enfant du bon Dieu. . . ."

And the great mannish woman, with her bony nose and her square military shoulders, began:

> "L'enfant perdu que sa mère abandonne,
> Trouve toujours un asile au saint lieu.
> Dieu qui le voit le défend de son trône.
> L'enfant perdu, c'est l'enfant du bon Dieu."

Her voice trembled on certain words, lingered falteringly; she raised the corners of her eyes towards heaven, whilst she waved her right hand before her chest, and laid it on her heart with an affecting gesture. Gervaise, in a state of agony at seeing Lantier, could not restrain her tears; it seemed to her that the song was telling her her own sorrows; that she was this lost child, lost and forsaken, whose defence God was going to take up. Clémence, very drunk, burst into sobs; she laid down her head on the edge of the table, and stifled her hiccups in the table-cloth. There was a silence, in which the air seemed charged with emotion. The women had pulled out their handkerchiefs, and now wiped their eyes without disguise, as if the feeling did them honour. The men looked at the ground straight before them, blinking their eyelids. Poisson, choking and clenching his teeth, bit two pieces out of his pipe, which he spat out without ceasing to smoke. Boche, who had his hand on the coal-dealer's knee, gave over pinching it, seized with a vague feeling of remorse and respect, whilst two big tears trickled down his cheeks. These jolly dogs were simply as drunk as lords and as tender-hearted as lambs. The wine found its way to their eyes; and when the refrain began, slower and more tearful still, all gave way, and fairly blubbered into their plates, undoing another button to give vent to their tender feelings.

But Gervaise and Virginie, despite themselves, could not take their eyes off the pavement opposite. Madame Boche, in her turn, caught sight of Lantier, and gave a little cry, without ceasing to dabble her face with her tears. Then all three looked at one another anxiously, with an involuntary movement of the head. Good heavens! if Coupeau were only to turn, if Coupeau were only to catch sight of him! What a pitched battle there would be! what a to-do! And they exchanged such looks that presently Coupeau demanded:

"What are you looking at?"

He looked out and saw Lantier.

"What the hell!" he cried, "this is coming it a bit too strong! Ah, the dirty cad! ah, the dirty cad! No, this is too much! I'll soon put a stop to it!"

And he got up, stuttering out frightful threats. Gervaise in a whisper implored him:

"Listen to me, please. Put down your knife. Stay where you are; don't do anything rash."

Virginie had to take out of his hands the knife that he had caught up from the table. But she could not hinder him from going outside and going up to Lantier. The company, overcome by its own emotion, saw nothing, weeping louder then ever, whilst Madame Lerat sang with an expression of racking pathos:

> "Orpheline, on l'avait perdue,
>   Et sa voix n'était entendue
>   Que des grands arbres et du vent."

The last line sounded like the very breath of the storm.
Madame Putois, who was about to drink was so moved that
she upset her glass on the cloth. Meanwhile, Gervaise sat as
if turned to ice, her hand pressed tightly over her mouth to
keep herself from crying out, her eyelids blinking with fright,
expecting every second to see one of the two men strike the
other to the ground in the middle of the street. Virginie and
Madame Boche also followed the scene, profoundly interested.
Coupeau, going out into the fresh air, had nearly measured
his length in the gutter. as he was making for Lantier. Lantier,
his hands in his pockets, had simply stepped aside. And the
two men now slanged one another; the tinsmith especially
gave the other a good dressing, called him a filthy pig, talked
of eating his tripes. Their voices sounded loud and furious,
they made frantic gestures, as if they would whirl their arms
off. Gervaise sank back, closing her eyes; it went on longer
than she could endure to look at; it seemed to her that at every
moment they would fly at each other's throats, so close were
their faces together. Then, hearing nothing more, she opened
her eyes again, and sat there stupefied; they were quietly
talking to one another.

The voice of Madame Lerat, cooing and lachrymose, was
heard in a new verse:

> "Le lendemain, a demi morte,
>   Ou recueillit le pauvre enfant."

"Some women are bitches, no doubt about it," said Madame
Lorilleux, to the approval of everyone.

Gervaise exchanged glances with Madame Boche and
Virginie. They were making it up then! Coupeau and Lantier
continued their conversation on the edge of the pavement. They
still called each other names, but in a friendly way. They said
"damned fool" to each other in a tone which was almost
amiable. As the people were staring at them, they began to
walk up and down, slowly, side by side, along the pavement,
turning back again every ten yards. They had struck up a
lively conversation. All at once Coupeau seemed to get
angry again, whilst the other man refused and held back.
And it was the tinsmith himself who dragged Lantier across
the street, and forced him to enter the laundry.

"I tell you I mean it!" he cried. "You shall drink a glass of
wine. Men are men, eh? Why shouldn't we be friends?"

Madame Lerat had come to the end of the last refrain. All the women repeated together, while they twisted their handkerchiefs:

"L'enfant perdu, c'est l'enfant du bon Dieu."

The singer was much complimented, and she sat down, pretending that she was quite worn out with the exertion. She asked for something to drink, for she threw herself into the sentiment of the song too much, really too much, and she was afraid it was bad for her nerves. Meanwhile all eyes were fixed on Lantier, quietly seated by the side of Coupeau, and already eating the last fragment of the Savoy cake, which he dipped in his wine. With the exception of Virginie and Madame Boche, no one knew him. The Lorilleux scented something in the air, but they had no idea what it was, and they put on a quizzical air. Goujet, who had noticed Gervaise's emotion, looked askance at the newcomer. As there was an awkward silence, Coupeau said simply:

"This is a friend of mine."

Then, turning to his wife:

"Come, stir your stumps! Is there any more hot coffee?"

Gervaise gazed at them, one after the other, blandly and stupidly. At the first moment, when her husband had pushed her old lover into the shop, she had seized her head in both hands, instinctively, as she did in a thunder-storm, at every peal of thunder. It could never be possible; surely the walls would give way, and bury them all in their ruins! Then, seeing the two men seated there, without so much as a fold of the curtains having shaken, it all suddenly seemed to her quite natural. The goose had not quite agreed with her; she had certainly eaten too much; and it hindered her from thinking. A pleasant idleness weighed upon her, seemed to nail her there to the edge of the table, wanting nothing, only to be not worried. Good Lord! what was the use of keeping up old grudges when other folk didn't, and things seemed to settle down of themselves to the general satisfaction? She got up and went to see if there was any coffee left.

In the back room the children had fallen asleep. The cross-eyed Augustine had terrorized over them during all the dessert, pinching their strawberries, frightening them with horrible threats. By this time she was very ill, all doubled up on a little stool, quite white and saying nothing. Fat little

Pauline's head had sunk down on Étienne's shoulder; Étienne himself was asleep with his head on the table. Nana was sitting on the edge of the bed, holding Victor close against her, one arm round his neck; and, half asleep, her eyes closed, she said over and over again, in a little weak voice:

"Oh! mamma, I ain't well; oh! mamma, I ain't well."

"Gracious!" murmured Augustine, whose head rolled to and fro on her shoulders, "they are all tight; they were singing just like grown ups."

Gervaise had another shock at the sight of Étienne. There was his father close by, eating a piece of cake, without ever having expressed a wish to give the little chap a kiss. She was on the point of awakening Étienne, and bringing him over to him. Then, once again, it seemed to her the best thing that, after all, the matter should have gone off so easily. It would have been out of place to break up the harmony of the dinner, now at the end. She came back with the coffee-pot, and poured out a glass of coffee for Lantier, who appeared to take no notice of her.

"Now it's my turn," said Coupeau, speaking very thick. "Eh! You've been keeping me for the tit-bit. Well, I'll sing you 'Qué cochon d'enfant'. "

"Yes, yes, 'Qué cochon d'enfant!' " cried everybody.

The uproar began again; Lantier was forgotten. The women got their glasses and knives ready, in order to join in the refrain. They laughed beforehand, and gazed expectantly at the tinsmith, who swayed from foot to foot in a manner of deliberate vulgarity, singing in an old woman's hoarse voice:

> "Tous les matins, quand je m' lève,
>   J'ai l'cœur sus d'sous;
> J' l'envoi' chercher contr' la Grève
>   Un poisson d'quatr' sous.
> Il rest' trois quarts d'heure en route,
>   Et puis, en r' montant,
> I' m' lich' la moitié d' ma goutte:
>   Qué cochon d'enfant!"

And the women, tapping on their glasses, took part in the chorus with roars of laughter:

> "Qué cochon d'enfant!
> Qué cochon d'enfant!"

The whole street now joined in, singing with one voice, "Qué cochon d'enfant!" Across the road the little watchmaker, the grocer's boys, the tripe-seller, the fruiterer, who all knew the song, all took up the refrain, slapping themselves in chorus. The whole street seemed to be drunk; the very smell of the feast had set them all reeling. And it must be said that the party itself was by this time awfully boozed. It had come on little by little, from the first glass of wine after the soup down to now, the finishing touch, when they all bawled together, all crammed with food, in the reddish haze of the two flickering lamps. The sound of this immense jollity deadened the very sound of the last vehicles passing in the street. Two policemen, thinking there was a row, hurried up; but catching sight of Poisson, they gave a little nod, and went on, slowly, side by side, along the shadow of the houses.

Coupeau was at this verse:

> "L'dimanche, à la P'tit'-Villette,
> Après la chaleur,
> J'allons chez mon oncl' Tinette,
> Qu' est maitr' vidangeur,
> Pour avoir des noyaux d' c'rise,
> En nous en r'tournant.
> I' s'roul' dans la marchandise.
> Qué cochon d'enfant!
> Qué cochon d'enfant!"

At that they fairly raised the roof, and so loud a burst of voices went up into the calm, damp air of the night that they fell to applauding themselves, feeling that that was an effort which it was impossible to beat.

Not one of the company ever remembered exactly how the feast came to an end. It must have been very late, no doubt, for there was not a cat stirring. And it seemed to them that they had danced round the table, hand in hand. It was all a yellow mist, with leaping crimson faces, grinning from ear to ear. They had certainly drunk sugared wine at the end; only, they were not quite sure if someone had not put salt into the glasses for a joke. The children had apparently undressed and gone to bed by themselves. Next day Madame Boche boasted that she had given two sound boxes on the ear to Boche, finding him chatting in rather too close proximity to the coal-dealer in a corner; but Boche, who had no recollection of it at all, looked on it as a mere bit of fake. What all joined in denouncing was the conduct of Clémence, really a person who ought not to be invited out; she had ended by showing all she had, and had been so badly upset as to completely ruin one of the muslin curtains. The men, at all events, went outside in the street; Lorilleux and Poisson, seized with qualms in the stomach, had managed to get as far as the pork-butcher's. Good breeding always comes out sooner or later. So, too, the ladies, Madame Putois, Madame Lerat, and Virginie, a little overcome by the heat, had merely gone into the back room to take off their stays; Virginie had even lain down on the bed just for a minute, so as to guard against any consequences. Then the party seemed to have somehow melted away, one after another, all in a body, disappearing into the darkness in a final uproar, a furious quarrel between the Lorilleux, an endless, dreary "trou la la, trou la la," of old Bru. Gervaise fancied that Goujet had burst into sobs on taking leave; Coupeau went on singing; as for Lantier, he must have stayed to the end. She had felt a hot breath against her hair at a certain moment, but if it came from Lantier or from the hot night air she could not say.

Madame Lerat had declared that she could not get back to Batignolles at that hour, and a mattress was taken out of the bed for her, and laid in a corner of the laundry, after the table had been pushed out of the way. She slept there, in the midst of the leavings of the great feast. And all night long, while the Coupeaus lay slumbering heavily, sleeping off the effects of the dinner, a neighbour's cat, taking advantage of an open window, went steadily to work on what remained of the goose, cracking the bones of the creature with the tiny sound of its sharp teeth.

CHAPTER EIGHT

On the Sunday after, Coupeau, who had not come back to dinner, brought in Lantier about ten o'clock. They had had some calves' feet at Thomas's, at Montmartre.

"You mustn't scold, missus," said the tinsmith. "You see we haven't been on the spree. Oh! there's no danger with him; he insists on keeping you straight."

And he told how they had met in the Rue Rochechouart. After dinner Lantier had refused to come and have a drink at the "Boule Noire", saying that when you are married to a nice, pretty woman you had no business to prowl about in low dancing-halls. Gervaise listened with a faint smile. No, indeed, she had no inclination to scold; she was far too much embarrassed for that. Ever since the party, she had been expecting to see her old lover one day or another; but at such an hour, just as she was going to bed, the unexpected arrival of the two men had flurried her, and with trembling hands she fastened up her back hair, which she had begun to let down.

"Look here," said Coupeau; "since he was nice enough not to take anything to drink outside, you must get something for us here. It's only fair."

The work-women had long since gone. Old Madame Coupeau and Nana had just gone to bed. Gervaise was in the act of putting up the shutters when they appeared. She left the place open, and brought some glasses and the remains of a bottle of brandy, which she laid out on the ironing-board. Lantier would not sit down, and he avoided speaking to her directly. However, when she was pouring out for him he said:

"A thimbleful, Madame, if you please."

Coupeau looked at them both and spoke his mind very bluntly. They were not going to behave like ninnies, surely! The past was the past; if one kept up a grudge after nine or ten years, you would finally have nobody you could speak to. No, no, he wore his heart on his sleeve; he knew very well whom he had to do with, a good honest man and a good

honest woman, eh? His mind was quite at rest, he knew he
could depend on both of them.

"Oh! indeed yes . . . indeed yes . . ." said Gervaise, looking
down, and not knowing what she was saying.

"I look upon her as a sister, merely a sister," murmured
Lantier.

"Shake hands then, damn it all!" cried Coupeau, "and
let the bloody fools say what they please! I call that better
than being a millionaire. For my part, a friend out-tops
everything, for a friend is a friend, don't you see? and there's
nothing better."

He slapped his chest so vigorously, and seemed so overcome,
that they had to calm him down. All three clinked glasses,
and drank in silence. Gervaise could at last look at Lantier
collectedly; on the night of the party she had seen him in a
mist. He had grown stouter, he was quite plump, his arms
and legs looked too thick for his small stature. But his face,
though puffed out with a life of idleness, still kept its regular
features; and as he trained his slight moustache very carefully,
he would not have been taken for more than his age, just
thirty-five. He was wearing grey trousers and a dark blue
overcoat, quite gentlemanly in cut, with a round hat; he had,
too, a watch and a silver chain, from which hung a ring, a
keepsake.

"I must go," he said. "I live a devil of a way off."

He was already outside, when the tinsmith called him back
to make him promise always to look in for a moment when he
was passing. Meanwhile, Gervaise, who had quietly left the
room, returned leading Étienne, who was in his shirt sleeves,
looking already asleep. The child smiled and rubbed his
eyes. But when he saw Lantier, he stood embarrassed and
trembling, glancing uneasily towards his mother and Coupeau.

"Don't you know this gentleman?" asked the latter.

The child looked down, without replying. Then he gave a
little nod to show that he recognized the gentleman.

"Well then, don't be a silly, go and give him a kiss."

Lantier quietly waited. When Étienne ventured near, he
bent down, held out both cheeks, and then gave the child a
big kiss on the forehead. Then the child looked up at his
father, and, all of a sudden, burst out sobbing, and rushed
out of the room like a mad thing. Coupeau scolded away,
declaring he was rude.

"It's emotion," said Gervaise, herself pale and agitated.

"Oh! he is generally as quiet as possible," explained Coupeau. "I know how to bring him up, you may depend. He'll get accustomed to you. He must get used to things. And, come now, if it were only for the youngster's sake, we couldn't always remain bad friends, could we? We should have had to make matters up one time or another, for I wouldn't for worlds keep a father away from his own son."

Thereupon he suggested that they should finish out the bottle. All three clinked their glasses again. Lantier showed no sort of surprise, took things quite calmly. Before taking his leave, in order to show himself as polite as possible to the tinsmith, he absolutely insisted on helping him to shut up shop. Then, brushing the dust carefully off his hands, he wished them good-night.

"A good night's sleep! I must try to catch my omnibus. I'll look you up again soon."

From that day forward, Lantier was often to be seen in the Rue de la Goutte-d'Or. He always came when Coupeau was there asking after him before he was well inside the door, pretending to have come entirely on his account. Then he would seat himself near the window, always in his overcoat, always shaved and combed; and he would talk politely, like an educated man. Little by little the Coupeaus learnt some of the details of his life during the last eight years. At one moment he had had control of a hat manufactory, and, when he was asked why he had given it up, he hinted at the roguery of a partner, a compatriot, a brute who had squandered all the money of the concern on women. But merely to have once been at the head of an establishment left a certain distinction about him, which was not to be gainsaid. He mentioned that he had nearly come to terms over a splendid affair; a new hatter was going to start in business, and put immense concerns into his hands. Meanwhile he did absolutely nothing; he simply strolled about with his hands in his pockets, like a gentleman of independent means. When he complained of his circumstances, and anyone ventured to tell him that some factory was in want of workmen, he smiled compassionately, and was by no means inclined to starve himself while he slaved for others. It was evident, in any case, as Coupeau declared, that the chap didn't live on air. Oh! he was a sly dog, he knew what he was about, he had other irons in the fire, for he looked the very picture of prosperity, and it must take some money to pay for all his white linen and his swell ties. One morning the tinsmith had seen him having his boots blacked on the Boulevard Montmartre. The truth was that Lantier, who gossiped very freely about others, told nothing, or told lies, on his own account. He would not even say where he was living. No, he was staying with a friend, a devil of a way off, until he could find a nice place to put up; and he declared it was useless for anyone to come to look for him, for he was never there.

"One finds plenty of places about," he exclaimed, "but then it is not worth the trouble of putting up where you are bound not to stay twenty-four hours. For instance, one Monday I went to Champion's at Montrouge. That evening Champion began to worry me about politics; he didn't look at things as I did; so, on Tuesday morning I left, for we are not in the times of slavery, and I have no notion of selling myself for seven francs a day."

It was then at the beginning of November. Lantier would bring bouquets of violets for Gervaise and the two work-women. Little by little he increased his visits, he came almost every day. He seemed to wish to get into the good graces of the whole neighbourhood, and he began with Clémence and Madame Putois, to whom he paid the most assiduous attentions, without distinction of age. At the end of a month the two work-women adored him. The Boches, whom he flattered greatly by going to pay his respects to them in their lodge, were enraptured with his politeness. As for the Lorilleux, when they discovered who it was that had arrived at dessert on the day of the party, they heaped up endless abuse on Gervaise for having had the impudence to take her old lover like that into her household. But one day Lantier went up to see them, and made such a good opening by ordering a chain for a lady of his acquaintance, that they asked him to sit down, and kept him for an hour, charmed with his conversation; they even wondered how such a gentlemanly man could ever have lived with Clop-clop. So it came about that the hatter's visits to the Coupeaus ceased to scandalize people, so well had he succeeded in getting into the good graces of the whole Rue de la Goutte-d'Or. Goujet alone held aloof. If he were there when the other arrived, he at once took his departure, so as not to be obliged to make the fellow's acquaintance.

Meanwhile, as Lantier came into favour on all sides, Gervaise, for the first few weeks, lived in a state of great distress. She still felt that burning sensation at the pit of the

stomach, which she had felt on the day when Virginie had
made her her confidences. What she feared above all was
that she might be powerless before him, if he should come in
some evening and find her alone, and kiss her. She thought
of him too much, she was too full of him. Slowly, however, her
mind quieted down, as she saw how well he behaved, never
looking her in the face, not so much as touching her with the
tip of his finger, when the others had turned their backs. Then,
too, Virginie, who seemed to read what was going on in
her mind, made her feel ashamed of such thoughts. What was
there to be afraid of? You couldn't come across a more
decent sort of man. And one day she managed to get them
both into a corner and start the conversation on matters of
sentiment. Lantier declared gravely, picking his words, that
his heart was dead, that he only wished now to give up his
life to the happiness of his son. He never alluded to Claude,
who was still in the south. He kissed Étienne every evening on
the forehead, not knowing what to say to him if he stayed in
the room, forgetting him entirely while he bandied compliments with Clémence. And Gervaise grew easy in her mind
once more. The presence of Lantier saved her from the
souvenirs of Plassans and the Hôtel Boncœur; seeing him so
constantly, she dreamed of him no longer. She even felt a
certain repugnance at thinking of their former relations. Oh!
that was all over, that was all over now. If he should ever dare
come after her again, she would simply box his ears for him,
she would tell her husband, if need be. And she turned again,
now without compunction, with a singular sweetness, rather,
to the friendship of her friend Goujet.

One morning, on coming to work. Clémence related that
the night before, about eleven, she had seen Monsieur Lantier
with a lady on his arm. She said it as coarsely as she could,
with a certain malicious insistence, to see how her mistress
would take it. Yes, Monsieur Lantier was climbing the Rue
Notre-Dame de Lorette; the woman was blonde, one of those
boulevard tarts with a bare backside under a silk dress. Just
for fun, she had followed them. The tart had gone into a
pork-butcher's to buy some shrimps and ham. Then, at the
Rue de la Rochefoucauld, Monsieur Lantier had waited on
the pavement, while the woman went up by herself, and then
beckoned to him from the window to come up. Clémence made
all sorts of unpleasant suggestions, but Gervaise went on
quietly ironing a white dress. At moments the story brought

H

a faint smile to her lips. Those Provençals, she said, were all
simply crazy after women; they would have them whether or
no; they were capable of picking them out of a dung-heap
with a shovel. And at night, when the hatter arrived, it
amused her to hear Clémence teasing him about his blonde.
He seemed quite pleased at having been seen. It was simply
an old friend whom he still saw from time to time, when he
could do so without difficulty; a very swell sort of girl, with
fine apartments, and he named certain of her old lovers, a
viscount, a big merchant in crockery, the son of a notary. He
liked women who used scent. And he put his handkerchief,
which the little woman had scented, under Clémence's nose.
Just then Étienne came in, and he put on his most serious air,
adding that a bit of fooling was of no consequence, but his
heart was dead. Gervaise, as she bent over her work, nodded
approval. And Clémence was nicely paid out for her malice,
for she had felt Lantier give her a pinch two or three times
already without anyone seeing it, and she was bursting with
envy because she didn't stink of musk like the little boulevard
tart.

When the spring came, Lantier, now quite one of the
family, talked of coming to live in the neighbourhood, so as
to be nearer his friends. He wanted a furnished room in a
decent house. Madame Boche, Gervaise as well, did their
utmost to find one for him. But he was extremely particular.
He must have a large court, he must have a ground floor, in
short, every possible convenience. And now, every evening,
at the Coupeaus, he seemed to be taking measure of the
height of the ceilings, studying the arrangement of the rooms,
longing for a place just like that. Oh! he would ask nothing
better than to find a resting place in this quiet, cosy corner.
And he always ended his scrutiny with this phrase:

"Heavens! but you are jolly well off here, no mistake!"

One evening when he had been dining there, and he came
to his phrase at dessert, Coupeau, who by this time had got
to thee-ing and thou-ing him, cried suddenly:

"You'd better stop here, old man, if you feel disposed. We
could arrange."

And he explained that the dirty clothes' room, properly
cleaned out, would make a nice little room. Etienne could
sleep in the laundry. They could put a mattress for him on the
ground; that was all.

"No, no!" said Lantier; "I can't accept. It would put you

out too much. I know you mean it kindly, but we should be crowded up too much. Then, you know, I should have to go through your room, and that wouldn't always be amusing."

"Oh! the beast!" cried the tinsmith with a roar of laughter, banging his fist on the table by way of clearing his throat, "he is always thinking of something dirty! But, you bloody fool, can't you see a way out of the difficulty? Look here; there are two windows in the room. Well, you knock out one and turn it into a door. Then, do you see? you come right in from the court, and we can even block up the door leading through, if we choose to. We needn't see one another unless we please, and we should have our own premises."

There was a silence. The hatter murmured:

"Ah! yes, if it could be like that, I don't say—— And yet, no, I should be too much in your way."

He avoided looking at Gervaise. But he was evidently waiting for a word from her in order to accept. She was quite taken aback at her husband's idea; not that the thought of seeing Lantier living in the house shocked or troubled her much; but she did not see where the dirty clothes were to be kept. But the tinsmith pointed out the advantages of the arrangement. The rent, five hundred francs, had always seemed rather high. Well, their pal should pay twenty francs a month for the room, furnished; it would not be dear for him, and it would come in handy for them at quarter-day. He added that he would undertake to knock up a big box under their bed, big enough to hold all the dirty clothes of the neighbourhood. Gervaise hesitated, and glanced at old Madame Coupeau, whom Lantier had quite won over, months back, by bringing her cough lozenges for her throat.

"You will not be in the way, certainly," she said at length. "We might manage it——"

"No, no, thanks," said the hatter. "You are too good, it would be taking advantage of you."

At this Coupeau burst out impatiently. How much longer was he going to shilly-shally? When they really wished it! He would be rendering them a service, there! Then he shouted in a furious voice:

"Étienne! Étienne!"

The boy was asleep with his head on the table. He jumped up with a start.

"Look here, say: 'You must.' Yes, to that gentleman. Say it aloud: 'You must!'"

"You must!" faltered Étienne, sleepily.

There was a general laugh. But Lantier soon relapsed into his former air of serious concern. He shook hands with Coupeau across the table, saying:

"I accept. We are to be good friends all round aren't we? I accept for the child's sake."

The very next day, as M. Marescot, the landlord, had come to see the Boches. Gervaise mentioned the matter to him. He seemed at first quite concerned, and refused angrily, as if they were asking him to knock down a wing of his house. Then, after a minute inspection, during which he gazed into the air to see if the upper storeys were not likely to be over-turned, he finally gave the authorization, but on condition that he was to incur no expense; and the Coupeaus had to sign a paper, in which they agreed to put things back as they were before, at the expiration of their lease. That very evening, the tinsmith brought in some of his mates, a mason, a carpenter, a painter, good chaps who would do the little job after working hours, in order to render him a service. The putting up of the new door, and the cleaning out of the room, cost none the less, a good hundred francs, without reckoning the drinks with which the work had to be washed down. The tinsmith promised to pay it later on, with the first money that he got from his lodger. Then there was the question of furniture. Gervaise left old Madame Coupeau's cupboard where it was; she added a table and two chairs, from her own room; and she had, in addition, to buy a toilet-table, and a bed and bed-clothes, a hundred and thirty francs in all, which she was to pay for at the rate of ten francs a month. Still, if Lantier's twenty francs would be swallowed up for the first ten months or so, in paying up these debts, later on there would be quite a little harvest.

It was just the beginning of June that Lantier took up his new abode. The night before, Coupeau had offered to go and help him carry his trunk, so as to save the thirty sous of a cab. But he had seemed rather embarrassed, and declared that his trunk was too heavy, as if he still wished to keep them from knowing where he was living. He came in the afternoon, about three, when Coupeau was not about. Gervaise, coming out to the door of the shop, turned pale as she caught sight of the trunk on the cab. It was their old trunk, the trunk which she had brought up from Plassans, now all battered and broken, held together by cord. She saw it reappear as she had dreamed, and she could have fancied that it was the very same cab in which that little tart Adèle had lured him away, the very same cab that was now bringing him back. Meanwhile, Boche lent a hand to Lantier. The laundress watched them in silence, an uneasy silence. When they had deposited the trunk in the middle of the room, she said, in order to say something:

"Well! there's a good job done."

Then, recovering herself as she saw that Lantier was busy undoing the cords, without taking the least notice of her, she added:

"Monsieur Boche, you'll have a glass?"

And she went to fetch a bottle and glasses. Just then Poisson, in his policeman's garb, passed outside. She gave him a little nod, with a wink and a smile. The policeman knew what that meant. When he was on duty, and you winked at him, that meant that you offered him a glass of wine. And he would pass and repass for hours together before the laundress's door, in expectation of that wink. Then, so as not to be observed, he came in by way of the court, and kept his glass out of sight as he sipped it.

"Ah! ah!" said Lantier, as he saw him come in," it's you, is it, Badingue?"

He called him Badingue for a joke, so as to make fun of the Emperor. Poisson took it in his stiff sort of way, without showing whether it really offended him or not. Besides, the two men, though disagreeing about politics, had become great friends.

"You know that the Emperor was a policeman himself when he was in London," said Boche. "On my word, he used to run in drunken women."

Meanwhile Gervaise had poured out three glasses. She could not take anything herself, she felt too overcome. But she stood there watching Lantier as he undid the last cords, longing to know what was in the trunk. She remembered, in a certain corner, a heap of socks, two dirty shirts, an old hat. Were they still there? was she once more to see those tattered relics of the past? Before lifting the cover, Lantier took his glass, and clinked.

"To your health."

"To yours," replied Boche and Poisson.

The laundress refilled the glasses. The three men wiped their lips with their hands. At last the hatter opened the

trunk. It was stuffed with a pell-mell of papers, books, old
clothes, bundles of linen. He took out, one after another, a
saucepan, a pair of boots, a bust of Ledru-Rollin, with the
nose broken, an embroidered shirt, a pair of workmen's
trousers. And Gervaise, leaning over, could distinguish a
smell of tobacco, the smell of a man who was slovenly in his
ways, who looked after the outside of his things, what people
could see of him. No, the old hat was not there, in the left
corner. Instead, there was a pin-cushion that was new to her,
some woman's present. Gradually she quietened down, feeling
only a sort of vague sadness, looking at the things, one after
the other, considering whether they belonged to her time or
to the times of others.

"I say, Badingue, do you know that?" enquired Lantier.

He shoved under his nose a little book, printed in Brussels,
Les Amours de Napoléon III, illustrated with woodcuts. Among
other anecdotes, there was one telling how the Emperor had
seduced the daughter of a cook, aged thirteen; and the
picture represented Napoleon III, bare-legged, wearing only
the order of the Legion of Honour, running after a little girl
who tried to escape from his lustful pursuit.

"Ah! that's it!" cried Boche, to whose slyly voluptuous
instincts the picture appealed. "That's always the way!"

Poisson was quite taken aback; he could not find a word
in defence of the Emperor. It was in a book, he could not deny
it. But as Lantier flourished the picture before him with
malicious delight, he finally threw out his arms, exclaiming:

"Well, and what of that? Isn't it human nature after all?"

Lantier could find no reply. He arranged his books and
newspapers on one of the cupboard shelves, and as he seemed
greatly distressed at not having a little hanging book-case to
put up over the table, Gervaise promised to get one for him.
He had the *Histoire de Dix Ans*, by Louis Blanc, all but the
first volume, which he had never had, the *Girondins* of Lamar-
tine, in penny numbers, Eugène Sue's *Mysteres de Paris* and
Le Juif Errant, besides a whole heap of philosophic and
humanitarian books which he had picked up in old rag
shops. But it was on his newspapers that he gazed with special
tenderness and respect. It was a collection that he had been
making for years. Whenever he read at a café an article in a
paper that seemed to him to express his own views in a
satisfactory manner, he bought and kept the paper. He had
thus got together an enormous bundle, papers of all sorts and

all dates, thrown together without any kind of order. He pulled up the package from the very bottom of the trunk, and gave it a friendly tap as he addressed the two other men·

"You see that? Well, that's my little lot, there isn't anybody who can boast of such a beauty. You'd never guess what there is in that. Why, if you put only half those ideas into practice, you'd make a clean sweep of half the social abuses. Yes, your Emperor and all his narks would have a nice dose."

But he was interrupted by the policeman, whose red moustache and imperial had begun to bristle in his pallid face.

"And the army, what would you do with that now?"

Lantier was carried away by his excitement. He banged his newspapers furiously, and shouted:

"I demand the suppression of the standing army, the fraternity of nations. I demand the abolition of privileges, of titles and monopolies. I demand equality of wages, the redistribution of benefices, the glorification of the proletariat. Liberty of all kinds, do you hear! all! and divorce!"

"Yes, yes, divorce, for moral reasons!" added Boche, by way of backing him up.

Poisson assumed a majestic air. He replied:

"Nevertheless, if I don't want your liberties, I am perfectly free."

"If you don't want them, if you don't want them," stuttered Lantier, choking with rage. "No, you are not free! If you don't want them, I'd pack you off to Cayenne—yes, I would, to Cayenne—with your Emperor and the whole bloody lot of them!"

They had a regular set-to, after that fashion, every time they met. Gervaise, who disliked arguments, generally had to interfere. She came out of the apathetic state into which she had been thrown by the sight of the trunk, about which lingered, now all spoilt, the perfume of their old love; and she recalled the men to their glasses.

"True," said Lantier, quieting down all of a sudden, and taking up his glass. "Here's yours."

"Yours," responded Boche and Poisson, clinking glasses with him.

Meanwhile Boche shifted a little uneasily from foot to foot, looking at the policeman out of the corner of his eye.

"All that is quite between ourselves, eh, Monsieur Poisson?" he murmured. "One lets you see and hear things. . . ."

But Poisson would not let him finish. He laid his hand on

his heart, as if to explain that it was all buried there. He was not going to play the spy on his friends, no indeed. Then Coupeau turned up, and a second bottle was emptied. Finally the policeman went out the back way and took up his former regular, mechanical march up and down the pavement.

At first everything was at sixes and sevens at the laundress's. Lantier had indeed his own room, his own entrance, his own key; but, as at the last moment they had decided not to fasten up the communicating door, it generally happened that he came in through the laundry. The dirty clothes, too, were a considerable trouble to Gervaise, for her husband had done nothing in regard to the big box he had talked of; and she was reduced to stowing the linen about everywhere, in all the corners, and especially under the bed, which was not quite pleasant in the summer nights. Then, too, she found it very tiresome to be obliged to make Étienne's bed every evening in the middle of the laundry; when they worked on late, the child went to sleep on a chair, as he waited up for them. So when Goujet spoke of sending Étienne to Lille, where his old master, a mechanician, was in want of apprentices, she was much inclined to listen to the suggestion, the more so as the boy, not happy at home, and anxious to be his own master, begged her to give her consent. She was only afraid that Lantier would flatly refuse. He had taken up his abode with them simply so as to be near his son; he would not want to lose him just a fortnight after he had come into the place. However, when she spoke to him timidly about the affair, he gave his entire approval, saying that young workmen ought to see a bit of the country. On the morning of Étienne's departure he discoursed to him about his rights, then he embraced him, and declaimed:

"Remember that the producer is not a slave, but that whoever is not a producer is a drone."

After that the household settled down into its usual train; things quietened down, and took on new habits without disturbance. Gervaise got used to seeing the dirty clothes lying about all over the place, to seeing Lantier going and coming. He still talked of his important affairs; he went out sometimes, combed and brushed, wearing his best linen, and he disappeared, sometimes stayed away the whole night; then he would come back pretending to be quite worn out, his head splitting, as if he had been discussing matters of the most serious interest for the last twenty-four hours. The truth was that he simply let things slide. Oh! there was no danger of his getting his hands galled with hard work. He generally rose about ten, went for a walk in the afternoon, if the weather was agreeable, or, if it was raining, stayed in the shop and read the newspaper. It was just the place for him, he was perfectly happy to have petticoats always about him, to be there in the midst of women; he delighted in their vulgarities, spurring them on to indulge in them while he himself always spoke with perfect correctness; and that explained why he was so much after laundresses, who are not by any means squeamish. When Clémence came out with her whole budget, he listened with his amiable smile, twisting his slight moustache. The smell of the workshop, the sweating work-women moving the irons to and fro with their bare arms, the whole place, like an alcove heaped up with the litter of all the women of the neighbourhood, seemed the very place he had dreamed of, a long-looked-for haven of idleness and enjoyment.

At first Lantier took his meals at François', at the corner of the Rue des Poissonniers. But he dined with the Coupeaus three or four days out of the seven; and finally he offered to board with them, he would give them fifteen francs every Saturday. After that he never left the house; he took up his position for good and all. He was to be seen from morning to night, in and out of the shop and the back room, in his shirt-sleeves, raising his voice, ordering them about; he even attended to the customers and took charge of the shop. He got tired of François' wine, and persuaded Gervaise to buy her wine from Vigouroux, the coal-dealer near, whose wife he would go and pinch, along with Boche, when he went to take orders. Then he decided that Coudeloup's bread was not properly baked; and he sent Augustine for the bread to Meyer's, the Viennese bakery in the Faubourg Poissonnière. He also changed Lehongre, the grocer, and only kept the butcher of the Rue Polonceau, the fat Charles, on account of his political opinions. At the end of a month he wanted all the cooking to be done with oil. As Clémence said in joke, the oilstain was always coming out with this damned Provençal. He made the omelettes himself, omelettes twice-turned, more browned than pancakes, and so hard that they were more like cakes. He watched old Madame Coupeau, insisting on the steaks being well done, till they were like leather; adding garlic everywhere, furious if they stinted the dressing in the salad, horrid stuff, he declared, which might turn out to be poisonous. But his great fancy was a certain soup, vermicelli cooked in water, very thick, into which he poured a good half bottle of oil. Only he and Gervaise could eat it; the others, Parisians, had one day ventured to take a taste of it, and had nearly thrown up all their insides.

Little by little Lantier had come, too, to mix himself up in the family affairs. As the Lorilleux always made a great fuss about paying up old Madame Coupeau's hundred sous, he had explained that one could bring an action against them. Were they making game of people? Why, they ought to contribute ten francs a month! And he went up himself to demand the ten francs, so boldly and so insinuatingly, that the chain-maker dared not refuse. Now Madame Lerat as well gave two pieces of a hundred sous. Old Madame Coupeau could have kissed Lantier's hands; and Lantier, too, played the *rôle* of mediator in the quarrels between the old woman and Gervaise. When the laundress lost her patience, and spoke roughly to her mother-in-law, and the old woman went off to bed crying, he gave them both a good lecture, and insisted on their making friends again, asking if they thought such nice humours were amusing for other people. Then Nana, too; she had been very badly brought up, in his opinion. Nor was he wrong, for when the father scolded the mother stuck up for her, and when the mother hit her the father made a scene. Nana, delighted at seeing her parents at variance, for that gave her her own excuse beforehand, simply did what she liked. At present her chief delight was to go and play in the farrier's opposite; she would swing all day long on the shafts of the carts; she would hide herself with a set of urchins in a corner of the dim court, lit only by the red light of the forge; and would suddenly rush out again, screaming and tousled, followed by the whole string of dirty brats, as if a shower of blows had sent the young vagabonds flying. Only Lantier could scold her; and even with him she generally had her answer ready. The little beggar, only ten years old as she was, strutted before him as if she were a lady, looked at him out of the corners of her eyes, eyes already full of vice. Finally he took charge of her education; he taught her to dance and to speak *patois*.

Thus a year passed by. In the neighbourhood it was generally supposed that Lantier had a private income, for nothing else could explain the rate at which the Coupeaus were living. No doubt Gervaise was still earning money, but now that she had to provide for two men who were doing nothing, the shop, surely, couldn't be enough; all the more as the business was not so good as it had been, the custom was falling off somewhat; the work-women fooled about from morning to night. As a matter of fact, Lantier paid for nothing, neither board nor keep. The first few months he had made part payment, then he referred vaguely to a considerable sum that was to come to him, which would enable him to pay later on in one lump. Gervaise dared not ask him for a penny. She took the bread, and wine, and meat, on credit. Bills were mounting up all around, at the rate of three or four francs a day. She had not paid a penny to the furniture-dealer, nor to the mason, the carpenter, and the painter. There were complaints on every hand; she was less politely treated in the shops. But she seemed intoxicated by the debts which crowded upon her; she lost her head, chose the most expensive things, gave way more and more to her love of good food, now that she had given up paying for things. All the same, her intentions were perfectly honest; she was always dreaming of earning hundreds of francs a day, she did not quite know how, so as to distribute handfuls of five-franc pieces to all her trades-people. She became more and more entangled, and the further she sank the more she talked of extending her business. However, Clémence had left her at midsummer; there was not enough work for two, and she had to wait weeks for her money. In the midst of this gradual collapse, Coupeau and Lantier had a fine time. The two jolly fellows, up to their chins in meat and drink, grew fat on the ruins of the establishment. They egged one another on to take two servings instead of one, and they patted their stomachs over the dessert for a joke, by way of digesting more quickly.

The great subject of converstaion among the neighbours was the question whether Lantier had really gone back to Gervaise. There were differences of opinion. According to the Lorilleux, Clop-clop did all she could to get back the hatter, but he would have nothing to do with her, he found her too seedy, he had his own girls about town, of a very different phiz from hers. According to the Boches, on the contrary, the laundress, from the very first night, had gone back to her old spouse, as soon as that ninny Coupeau had begun to snore. All that, however you took it, scarcely seemed the thing; but there are so many unpleasant things in life, and much worse than that, that the neighbours came to look upon the *ménage à trois* as quite natural, quite decent even; for there were no quarrels, and propriety was never outraged. Certainly if one were to pry into the interiors in the neighbourhood, you would find much worse things going on. At all events, every-thing went smoothly with the Coupeaus. All three did their little cooking together, drank together, and slept together, in the friendliest way, without keeping the neighbours awake. Then, too, everyone was still charmed by the pleasant ways of Lantier. He wheedled everybody into silence. And, in the general doubt as to his relations with Gervaise, when the fruit-erer denied these relations before the tripe-seller, the latter would intimate that it was really a pity, for if so, it made the Coupeaus less interesting.

Meanwhile Gervaise lived in peace and quietness, so far as this matter was concerned. Things indeed came to such a point that she was accused of being heartless. In the family they could not understand her grudge against her old lover. Madame Lerat, who delighted in mixing herself up with love affairs, came every evening; she always spoke of Lantier as someone quite irresistible, into whose arms the loftiest ladies were bound to fall. Madame Boche would not have answered for her virtue, if she had been ten years younger. A slow, underhand conspiracy seemed to be gradually urging Gervaise onward, as if all these women about her were doing her a service in giving her a lover. But Gervaise could not understand it, she did not see so many charms in Lantier. No doubt he had altered to his advantage; he always wore an overcoat, he had picked up some education in the cafés and political clubs. Only, she who knew him so well, she could look right into his soul, through the windows of his eyes, and she found there many things which gave her a shiver. Well, if it pleased the others so much, why didn't they have a try for him themselves? That was what she declared one day to Virginie, who was the most pressing of them all. Thereupon, Madame Lerat and Virginie, in order to excite her, told her how Lantier and Clémence were carrying on. No, she had seen nothing of it; but if ever she went out, the hatter was sure to take the girl into his room. Now they were seen about together, he apparently went to see her where she was living.

"Well," said the laundress, her voice trembling a little, "what has that to do with me?"

And she looked straight into Virginie's light brown eyes, in which sparkles of gold danced, as in the eyes of cats. Had the woman a spite against her, so anxious was she to make her jealous? But the sempstress put on her most expressionless air, and replied:

"Of course it's nothing to do with you; only you ought to advise him to let the girl alone, or he will certainly get himself into some unpleasantness or other."

The worst of it was that Lantier took encouragement from all this, and changed his manner with Gervaise. Now, when he shook hands with her, he held her hand in his for an instant. He wearied her with the fixity of his gaze, looking at her with audacious eyes, in which she could read clearly enough what he asked for. If he passed behind her, he pressed against her with his knees, breathing on her neck as if to send her to sleep. However, he still bided his time before declaring himself brutally. But one evening, when he was alone with her, he pushed her before him, tremblingly, into a corner, and would have kissed her. It chanced that Goujet entered just at this moment; thereupon she struggled and got away from him. And the three exchanged a few words as if nothing had happened. Goujet's face was quite white, and he looked on the ground, thinking that he had disturbed them, and that she had struggled merely so as not to be kissed in public.

Next day Gervaise moved uneasily about the laundry, very miserable, incapable of ironing a handkerchief; she wanted to see Goujet, and explain to him how Lantier had driven her into the corner. But since Étienne had gone to Lille she dared not enter the forge, for Bec-Salé, otherwise Boit-sans-Soif, greeted her with his eternal snigger. However, that afternoon she gave way to her inclination, and taking an empty basket she went out under the pretext of fetching some petticoats from her customer in the Rue des Portes-Blanches. Then, when she reached the Rue Marcadet, she walked slowly along in front of the bolt manufactory, counting on the good luck of a meeting. Evidently Goujet, on his side, was looking out for her, for she had not been there five minutes when he came out, as if by chance.

"Ah!" he said, with a faint smile, "you are out for a walk; going home, I suppose?"

He said that, in order to say something; Gervaise was going in quite the opposite direction. And they went on together towards Montmartre, side by side, without taking one another's arm. They merely wanted to get as far from the workshop as possible, so as not to look as if they had had a rendezvous outside the door. Both looking on the ground, they followed the rutted pavement in the midst of all the snorting factories. Then, two hundred yards away, instinctively, as if they knew the spot, they turned to the left, still in silence, and made their way to a piece of waste land. Between a steam saw-mill and a button manufactory there was a little patch of green meadow with yellow circles of scorched grass; a goat, tied to a stake, walked round and round, bleating; at the other end a dead tree crumbled away in the sun.

"Why!" murmured Gervaise, "it's almost like country here."

They sat down under the dead tree. The laundress laid her basket at her feet. Over against them the Buttes Montmartre towered up in rows of tall grey and yellow houses, one above another, amidst clusters of stunted foliage; and when they leaned back a little they could see the broad sky, fiery clear above the city, spotted on the north by a flight of little white clouds. But the vivid light dazzled them, they looked along the flat horizon to the chalky distance of the suburbs, they followed the smoke which came in a cloud from the thin chimney of the steam saw-mill, breathing out like great sighs, which seemed to ease the burden that oppressed them.

"Yes," said Gervaise, embarrassed by the silence, "I was passing, I went out. . . ."

After having wished for a chance of explaining things, she found herself unable to say a word. She felt overcome with confusion, and yet she knew that they had come there for that very purpose, to talk over just that; indeed, it was of that that they conversed, without a word said. Last night's incident lay between them like a weight, troubling them.

Then, overcome with a great sadness, with tears in her eyes, she told how Madame Bijard, her washerwoman, had died that morning, after frightful agonies.

"It all came from a kick that Bijard gave her," she said, in a low, monotonous voice. "Her body swelled up; something must have broken inside. For three days she simply lay and writhed. Ah! and there are scoundrels in the alleys who have done nothing like that. But the law would have its hands full indeed, if it took any heed of all the women who are kicked to death by their husbands. A kick more or less hardly counts, does it? when you get them every day. And the poor woman, too, in order to save her man from the scaffold, explained that she had hurt herself by falling on the edge of a tub. She screamed all night long, the night before she died."

The blacksmith was silent, tearing up blades of grass, nervously, with his fingers.

"It's only a fortnight ago," continued Gervaise, "since she weaned her last child, little Jules; and that's one good thing, for the child won't suffer by it. However, there's poor little Lalie with two mites to look after. She isn't eight yet, but she is as serious and sensible as a little mother. And her father is always battering her about too. Well, there are some people who seem born to suffer."

Goujet looked at her, and said suddenly, his lips trembling:

"You pained me very much yesterday; I can't tell you how much you pained me."

Gervaise turned pale, and clasped her hands. But he went on:

"I know that was sure to come. Only you might have trusted me; you might have told me how things were, and not let me think . . ."

He could not finish the sentence. She rose; she saw he believed that she had gone back to Lantier, as the neighbours declared. And stretching out her hands she cried:

"No, no, I swear to you. He had pushed me into a corner, he was going to kiss me, true; but his face never even touched mine, and it was the very first time he ever tried. Oh! I swear, on my life, on my children's, on all that is most sacred to me!"

But the blacksmith shook his head. He distrusted her, for women always deny everything. Then Gervaise, with profound seriousness, said slowly:

"You know me, Monsieur Goujet; you know I don't tell lies. Well, it isn't so, really, on my word of honour. And it never will be, I assure you, never! If it should ever come to that I should be the vilest of the vile, and I should not deserve the friendship of an honest man like you."

She had looked at him so openly, so frankly, as she spoke, that he took her hand and made her sit down again. Now he breathed freely again, he laughed in his heart. It was the first time that he had held her hand like that, clasped in his. Both remained silent. In the sky the flight of white clouds swam slowly across, like a slow flight of swans. In the corner of the field the goat had turned in their direction, and gazed at them, bleating softly, at long regular intervals. And, hand in hand, their eyes full of tenderness, they gazed into the distance, off to the grey slope of Montmartre, between the high forest of factory chimneys that cut off the horizon, here in these dingy and desolate outskirts, where the little green clumps of trees about the low taverns brought tears into their eyes.

"Your mother doesn't like me, I know," went on Gervaise, in a low voice. "Don't say no. We owe you such a lot of money."

But he stopped her brutally, squeezing her hand till he hurt her; he would not have her speak of money. Then he hesitated, and at last stammered out:

"Listen to me. I have been wanting to say something to you for a long time. You are not happy. My mother is sure that things are going badly with you."

He stopped, then in a choking voice he said:

"Well, we must go away together."

She looked at him for a moment without understanding, surprised by this abrupt declaration of love—a love on which he had never opened his lips.

"How do you mean?" she asked.

"Yes," he went on, looking down, "we'll go away and live somewhere, in Belgium if you like. It is almost my own country. If we both work, we shall soon be quite well off."

At that she went red all over. If he had taken her in his arms and kissed her, she would have been less taken aback. He was an odd chap, certainly, to propose an elopement, like what goes on in novels and in the upper classes. She was quite used to seeing workmen, all about her, making love to married women; but they did not so much as take them to Saint-Denis; it went on on the spot, and very straight indeed.

"Oh! Monsieur Goujet, Monsieur Goujet!" she murmured, without finding another word.

"Come now, you see, there will be only the two of us then," he went on. "Other people distress me, do you see? When I like anyone, I can't bear to see them with others."

But she collected herself, she refused, quite composedly.

"It isn't possible, Monsieur Goujet. It would be very wrong. Don't you see, I am married, I have children. I know quite well that you care for me, and that I give you pain. Only, we should repent of it, we should get no pleasure out of it. I too care for you, and I care for you too much to let you do anything so foolish. For it would be foolish indeed. No, no, it is better to stay as we are. We respect each other, we feel for one another. That's a good deal; it has helped me many a time. When one keeps straight, in our position, one is well repaid for it."

He shook his head as he listened to her. He approved of what she said, he could not contradict her. All at once, there in broad daylight, he took her in his arms, he crushed her in his arms, he kissed her furiously on the neck, as if he would eat the skin. Then he let her go, asking nothing further; and he said no more of his love. She shook herself, she was not at all angry, she felt that they had both earned that little pleasure.

Meanwhile the blacksmith, quivering from head to foot turned away from her, so as to keep down his intense desire to take her in his arms again; and he went down on his hands and knees, and, not knowing what to do with his hands, he began picking dandelions, and throwing them from some way off into her basket. Some splendid golden dandelions grew there, in the midst of the scorched grass. Little by little it amused him, quieting him down. He picked the flowers delicately with his great fingers, stiffened by the handling of hammers, and threw them one by one; and his eyes laughed, the eyes of a good faithful dog, when he did not miss his aim. The laundress leant up against the dead tree, peaceful and happy, raising her voice as she spoke, on account of the shrill hiss of the steam saw-mill. When they left the waste ground, side by side, talking of Étienne, who liked it very much at Lille, the basket in her arms was full of dandelions.

At the bottom of her heart, Gervaise was not so confident of herself before Lantier as she said. She had indeed quite made up her mind not to allow him to touch her with the tip of his finger; but she feared, if he were ever to touch her, her old cowardice, her easy-going way of taking things, of wanting to please people. Lantier, however, had not made any other attempt. He had been alone with her several times, and had done nothing. He seemed now to be occupied with the tripe-seller, a woman of forty-five, very well preserved. Gervaise referred to the tripe-seller before Goujet, so as to reassure him. When Virginie and Madame Lerat started on their eulogies of the hatter, she replied that he could get on all right without any admiration on her part, as all the neighbours seemed to have a fancy for him.

Coupeau, for his part, declared everywhere that Lantier was a real good fellow. People could jaw about them as much

as they pleased; he knew what was what, and didn't care a
straw for all their chatter, when he had the right on his side.
When the three of them went out together on Sundays, he
insisted on his wife and Lantier going in front, arm in arm,
just out of bravado; and he glared at everybody, ready to hit
out right and left if there was the slightest joking on his
account. Certainly, he found Lantier a little stuck-up, accused
him of being a molly-coddle in regard to drinks, and sneered
at him because he knew how to read, and talked like a lawyer.
But, apart from that, he declared him a damned good fellow.
You couldn't find a couple of better chaps if you hunted all
through La Chapelle. In a word, they understood one another;
they were bound to be friends. And friendship with a man is
more substantial than love with a woman.

Then, it must be added, Coupeau and Lantier were almost
always on the bust. Lantier was now accustomed to borrow
money from Gervaise—ten francs, twenty francs—whenever
there was any money about. It was always for his important
business. Then, on those days, he got Coupeau to come
along with him, talked of a long distance he had to go, and
then, sitting opposite one another in the corner of some
restaurant near, they were soon over head and ears in dishes
that one can't get at home, washing them down with expensive
wine. The tinsmith would have preferred to do the thing with
less splash, but he was much impressed by the hatter's swell
tastes, his way of finding extraordinary names of sauces on the
bill of fare. You couldn't imagine how dainty and particular
he was. They were all like that, apparently, in the south. He
would have nothing too heating; he argued over every stew
from the point of view of health, sending back a dish when it
was too salt or too peppery for him. It was still worse in regard
to draughts; he was always in a blue funk about them. He
would call the whole establishment over the coals if a door
was left ajar. And, with all that, he was very close, and would
give the waiters two sous for a dinner of seven or eight
francs. They trembled before him, all the same, and the two
of them were well known from Batignolles to Belleville, all
along the outer boulevards. They went to the Grande Rue
des Batignolles, where they served tripe à la mode de Caen on
little braziers. In the lower part of Montmartre they found
the best oysters in the quarter at the "Ville de Bar-le-Duc".
When they found their way to the top of the Butte, they
would have jugged hare at the "Moulin de la Galette". In

the Rue des Martyrs, the "Lilas" made a specialty of calves'
head, whilst in the Chaussée Clignancourt, the restaurants of
the "Lion d'Or" and the "Deux Marronniers" provided
stewed kidneys that were simply delicious. But more often
they went leftward, Belleville way, and had their table
reserved for them at the "Vendanges de Bourgogne", at the
"Cadran Bleu", at the "Capucin", well-known houses where
you could ask for anything and everything with your eyes
shut. These were little jaunts on the sly, to which they made
covert allusions next day, while they trifled over Gervaise's
potatoes. One day, Lantier brought a woman with him to one
of the arbours of the "Moulin de la Galette", and Coupeau
left them together after the dessert.

Naturally, one cannot revel and work at the same time.
Since Lantier's entrance into the household, the tinsmith,
already idle about half his time, had never touched a tool.
If, finding himself in straits, he did get a job, the other man
would go round to the yard, and jeer at finding him strung
on the end of his knotted rope like a smoked ham, calling to
him to come down and have a drink. That settled it, the
tinsmith left his job, and started off on a booze which would
last for several days and weeks. Oh! a famous booze, a general
survey of all the pubs of the quarter; the night's drunkenness
slept off at midday, and taken on again at night; drink
following drink into the depths of night, like the lights of a
feast, till the last candle went out with the last glass. The
hatter always pulled himself up in time. He left the other to
get tight, and came back smiling, with his amiable air. When
he got a bit screwed himself, he did it decently, without
letting anyone see it. If you knew him well, you could just
distinguish it by a little contraction of the eyes, and by his
more venturesome manners with women. The tinsmith, on
the contrary, became disgusting, and now could scarcely
drink without getting into a beastly state.

Thus in the early part of September, Coupeau went on a
booze which ended disagreeably enough both for him and
others. The day before, he had got a job. This time Lantier
was full of fine sentiments; he sang the praises of work, work
which ennobles man. He even got up before daybreak, in
order to accompany his friend, and do honour, in him, to the
workman really worthy of the name. But, on reaching the
"Petite Civette", which was just opening, they went in to have
a prune, one only, with the sole purpose of drinking to their

firm resolutions of good conduct. Opposite the counter, on a bench, with his back against the wall, sat Bibi-la-Grillade, sulkily smoking his pipe.

"Hallo! Bibi's off on his rounds," said Coupeau. "Feel slack, old pal?"

"No," said the workman, stretching himself. "It's the beastly people you work for. I gave mine the chuck yesterday. All sots and cads."

And Bibi-la-Grillade accepted a prune. He was evidently there waiting for someone to come and stand drinks. However, Lantier stood up for the masters; they were sometimes very badly treated, he ought to know something about it, with his experience of business. It was the workmen who are a jolly bad lot; always boozing, shirking work, leaving you in the lurch when you had a pressing order, turning up again when they were cleaned out. He had for instance, a little Picard, whose hobby was to be trotted about in cabs; as soon as he had his week's money, he would take cabs for days together. That was a nice fancy on the part of a workman! Then, all at once, Lantier began to attack the masters. Oh! he had his eyes open, he told everybody the truth straight. A dirty lot, after all, using you shamelessly for their own ends, making their living out of you. He, thank God! could sleep with a clear conscience; he had always treated his men as his friends, preferring not to gain his millions like certain others.

"Come along now, old chap," he said, turning to Coupeau. "We're on our best behaviour, mustn't be late."

Bibi-la-Grillade, his arms hanging limply by his side, came out with them. Outside it was scarcely light, a sort of twilight, rendered all the dingier in the reflection of the muddy pavement; it had rained the night before; it was very mild. The gas-lamps had just been put out; the street wavered in shadow, filling already with the concourse of workmen going down towards the city. Coupeau, bag on back, marched with the resolute air of a man who means business, for once in a while. He turned and asked:

"Bibi, do you care to come along with me? I was told to bring a mate with me if I could."

"Thanks," replied Bibi-la-Grillade, "not taking any! You'd better suggest it to Mes-Bottes, who was looking out for something yesterday. Wait a minute Mes-Bottes is sure to be in there."

And as they reached the bottom of the street they saw

Mes-Bottes, sure enough, inside old Colombe's. Despite
the early hour, the bar was already a-glare, the shutters
down, the gas lit. Lantier waited at the door, telling
Coupeau to be as quick as possible, for they had only just
ten minutes.

"What! you are going to that dirty spy of a Bourguignon's,"
cried Mes-Bottes, when the tinsmith had spoken to him.
"You won't find me in that hole again! No, I'd rather
starve till next year. Why, old chap, you won't stay there
three days, I'm pretty sure of that."

"Such a dirty hole as all that?" asked Coupeau uneasily.

"Dirtiest hole you ever saw. You aren't allowed to move.
The boss is after you every minute. And his ways too, and his
missus, who treats you as a tippler, and a shop where you
aren't allowed to spit! I sent them packing the very first
night, you may be sure."

"Good! now I know beforehand, I'm not likely to eat a
bushel of salt while I'm with them. I'll go and see what
they're like this morning; but if the boss isn't to my taste, I'll
pick him up and seat him on his missus, as neat as a pair of
soles!"

The tinsmith shook his mate's hand by way of thanks for
his information, and was on the point of going, when Mes-
Bottes grew angry. Blast it all! was the Bourguignon going to
hinder them from having a glass together? Wasn't a man a
man, eh? The boss could very well afford to wait five minutes.
Lantier came in to have his share in the drink, and the four
men stood in front of the bar. But Mes-Bottes, his shoes down
at heel, his blouse black with dirt, his cap flattened down on
the back of his head, bawled vigorously, and rolled his eyes,
as if he were the lord and master of the bar. He had been
proclaimed king of sots, and emperor of gormandizers, for
having eaten a salad of live cockchafers, and bitten a piece
out of a dead cat.

"I say you old Borgia!" he cried to old Colombe, "give
me some brandy, some of your three-star mule's piss."

And when old Colombe, pale and quiet in his blue knitted
vest, had poured out the four glasses, they were drained at a
gulp, so as not to let them get flat.

"That does you good, eh, where it goes down," murmured
Bibi-la-Grillade.

But the creature Mes-Bottes had a droll tale to tell. Last
Friday he was so drunk that his mates had fastened his pipe

into his mouth with a handful of plaster. It was enough to
finish up anyone else; as for him, he simply gloried in it.

"Do these gentlemen require any more?" asked old
Colombe, in his oily voice.

"Yes, another drink all round," said Lantier. "It's my turn."

They began to talk of women. Bibi-la-Grillade, last Sunday,
had sent his wife to Montrouge, to stay with an aunt. Coupeau
inquired after *Malle des Indes*, a Chaillot laundress, known in
the establishment. They were just going to drink, when
Mes-Bottes yelled out to Goujet and Lorilleux, who were
passing. They came to the door, but refused to enter. The
blacksmith didn't feel inclined for anything; the chain-maker,
haggard and shivering, thrust the chains he was carrying deep
down into his pocket; and he coughed, excusing himself on
the ground that a drop of brandy quite upset him.

"Humbug!" muttered Mes-Bottes. "They're only off to
have a drink on the sly."

He had no sooner lifted the glass to his lips than he went
for old Colombe.

"You old cheat, you've changed the bottle! No fake with
me, if you please!"

The light was now broadening, a doubtful glimmer began
to make its way into the bar, and the landlord turned out the
gas. Coupeau, meanwhile, made excuses on behalf of his
brother-in-law, who couldn't drink; it was not his fault, he
even approved of Goujet, for it was very lucky for you if you
were never thirsty. And he spoke of setting out for his work,
when Lantier, with his grand air, read him a lesson: he must
stand drinks, in his turn, before decamping; you can't leave
your friends in the lurch, even at the call of duty.

"How long is he going to worry us with his work?" cried
Mes-Bottes.

"This gentleman stands drinks, then?" said old Colombe to
Coupeau.

Coupeau paid his turn, but when it came to the turn of
Bibi-la-Grillade, he leaned over the bar and whispered to the
landlord, who mildly shook his head. Mes-Bottes saw what
was meant, and returned to his invectives against that old
gawk of a Colombe. What! an old ragamuffin like him to turn
crusty with a mate! Every booze-seller lets you have tick. You
had to come into low pubs like that if you wanted to be
insulted! The landlord took it all very quietly, leaning on his
great fists, on the edge of the bar and reiterating politely:

"Lend the gentleman some money; that will be more simple."

"Damnation! well, I'll lend it to him," yelled Mes-Bottes. "Here! Bibi, chuck the tin into his lying old jaws!"

Then, fairly started, and worried by the bag that Coupeau still carried on his back, he continued, turning to the tin-smith:

"You look like a nurse. Put down the kid. Makes you hump-backed."

Coupeau hestitated an instant; then, calmly, as if he had decided after mature consideration, he put his bag on the ground, saying:

"It is too late now. I'll go in after lunch. I can say that the missus had the colic. Look here, old Colombe, I'll leave my tools under the seat here, and I'll come for them at twelve."

Lantier nodded approval of this arrangement. People should work, without a doubt; only when you are with friends, politeness before everything. An inclination for a good time had gradually tickled the fancy of all four; their hands hung heavily, and they looked enquiringly at one another. And, once having decided that there were five hours of idleness before them, they were seized with an explosive joy, slapped one another on the back, addressed one another in the most affectionate terms, Coupeau especially, who seemed to have grown younger now that such a load was taken off his mind, and who called the others "old cock!" They had another drink all round, then they went on to the "Puce qui renifle", a little pub where there was a billiard-table. The hatter was at first inclined to turn up his nose, because the place was none too swell; the brandy cost a franc a bottle, ten sous a pint, in two glasses, and the people who frequented the place had made such a mess on the billiard-table that the balls were stuck to it. But, the game once started, Lantier, who had a remarkably fine stroke, became as amiable and elegant as usual, puffing out his chest, and accompanying his cannoning with a graceful movement of the hips.

When it came to the hour for lunch, an idea occurred to Coupeau. He stamped his feet, crying:

"Let's go and hunt up Bec-Salé. I know where he works. We'll take him along to have some calves' feet with poulette sauce at old Madame Louis'."

The idea was applauded. Yes, Bec-Salé, otherwise Boit-sans-Soif, must come and have something to eat. They set out. The streets were yellow, a little rain fell; but they were too well warmed inside to mind this little sprinkling. Coupeau led the way to the bolt factory in the Rue Marcadet. As they got there a good half-hour before the time for coming out, the tinsmith gave two sous to a boy to go in and tell Bec-Salé that his missus wasn't well, and wanted to see him at once. The blacksmith appeared immediately, with an air of great calmness, scenting a lay of some sort.

"Ah! you guzzlers!" he said, when he discovered them hidden away in a doorway. "I knew what was up. Well! what are we to have today?"

At old Madame Louis', while they munched their calves' feet, they returned to the attack on the masters. Bec-Salé, otherwise Boit-sans-Soif, mentioned that there was an urgent order at his place. Oh! the boss was a decent enough chap; if you didn't turn up, he was good-tempered all the same, and he ought to think himself very lucky when you did turn up. And at all events there was no danger that any master would turn off Bec-Salé, otherwise Boit-sans-Soif, for you wouldn't easily find other chaps of his metal. After the calves' feet they had an omelette. Each had his bottle to himself. Old Madame Louis got her wine from Auvergne, wine as red as blood, wine you could cut with your knife. They began to grow merry over it.

"Who cares for the bloody boss, I should like to know," cried Bec-Salé at dessert. "Hasn't he had the cheek to hang up a bell in his place? A bell! all very well for slaves! Well, it can ring as long as it likes today. May I be damned if you catch me at that anvil again! Here have I been sticking at it for five days; it's about time I had a change. If he blows me up for it, I'll send him to Jerico."

"Now," said Coupeau, with an air of importance, "I have to leave you, I must be off to work. I promised my wife I would. Good luck to you, mates, I only wish I could stay."

The others laughed at him. But he seemed so decided, that they all went along with him, when he spoke of going to fetch his tools from old Colombe's. He took out his bag from under the seat, and placed it before him while they had a final drink. At one o'clock they were still continuing the round of drinks. Then Coupeau, with an air of boredom, stowed away the tools under the seat again; they were in his way, he could not get to the bar without stumbling over them. It was too absurd, he would go to Bourguignon's tomorrow. The four

others, who were arguing over the question of wages, were
not at all surprised when the tinsmith, without a word of
explanation, proposed that they should take a little stroll
along the boulevards, to stretch their legs a bit. The rain had
ceased. The little stroll took them no further than two hundred
yards, lounging along all in a row, and in silence, rather
overcome by the fresh air, and bored at finding themselves
out of doors. Slowly, without even a nudge from one to another,
they turned instinctively up the Rue des Poissonniers, where
they went into Francois' to have a drink. They really needed
it to set them up. It was too dismal in the street; it was so
muddy you'd hardly turn a policeman out of doors. Lantier
led the way into the back parlour, a little room, in which
there was one table, separated from the bar-room by a
partition of frosted glass. He generally chose the back parlours,
because it was more comfortable. Wasn't it all right for the
others? You might be in your own house; you could have a
snooze if you liked without being in anybody's way. He asked
for the paper, spread it out to its full extent, and looked it up
and down with knitted brows. Coupeau and Mes-Bottes began
playing piquet. There were two bottles and five glasses on
the table.

"Well, what does it say in your paper, eh?" asked Bibi-
la-Grillade.

Lantier did not reply at once. Then, without raising his
eyes:

"I'm looking at the parliamentary news. Pretty Republicans
they are, those blasted lazybones of the Left! Do they think
the people sends them up to spout their sugary rot? Here's a
gentleman who believes in God, and makes love to the
beastly ministers! For my part, if I were nominated, I would
stand up in the House and say, 'Shit!' Not a word more.
That's just what I think."

"You know that Badingue fell out with his missus the
other day, before the whole Court," remarked Bec-Salé,
otherwise Boit-sans-Soif. "My word! and about nothing, a
mere tiff! Badingue was a bit screwed."

"Shut up with your politics!" cried the tinsmith. "Read
about the murders; that's more fun."

And going back to his game, he called:

"I have three nines and three queens. Always queens!"

They emptied their glasses. Lantier began to read aloud:

" 'A horrible crime has recently thrown consternation over

the whole Commune of Gaillon (Seine-et-Marne). A father has been murdered by his son with a spade, in order to steal thirty sous——' "

They all uttered a cry of horror. There was a man, now, whom they would like to go and see guillotined. No, the guillotine wasn't enough; he ought to be chopped in bits. A story of infanticide revolted them equally; but the hatter, looking at it from the moral point of view, defended the woman by throwing all the blame on the seducer; for if some brute of a man hadn't got the poor woman into the family way, she would never have shoved the new-born down the water-closet. But what delighted them were the exploits of the Marquis de T——, who had been attacked by three black-guards as he came away from a ball at two o'clock in the morning, on the Boulevard des Invalides; without so much as taking off his gloves, he had got rid of the first two with a blow of the head in the pit of the stomach, and had marched the third man off to prison by the ear. What a wrist the man must have had! Pity he was a nobleman!

"Now listen to this," continued Lantier. "This is the society news. 'The eldest daughter of the Comtesse de Brétigny is about to be married to the young Baron de Valancay, aide-de-camp to His Majesty. Among the wedding presents there are more than three hundred thousand francs' worth of lace——' "

"Well what of that?" interrupted Bibi-la-Grillade. "We don't want to know the colour of their chemises. Lace won't help her, she'll see the moon just the same through the same hole as the rest."

As Lantier seemed on the point of going on with his reading Bec-Salé, otherwise Boit-sans-Soif, snatched the paper out of his hands and put it under him saying:

"Enough of that now! I'll dispose of it for you. That's all a paper's good for."

Meanwhile Mes-Bottes, who was considering his hand, thumped the table triumphantly. He made ninety-three points.

"The Revolution!" he cried. "Quinte major, twenty; tierce major, diamonds, twenty-three; three of kings, twenty-six; three of knaves, twenty-nine; three aces, ninety-two; and I play Year One of the Republic, ninety-three!"

"You're done, old chap," cried the others to Coupeau.

They ordered two more bottles. The glasses were now never

empty, and they grew more and more elevated, By five
o'clock it became quite an orgy; Lantier held his tongue, and
waited his moment to slip away; when people get to the point
of shouting at one another and spilling the wine over the
floor, he was quite out of his element. And, indeed, Coupeau
had just risen to make the drunkard's cross. On his head he
pronounced Montparnasse; on the right shoulder, Menilmonte;
on the left shoulder, La Courtille; between his legs, Bagnolet;
and in the pit of the stomach, *lapin sauté*, three times. The
hatter seized the occasion of the uproar caused by this little
ceremony and quietly made his escape, without anyone even
noticing that he had gone. He was himself by this time half
seas over. But, once outside, he pulled himself together, and
quietly returned to the laundry, where he told Gervaise that
he had left Coupeau with friends.

Two days passed. The tinsmith had not returned. He was
on the booze somewhere about, no one knew exactly where.
Some, however, said that they had seen him at old Baquet's,
at the "Papillon", at the "Petit Bonhomme qui tousse".
Only, some declared that he was alone, whilst others had met
him in company with seven or eight tipplers like himself.
Gervaise shrugged her shoulders with an air of resignation.
Fine habits these were! She did not run after him, she even
made a détour if she saw him in at a pub, so as not to anger
him, and she was always expecting him to return, listening at
night to hear if he wasn't snoring outside the door. He slept
on a dust-heap, on a seat, on a piece of waste land, in the
gutter. Then, next day, having hardly slept off last night's
drunkenness, he set off again on a new round of refreshers, a
furious reel of little glasses, big glasses, and bottles; losing
sight of his companions and finding them again, wandering
about in a muddle-headed sort of way, seeing the street dance
before his eyes, seeing the night fall and the day dawn
without any other thought than to drink himself drunk, and
to sleep it off on the spot. The sleeping it off was the finishing
touch. On the second day Gervaise went to old Colombe's bar
to make enquiries; they had seen him there five times, that
was all they could say. She had to content herself with bringing
back his tools, which had been left under the seat.

Lantier, that evening, seeing her somewhat out of sorts,
offered to take her to the music-hall, just for a change. At
first she declined, she was not in a laughing humour. But for
that, she would not have said no, for the hatter made the

suggestion in too frank a manner for her to suspect anything
wrong. He seemed touched by her distress, and showed himself quite paternal. Never had Coupeau stayed out for two
whole nights before. And, despite herself, she would go to the
door every five minutes, iron in hand, looking up and down
the street to see if he was anywhere to be seen. It was merely
something in her legs, she said, that would not let her be still.
Coupeau might break his leg, or fall under a cart and stay
there, for all she cared; she would be jolly well rid of him;
she had no feeling left, she declared, for a dirty brute like that.
But it was very annoying to be always wondering if he was
going to come in or not; and when the gas was lit, and Lantier
spoke to her again of the music-hall, she accepted. After all,
it would be very silly to refuse herself a pleasure when her
husband had been on the loose for the last three days. Since he
wouldn't come in, well, she would go out too. The house
might catch fire if it liked. She would have liked to set it
ablaze herself, so heavily did the dreariness of her life begin
to weigh upon her.

They had a hasty dinner, and before she set out, at eight
o'clock, Gervaise told old Madame Coupeau and Nana they
had better go to bed straight away. The shop was shut up;
she went out by the back way, and gave the key to Madame
Boche, saying that if her old man turned up, she might be
good enough to put him off to bed. The hatter waited for her
under the porch, in his best things, whistling a tune, She had
on her silk dress. They went slowly along the pavement,
leaning upon one another, lit up from time to time by the
lighted windows of shops; they were talking in low voices,
smilingly.

The music-hall was on the Boulevard de Rochechouart,
a little old café that had been enlarged by a wooden erection
over part of the court. At the door there was a string of glass
globes, making an illuminated portico. Long posters, pasted
upon boards, were placed on the ground, just out of the
gutter.

"Here we are," said Lantier. "Tonight, first appearance of
Mademoiselle Amanda, song and dance artist."

But he caught sight of Bibi-la-Grillade, who was also
reading the poster. Bibi had one eye in mourning, he had
evidently got into hot water the night before.

"Well, and where's Coupeau?" asked the hatter, looking
round him, "have you lost Coupeau!"

"Oh! we've had a nice time of it, since yesterday," replied the other. "We had a bit of a scuffle coming out of old Baquet's. I don't like to see the mawleys on the job. You see, it was through old Baquet's boy we got into a row, he wanted to make us pay twice for one bottle. So I slung my hook, and had a bit of a snooze."

He still yawned, he had slept for ten hours. But he was quite sober, had a hang-dog look about him, and his old jacket was covered with bits of fluff; he had evidently gone to bed in his clothes.

"Then you don't know where my husband is, Monsieur?" asked the laundress.

"No, not in the least. It was five o'clock when we came out of Baquet's. Very likely he went down the street. Yes, I do almost fancy I saw him go into the "Papillon" with a cabby. Oh, what fools! One feels fit for nothing!"

Lantier and Gervaise spent a very pleasant evening at the music-hall. At eleven, when the place shut, they strolled homewards, taking their time over it. There was a sharp, clear cold; the company went off in bands; and one could hear shrieks of laughter coming from the girls under the shadow of the trees, as the men made up to them a little too closely. Lantier hummed one of Mademoiselle Amanda's songs, "C'est dans l'nez qu'ça me chatouille". Gervaise, scarcely knowing what she was doing joined in the refrain. She had been very hot. Then, too, the two drinks she had had made her feel a little upset, especially with the smoke of pipes and the odour of the packed mass of people. But she had been particularly impressed by Mademoiselle Amanda. Never could she have ventured to appear in public so naked as all that. But, in all justice, one must admit that anyone would envy her such a skin. And she listened, with a sensual curiosity, to the details which Lantier gave concerning the person in question, with the air of one who could have told more if he pleased.

"They're all asleep," said Gervaise; and she had to ring three times before the Boches released the catch.

The door opened, but the porch was in darkness, and when she rapped at the window of the lodge to call for her key, the *concierge*, half asleep, had some story to tell, which at first she could not make out. However, she understood at last that Poisson the policeman had brought back Coupeau in a very queer state, and that the key ought to be in the lock.

"Ugh!" murmured Lantier when they had entered, "what has he been up to? It stinks like poison."

And indeed it stank strong. Gervaise, hunting about for the matches, stepped in something sloppy. When she had lit a candle, they had a pretty sight before them. Coupeau had thrown up everything; it was all over the room; the bed was plastered with it, and the carpet, right to the very chest of drawers, which was all splashed. And he had fallen off the bed, where Poisson must have laid him, and snored there, in the very midst of his own filth. He sprawled at full length, wallowing in it like a pig, one cheek all dabbled in it, breathing a foul breath out of his open mouth, sweeping with his hair, already grey, the pool that had formed all round his head.

"Oh! the beast! the beast!" cried Gervaise, indignant and exasperated. "He has messed everything. A dog wouldn't have done that, a dead dog is a decenter sight than that."

Neither dared move, not knowing where to put their foot. Never before had the tinsmith come back in such a state, or put the room in such a filthy condition. And the sight struck a rude blow to whatever sentiment his wife might still have for him. Before, when he had come back tipsy, she had excused him, and had not been disgusted. But this was too much, it almost made her sick. She would not have touched him with tongs. The mere idea of the skin of this blackguard touching hers revolted her, as if she had been expected to lie down by the side of a dead man, dead of some foul disease.

"I must sleep somewhere," she murmured, "I can't sleep in the street. I'd better get over him."

And she tried to step over the drunkard, and had to catch hold of the corner of the chest of drawers, so as not to slip in the filth. Coupeau completely blocked up the bed. Then Lantier, who laughed to himself as he saw that she would not sleep sound on her pillow that night, took her hand, and said in a low and ardent voice:

"Gervaise, listen to me, Gervaise."

But she understood what he meant, she wrenched herself free, all aghast, and dropping, like him, into the familiar second person, as of old.

"No, let me go. I implore you, Auguste, go to your room. I shall manage, I will get into bed at the foot."

"Gervaise, look here, don't be silly," he said, "The smell is too bad, you can't stay here. Come! What are you afraid of? *He* can't hear us!"

She struggled, she shook her head energetically. In her confusion, as if to show that she meant to stay there, she undressed, flung her silk dress over a chair, stripped to her chemise and petticoat, all white, her neck and arms bare. Her bed was her own, wasn't it? she would sleep in her own bed. Twice she tried to find a clean corner, and to make her way there. But Lantier would not let her go, he seized her by the waist, saying things to set her blood a-fire. Ah! she was in a fix, indeed, with a good-for-nothing of a husband before her, who kept her out of her honest bed, and a low brute behind her, who only wanted to take advantage of her distress to get her back again! As the hatter raised his voice, she begged him to be silent. And she listened, straining her ears towards the little room where Nana and old Madame Coupeau slept. The child and the old woman seemed to be asleep; they breathed loudly.

"Auguste, let me go, you will wake them!" she went on, clasping her hands. "Do be reasonable. Some other day— somewhere else. . . . Not here, before my girl."

He said nothing, only smiled; and he gave her a long, slow kiss on the ear, as he used once to kiss her, to tease and dizzy her. Then she felt her strength leave her, the air seemed to buzz, a long shiver ran through her body. Still she made one step more. But she had to draw back; it was impossible, the repulsion was too strong. The smell was so insupportable that she would herself have been sick between the clothes. Coupeau, as though on a bed of down, prostrate with drink, slept off his liquor, absolutely dead drunk. The whole street might have come in and embraced his wife, he would never have moved a muscle.

"So much the worse," she faltered; "it is his fault. I can't. . . . Oh, God! oh, God! he turns me out of bed—I haven't a bed to go to! No, I can't!—it is his fault!"

She trembled, she knew not what she was doing. And, as Lantier pushed her before him into his room, the face of Nana appeared at the glass door of the little room, behind one of the panes. The child had just woken up, and she got up softly in her nightdress, pale with sleep. She saw her father wallowing in his vomit; then, with her face against the glass, she stood there waiting until her mother's petticoat had disappeared into the other man's room opposite. She stood there very seriously. She opened her eyes wide, vicious young eyes, lit now with a sensual curiosity.

CHAPTER NINE

THAT winter, old Madame Coupeau came near dying in a fit of choking. Every year, in the month of December, her asthma was sure to lay her on her back for two or three weeks. She wasn't as young as she once was; she would be seventy-three come St. Anthony. And she was now quite broken down; a mere nothing would bring her to death's door, though she was still plump and substantial. The doctor declared that her cough would carry her off some fine day before you could say Jack Robinson.

When she was laid up in bed, old Madame Coupeau got as spiteful as a cat. It must be said that the little room where she slept with Nana was not very lively. Between the child's bed and hers there was just room for two chairs. The paper on the walls, an old faded grey paper, hung in strips. The little round window near the ceiling let in only a faint and cavernous light. It made you feel old enough in there, especially when you could hardly breathe. At night, when she lay awake, she could hear the child breathing in her sleep, and that was some sort of distraction. But, by day, as people couldn't keep her company from morning to night, she grumbled, and wept, and said over and over for hours together, rolling her head to and fro on the pillow:

"Oh God! how miserable I am! Oh God! how miserable I am! They've shut me up in prison, they'll kill me in prison!"

And whenever a visitor came to see her, Virginie or Madame Boche, and asked her how she was, she would make no reply, but would begin at once upon the chapter of complaints.

"Ah! it's dearly bought, is the bread that I eat here! No, no, I shouldn't suffer so much among strangers! Look here, I wanted a cup of broth, and they brought me a whole jugful, so as to make out I drink too much. And Nana, too, the child I brought up myself, she runs off barefoot in the morning, and I never see her again. One would think I smelt bad. But at night, though, she sleeps as sound as you like; she never wakes up to know if I'm in pain. You see, I'm in the way; they're only waiting for me to be gone. I haven't even a son now, that wretched little laundress has taken him away from me. She would beat me, she would finish me off, if she wasn't afraid of the law."

And indeed Gervaise was at times somewhat rough with her. The business was going badly, their tempers were all souring, they sent one another about their business at the least excuse. Coupeau, one morning when he had a head, had cried, "The old woman is always saying she is dying, and yet she never dies," an expression which had struck old Madame Coupeau to the heart. They complained of what she cost, remarking calmly that they would spend a lot less if she were not there. But on her side, too, she went on in a way she ought not to have done. Thus, when she saw her eldest daughter Madame Lerat, she made a great fuss, accusing her son and daughter-in-law of letting her die of starvation, all for the sake of getting a piece of twenty sous, which she spent on little delicacies for herself. And she kicked up an awful rumpus with the Lorilleux, telling them how their ten francs were spent on the laundress's whims and fancies, on new bonnets, on cakes eaten on the sly, on dirtier things still, things that one couldn't allude to. Two or three times she nearly brought the family to blows. Sometimes she was for one, sometimes for another; till at last things got in a regular mess.

When she was at her worst, that winter, one afternoon when Madame Lorilleux and Madame Lerat had met at her bedside, old Madame Coupeau blinked her eyes at them to make them bend down. She could scarcely speak. She whispered, with difficulty:

"Here's a nice thing. I heard them the other night. Yes, yes, Clop-clop and the hatter. And they're going it. Coupeau's all right. 'Tis a nice thing."

She related in short phrases, coughing and choking, that her son had come in dead drunk one night. Then as she could not sleep, she had heard every sound, Clop-clop's bare feet on the floor, the hissing voice of the hatter calling her, the door of communication opened softly, and the rest. It must have lasted till daylight, but she did not know exactly when, because, despite her efforts, she had finally gone off to sleep.

"The most shocking part of it is, that Nana must have been able to hear it too," she continued. "And, as a matter of fact, she was restless all night, she who generally sleeps so sound; she tossed and turned as if she had live coals in her bed."

The two women did not seem at all surprised.

"Good heavens!" murmured Madame Lorilleux, "it's no doubt been going on from the first day. If it pleases Coupeau we have no cause to complain. Only, it is not at all to the credit of the family."

"For my part," explained Madame Lerat, pursing up her lips, "if I had been there I should have given them a fright, I should have called out something, no matter what: 'I see you,' or, 'Here are the gendarmes.' A doctor's servant told me that her master had told her that that could strike a woman dead, at a certain moment. And if she were struck there and then it would have served her right, she would have been punished where she had sinned."

The whole neighbourhood soon knew that Gervaise went into Lantier's room every night. Madame Lorilleux, before the neighbours, showed a violent indignation; she compassionated her brother, a ninny who let his wife paint him yellow from head to foot; and, on her own account, if she ever went into such a dirty hole, it was simply on account of her poor mother, who was forced to live in the midst of such abominations. Thereupon the neighbours fell with one accord upon Gervaise. It must be she who had led the hatter astray. You could see it in her eyes. But, despite these evil rumours, Lantier, the sly dog, remained popular, because he still kept up his swell airs with everybody, walking along in the street reading the newspaper, polite and attentive to the ladies, always with sweets and flowers to give away. As for him, no doubt he took what was given him; a man was a man, he couldn't always be expected to resist women who throw themselves at his head. But as for her, she had no excuse; she was a disgrace to the Rue de la Goutte-d'Or. And the Lorilleux, as godfather and godmother, got Nana to come and give them the details. When they questioned her in a roundabout way, the child put on an air of ignorance, and lowered her long soft eyelashes, as if to extinguish the flame of her eyes.

In the midst of all this public indignation Gervaise went on her way quietly, only a little weary and sleepy. At the beginning, it seemed to her that she was very wicked, very shameless, and she had a disgust of herself. When she came from Lantier's room she washed her hands, she damped a towel and rubbed her shoulders, almost hard enough to rub the skin off, as if she would cleanse herself from her pollution. If Coupeau began to fool about with her, she would fire up and run shivering to dress herself at the other end of the laundry; nor would she allow the hatter to touch her, when her husband had just given her a kiss. She would fain have had a change of skin for the change of men. But gradually she got accustomed to it. It was too fatiguing to make herself clean every time. Her instincts of idleness had their way with her, her desire to be happy brought her to get all the happiness she could out of all these bothers. She made allowances for herself and for others; only anxious to arrange things so as not to give anybody annoyance. So long as her husband and her lover were quite content, so long as the household went on its accustomed way, and everything was jolly and comfortable from morning to night, and everyone took life easily, there was really no cause for complaint. Then, after all, it could not be so wrong, for things fell out quite to everyone's satisfaction; and generally, when you do wrong, you suffer for it. Thus, her shamelessnes had become a sort of habit. Now it was all arranged as simply as eating and drinking; every time that Coupeau came home drunk, she slept with Lantier, and that happened at least every Monday, Tuesday and Wednesday of the week. She apportioned out her nights; she had even begun to leave the tinsmith in the middle of the night, if he snored too loudly; and she would finish her sleep composedly on the neighbouring pillow. It was not that she cared any more for the hatter. No, she simply found him nicer and cleaner, she could rest better in his room, it was like taking a bath. In a word, she was like cats, with their fancy for curling up and going to sleep on white linen.

Old Madame Coupeau never ventured to say anything about it openly. But after a quarrel, when the laundress had given her a shaking, the old woman came out pretty definitely about it. She declared that she knew some men who were fine and thick-headed, and some women who were fine and sly; and she mumbled out other sayings, cruder still, with all the free-spokenness of an old waistcoat hand. At first Gervaise simply gave her a stare, without replying, then, as indefinitely as the other, she defended herself on general grounds. When a woman's husband was a drunkard, a dirty brute, who wallowed in beastliness, the woman was justified in looking about for something more decent elsewhere. She went further, and gave it out that Lantier was her husband as much as Coupeau, perhaps more so. Hadn't she known him when she was fourteen? Hadn't she had two children by him? Well, under those circumstances, everything was justifiable; no one could throw a stone at her. It was only what was quite natural. Besides, she would like to see anyone interfere with her; she would soon give them all a dose of their own. The Rue de la Goutte-d'Or was not so very proper! Little Madame Vigouroux cut fine capers among her coal from morning to night. Madame Lehongre, the grocer's wife, went to bed with her brother-in-law, a great slobbering lout that you wouldn't have picked up on a shovel. The watchmaker opposite, that neat-looking little man, had nearly been brought before the assizes for something abominable; he went with his own daughter, a loose girl who walked the streets. And she waved her arm as if to take in the whole quarter; it would take her a good hour to exhibit all the dirty linen of these folks, a lot of people all heaped pell-mell, fathers and mothers and children, in their own filth. Ah! she knew all about it, all the goings-on everywhere about; the very place stank of it! Yes, yes, a very nice thing, men and women, thereabouts, where poverty crowded one on top of the other! If you were to pound them all up, men and women together, in a mortar, you would get enough out of them to dung all the cherry trees in the Plaine Saint-Denis.

"Best not spit in the air, or it'll fall back on your own nose," she cried, when she was driven to extremities. "Let everybody mind his own business, and let other people live as they please, if they wish to live as they please themselves. For my part I don't object to anything, so long as I'm not dragged in the gutter by people who have pitched into it themselves, head foremost."

And one day, as old Madame Coupeau spoke out more definitely, she said to her, through her clenched teeth:

"You are laid up in bed, and you get the benefit of that. Listen to me, you make a great mistake. You know very well that I treat you better than you deserve, for I have never said anything to you about your own carryings-on. Oh, I know, nice carryings-on, two or three men, while Coupeau was alive. No, you needn't begin to cough, that's all I have to say. I merely want you to shut up for good, that's all."

The old woman nearly choked over it. Next day, as Goujet called for the clothes while Gervaise was out, old Madame Coupeau called him over, and kept him a long time by her bed. She knew the friendship that the blacksmith had for Gervaise, she had noticed that for some time he had been gloomy and unhappy, suspecting what was going on. And for

the pleasure of talking, the pleasure of avenging herself for
last night's quarrel, she told him the truth straight, crying
and complaining, as if the bad conduct of Gervaise affected
her the most. When Goujet left the little room he had to hold
on to the wall, choking with vexation. As soon as the laundress
had returned, old Madame Coupeau called to her that she
was wanted at once at Madame Goujet's with the linen,
ironed or not; and she appeared so lively that Gervaise
guessed she had been tattling, and saw well enough the
heart-breaking scene that lay before her.

Very pale and shaking, she put the clothes into her basket
and set out. For years past she had not paid the Goujets a
sou. The debt amounted to four hundred and twenty-five
francs. Every time she took the money for the washing,
saying that she was in difficulties. She was ashamed to do it,
because it seemed as if she were taking advantage of the
blacksmith's friendship in order to do him. Coupeau, now
less scrupulous, jeered, and said he had no doubt fooled about
with her a bit in the corners, and now he paid for it. But she,
despite the relations with Lantier into which she had
succumbed, was up in arms at once, and asked her husband
if he would like to eat that sort of bread. She would not
allow anyone to speak ill of Goujet in her presence; her
affection for the blacksmith still lingered, like a remnant of
her own honour. And every time that she took back the
clothes to these honest people, her heart failed her the
moment she set foot on the stairs.

"Ah! you have come at last!" said Madame Goujet, dryly,
as she opened the door. "When I want to order my coffin, I
will send you for it."

Gervaise came in looking very much embarrassed, without
even daring to make an excuse. She was not punctual any
longer now, never turned up at the proper hour, kept people
waiting for a whole week. Little by little everything with her
was falling into disorder.

"Here have I been looking out for you for a week," continued
the lace-maker. "And you tell me lies too, you send your
apprentice to me with all sorts of stories; you are just going to
set about the things, you will let me have it that very evening,
or there has been a mishap, the bundle has fallen into a pail
of water. All this while I am wasting my time, nothing comes,
and I get anxious. No, you are very foolish. Come now, what
is it you have in the basket? Have you, at all events, got

everything? Have you brought back the pair of sheets of mine that you have had for the last month, and the chemise which didn't turn up at the last washing?

"Yes, yes," murmured Gervaise, "I've got the chemise, here it is."

But Madame Goujet uttered an exclamation. The chemise was not hers, she wouldn't take it. Now her linen was changed, that was the finishing touch! Only the other week she had had two handkerchiefs which hadn't got her mark. She didn't at all relish that sort of thing, linen coming from nobody knows where. Then, too, she didn't wish to lose her own property.

"And the sheets?" she went on. "They are lost, I suppose? Well, my good woman, you must manage as you please, but I insist on having them back, without fail tomorrow morning, do you understand?"

There was a silence. What especially troubled her was to feel that the door of Goujet's room was ajar, just behind her. She was sure that he was in there; and how annoying if he was listening to these well-merited reproaches, to which she could answer nothing. She took it all as mildly and cringingly as possible, and she bent over the basket, taking out the things and putting them on the bed as quickly as she could. But it was no better than before, for Madame Goujet began to turn over the articles one by one. She took them, put them down again, and said:

"Ah! you are getting quite out of it. I can't pay you compliments every day now. You mess the things about, you get them in a state! Look here, just look at that shirt-front, it is singed; the iron has left a mark on the folds. And the buttons are all torn off. I don't know how you manage; you never leave a button. Now, look here, here is a bodice that I certainly shall not pay for. Do you see that? The dirt is all left on it, you have only spread it further. Very good, if the linen is not even clean. . . ."

She stopped, and began counting it over. Then she cried——

"What! what are you bringing me? There are two pairs of stockings wanting, six towels, a tablecloth, dusters. . . . That's the way you treat me, is it! I told you to bring it all back, ironed or not. If your apprentice isn't here with all the rest within an hour, we shall have a disagreement, Madame Coupeau, I give you due warning."

At that moment Goujet coughed in his room. A little shiver went through Gervaise. What a way to be treated before him! And she stood there in the middle of the room, all confused, waiting for the dirty clothes. But as soon as she had made out the account, Madame Goujet had quietly returned to her place by the window, where she was mending a lace shawl.

"And the clothes?" asked the laundress timidly.

"No, thank you," replied the old woman, "there are none this week."

Gervaise went quite pale. So they took away their custom from her! At that she completely lost her self-possession, and she had to sit down on a chair, her legs gave way under her. And she made no attempt to excuse herself, she could say nothing but:

"Monsieur Goujet is ill?"

Yes, he was not well, he had had to come home instead of going to the forge, and he was lying down to rest. Madame Goujet spoke gravely, as she sat there in her invariable black dress, her white face framed in by its nun-like coif. They had lowered the wages of the bolt-makers again; it had fallen now from nine francs to seven francs, on account of the machines, which did everything. And she explained that they had to economize all round; she was going to do the washing herself, as she had done before. Naturally it would have come in very handy if the Coupeaus had paid back the money that her son had lent them. But she certainly had no intention of setting the bailiffs upon them because they couldn't pay. While she spoke of the debt, Gervaise, with downcast eyes, seemed to follow the agile movement of the needles picking up the stitches one by one.

"However," continued the lace-mender, "if you would stint yourself a little, you could soon pay it off. You live very well, you spend a lot of money, I am sure. If you were only to give us ten francs a month. . . ."

She was interrupted by the voice of Goujet calling her:

"Mother! Mother!"

She came back in a minute, and changed the conversation. Goujet had evidently begged her not to ask Gervaise for money. But in spite of herself, after five minutes she was speaking once more of the debt. Oh! she had seen for a long time what would happen; the tinsmith was drinking up everything, and he would bring her down yet further. And her son would never have lent the money if he had listened to her. By this time he would have been married, he would not be in the state he was now, with the prospect of lifelong unhappiness. She grew warm, she spoke very severely, accusing Gervaise, definitely enough, of having plotted with Coupeau all along to take advantage of her poor fool of a son. Yes, there were women who played the hypocrite for years; but it all came out at last.

"Mother! Mother!" called Goujet a second time, more violently.

She got up, and when she returned she said, as she sat down to her work:

"Go in, he wishes to see you."

Gervaise was all of a tremble; she left the door open. The scene affected her all the more because it was a sort of avowal, before Madame Goujet, of their affection for each other. She found herself again in the little quiet room, papered with pictures, with its little narrow iron bed, like the room of a boy of fifteen. Goujet lay at full length on the bed, overcome by old Madame Coupeau's revelations; his eyes were red, and his golden beard was still wet with tears. He must have attacked his pillow with his terrible fists in the first moment of rage, for the pillow-case was all rent and the feathers coming through.

"Listen to me, mother is in the wrong," he said to the laundress, almost in a whisper. "You owe me nothing, and I won't have anything more said about it.

He raised himself up and looked at her. Big tears came into his eyes.

"You are not well, Monsieur Goujet?" she murmured. "What is the matter?"

"Nothing thanks. I fatigued myself too much yesterday. I am going to sleep a bit."

Then he could contain himself no longer, he cried:

"God! God! you should never have done it, never! You swore to me. And now you have done it, you have done it. Oh, God! how you have made me suffer; go, go!"

And he waved to her to go, gently, supplicatingly. She did not go near him, she turned and went as he bade her, stupidly, without a word to say to him, to comfort him. In the next room she took up her basket, but she made no move to go, standing as if she wanted to say something. Madame Goujet went on with her work, without raising her head. At last she said:

"Well, good-night! send me my linen, we will settle up afterwards."

"Yes, I will, good-night!" faltered Gervaise.

She closed the door, slowly, giving a final look round the neat and orderly interior in which she seemed to leave behind her something of her better self. She went back to the laundry finding her way mechanically, stupidly, as a cow wanders homeward, without heeding the way it goes. Old Madame Coupeau had left her bed for the first time, and was sitting on a chair by the stove. But the laundress did not even scold her; she was too weary; her bones ached as if she had been beaten; it seemed to her that life was harder than one could bear, and that unless you died right away, you could not get rid of your own heart as you pleased.

And now Gervaise grew utterly heedless. She had a vague way of waving her hand as if to send everybody about their business. At every new worry she fell back on her one remaining pleasure, her three good meals a day. The shop might crumble to ruin; provided she was not underneath it, she would have let it crumble willingly. And it crumbled away, not all at once, but a little more, little by little. One by one her customers quarrelled with her, and took their custom elsewhere. M. Madinier, Mademoiselle Remanjou, the Boches themselves, had all gone back to Madame Fauçonnier, where things were attended to more punctually. After a time people get tired of asking for a pair of stockings for three weeks, and of putting on a shirt with the grease-spots of the other Sunday still on it. Gervaise bid them good riddance, ill-temperedly enough, telling them she was jolly glad not to have to mess about in their beastliness any longer. Very well, the whole quarter could go, if they pleased; it would rid her of a nice lot of filth, and it would always be so much the less work. Meanwhile, she only retained the bad-paying people, the disreputable ones, and people like Madame Gaudron, whom not a single laundress in the Rue Neuve would wash for, her linen stank so. The shop was so run down that she had to dismiss her last work-woman, Madame Putois, and she was left now with only her apprentice, the cross-eyed Augustine, who got more stupid every day. And even these two had not always enough work; they had to dawdle about whole afternoons. It was far on in the downward course, not far from ruin.

Naturally, when idleness and poverty come in at the door, cleanliness went out at the window. The beautiful blue shop, the colour of azure, once the pride of Gervaise, was scarcely recognizable. The wood and panes of the windows, which were

never cleaned, were all splashed from top to bottom by the
mud of passing vehicles. On a brass wire along the window-
frame still hung three grey rags, left by customers who had
died in hospital. And inside it was shabbier still; the damp
linen drying on lines had unstuck the paper; the Pompadour
chintz hung in strips, like cobwebs heavy with dust; the stove,
broken, and poked all in holes, looked like a fragment of old
iron in a second-hand dealer's; the ironing-board seemed to
have served for table to a whole garrison, spotted as it was
with coffee and wine, plastered with jam, slobbery with
Monday's grease stains. With all that mingled a sharp odour
of starch, a smell made up of must, of burnt fat, and of general
dirt. But Gervaise was quite comfortable in the midst of it all.
She never saw the shop get dirty; she got accustomed to the
torn paper, the greasy woodwork, as she got accustomed to
wearing torn skirts, and to not washing her ears. The very
dirt itself made a warm nest where she squatted down contentedly. To let things go as they would, to wait until the dust
filled every crevice and coated everything, to feel the house
drowse about her in a heavy idleness like her own; that was a
sort of delight, a kind of intoxication to her. Peace and
quietness first of all; the rest, she wouldn't give a wink for.
As for her debts, now constantly increasing, she had given
up caring for them. She lost her sense of honesty; she would
pay or not, as it happened, and she preferred not to know.
When the credit was closed to her in one shop, she opened a
fresh credit in the shop next door. She was in debt all around,
she was dunned on every side. Merely in the Rue de la
Goutte-d'Or, she dared not go past the coal-dealer's, nor the
grocer's, nor the fruiterer's; and for this reason she had to go
round by way of the Rue des Poissonniers, when she went to
the wash-house, a few minutes' run. The shop-keepers accused
her of roguery. One night, the man who had sold her Lantier's
furniture made a regular rumpus in the street; he swore he
would turn her up and give her a good hiding, if she didn't
hand over his money on the spot. Scenes like this did, indeed,
leave her all of a tremble; but she would shake herself like a
beaten cur, and it was all over. She had just as good an appetite
for her dinner that evening. Cheeky it was of them! She had
no money, and she couldn't manufacture it! Then the shop-
keepers were all thieves; they were made to be kept waiting.
And she turned over and went to sleep composedly, refusing
to consider what was sure to happen sooner or later. She

would be broke, no doubt; but, till then, she meant not to worry herself.

Meanwhile, old Madame Coupeau was on her legs again. For another year the business just kept going, During the summer, naturally, there was always a little more work, the white petticoats and cotton dresses of the girls who walked the outer boulevards. Things went steadily down-hill, a little deeper down in the mire every week, with some ups and downs all the same, nights when you had to fold your hands before an empty table, and others when you had stuffed away over your veal till you could stuff no longer. Old Madame Coupeau was now for ever to be seen on the pavement, with bundles hidden away under her apron, strolling along to the pawnshop of the Rue Polonceau. She went off, rounding her back, looking as prim and proper as a pious old lady going to mass; and she quite enjoyed it, it amused her to go on the job for money, all this trucking of second-hand goods quite tickled the fancy of the cunning old person. The clerks at the Rue Polonceau knew her well; they called her "Mother Four Francs", because she always asked four francs when they offered three, on her bundles, no bigger than a pennyworth of butter. Gervaise would have bartered the whole house, if she could; she was seized with a perfect mania for putting things up the spout; she would have shaved her head if they had offered her a loan on her hair. It was such a nice easy method. one couldn't help going there to get some small change, if one only wanted a four-pound loaf. The whole blessed lot went; linen, and clothes, and tools and furniture. At first she took advantage of a good week to get out her things, ready to put them in again next week. Then she merely laughed and let things slide, selling her pawn-tickets. Only one thing went to her heart, that was to put her clock in pawn, in order to pay a bill of twenty francs to a bailiff who came to distrain her. Till then she had sworn that she would die of hunger rather than touch her clock. When old Madame Coupeau took it off in a bandbox she sank helpless on a chair, with tears in her eyes, as if her whole fortune were taken from her. But when old Madame Coupeau came back with twenty-five francs, the unexpected five francs over consoled her, and she sent off the old woman for four penn'orth of brandy in a glass, simply in order to drink to the five-franc piece. Often, nowadays, when they were on friendly terms, they had their little drop together, on a corner of the ironing-board, a mixture, half brandy and half cassis. Old Madame Coupeau had a knack of carrying a full glass in her apron pocket without spilling a drop. The neighbours needn't know, at all events. As a matter of fact, the neighbours knew perfectly well. The fruiterer, the tripe-seller, the grocer's boys said:

"Hallo! the old woman is off to uncle's," or "Hallo! the old woman's bringing her little drop in her pocket."

And, naturally, that roused popular feeling against Gervaise. She was gobbling up everything; she would soon finish up the lot. A few more mouthfuls and the place would be nicely cleaned out.

Amidst this general downfall Coupeau flourished. The boozy brute seemed to bear a charmed life. The wine and brandy positively fattened him. He ate enormously, and made great game of the skinny Lorilleux, who declared that drink killed people; by way of answer he tapped his stomach, which the fat had stretched tight, like the skin of a drum. At the end of a night's debauch, he would play a tune on it, the roll of a big drum, enough to make the fortune of an itinerant tooth-drawer. But Lorilleux, annoyed at not having much of a stomach himself, declared that it was yellow fat, unhealthy fat. However, Coupeau drank deeper than ever, for his health, he said. His pepper-and-salt hair, brushed right back, flamed like a torch. His face, with its ape-like jaws, looked more and more drunken, took more and more a vinous colour. And he was still, as ever, a jolly dog; he sent his wife packing when she spoke to him of their difficulties. As if men had anything to do with those tiresome little details! The crib might go bare, that was no concern of his. He must have his good things to eat, morning and evening, and he never concerned himself as to where they came from. When he had not done a stroke of work for a week, he became more exacting than ever. However, he still patted Lantier on the back, as friendly as ever. Evidently he was quite unconscious of his wife's misconduct; at least, various people, the Boches, the Poissons, would take their oath he suspected nothing, and a great pity it would be if he ever were to. But Madame Lerat, his own sister, shook her head, and declared she knew of husbands who didn't mind it at all. One night Gervaise herself, coming back from the hatter's room, had a terrible shock on feeling in the darkness, a little kick from behind; then she reassured herself by the thought that she had merely knocked against the frame of the bed. The situation was really too awful; it could not be that her husband amused himself over it.

Lantier, too, was far from being badly looked after. He was very careful of himself, measured his girth by the girth of his trousers, constantly afraid of being obliged to tighten or loosen the waist-band; it seemed to him he was just right, he wished neither to go fatter or thinner, for looks' sake. This made him very particular about what he ate, for he calculated every dish so as not to alter the size of his waist. Even when there was not a penny in the house, he must have his eggs and his chops, things that were light and nourishing. Ever since he had been sharing the wife with the husband, he considered that he had a good half share in the household; he picked up the money that lay about, had Gervaise at his beck and call, and grumbled and growled, and seemed to be more at home than the master of the house. But indeed there were two masters of the house, and number two managed to get the best of everything, the wife, the table, and all the rest. He took the cream off the Coupeaus; and why not? He now cared very little about letting people see how things stood. Nana was his favourite; he liked pretty little girls. He took less and less heed of Étienne, for boys, according to him, ought to fight their own way. When anyone came to see Coupeau, Lantier was always there, in slippers and shirt sleeves, coming out of the back parlour with the bored air of a husband who is disturbed; and he answered for Coupeau, he said that it was the same thing.

Between the two of them, Gervaise had not always the merriest conceivable time of it. She had nothing to complain of as regarded her health, God be thanked! She, too, had become rather too plump. But with two men on her hands, both wanting to be looked after, both wanting to be pleased, she had sometimes more than she could do. One husband, confound it all, fagged you quite enough! And the worst part of it was that they hit it off very well together, the two black-guards. They never had a dispute about anything; they laughed in one another's faces after dinner, with their elbows on the table; they were rubbing up against each other all day, like cats who are after their kind. And when they came home in a bad temper, it was on her that they fell. Go for her, she could stand it all right; it made them better friends to have their jaw together. And it was no good for her to show her teeth. At first, when one of them went for her, she looked

at the other out of the corner of her eye to get him to side
with her. But it didn't always succeed. She took things meekly
now, she bent her back to the burden; she saw that it amused
them to knock her about, she was so plump and round, a
regular ball. Coupeau, who was very foul-mouthed, used the
most filthy language against her. Lantier, on the contrary,
said his nasty things carefully, saying things that no one else
said, and that cut her more keenly. Happily, one gets used to
everything; the bad words, the injustice of the two men,
finally ran off her like water off a duck's back. And she even
came to prefer them when they were angry, because when
they wanted to be nice they bothered her more than ever,
always after her, not leaving her in peace even to put on her
bonnet. Then, too, they wanted tasty dishes, she must salt
things, and not salt things, blow hot and cold at once, pet
them, and put them in cotton wool one after the other. By the
end of the week her head ached and her bones ached, she was
half bewildered, her eyes looked half crazy. That sort of thing
uses up a woman.

Yes, Coupeau and Lantier used her up, that was the word;
they burnt her at both ends, as one says of the candle. The
tinsmith, of course, was quite uneducated, but the hatter was
a bit too much so, or at least he had a sort of education, as
people who are not clean have a white shirt, dirty underneath.
One night she dreamt that she was at the edge of a pit;
Coupeau drove her towards it with a blow of his fist, while
Lantier tickled her sides to make her jump quicker. Well,
that was just like her life. Ah! she was in for it, it was no
wonder if she went to the bad. The neighbours were far from
just when they were down upon her for the bad habits into
which she had fallen, for it was not her own fault. Sometimes,
when she thought it over, a shiver ran through her. It seemed
to her that things might have turned out even worse than they
did. It was better to have two husbands, for example, than to
lose one's two arms. And her position seemed to her natural
enough, a position in which people often found themselves;
she did her best to get her own share of happiness out of it.
What proved how homely and comfortable she had come to
be, was that she now disliked neither Coupeau nor Lantier.
In a piece at the Gaieté she had seen a loose woman who
loathed her husband, and poisoned him for the sake of her
lover; and she was disgusted with it, for she herself felt nothing
at all like that. Was it not much more reasonable to live

comfortably all three? No, no, none of that silliness for her; her life was quite dreary enough as it was. In short, despite her debts, despite the poverty which threatened her, she would have considered herself quite happy and content if the tinsmith and the hatter had been a little less hasty and rough with her.

Towards the autumn, unfortunately, affairs got rather worse. Lantier declared he was going thin, and pulled a longer face every day. He grumbled about everything, growled over the potatoes, a nasty mess he couldn't eat, he declared, without getting a stomach-ache. The least bit of bickering now came to a regular rumpus; everybody accused everybody else of being the ruin of the house, and it was the very devil to make up matters again before getting off to bed in peace and comfort. When the brass is all gone the most patient of people get to blows. Lantier saw Queer Street before him, and it exasperated him to feel that the house was on its last legs, so much so, indeed, that he saw the day when he would have to take his hat, and go elsewhere for his bite and sup. And by this time he had got so accustomed to his little corner, to his little ways there, to being petted by everybody, a regular land of plenty, which he would not easily find again. Lord! you can't eat your cake and have it. And he was angry with his own stomach, for the house after all was there; he had gobbled it all up. But he did not confine himself to that; he was furious with the two others for having let the place go to pot in two years. Really the Coupeaus were good for nothing. And he declared that Gervaise was not economical. What the hell was going to become of them? Now his friends gave him the go-by, just at the moment when he was on the point of coming to terms over a splendid affair, a situation at six thousand francs in a factory, enough to put them all in clover.

One evening in December the cupboard really was bare. There was not a scrap of bread in the place. Lantier was very gloomy, he went out early, longing to make tracks for another crib, where there was a good wholesome smell of cooking. He sat by the stove for hours together, thinking it over. Then all at once he began to be very friendly with the Poissons. He gave up calling the policeman Badingue, he went so far as to admit that the Emperor wasn't a bad fellow, perhaps. He seemed specially drawn to Virginie, a clever woman, he said, who knew jolly well which way the wind was blowing. It was quite evident, he was simply stuffing them with

blarney. It even looked as if he wanted to board with them.
But he had a much better notion than that in his pate.
Virginie had told him that she would like to set up a shop of
some kind, and he kept the project constantly before her,
declaring it was an excellent one. She seemed quite cut out
for a business, she was tall, prepossessing, active. Oh! she
could get as much money as ever she liked. Since she had the
money lying idle, an aunt's legacy, she would do well to leave
the four dresses she would patch up in a season, and launch
into business; and he gave her instances of people who were
in a fair way of making their fortunes, the fruiterer at the
corner of the street, a little crockery dealer on the outer
boulevard; it was just the very moment, you could sell the
very sweepings of the counter. However, Virginie hesitated;
she looked about for a shop she could take, somewhere near;
she did not want to leave the neighbourhood. Then Lantier
would take her aside, and have a little talk with her in the
corner. He seemed to urge something upon her, and she did
not say no, she seemed to authorize him to act on her behalf.
It was a sort of secret between them; there were winks and
hurried words; their very ways of shaking hands seemed to
be plotting something. From that time, as the hatter ate his
meagre rations with the Coupeaus, he kept a wary eye upon
them, and he had now become very talkative again, was for
ever dinning them with endless complaints. All day long
Gervaise had to hear him dilating on their poverty. Good
Lord! it wasn't on his own account that he spoke; he would
share his dry bread with them as long as ever they liked.
Only, it was wise to look the situation fairly in the face. They
owed at least five hundred and fifty francs in the neighbourhood, to the baker, the coal-dealer, the grocer, and others.
Besides, they were two quarters behindhand with the rent,
which meant two hundred and fifty francs more; the landlord,
M. Marescot, even spoke of turning them out, if they did not
pay before the 1st of January. Then everything had gone to
the pawnshop, there was not three francs' worth of odds and
ends left, so thoroughly had the place been cleaned out; there
were the nails in the walls, that was all, and two books, worth
three sous. Gervaise was quite bewildered, all the strength
taken out of her, by this reckoning; and she would lose her
temper, and bang the table, or else cry like a ninny. One
evening she declared:

"I shall turn out of the place tomorrow! I would rather

put the key under the door, and sleep in the street, than go on living in such a funk."

"It would be better," said Lantier, slyly, "to get someone else to take the place, if you could. If you were both to make up your minds to give up the shop. . . ."

She interrupted him more violently than ever.

"Why, at once, at once!—I should be jolly glad to!"

Then the hatter showed himself very business-like. By giving up the lease, they would no doubt get the new tenant to pay the two terms in arrears, and he ventured to allude to the Poissons; he remembered that Virginie was on the look-out for a shop; perhaps it would do for her. It even occurred to him that he had heard her make some such suggestion. But the laundress, at the name of Virginie, recovered herself at once. They would see. When one was in a rage, one always talked of chucking things, only it did not seem quite so plausible when you thought over it.

For the next few days, whenever Lantier started the subject again, Gervaise replied that she had looked into it more closely and changed her mind. A nice thing it would be for her not to have any shop at all! That wouldn't bring her in her living. On the contrary, she meant to take back her work-women and get new customers. She said that to combat the hatter's plausible arguments; he showed her how she would be situated, with fresh expenses, and not the least chance of getting back where she was before. But he was tactless enough to mention again the name of Virginie, and at that she revolted furiously. No, no, never! She had always had her doubts of Virginie's friendliness, and if Virginie wanted to have the shop it was for the purpose of humiliating her. She would let it go to the first woman in the street, rather than to that great hypocrite, who had been waiting for years in the hope of seeing her come to smash. Oh! she saw it all now. She understood now why those yellow sparks came into the cat's eyes of the chatterer. Yes, Virginie still had on her conscience that good hiding she had given her in the wash-house, and she still fanned the old grudge she had against her. Well, she had better stow her hiding away in safety, or she was likely to get another. And pretty soon too; she could have her backside ready. Lantier, at this outburst, at first gave her back her own. He called her cabbage-head, humpty-dumpty, Madame Fine-airs, and he went to the extent of calling Coupeau clodhopper, who couldn't make his

wife treat friends decently. Then, realizing that he was
endangering everything by his anger, he declared that he
would never mix himself in other people's affairs again; one
got paid out for it. And indeed he seemed to have let the
matter drop, really waiting for an opportunity to bring the
laundress to the decisive point.

January had come, with wretched weather, cold and wet.
Old Madame Coupeau, who had been coughing and choking
all December, had had to stay in bed since Twelfth Night. It
was chronic with her; it came on regularly every winter. But
this winter everyone said that she would never leave her room
again, until she left it feet foremost; and she had indeed an
ominous rattle in the throat, yet she was still plump and
substantial, with one eye already extinct, and her face all
drawn aside. Certainly her children did not exactly wish her
to die; still, she had been hanging on by a thread for so long,
she was really such a burden to them, that, in the depths of
their hearts, they thought of her death as a deliverance for
everybody. It would be much better for her too herself, for
she had had her time, and when you have had your time there
is nothing to regret. The doctor had called once, but he had
not come back again. They gave her her broth, so as not to
abandon her altogether. And every hour they looked in to
see if she was still alive. Her breath was so bad that she could
not speak; but out of her one eye, still clear and living, she
gazed at them fixedly; and there were many meanings in that
gaze, regrets after her lost youth, grief at seeing her own
children so anxious to get rid of her, wrath against that
vicious little rascal of a Nana, who would go as coolly as
possible now, at night, to spy at the glass door in her night-
dress.

One Monday evening, Coupeau came home drunk.
Since his mother had been in danger, he lived in a continual
state of solicitude. When he was in bed, snoring with all his
might, Gervaise hesitated for a moment. She watched up with
old Madame Coupeau a part of the night. Besides, Nana was
very courageous, and slept, as before, by the old woman's
side, saying that if she heard her dying she would soon call
them. That night, as the child slept and the sick woman
seemed to be slumbering peacefully, the laundress finally
gave way to Lantier, who called to her from his room, where
he advised her to come and have a bit of rest. They would
keep a candle lit on the ground, behind the cupboard. But,

about three o'clock in the morning, Gervaise jumped out of bed all of a sudden, quaking and seized with fright. She seemed to have felt a cold breath pass over her body. The candle-end was burnt out, she hitched her petticoats about her in the dark, feverishly. She hurried into the little room, knocking against the furniture, and lit a small lamp. In the dead silence, the heavy darkness, the tinsmith's snore sounded out, two deep notes. Nana lay on her back, a little breath coming through her swollen lips. And Gervaise, lowering the lamp, which set the shadows dancing, lit up the face of old Madame Coupeau; it was quite white, the head had rolled over on one shoulder, the eyes were wide open· Old Madame Coupeau was dead.

Quietly, without a cry, frozen and cautious, Gervaise went back to Lantier's room. He had gone to sleep again. She leaned over him and whispered:

"I say, it's all over, she is dead."

Heavy with sleep, and only half awake, he growled out:

"Shut up; come to bed. We can't do anything for her if she is dead."

Then, raising himself on his elbow, he asked:

"What time is it?"

"Three."

"Only three! Come to bed, then. You'll make yourself ill. When it's morning, we'll see."

But she paid no heed to him, she put on all her things. He pulled the clothes up over him again, and turned towards the wall, saying what damned fools women were. What was the hurry of telling everybody that there was a death in the house? It wasn't such specially lively news in the middle of the night; and he was exasperated to see his sleep spoilt by such gloomy ideas. Meanwhile, when she had taken all her things back into her room, down to the very hair-pins, she sat down and sobbed at her ease, not fearing now to be caught with the hatter. In her heart she was really fond of old Madame Coupeau, she felt a real grief, though at the first stroke she felt nothing but fright and dissatisfaction at her choosing her time so badly. And she wept all alone, the sound of it quite loud in the silence, while the tinsmith went on snoring; he heard nothing, she had called and shaken him, and then thought it just as well to let him be, for if he woke up it would only be one bother the more. When she went back to the body, she found Nana sitting up, rubbing her eyes. The child understood, and she craned her neck to get a better view of her grandmother, with her vicious child's curiosity; she said nothing, she trembled a little, frightened and pleased at once with this sight of death, which she had promised herself for days as something naughty, which children were not allowed to see; and, as she gazed at the pallid mask, drawn at the last gasp by the passion of life, her cat-like eyes grew larger, and she had that shiver down her spine which nailed her to the glass of the door, when she was spying out for things that don't concern brats.

"Come, get up," said her mother, in a low voice. "I won't have you staying here."

She got out of bed regretfully, turning her head, not taking her eyes off the dead woman. Gervaise was puzzled to know what to do with her till daylight. She had decided to dress her when Lantier, in slippers and trousers, came in; he could not go to sleep again, he was a little ashamed of his conduct. It was all right then.

"She can sleep in my bed," he murmured. "There's plenty of room."

Nana lifted her big bright eyes on her mother and Lantier, and put on her silliest air, as she did on New Year's Day, when they gave her chocolate. There was no need to drive her; she trotted off in her night-dress, her little bare feet scarcely touching the ground; and she glided like a snake into the bed, which was still warm, and lay buried there at full length, her slim body scarcely raising the quilt at all. Whenever her mother came in, she saw her lying there silent, with shining eyes, wide awake, and motionless, very red, and apparently thinking over things.

Meanwhile Lantier had helped Gervaise to dress old Madame Coupeau; and it was no small job, for the dead woman was a pretty weight. No one would have thought that the old woman was so plump and so white. They put on her stockings, her white petticoat, her under-bodice, and her cap; all her best linen. Coupeau still snored, two notes, one deep, which went down, the other sharp, which went up; a sort of church music, like that which goes with the ceremonies of Good Friday. When the dead woman was properly dressed and laid out, Lantier poured himself out a glass of wine, to pick himself up, for he felt rather upset. Gervaise hunted about in the chest of drawers, looking for a little brass crucifix that she had brought from Plassans; but she remembered that old Madame

Coupeau had sold it herself. They lit the stove, and passed the rest of the night half asleep on chairs, finishing up the bottle of wine, wearied and fretful, as if it was their fault.

About seven o'clock, before it was light, Coupeau woke up. When he learnt what had happened, he seemed at first unconcerned enough, faltering out a few words, fancying they were making game of him. Then, he flung himself on the ground, he threw himself before the dead woman; and he kissed her, he cried like a child, weeping big tears, so that he made the sheets quite wet when he wiped his face on them. Gervaise had begun to sob again; she was deeply affected by her husband's sorrow, she felt friends with him again; yes, at heart he was better than she had believed him. Coupeau's despair brought on a violent headache. He pushed his fingers through his hair, his mouth was still out of taste after his night's debauch, and he had not quite got over his intoxication, despite his ten hours' sleep. And he clasped his hands and broke out into lamentations. Damnation! his poor mother, whom he loved so much, she was gone! Ah! his head was splitting, it would finish him off! A regular helmet of fire about his head, and his heart too was torn out of him! No, Fate had no right to punish a man so hardly.

"Come, come, courage, old man," said Lantier, getting up. "You must pull yourself together."

He poured out a glass of wine, but Coupeau refused to drink.

"What is the matter with me? I seem to have copper in my mouth. It's mother; when I saw her, I had that taste of copper. Mother, oh, my God! mother! mother! . . ."

And he began again, crying like a child. He drank the glass of wine all the same, to put out the fire that burnt inside him. Lantier soon went out under the pretext of giving the news to the family, and then going on to make the declaration at the mayoralty. He felt the need of a little fresh air, and when he got outside he was in no hurry, he began to smoke cigarettes, enjoying the sharp cold of the morning. On his way from Madame Lerat's he even went into a dairy shop at Batignolles to have a hot cup of coffee; and he stayed there a good hour thinking over things.

About nine the whole family was assembled in the laundry, of which they did not take down the shutters. Lorilleux shed no tears, besides, he had an urgent job, and he went back to his work-room again almost immediately, after having posed a minute or two in what he thought the proper way. Madame Lorilleux and Madame Lerat embraced the Coupeaus, and dabbed their handkerchiefs over their eyes, from which some little tears ran. But the former, when she had glanced hastily round the room, suddenly raised her voice to say that "you never put a lighted lamp by the side of a body; you must have candles;" and Nana was sent out for a packet of candles, big ones. Well, well, if you died at Clop-clop's, she would lay you out in a queer sort of way. What a booby! She didn't even know what to do with a dead body. Hadn't she ever buried anybody in all her life? Madame Lerat went up to borrow a crucifix from somebody; she brought back one that was too big, a cross of black wood, on which was nailed a Christ of painted cardboard, which covered old Madame Coupeau's whole chest, and seemed to crush her with its weight. Then they looked about for some holy water, but there was none to be had, and again Nana was sent out to the church to bring some home in a bottle. In a few minutes the little room had quite a different air; on a little table there was a candle burning, by the side of a glass full of holy water, in which was placed a sprig of box. Now, if people came in, it would at all events look decent. And the chairs were ranged all round the walls in the laundry, as if for a reception.

It was eleven when Lantier came back. He had got information from the undertaker's office.

"The bier is twelve francs," he said. "If you want a mass that will be ten francs more. Then there is the hearse, which you pay for according to the ornaments."

"Oh! that is quite useless," murmured Madame Lorilleux, raising her head with a surprised and indignant air. "It won't bring back mother, will it? We mustn't do more than we can afford."

"Certainly, that is just what I mean," said the hatter. "I merely got the figures for your guidance. Tell me what you want: after dinner I will go and see about it."

They spoke in half whispers, in the dim light which came through the slits in the shutters. The door of the little room was left wide open; and from this opening seemed to issue the heavy silence of death. The children went up in the court outside, a ring of children raced round in the pale winter sunlight. All at once they heard Nana, who had made her escape from the Boches, where they had sent her. She led with her shrill voice, and all the heels tapped on the pavement, whilst the words of their song went up like a noise of brawling birds:

> "Notre âne, notre âne,
> Il a mal à la patte.
> Madame lui a fait faire
> Un joli patatoire,
> Et des souliers lilas, la, la,
> Et des souliers lilas!"

Gervaise waited her turn to say:

"We are not rich, certainly; but we should like to do things decently. If old Madame Coupeau has not left us anything, that is no reason why we should put her into the earth as if she were a dog. No, we must have a mass, and a nice hearse."

"And who is to pay for it?" asked Madame Lorilleux violently. "Not us, we lost more money last week; certainly not you, for you are cleaned out yourself. Now you see what you have come to, with your craze for showing off before people."

Coupeau, when they consulted him, simply stammered out a few words, with a gesture of profound indifference; then he dozed off again on his chair. Madame Lerat said she would pay her share. She agreed with Gervaise, that one ought to do things decently. Then the two of them calculated it up on a scrap of paper; it mounted up to about ninety francs, for they decided, after long discussion, to have a hearse with a narrow pall.

"There are three of us,' said the laundress, in conclusion. "We will each give thirty francs. That won't ruin us."

But Madame Lorilleux burst out furiously:

"All very well, but for my part I refuse, I tell you, I refuse! It is not the thirty francs. I would give a hundred thousand if I had them, if that would bring mother back to life. Only I don't care about being stuck-up. You have your shop, you like to crow over the neighbours. But we people have nothing to do with all that. We don't take up any pose. Oh! you can do as you please. Put plumes on the hearse, if that amuses you."

"We don't ask you for anything," said Gervaise, at last. "If I had to sell myself, I wouldn't have anything to reproach myself with. I kept old Madame Coupeau without you while she was alive, and I'll bury her now she's dead. Once more, I'm not going to mince matters: I would take in a lost cat, and I wouldn't leave your mother in the gutter."

At that Madame Lorilleux began to cry, and Lantier had difficulty to keep her from leaving them on the spot. The discussion became so heated, that Madame Lerat, with an energetic hush! hush! went into the next room, and gave an anxious look at the dead woman, as if she feared it would waken her, hearing what was being said all round. At this moment the little girls began dancing again in the court outside, the shrill voice of Nana louder than all the rest:

> "Notre âne, notre âne,
> Il a bien mal au ventre.
> Madame lui a fait faire
> Un jolie ventrouilloire
> Et des souliers lilas, la, la,
> Et des souliers lilas."

"Oh Lord! how tiring those children are, with their song," said Gervaise to Lantier, almost crying with impatience and sorrow. "Do make them be quiet, and give Nana a slap and send her back to the *concierge*."

Madame Lerat and Madame Lorilleux went off to get some dinner, promising to come back again. The Coupeaus sat down to table; they had something in from the pork-butchers, but they could summon up no appetite, they scarcely dared tap their plates with their forks. They were worried and oppressed with poor old Madame Coupeau, who seemed to weigh them down, and to fill every corner of the house. The course of their existence was quite upset, they looked about for things and could not find them, they felt quite done up, as if after a night's dissipation. Lantier went out immediately to the undertaker's, with the thirty francs of Madame Lerat, and the sixty francs that Gervaise had rushed off, bare-headed and like a crazy thing, to borrow from Goujet. In the afternoon some visitors arrived, neighbours, full of curiosity, coming sighing, and rolling their eyes pathetically; they went into the little room, had a look at the dead body, and made the sign of the cross, and stirred the bit of box in the holy water; then they sat down in the shop, where they spoke of the dear woman interminably, repeating the same phrase for hours together. Mademoiselle Remanjou observed that her right eye remained open, Madame Gaudron declared that she had a good colour for her age, and Madame Fauconnier was stupefied at having seen her take her coffee only three days before. How quickly one went off! everybody ought to prepare for kingdom-come. By evening the Coupeaus had had quite enough of it. It was too great a nuisance to have to keep a body so long. The Government ought to make a new law on the subject. The whole evening, another night, and a whole morning—really, it would never be over. When you have done crying, one's sorrow gets a sharp edge on it, and you behave as you ought not to. Old Madame Coupeau, stiff and still in her narrow room, weighed on them more and more intolerably. And, in spite of themselves, they got back into their usual ways once more, they lost their first feeling of reverence.

"You will stop and have something to eat with us," said Gervaise to Madame Lerat and Madame Lorilleux when they returned. "It is too sad by one's self."

They laid the things on the ironing-board. Everyone on seeing it thought of the big spreads they had seen there before. Lantier had come back. Lorilleux came downstairs again. Just as they were sitting down, Boche came in to say that M. Marescot wished to come in, and the landlord entered with an air of solemnity, his large decoration in his frock-coat. He bowed in silence, went straight to the little room, where he knelt down. He had a very pious air, he prayed with all the absorption of a priest, then made a cross in the air, and sprinkled the corpse with the sprig of box. The whole family had left the table, and stood up greatly impressed. M. Marescot, his devotions once over, returned to the laundry and said to the Coupeaus:

"I have come for the two terms in arrears; can you pay up now?"

"No, Monsieur, not the whole of it," stammered Gervaise, very much annoyed at hearing the matter referred to before the Lorilleux. "You understand, with the troubles we have had. . . ."

"No doubt; but everyone has his own troubles," said the landlord, spreading out his huge workman's hands. "I am very sorry, but I can't wait any longer. If I am not paid by the day after tomorrow morning, I shall be forced to have recourse to a distraint."

Gervaise clasped her hands, the tears in her eyes, mute and supplicating. He shook his great bony head energetically, to intimate that all expostulation was useless. However, the respect due to the dead forbade all discussion. He withdrew discreetly, bowing himself out.

"A thousand pardons for having disturbed you," he murmured. "The day after tomorrow morning, don't forget."

And as, on his way out, he had again to pass before the little room, he saluted the body once more with a devout genuflexion, through the doorway.

At first they ate quickly, so as not to seem as if they found any pleasure in it. But, by the time they had come to the dessert, they went a bit slower, feeling in the mood to take things more comfortably. From time to time Gervaise, or one of the two sisters, would get up, her mouth full, and her serviette still in her hand, and give a look into the little room; when she sat down again, finishing her mouthful, the others would look at her for a second, to see if things were all right. Then the women got up somewhat less often, old Madame Coupeau was forgotten. They had made some coffee, very strong coffee, so as to keep them awake all night. The Poissons came about eight. They were invited to come and have a glass. Thereupon Lantier, who had kept his eye on Gervaise seemed to seize an occasion that he had been looking out for all day. Apropos of the hard-heartedness of landlords who came for money when there was death in the house, he said all of a sudden:

"He's a regular Jesuit, that old scamp, with his pious airs! But if I were you I should get out of the place as quick as possible."

Gervaise, overcome with fatigue, tired and worn, replied helplessly:

"Oh, for certain I shall not wait till they come to turn me out. I have had quite enough of it, quite."

The Lorilleux, delighted at the idea of Clop-clop giving up her laundry, were loud in their approval. No one would ever believe what a shop cost. If she were to gain no more than three francs by going out, at least she would have no expenses, and there would be no big risks. They drove home this argument to Coupeau; he drank deep, and was in a very emotional state, weeping into his plate, all by himself. As the laundress seemed to be giving way, Lantier gave a wink to the Poissons; and Virginie struck in, in the most amiable way.

"You know, it could easily be arranged. I will take on the

lease, if you like, and settle it all for you with the landlord. That would be more comfortable for you."

"No, thanks," replied Gervaise, with a sort of shiver. "I know where to get the money for the rent, if I wish to. I shall work; I have my two arms, thank God! to take my part."

"We will talk about it later on," said the hatter, hastily. "It isn't quite the thing tonight. Later on, tomorrow, perhaps."

At this moment Madame Lerat, who had gone into the next room, uttered a little shriek. She was quite frightened, she said, for she had found the candle had gone out; it had burnt to the very end. They hurriedly lit another; and heads were shaken, it was a bad omen when the light went out by a dead body.

The night-watch began. Coupeau had stretched himself out, not to sleep, he said, but to meditate; and in five minutes he was snoring. Nana cried when they sent her in to sleep at the Boches'; she had been looking forward ever since the morning to the delight of being nice and warm in the big bed of her friend Lantier. The Poissons stayed till midnight. They had finally made some wine punch in a salad-bowl, because the coffee was too much for the women's nerves. Their conversation took a somewhat tender turn. Virginie spoke of the country; she would like to be buried in the corner of a wood, with wild flowers on her tomb. Madame Lerat had already laid away in her cupboard the sheets in which she was to be laid out, and she kept it scented with lavender-water; she would like to have a nice scent in her nostrils when she came to eat the wild flowers by the roots. Then, without transition, the policeman told how they had arrested a fine tall girl that morning, who had been stealing from a pork-butcher's shop; when she was searched, they found ten sausages hung round her waist, before and behind. Madame Lorilleux declared in a tone of great disgust, that she would not like to have those sausages to eat, and they all began to laugh, very quietly. The night-watch livened up a bit, while preserving the proprieties.

But as they finished the wine punch, a singular sound, a dull, trickling sound, was heard from the little room. They all looked up at one another.

"It is nothing," said Lantier composedly, lowering his voice. "She is emptying herself."

The explanation made them shake their heads with an air of relief, and they set down their glasses on the table.

Finally the Poissons took their leave. Lantier went with them; he was going on to a friend's, he said, so as to let the ladies have his bed, where they could lie down for an hour, in turn. Then Gervaise and the two sisters, by the side of the sleeping Coupeau, seated themselves around the fire, on which they kept some hot coffee. They sat there crouching together, their hands under their aprons, their faces bent over the heat, talking in whispers, in the silence of the whole quarter. Madame Lorilleux complained that she had no black dress, and she didn't want the expense of buying one, for they were hard up, very hard up; and she questioned Gervaise as to whether old Madame Coupeau had not left a black skirt they had given her for her birthday. Gervaise went to look for it. If it were taken in at the waist, it would do all right. But Madame Lorilleux wanted too some old linen, she spoke of the bed, the cupboard, the two chairs, looking around for any small articles there might be to be divided. They nearly quarrelled over it. Madame Lerat acted as peacemaker; she was more just; the Coupeaus had looked after their mother, her few belongings were certainly theirs by right. And the three of them crouched down again over the stove, with monotonous little bickerings. The night seemed to them terribly long. For some time they gave themselves a shaking, drank some coffee, and put their heads in at the door of the next room, where the candle, which mustn't be snuffed, burned with a long red flame, thickened by the smoky thief which had come into the wick. Towards morning they began to shiver, despite the intense heat of the stove. A trouble, a weariness at having talked too much, gave them a feeling of suffocation, their tongues dry, their eyes aching. Madame Lerat threw herself on Lantier's bed, and began snoring like a man; whilst the two others, their heads touching their knees, slept before the fire. In the early morning twilight they awoke with a start. The candle of old Madame Coupeau had gone out again. And as they heard once more, in the darkness, the dull trickling sound, Madame Lorilleux gave the explanation aloud for her own reassurance.

"She's emptying herself," she repeated, as she lit another candle.

The funeral was to be at half-past ten. A nice forenoon they were going to have, after such a night and day as they had had. And Gervaise, penniless as she was, declared she would give a hundred francs to anyone who would come and take off old

Madame Coupeau three hours earlier. No, however much you may care for people, they are too much for you when they are dead; and the more you care for them, the more you wish to have them out of the way.

Fortunately, the morning of a funeral is full of distractions. There are all sorts of preparations to be made. First there was the luncheon. Then old Bazouge turned up, the undertaker's man on the sixth storey, bringing the bier and the bag of bran. The old chap was never sober, and that day, at eight in the morning, he was still jolly with last night's drink.

"It's for here, isn't it?" he said.

And he set down the coffin, the new wood creaking.

But as he put down the bag by the side of it, he gaped with open eyes and open mouth as he caught sight of Gervaise before him.

"I beg your pardon; excuse me, I've made a mistake," he stammered. "They told me it was for you."

He had already taken up his bag when the laundress cried:

"Stop! stop! it is for here."

"Blast it all! Why can't people explain things?" he went on, smacking his thigh. "I see, it's the old woman."

Gervaise had turned quite white. Old Bazouge had brought the coffin for her. He went on in his politest way, trying to make excuses.

"Well, you see, they told me yesterday that there was someone gone on the ground floor. So then, I thought. . . . You know, in our profession, those things go in at one ear and out at the other. Here are my best compliments all the same. Well, the later the better, though life isn't all smiles, you know. Oh! far from it."

She listened, drawing back for fear he would seize her in his great dirty hands and take her away in his box. Once before, on her wedding-night, he had told her that he knew women who would thank him if he would only come and take them. Well, she had not reached that point yet, and it sent a cold shudder down her spine. Her life was spoilt, but she did not want to leave it just yet; she would starve for years and years rather than have the quick relief of death.

"He's tight," she muttered, with an air of disgust and terror. "They might at least not send us tipplers; we pay dear enough."

At that the man turned crusty and quizzical.

"I say, my good little woman, it'll be your turn another time. I'm at your service, remember. You have only to give me a wink. It's I'm the ladies' comforter. And don't you spit upon old Bazouge, either, for he's held in his arms people much more swell than you, and they let themselves be put straight without making any complaints, glad enough to go on with their sleep in the dark."

"Be quiet, Bazouge," said Madame Lorilleux severely; she had come in on hearing the sound of voices. "Your jokes are not seemly. If we were to make a complaint against you, you would be turned off. Get out of the place, you unprincipled lout."

The undertaker's man went off, but as he made his way along the pavement he could be heard muttering:

"Unprincipled! I don't know about unprincipled—I don't know about unprincipled. I only know about being honest."

Ten o'clock struck. There was some delay about the hearse. There were already several people in the shop, friends and neighbours. M. Madinier, Mes-Bottes, Madame Gaudron, Mademoiselle Remanjou; and every few minutes a man or woman's head was put out between the closed shutters in the opening of the door, to see if the laggard of a hearse was in sight. The family, gathered together in the back room, pressed each other's hands. There were short silences, interrupted by rapid whispers, an uneasy, feverish air of expectancy, with the sharp, sudden rustle of a dress. Madame Lorilleux had forgotten her handkerchief, or Madame Lerat looked about for a prayer-book to take with her. Each, as they came in, noticed before the bed, in the middle of the room, the open coffin; and, despite themselves, each stopped and gave it a sidelong glance, calculating whether big old Madame Coupeau would ever be able to get into it. They all looked at each other with this thought in their eyes, without confessing it. But someone was heard at the street door. M. Madinier came in and announced in a solemn and formal voice, with a fine gesture:

"They are here."

It was not as yet the hearse. Four mutes entered, one after another, hurriedly, with the red faces and lumpish hands of removal carriers, in dirty black clothes, worn and whitened with the rubbing of coffins. Old Bazouge walked first, very drunk and very respectable; he always pulled himself together the moment he was at work. They did not say a word, hanging their heads a little, they seemed already to weigh old Madame Coupeau with their eyes. And there was no delay; the poor old soul was packed up in no time. The shortest of the men, a squint-eyed young fellow, emptied the bran in the coffin, and spread it out, kneading it as if he were making bread. Another tall thin fellow, with a jocose air, spread out the winding-sheet. Then, one—two—and away! all four seized the body and hoisted it, two at the head, two at the feet. You couldn't have turned a pancake more quickly. If anyone had turned away, they might have imagined that old Madame Coupeau had jumped into her coffin herself. She slipped into it as if she were quite at home there—oh! exactly, so exactly that they heard her rub against the new wood. She touched all round like a picture in a frame. But she got in, much to the surprise of the onlookers; certainly, she must have shrunk since the night before. Meanwhile the mutes got up and waited. The little squint-eyed fellow took up the cover, as if to summon the family to take their last farewell, whilst Bazouge put the nails in his mouth and got his hammer ready, Then Coupeau, his two sisters, and Gervaise, with others as well, flung themselves on their knees, and kissed the old mother who had gone, with big tears, which fell and rolled in warm drops on the stiffened face, cold as ice. There was a prolonged sound of sobbing. The cover was lowered, old Bazouge drove in his nails with the skill of a packer, two blows to every nail; and the sound of weeping became inaudible in a noise like the noise of furniture being repaired. It was done. They set out.

"The idea of making such a to-do, at a time like this," said Madame Lorilleux to her husband, when she saw the hearse outside the door.

The whole neighbourhood was in a state of excitement over the hearse. The tripe-seller called the grocer's boys, the little watchmaker came out on the pavement, the neighbours leant out of their windows. And everyone talked of the pall, with its white cotton fringe. The Coupeaus would have done better to pay off their debts! But, as the Lorilleux said, when you're puffed up with pride, it shows itself on every occasion.

"It is shameful!" said Gervaise, at the same moment, speaking of the chain-maker and his wife. "To think that those skinflints have not so much as brought a bouquet of violets for their mother!"

The Lorilleux, indeed, had come empty-handed. Madame Lerat had brought a crown of artificial flowers, and there was

also on the bier a crown of immortelles and a bouquet bought
by the Coupeaus. The undertaker's men had had to make a
fine effort to lift and carry the coffin. The procession was slow
in getting in order. Coupeau and Lorilleux, in frock-coats,
hat in hand, led the mourners; the former, in a melting mood,
maintained by two glasses of white wine in the morning, held
his brother-in-law's arm; his legs shook under him, and he had
a splitting headache. Then came the men, M. Madinier, very
solemn, and all in black, Mes-Bottes, a great-coat over his
blouse. Boche, whose yellow trousers seemed quite out of
keeping, Lantier, Gaudron, Bibi-la-Grillade, Poisson, and
others. The ladies followed; first Madame Lorilleux, trailing
the dead woman's dress, which she had done up for the
occasion, Madame Lerat, with a shawl covering her improvised
mourning, a dress trimmed with lilac, and at the end Virginie,
Madame Gaudron, Madame Fauconnier, Mademoiselle
Remanjou, and the others of the party. When the hearse
started on its way down the Rue de la Goutte-d'Or, whilst
the people made the sign of the cross, and raised their hats,
the four mutes led the way, two in front, the two others on the
right and left. Gervaise had stayed behind to lock up the
shop. She put Nana in Madame Boche's care, and she caught
up the procession running, whilst the child, whom the *concierge*
held in the porch, looked with immense interest at her
grandmother going out of sight down the street, in that fine
carriage.

Just at the moment when Gervaise, quite out of breath, had
caught up the procession, Goujet arrived from the opposite
direction. He joined the men, but he turned and nodded to
her so kindly, that all her unhappiness came back to her all
at once, and she began to cry once more. She was not crying
only on account of old Madame Coupeau, but for something
abominable, she could not say what, which stifled her. All
the way she held her handkerchief to her eyes. Madame
Lorilleux, whose cheeks were dry and inflamed, looked
askance, as if she fancied it was done for show.

At the church the ceremony was soon hurried through.
The mass, however, dragged a little, for the priest was very
old. Mes-Bottes and Bibi-la-Grillade had preferred to wait
outside, on account of the collection. M. Madinier, all the
time, studied the priests, and he communicated his observa-
tions to Lantier: those jokers mumbled out their Latin without
knowing what they were gabbling; they buried you a person

as they would have baptized or married them, without the least real feeling. Then M. Madinier blamed the heap of ceremonies, the lights, the mournful voices, the whole parade. One really lost one's friends twice over, at home and in church. And all the men agreed with him, for it was a painful moment to all, when, at the end of the mass, there was a hurry-skurry of prayers, and the assistants filed by the body and cast the holy water over it. Happily the cemetery was not far distant, the little cemetery of La Chapelle, a bit of garden which opens on the Rue Marcadet. The procession reached it in disorder, walking noisily, and chatting of their own affairs. The hard soil sounded out, they would like to have stamped their feet. The gaping hole, beside which the coffin was laid, was already frozen, white and stony as a chalk-quarry; and those present, ranged around the hillocks that had been thrown up, found it anything but agreeable to wait there in such cold weather, looking uncomfortably into the hole before them. At last a priest in surplice came out of a little house, shivering, his breath steamed at every *De Profundis* that he uttered. At the last sign of the cross he hurried off, without the least desire to go over it again. The grave-digger took his spade; but, on account of the frost, he detached the earth in great heavy clods, which clattered down on the coffin like a regular bombardment, a cannonade enough to break through the wood. However selfish one may be, that sound does go to your heart. The tears began to flow again. Even after they had gone, after they were outside, they could still hear the detonations. Mes-Bottes, blowing in his hands, made the observation:

"Blast it all! poor old Madame Coupeau won't have a warm time of it!"

"Ladies and gentlemen," said the tinsmith to the few friends who remained behind with the family, "if you will kindly allow me to offer you something. . . ."

And he led the way to a public-house in the Rue Marcadet, "A la Descente du Cimetière." Gervaise, waiting outside, called to Goujet, who was moving off after having again saluted her with a nod. Why would he not accept a glass of wine. He was busy, must get back to work. Then they looked at one another for a moment without speaking.

"I beg your pardon about the sixty francs," murmured the laundress. "I was half beside myself I thought of you——"

"Oh, that's nothing; it's granted," interrupted the blacksmith. "And, you know, I am always at your service if you are in trouble. But say nothing to mother, because she has her own ideas, and I don't want to vex her."

She gazed into his face, and, seeing him there so good, so mournful, with his golden beard, she was on the point of accepting his old proposition to go away with him and be happy together somewhere. Then another wicked idea came into her head, to borrow the two quarter's rent from him, at no matter what price. She trembled; she went on in a caressing voice:

"We are good friends all the same, though?"

He nodded, and replied:

"Yes, indeed, we shall always be good friends. Only, you understand, all is over between us."

And he went off with great strides, leaving Gervaise as if stunned; his last words seemed to ring in her ears like a tolling of a bell. And as she went into the public-house, she heard, deep down in the depths of her heart:

"All is over, well, all is over; there is nothing for me to do if all is over!"

She sat down, swallowed a mouthful of bread and cheese and drained a full glass that she found before her.

It was a long room on the ground floor; it had a low ceiling, and there were two large tables. Bottles, quarterns of bread, triangles of Brie on three plates, were laid out in order. The company ate hastily, without table-cloth or covers. Further on, near the stove which was snorting furiously, the four mutes were finishing their dinner.

"Well, well," said M. Madinier, "we all have our turn. The old give place to the young. Your place will seem quite empty when you go back to it."

"Oh! my brother is giving it up," said Madame Lorilleux quickly. "The shop is ruinous."

They had been working away on Coupeau, all advising him to give up the lease. Madame Lerat herself, who for some time had been on the best of terms with Lantier and Virginie, tickled by the idea that they were mashed on one another, spoke of bankruptcy and prison with an air of terror. And the tinsmith all at once grew angry; his melting mood turned to rage under the influence of too many glasses of wine.

"Look here," he shouted in the face of his wife, "you've got to listen to me! You always go on your way like a damned

fool but this time you'll have to go *my* way; I give you
warning!"

"Oh! I say," said Lantier, "as if one ever made an impression on her by soft words! You want a mallet to knock it
into her."

And they both began on her at once. All this did not hinder
the eating. The Brie disappeared, the bottles flowed freely,
and Gervaise began to give way under all this pressure. She
said nothing; she went on eating very hurriedly, as if she were
very hungry. When they came to a pause she looked up
quietly and said:

"Well, is that enough? I don't care a straw about the shop.
I don't want to have anything more to do with it. Do you
understand? I don't care a straw! I've done with it."

Then they ordered more bread and cheese, and had a
serious talk. The Poissons would take on the lease, and were
willing to make up the two terms in arrears. Boche agreed to
the arrangement with an air of importance, in the landlord's
name. He even allotted to the Coupeaus, as a temporary
thing, the vacant rooms on the sixth floor in the Lorilleux's
corridor. As for Lantier, he would be very glad to keep his room
if he wouldn't be in the way of the Poissons. The policeman
bowed, he would not be in the way at all; friends can always
get on together, despite their political differences. And
Lantier, without concerning himself further about the transfer,
now that he had settled his little piece of business, made himself a huge slice of bread and cheese, and lay back in his chair,
eating it luxuriously, his face flushed, his eyes burning with a
sly delight, while he winked now at Gervaise, now at Virginie.

"Hi! old Bazouge!" Coupeau called out, "come and have
a drink. We are not proud, we all work for our living."

The four mutes, who were on the point of going, came back
and clinked glasses with the company. It was no reproach, but
the lady weighed a good lot; they deserved a glass of wine.
Old Bazouge looked fixedly at Gervaise, without misplacing
a word. She got up uneasily and left the men, who were all
getting their fair dose. Coupeau, as drunk as a lord, began to
blubber, and declared that it was all grief.

That evening, when Gervaise returned home, she sat down
as if stupefied. It seemed to her that the rooms were huge and
empty. It really cleared a lot of space. But it was not only old
Madame Coupeau whom she had left in the hole in the little
garden of the Rue Marçadet. All sorts of things had gone with

her, a piece of her very life, and her shop too, and her pride as the mistress of an establishment, and other feelings, too, had been buried that day. Yes, the walls were bare now, and her heart too; it was a general moving out, a general sliding down-hill. And she felt too tired to pick herself up again; she would do that later on if she could.

At ten o'clock, when they undressed her, Nana screamed and kicked. She had wanted to sleep in old Madame Coupeau's bed. Her mother tried to frighten her; but the child was too precocious; the dead awoke only curiosity in her, and at last, to restore peace, they let her lay herself out in old Madame Coupeau's place. She liked big beds, the little rogue; beds that she could roll about in. That night she slept soundly indeed, in the dainty warmth and softness of the feather-bed.

CHAPTER TEN

THE Coupeaus' new lodgings were on the sixth floor, staircase
B. When you had passed in front of Mademoiselle Remanjou's,
you turned into the passage on the left. Then you had to turn
again. The first door was the Bijards'. Almost opposite, in a
little close hole, under a little staircase that led to the roof,
slept old Bru. Two doors further on was Bazouge's. Then,
over against Bazouge, was the Coupeaus', a room and a little
room looking on the court. And there were only two other
households further on, before you reached the Lorilleux,
right at the end.

One room and a little room, that was all. The Coupeaus
had to perch there now. And the larger of the two rooms was
a mere handbreadth. Everything had to be done in it; you
had to sleep, eat, and all the rest. In the little room there was
just space enough for Nana's bed; she would have to undress
in her father and mother's room, and the door had to be
left open at night, for fear she should be stifled. It was so small
that Gervaise had turned over her things to the Poissons with
the shop; there was no room for them. The bed, the table,
four chairs; the place was quite full. All the same, she could
not give up her chest of drawers, and she had squeezed in the
great lumbering thing, which blocked up half the window.
One wing of the window couldn't be opened, and some of the
light and cheerfulness was cut off. When she wanted to look
down in the court, as she was now very stout, she had not
room for her elbows, and she had to look out sideways,
screwing round her neck.

For the first few days, she simply sat and cried. It seemed
too hard, not to be able to stir, after you had been used to
plenty of space. She felt stifled, she spent hours together at the
window, squeezed in between the wall and the chest of
drawers, until her neck was quite stiff. It was only then that
she was able to breathe freely. The court however, always
had a sad aspect for her. Over opposite, on the sunny side, she
saw what she had longed for of old, the fifth-floor window,
where the scarlet runners every spring twined their thin

tendrils about the trellis-work of string. Her own room was on
the shady side, where a pot of mignonette died in a week. Ah,
no, the pleasure of life was over now; it was not this sort of
existence that she had hoped for. Instead of having a bed of
roses for her old age, she had to make her bed in no very
sweet place. One day as she was leaning out, she had a very
queer sensation; she seemed to see herself down there below,
under the porch, near the *concierge's* lodge, looking up and
examining the house for the first time; and that jump of
thirteen years backwards gave her quite a start. The court had
not changed, the walls were hardly more black and streaked
than before; a stink came up from the rusty gutters; there were
clothes hung out to dry on lines, a child's clouts plastered with
filth; below, the battered pavement was still littered with the
locksmith's cinders and the carpenter's shavings; even the
dyer's stream in the damp corner had a beautiful blue tinge,
as delicate a blue as it had been of old. But she herself, how
changed and jaded she seemed to herself to be! She was no
more down below, her face to the sky, courageous and content,
longing for a fine place to live in. She was up under the roof,
in the lousiest corner, the dirtiest hole of the place, where not
a ray of sunlight could ever penetrate. And it was only natural
that she should cry; her fate left her nothing to be pleased with.

However, when Gervaise had got a little used to things,
the beginnings of the housekeeping in the new place were not
so bad after all. The winter was nearly over, the little money
they had got from Virginie for the furniture helped them to
get things straight. Then, when the fine weather came on,
they had a stroke of luck: Coupeau was hired to do some
work in the country, at Estampes; and he was there for nearly
three months without giving way to drink, cured for the
moment by the country air. You would never think how it
quenches a drunkard's thirst to get out of the atmosphere of
Paris, where there is a regular fume of wine and spirits in the
very streets. When he came back he was as fresh as a rose.
And he brought back with him four hundred francs, with
which they paid the two quarters of rent for which the
Poissons had made themselves responsible, as well as the
little debts of the neighbourhood, the most crying ones.
Gervaise was thus able to enter two or three streets which she
had not been able to pass through. Naturally, she had gone
back to her ironing work by the day. Madame Fauconnier,
an excellent woman when you flattered her, had agreed to

take her back. She even gave her three francs, as to a principal
hand, in consideration of her former position as mistress. So
the household seemed to be getting on a bit. Even, with hard
work and strict economy, Gervaise saw the day when they
could pay everybody, and get once more into a decent way of
living. But she only said that to herself in the fever of delight
at the big sum that her husband had earned. Looking at it
coldly she said that good things never last.

What wounded the Coupeaus the most was to see the
Poissons installed in their old shop. They were not too envious
in the general way, but people teased them, expatiating
deliberately before them on the improvement that had been
made by their successors. The Boches, the Lorilleux more
particularly, were never at an end. To hear them you would
think there never had been such a lovely shop. And they told
how dirty everything had been when the Poissons came in,
so that the cleaning it out had cost thirty francs by itself.
Virginie, after much hesitation, had decided upon a little
business in the grocery line, sweetmeats, chocolates, coffee,
tea. Lantier had urged her to go into this business, for, he
said, there were immense sums to be gained out of delicacies.
The shop was painted black, relieved with gilt mouldings,
two colours that were in very good taste. Three carpenters
worked for a week at fixing up the shelves, the windows, the
counter with shelves for the glass jars, as you see them at
confectioners. Poisson's little legacy in reserve must have
been considerably broken in upon. But Virginie was in
triumph, and the Lorilleux, assisted by the porters, spared
Gervaise no detail, not a shelf, nor a window arrangement,
nor a glass jar, amused at seeing her change countenance.
You may not fancy yourself envious, but you are furious when
other people get into your slippers and kick you out.

There was also another question underneath. It was
reported that Lantier had left Gervaise. The neighbours
declared that it was a very proper thing. It was quite a moral
lesson to the street. And all the credit of the separation went
to the artful Lantier, whom the ladies were still mashed upon.
There were definite details; he had had to box her ears to
make her leave off, so set upon him was she. Naturally, no one
said the exact truth; those who might have known it, found
it too simple and not interesting enough. Lantier had indeed
left Gervaise, in the sense that he had not got her at his beck
and call day and night; but he certainly went up sometimes to

see her on the sixth floor, for Mademoiselle Remanjou had met him coming out of the Coupeaus' at unusual hours. In short, the connection went on, anyhow, in a sort of go-as-you-please way, without either of them finding much pleasure in it; a sort of habit, a way of making one's self agreeable to each other, not more. Only what complicated the situation was that the neighbours spread the report that Lantier and Virginie were now bedfellows. Here, too, the neighbours were a little ahead in their reckoning. No doubt the hatter was paying court to her, and it was likely enough, since she replaced Gervaise in every respect in the house. There was even a story that one night he had gone to find Gervaise on his neighbour's pillow, and had taken off Virginie and kept her, without finding out his mistake till the morning, on account of the dim light. The story caused much amusement, but he was not really so far on; he had only got to the point of giving her a pinch now and then. The Lorilleux, too, were always talking before the laundress of the love-affairs of Lantier and Madame Poisson in a very satisfied tone, so as to make her jealous. The Boches too, declared that they had never seen a finer couple. What was odd was that the Rue de la Goutte-d'Or did not frown upon this new *ménage à trois*; no, morality, which had been severe with Gervaise, was lenient with Virginie. Perhaps the smiling indulgence of the street was due to the fact that the husband was a policeman.

Happily, Gervaise was not at all given to jealousy. Lantier's infidelities left her quite tranquil, for it was long since she had had any real feeling for him in this respect. She had heard, without wishing to hear them, dirty stories enough, how Lantier went off with all sorts of girls, the first frizzly-headed creature that he came across in the street; and it affected her so little that she went on letting him have his way, without being able to work up enough anger to break with him. However, she did not accept so easily his cottoning on to Virginie. With Virginie it was quite different. They had taken up with one another simply in order to tease her, and if she took precious little heed of trifles, she wished to be respected. So, when Madame Lorilleux, or some other malicious creature, made a point of saying in her presence that Poisson could now no longer pass under the Porte Saint-Denis, she went quite white, she felt a sort of tightening across the chest, a burning in the pit of the stomach. She bit her lips, and kept in her anger, not wishing to give her enemies so much gratification. But she evidently was on bad terms with Lantier, for Mademoiselle Remanjou thought she heard the sound of a slap, one afternoon; any way there was certainly a quarrel. Lantier never spoke to her for a fortnight, then he came back and made it up, and the course of things went on as if nothing had happened. Gervaise wished to get what she could out of it; at all events to avoid a clawing of chignons, desiring at all events not to make her life worse than it had been. Ah! she was not twenty years old any longer, she did not care about men to the point of blacking other people's eyes for them and getting run in. Only, she added it up with the rest.

Coupeau made fine fun of the situation. This confiding husband, who had not chosen to see his own cuckoldom, laughed himself hoarse over Poisson's pair of horns. In his own household it was a matter of no consequence, but in other people's it seemed to him very funny, and he took no end of trouble to spy upon those little accidents when the neighbours were a bit free with their favours. What a ninny Poisson was! and he carried a sword, too, and hustled people on the pavement. And Coupeau pushed his impudence to the point of joking Gervaise on the subject. Well! her lovers were jolly glad to give her the slip. She had very bad luck: first of all she had not succeeded with blacksmiths, and then for the second time it was a hatter who gave her the go-by. But she went in for professions which were really not serious. Why did she not take up a mason, a binding sort of a man, a man accustomed to mix his mortar solidly. No doubt he only said these things for fun, but Gervaise, none the less, turned green, for he stared at her with his little grey eyes, as if he would drive his words into her with a gimlet. When he began on this sort of nastiness, she never knew if he meant it quite in fun or at all seriously. A man who is drunk from year's end to year's end is not himself, and there are certain husbands, jealous enough when they are twenty, whom drink, at thirty, renders very accommodating indeed on the chapter of conjugal fidelity.

You should have seen Coupeau strut about in the Rue de la Goutte-d'Or! He spoke of Poisson as the cuckold. That nicely did for all the gossips; it wasn't he this time who was the cuckold. Oh! he knew what he knew. If he sometimes didn't pretend to, it was because he didn't care to spread scandal. Every man knows his own business, and can scratch himself where he itches. There was no itch about him, and he couldn't scratch himself, even to please people. But as for the policeman, was he really aware of it? There it was, anyway, this time; the lovers had actually been seen together, there was no mere rumour here. And he got quite excited, he couldn't see how a man, a Government official, could let such things go on in his home. Apparently the policeman liked second-hand goods, that was all. In the evening, however, when Coupeau was bored at sitting with his wife in their little room under the roof, he would go downstairs, all the same, and fetch Lantier, insist on his coming up and joining them. He found the crib a bit dreary, since his pal was there no more. He patched up his relations with Gervaise, when they were at loggerheads. Blast it all! what was the use of sending everybody about their business? mayn't you amuse yourself as you please? He laughed to himself, vast ideas seemed to loom up in his vague drunken eyes, and he seemed longing to share his all with the hatter, and give a brighter colour to his life. And it was especially on such occasions as these that Gervaise did not know if he spoke in jest or in earnest.

Meanwhile, Lantier assumed an air of great importance. He put on a dignified and paternal manner. Three times over he had patched up the quarrels of the Coupeaus and the Poissons. He like to see the two households at peace with one another. Thanks to his kind, yet strict supervision, Gervaise and Virginie always professed the greatest friendship for one another. And he ruled over blonde and brunette alike, with the tranquillity of a pasha, fattening over his tricky dealings. The rascal had not given over digesting the Coupeaus when he had already begun upon the Poissons. Oh! he was quite up to it! he had already disposed of one shop, he was quite ready for another. Well, it is only this kind of man who is always lucky.

It was in this year, in June, that Nana was confirmed. She was then going on for thirteen, she had suddenly shot up very tall, with a cheeky sort of air; last year, she had been dismissed from the catechism class, on account of her misconduct; and if the vicar admitted her this time, it was only for fear she would go for good and all, and be one little heathen the more on the streets. Nana jumped for joy when she thought of the white dress. The Lorilleux, as godfather and godmother, had promised her the dress, and they talked of their present all over the house; Madame Lerat was to give her the veil and

cap, Virginie, the purse, Lantier, the prayer-book; so that the
Coupeaus looked forward to the ceremony without too much
uneasiness. Even the Poissons, who wanted to have a house-
warming, chose this as the occasion, no doubt on the suggestion
of Lantier. They invited the Coupeaus and Boches, whose
little child was also being confirmed. They would have a leg
of mutton, and something with it.

The night before, as Nana gazed rapturously at the presents
laid out on the chest of drawers, Coupeau came back in a
beastly state. The Paris air had got him in its clutches again.
And he went for his wife and child, with drunkard's arguments, disgusting phrases which were not quite the thing for
such an occasion. But Nana herself was getting foul-mouthed
in the midst of all the dirty talk that she heard going on around
her continually. When quarrels broke out she was quite ready
to call her mother bitch and hag.

"Well! what next?" grumbled the tinsmith. "I want my
soup, you pack of jades! Look at the females with their flum-
meries! I'll over with the whole blooming lot if you don't give
me my soup!"

"What a nuisance when he is tight!" murmured Gervaise
impatiently.

Then, turning towards him:

"She's excited; don't bother us."

Nana had put on a modest air because she thought it
looked pretty on a day like that. She went on looking at the
presents on the chest of drawers, making a pretence of casting
down her eyes and not understanding her father's bad words.
But the tinsmith was very quarrelsome that night, after his
drink. He came up close to her and went on:

"I'll give it to you, with your white dresses! Do you want
to make titties again with lumps of paper inside your stays, as
you did the other Sunday? You wait a bit! I see you wriggling
your backside! Tickles you nicely, all that toggery! sets your
pate agog. Will you get out of it, you blasted little slut! Leave
that alone, put it in the drawer, or I'll wipe your face with it!"

Nana still kept her eyes lowered, and replied nothing. She
had taken up the little tulle cap, and she asked her mother
how much it cost. As Coupeau stretched out his hand to tear
it from her, it was Gervaise who thrust him back saying:

"Will you leave the child alone! she is all right, she isn't
doing any harm."

Then the tinsmith burst out more furiously than ever:

"Ah! the whores! Mother and daughter, a nice pair they are. Very nice it is to go and pretend to be so pious, when you only want to make eyes at the men. Dare to deny it, you little slut! I'll dress you in an old sack and see if that tickles your hide. Yes, a sack, to sicken you of it, you and your priests! Do you think I want to have vice put into you?"

Nana suddenly turned furiously, while Gervaise stretched out her arms, to protect the things that Coupeau talked of tearing up. The child stared hard at her father; then, forgetting the modesty recommended by her confessor:

"Swine!" she said, through her clenched teeth.

As soon as the tinsmith had finished his soup, he was snoring. Next morning he awoke in an excellent humour. He had just enough of his night's dose still on him to put him in a good temper. He helped to dress the child, much moved by the white dress, declaring that a mere nothing gave the little object quite the air of a young lady. In short, as he said, a father was naturally proud of his child, on a day like that. And it was a sight to see the way Nana carried it off, with the embarrassed smiles of a bride, in her white dress, a little too short for her. When they went down, and she saw Pauline on the doorstep, also all ready dressed, she gave a good look up and down her, and then was as amiable as possible, for she saw that the other did not look so well as herself, was all bundled up. The two families set out for the church. Nana and Pauline walked first, prayer-books in hand, holding in their veils, puffed out by the wind; and they did not say anything to each other, they were bursting with pride at seeing the people come out of their shops, and they put on a pious air, in order that they might hear the people say as they passed: how nice they are behaving! Madame Boche and Madame Lorilleux stayed behind, in order to give one another their opinions in regard to Clop-clop, a spendthrift, whose daughter would never have been confirmed if her relations had not given her everything, yes, everything, even a new chemise, out of respect for the holy table. Madame Lorilleux was specially concerned for the dress, her own present, and she gave Nana a rating and called her "dirty beast" every time that the child picked up any dust with her skirt, by going too near the shops.

In church, Coupeau wept the whole time. It was silly, but he couldn't help it. It all came over him, the vicar spreading out his arms, the little girls like little angels going in procession with joined hands, and the organ gave him a queer sensation inside, the good smell of the incense made him sniff, as if one had put a bouquet before his nose. Everything looked heavenly, he was touched to the heart. There was in particular a psalm, something smooth and sweet, while the children took the sacrament, which seemed to trickle down his neck, sending a shiver all along his spine. All round him, too, there was a general display of damp handkerchiefs. It was a great occasion, a unique occasion. Only, when he came out of church, and went for a drink with Lorilleux, who had not been at all impressed and who laughed at him for it, he accused the "crows" of burning wizard's herbs in order to make fools of men. Then, after all, he did not conceal the fact, he had cried a bit; well, it merely proved that he was not as hard as a stone. And he ordered another drink.

That evening the house-warming at the Poissons' was very gay. Everything went off without a hitch from beginning to end. However unlucky you may be, there are always good times now and then when you can get on even with the people you detest. Lantier had Gervaise on his left and Virginie on his right, and he made a great deal of both of them, like a cock who wishes to have peace in the hen-coop. Opposite, Poisson preserved his calmly and severely meditative air, the air of a policeman on duty, his eyes lowering, thinking of nothing. But it was the two children, Nana and Pauline, who were the central figures of the feast; they had been allowed to keep on their things, and they sat stiffly, for fear of spotting their white dresses, and at every mouthful they were told to keep their chins up, so as to swallow properly. Nana got worried, and finally spilt all her wine over her bodice. It was quite a to-do; she had to have it taken off and washed at once in a glass of water.

Then, over the dessert, they had a serious talk about the children's future. Madame Boche had made up her mind. Pauline was to be sent to a place where they did open-work in gold and silver; it brought in five or six francs. Gervaise had not yet settled, Nana had not shown any particular inclination. Oh! she was just running about the place. She would show some inclination; but, all the same, she was a regular butter-fingers.

"If I were in your place," said Madame Lerat, "I would let her be a flower-worker. It's a nice, decent trade."

"Flower-workers!" murmured Lorilleux; "a gay lot they are, all of them."

"Well, and what about me?" said Madame Lerat, pursing up her lips. "You are polite. All the same, I'm not a bitch: I'm not on my back at the first whistle."

Everyone hushed her up.

"Madame Lerat! Madame Lerat!"

And they glanced out of the corners of their eyes at the two children just come from confirmation, who were sticking their noses into their glasses to keep from laughing. Even the men had, so far, had the decency to pick their words. But Madame Lerat would not take the lesson. What she had just said she had heard in the best society. Besides, she flattered herself that she knew how to put things; people had often complimented her on the way in which she could say everything, even before children, without ever outraging propriety.

"There are very decent women among flower-workers, let me tell you!" she cried. "They are made like other women, they aren't hide-bound, I know very well. Only they look after themselves, they know how to make a good choice when they want to go off the lines. Yes, that comes from the flowers. For my part, it is that which has kept me. . . ."

"Good gracious!" interrupted Gervaise, "I haven't any objection to flowers. I only want something which Nana would like, that's all; it isn't good to put children to what doesn't suit them. Look here, Nana, don't be silly, tell me. How would you like to work at flowers?"

The child, bending over her plate, picked up crumbs of cake with her wetted finger, which she sucked. She did not answer at once. She only gave her little vicious smile.

"Yes, mamma, I should like it," she said at last.

So it was settled straight off. Coupeau wanted Madame Lerat to take the child to her workshop, Rue du Caire, the very day after. And the company talked gravely of the duties of life. Boche said that Nana and Pauline were women, now that they had been confirmed. Poisson added that they ought now to know how to cook and mend and look after a house. They even spoke of when they would get married and have children. The urchins listened and laughed within themselves, rubbing against one another, puffed up at the idea of being women, red and awkward in their white dresses. But what tickled them the most was when Lantier began to tease them, asking them if they had not already got their little husbands. And they insisted on Nana confessing that she was very fond of Victor Fauconnier, the son of her mother's mistress.

"Well," said Madame Lorilleux before the Boches, as they were all leaving, "she is our godchild, but from the moment they make her a flower-worker we have nothing more to do with her. One more draggle-tail for the streets. They'll have her pissing pepper before six months are out, you'll see!"

When they went upstairs to bed, the Coupeaus decided that everything had gone off very well, and the Poissons were a better sort than they had fancied. Gervaise even admitted that the shop was nicely arranged. She had expected to have a very bad time in spending the evening in her old home, now in the hands of others; and she was surprised at herself for not having had a moment's annoyance. When Nana was undressing she asked her mother if the dress of the young lady on the second floor, when she was married last month, had been muslin like hers.

But this was the last really happy day they were to have. Two years passed, and they sank deeper and deeper. The winters, in particular, tried them. If they had something to eat during fine weather, the pang of hunger came with the rain and cold; then began the dance before the sideboard, the dinners by heart, in the little Siberia of their domain. The villainous December made its way throught their door, bringing all kinds of hardship, putting people out of work, numbing them with the frost, and the black misery of wet weather. The first winter they were still sometimes able to have a fire, and they would crouch around the stove, finding it better to keep warm than even to have something to eat; the second winter the stove stood cold and rusty, freezing them with its dismal air of desolation. But what gave them the most bother, what brought them to the final point of distress, was to pay their rent. Oh! the January quarter, when there was not a scrap of bread in the place, and old Boche came with the receipt! It brought in the cold more than ever, a very northern tempest. M. Marescot turned up the Saturday after, wrapped in a big overcoat, his great hands cased in woollen gloves, and he always spoke of turning them out, while the snow fell outside, as if it were making a bed for them on the pavement, laying the white sheets. They would have sold themselves in order to pay the quarter's rent. It was the quarter's rent that kept the cupboard and the stove empty. And throughout the whole house there was a general lamentation. There was a sound of weeping in every storey, a music of misery wailed through staircase and corridors. If there had been a death in every home, there could scarcely have been such an abominable organ music everywhere. The last day had come, the end of all things, the extinction of poor folk. The woman on the third went out for a week to walk the corner of the Rue Belhomme. A workman, the mason on the fifth, had stolen from his master.

No doubt the Coupeaus had only themselves to blame. However badly off you may be, you can always make your way, with order and economy, like the Lorilleux for instance, who sent in their quarter's rent punctually, folded in bits of dirty paper; but the Lorilleux led a life that was enough to disgust you with work. Nana was not yet earning anything with her flowers; she even required not a little money for her keep. Gervaise had by this time got to be held in very little esteem at Madame Fauconnier's. She lost her skill more and more, she bungled the work, until the mistress had to reduce her pay to two francs, a botcher's pay. Notwithstanding, she was very stuck-up, very sensitive, posing before everybody on the strength of her former position. She sometimes stayed away a day, she would go off in a huff; thus, on one occasion, she was so disgusted at Madame Fauconnier taking on Madame Putois, and having to work side by side with her former work-woman, that she stayed away for a whole fortnight. After these whimsies they took her back out of charity, which irritated her still more. Naturally, at the end of the week, the pay was not very large; and, as she said bitterly, it was she who would be in her mistress's debt some Saturday or other. As for Coupeau, he did some work perhaps, but if so he certainly made a present of his work to the Government, for Gervaise, since the Estampes expedition, had not seen the colour of his money. On pay-day she now never even looked at his hands when he came in. He would come lounging along, his pockets empty, often even without his handkerchief; Lord! why he had lost his wipe, or some joker had prigged it for fun. At first, he would make out calculations, and invent fibs, ten francs for a subscription, twenty francs that had slipped out of his pocket through a hole that he showed, fifty francs that had gone to pay some imaginary debts. But after a time, he did not take the trouble. He had nothing in his pocket, he had it inside him, not at all a bad way of bringing it home to the missus. The laundress, at Madame Boche's suggestion, sometimes went to wait for her man on the way out from work, so as to seize the nest-egg fresh laid; but it was no use whatever, Coupeau's pals told him she was there, and the money made its way down into his shoes, or some other less decent hiding-place. Madame Boche was very artful in this respect, for Boche had a way of making ten-franc pieces disappear, little sums intended to stand treat to certain amiable ladies of his acquaintance; she searched every corner of his clothes, and generally found the missing piece in the front of his cap, sewn in between the leather and the cloth. It wasn't in the tinsmith's line to pad his togs with gold; he stowed it away under his skin, and Gervaise couldn't very well take the scissors and unstitch that!

Yes, it was their own fault no doubt, if they went on from bad to worse. But people never say those things, especially when they are on their downward roads. They declared it was their bad luck, that God was very unjust to them. They kicked up a regular shindy now, indoors; they were at it the whole day. But they had not yet come to blows, except for an occasional one in the heat of discussion. The worst of it was that they had opened the door of the cage to all the kind feelings that remained to them, and they had all flown away, like canaries. The comfortable warmth of father, mother, and children, when all hold together, had gone out of them, and left them shivering, each in a different corner. All three Coupeau, Gervaise, and Nana, had turned crusty, and their eyes were full of hate; and it seemed as if something had broken the mainspring of the family, the piece of mechanism which, in happy people, makes hearts beat in unison. Ah! it was quite certain that Gervaise was not so terrified as she once was, when she saw Coupeau at the edge of gutters, thirty or forty feet from the ground. She would not have given him a push herself; but if he had fallen of his own accord, well, that wouldn't have taken anything very valuable out of the world. When they were nagging at one another in the house, she asked how long it would be before they brought him back to her on a stretcher. That was just what she was waiting for, tt would be the greatest good luck she could get. What was ihe good of the tippler? to cause her tears, to eat up every-thing, to bring her to the bad. Why! men who were of no more use than that, they were put underground as soon as possible, and you danced over them a polka of deliverance. And when the mother said, "Kill!" the daughter replied, "Bash him!" Nana read the accidents in the papers, and made her own reflections on them, like an unnatural daughter. Her father had such good luck, that he had been knocked down by an omnibus without it's even sobering him. When would the lazy brute be finished off?

In the midst of this existence, soured by poverty, Gervaise suffered too on account of the starving people she found all around her. It was the lousy corner of the house, where three or four households seemed to have agreed not to indulge in a meal every day. The doors might open, it was not often they let out a smell of cooking. All along the corridor, there was a deathly silence, and the walls rang hollow, like empty stomachs. Now and again there was a bit of a row, women crying, hungry brats screaming, families, who went for each other tooth and nail, in default of anything else to use their jaws upon. A sort of general cramp seemed to yawn from all those gaping mouths; and chests grew hollow, merely with breathing the air of the place, an air in which a gnat could hardly live. But Gervaise specially pitied poor old Bru in his hole under the little staircase. He hid himself away there like a marmot, and he rolled himself up in it so as not to be so cold; he stayed there whole days without ever coming out, on his heap of straw. Not even hunger drove him out, for it was useless to go out and get an appetite, when nobody had invited him out to dinner. When he had not been seen for three or four days, the neighbours pushed open his door, and looked in to see if it was all over. No, he lived still, not much, but a little, he was not quite gone; even death seemed to have forgotten him! Whenever Gervaise had any bread, she threw him the crusts. If she turned sour and loathed men, on her husband's account, at all events she was really sorry for animals; and old Bru, poor old fellow, who was left to starve because he could no longer hold a tool, was like a dog to her, a beast too old for work, of which even the knackers wouldn't buy the skin or the fat. It was a weight on her mind to know he was always there, on the other side of the passage, forsaken of God and man, living on himself, shrunk now to the stature of a child, dried and shrivelled as an orange over the fire-place.

The laundress suffered equally from the nearness of Bazouge, the undertaker's man. A mere partition, quite a thin one, separated the two rooms. He could not put his finger in his mouth without her hearing it. As soon as he came in at night, she listened, despite herself, to every sound that came from his room, the black hat sounding on the chest of drawers like a clod of earth, the black cloak, as it was hung up, scraping against the wall like the sound of some night-bird's wings, all the black things thrown all about the room, like mourning being unpacked. She heard him moving about, worried by his slightest movement, starting if he knocked against a piece of furniture or rattled his crockery. She could not help thinking of the infernal drunkard with a sort of fear mixed with a certain curiosity. He was always jolly, a bit screwed every night, and quite far gone always on Sunday; he coughed and spat, and sang, made the most unseemly noises, and fought with the four walls before he could find his bed. And she would turn quite pale, wondering what he was up to now; she had the most horrible fancies, would get it into her head that he had brought home a corpse with him and that he was stowing it away under his bed. Why, wasn't there a story in the papers about an undertaker's man who had quite a collection of children's coffins in his house, which he had made to save the trouble of going to the cemetery more than once. Certainly, when Bazouge arrived, he brought with him the scent of death on the other side of that partition. It was like living opposite Pére-Lachaise, in the very land of moles. The creature was a perfect terror, always laughing to himself when he was alone, as if his profession amused him. Even when he had finished kicking up a row, and had gone to bed, he snored in an extraordinary way, which made Gervaise hold her breath. She listened, straining her ears for hours together, fancying that a funeral procession was passing through the next room.

And the worst of it all was that Gervaise, for all her terror, felt drawn to lay her ear against the wall, so as to hear better. Bazouge affected her as a handsome man does an honest woman; she would fain have a taste, but dares not; her good bringing-up holds her back. Well, if fear had not held her back, Gervaise would fain have had a taste of death, would fain have known what it was like. She was sometimes so queer, with bated breath, waiting and watching for the meaning of one of Bazouge's movements, that Coupeau asked her, with a chuckle, if she was mashed on the mute. It angered her, and she talked of moving, so repugnant was it to be in such close quarters with him; and, despite herself, no sooner had the old man arrived, with his scent of the graveyard, than she fell back once more into her reflections, wearing the fearful and alert air of a wife who

dreams of slashing into her marriage lines. Had he not twice
offered to pack her up and take her away with him somewhere
for a sleep, where you slumber so soundly that you forget
your miseries at once? Perhaps there was really nothing
better. Little by little there came to her a burning desire of it.
She would like to have tried it for a fortnight, for a month. Oh!
to sleep for a month, especially in winter, the month when the
quarter-day came, when the troubles of life crushed her to
the ground! But it was impossible; you must go on sleeping
for ever if you begin to sleep for one hour. And the thought
froze her; her letch of death evaporated before the endless
and relentless friendship claimed by the earth.

One night in January she set to banging her fists against
the partition. She had spent a frightful week, hustled about on
all sides, penniless and helpless. That night she was not well,
she shook with fever, and saw lights dancing before her.
Then, instead of throwing herself out of the window, as she
had been tempted to do for a moment, she began to bang and
call:

"Bazouge! Bazouge!"

The mute was taking off his shoes, singing "Il était trois
belles filles". He must have had plenty of work that day, for
he seemed more overcome than usual.

"Bazouge! Bazouge!" cried Gervaise, raising her voice.

Would he not hear her? She gave herself up completely, he
could take her on his back and carry her where he carried his
other women, the poor and the rich, that he comforted. His
song, "Il était trois belles filles", distressed her, for she saw in
it the disdain of a man who has too many lovers.

"What's up? What's up?" stuttered Bazouge. "Anybody
ill? I'm ready, my good woman."

But, at the sound of this hoarse voice, Gervaise awoke from
her nightmare. What had she done? she had knocked at the
partition, evidently. And she started in terror, she recoiled, as
she seemed to see the great hands pass through the wall to
seize her by the hair. No, no, she would not go, she was not
ready. If she had knocked, it must have been with her elbow,
in turning, without intending to. And a horror mounted
slowly from her knees to her shoulders, at the thought of
seeing herself trailed along in the old man's arms, stiff and
rigid, her face white as a sheet.

"Well! nobody?" said Bazouge in the silence. "I'm waiting.
I'm always attentive to the ladies."

"Nothing, nothing," said the laundress at last, in a choking voice, "I don't want anything, thanks."

While the mute went off to sleep, grumbling and growling, she lay there anxiously listening, not daring to move, for fear he should imagine he heard her knocking again. She swore to herself that she would take good care now. If she were at her last gasp, she would not ask help from her neighbour. And she said that to reassure herself, for at certain moments, despite the funk she had been in, she still kept her timorous letch.

In the midst of all this misery, her own and others, Gervaise found a fine example of courage in at the Bijards'. Little Lalie, a child of eight years old, a tiny thing, looked after the household as nicely and neatly as a grown-up person; and it was no small task, she had to see after two little urchins, her brother Jules and her sister Henriette, two little brats of three and five, whom she had to keep her eye upon all day, even when she was sweeping and washing up. Since old Bijard had killed his wife with a kick in the stomach, Lalie had acted as the little mother of the family. Without a word said, quite of her own accord, she took the dead woman's place, to such an extent that her foolish brute of a father, to make the likeness complete, battered about the daughter now as he had battered the mother before. When he came in drunk he felt the need of a woman to attack. He did not even notice what a tiny little thing Lalie was; he hit her as he would have hit a grown woman. If he gave her a box on the ear, he covered her whole face, and the flesh was still so tender that the mark of his five fingers remained for two days. He beat her shamelessly, he kicked her for a yes or a no; it was the raging wolf falling on to a poor little timid cat, so thin, that she brought tears to your eyes; and she took it all with a resigned look in her beautiful eyes, without a murmur. Never did Lalie utter a complaint. She bent her head a little to protect her face; she kept herself from crying out, so as not to stir up the house. Then, when her father was tired of kicking her from corner to corner of the room, she waited until she had the strength to pick herself up; and she went back to her work, washing the children, making the soup, leaving not a speck of dust on the furniture. It was part of her daily task to be beaten.

Gervaise had taken a great liking for her little neighbour. She treated her as her equal, a woman of her own age, who had had experience of life. It is true that Lalie had a pale and serious air, the look of an old maid. To hear her talk, you

would have said she was thirty. She knew how to buy things,
to mend, to keep a home in order, and she spoke of children
as if she had had two or three in the course of her life. For a
child of eight, it made people laugh to hear it; then it made you
choke, and turn away to keep from crying. Gervaise got her to
come and see her as much as she could, gave her what she
was able to, things to eat, and old dresses. One day, as she was
trying on to her an old dress of Nana's, she was quite overcome
when she saw her spine all blue, her elbow with the skin
knocked off, and still bleeding, all her little innocent body
scored all over, and sticking to her bones. Well, old Bazouge
might bring his coffin this way, it would not have long to
wait at this rate! But the child begged her not to say anything
about it. She did not want anyone to be unkind to her father
on her account. She made excuses for him, she declared
that he would not be bad if he had not drank. He was mad,
he did not know what he was doing. Oh! she forgave
him, for one must forgive everything to people who are
mad.

After that Gervaise watched over her, and tried to interfere,
when she heard old Bijard coming upstairs. But for the most
part she only got a blow on her own account. During the day,
when she went in, she often found Lalie tied to the foot of the
iron bed; an idea of the fitter, who, before going out, tied
her round the legs and waist with stout cord, no one could
tell why; a whim of his drunken brain, probably a way of
tyrannizing over the child even when he was not there.
Lalie, as stiff as a poker, her legs tingling, was kept there, at
the bed post, for whole days; she even stood there all through
one night, Bijard having forgotten to come in. When Gervaise
spoke indignantly of untying her, she begged her not to
touch a single cord, because her father was furious, if he did
not find the same knots when he came back. She was really
all right, it rested her; and she said it with a smile, her poor
little legs all swollen and numbed. What distressed her was,
that the work got behind while she was tied like that to the
bed, with all the disorder before her. Her father might just
as well have invented something else. She kept her eye on the
children all the same, made them do as she told them, called
over Henriette or Jules to wipe their noses. As she had her
hands free, she knitted while she was waiting to be let loose,
so as not to lose the time altogether. And she suffered most of
all when old Bijard untied her; she dragged herself along the

ground for a good quarter of an hour, without being able to stand upright; her blood had stopped circulating.

The fitter had also invented another little diversion. He put sous into the stove until they were red-hot, then laid them on a corner of the chimney-piece. And he called Lalie and told her to go and fetch two pounds of bread. The child took the sous unsuspiciously, uttered a cry and dropped them to the ground, shaking her poor little burnt fingers. At that he began to storm. What did she mean by it, the baggage? Now she was losing good money, and he threatened to have her backside off if she didn't pick up the money at once. If she hesitated she had a first warning in the shape of so vigorous a cuff that everything danced before her. In silence, with two big tears in her eyes, she picked up the sous and carried them off, making them jump in the palm of her hand to cool them.

One would never think what ferocious ideas come into a drunkard's brain. One afternoon, for instance, after Lalie had finished tidying up, she was playing with the children. The window was open, there was a draught, and the wind outside in the passage kept pushing the door a little bit open.

"It is Monsieur Hardi," said the child. "Come in, Monsieur Hardi. Be so kind as to come in."

And she made curtsies before the door, bowing to the wind. Henriette and Jules, behind her, bowed too, enchanted with the game, screaming with laughter as if someone had tickled them. She was beaming at seeing them so full of fun, she even got a little fun out of it on her own account, which happened to her on the thirty-sixth of every month.

"Good day, Monsieur Hardi. How do you do, Monsieur Hardi?"

But a brutal hand drove the door open, old Bijard entered. Then the scene changed, Henriette and Jules fell down against the wall, whilst Lalie, terrified, stopped short in the very midst of a curtsy. The fitter was carrying a great carter's whip, brand-new, with a long handle of white wood, a leather lash, ending in a bit of thin cord. He put down the whip on the edge of the bed, and he did not give his usual kick to the child, who prepared for it instinctively, presenting her hips. He chuckled, and showed his black teeth, and he was very jovial, very drunk; he had the idea of a fine joke in his pate.

"Eh!" said he, "so you're doing the trull, are you, bloody slut! I heard you dancing as I came up. Now come here!

Closer, damnation! and turn this way; I don't want to sniff
your mustard-pot! I'm not touching you, you needn't shake
in your shoes like that. Take off my shoes."

Lalie, frightened at not receiving her usual thrashing, had
turned quite pale; she took off his shoes. He sat down on the
edge of the bed, he lay down on it in his clothes, with his
eyes open, watching every movement that she made. She was
quite stupefied under his gaze, and she shook with such a
fright that finally she dropped a cup. Then, without raising
himself, he took the whip and held it up to her.

"I say, youngster, look here: that is a present for you. Yes,
you've cost me fifty sous for that. With this plaything I shan't
need to run, and you won't be able to screw yourself into the
corners. Won't you have a try? Ah! you break the cups, do
you? Come now, gee-up, dance, make your curtsies to Monsieur
Hardi!"

He did not even raise himself in bed, but lay there sprawling,
his head buried in the pillow, cracking his great whip in the
room, with the sound of a postilion who is setting his horses
going. Then, lowering his arm, he sent the lash round Lalie's
waist winding and unwinding her like a top. She fell, and
tried to crawl away on her hands and knees; but he caught her
again with the lash, and set her on her legs once more.

"Gee-up! gee-up!" he shouted, "it's the donkey-race! Eh!
a jolly lark of a winter morning; I lie down, I don't catch
cold, and I catch the jade a good way off, without barking
my chilblains. Got you there, chatterbox! And got you there,
too! And got you there, again! Ah! if you get under the bed,
I'll have you with the handle. Gee-up! gee-up! ride a cock-
horse! ride a cock-horse!"

A little foam came to his lips, his yellow eyes nearly started
out of their sockets. Lalie, maddened with pain, screaming
aloud, rushed from corner to corner, grovelled on the floor,
squeezed herself flat against the walls; but the sharp lash
caught her wherever she went, cracking in her ears with the
sound of a bomb-shell, bringing out long weals all over her
skin. It was like the dance of an animal who is being taught
to do tricks. The poor little thing jumped and jumped—a
sight it was!—like children with a skipping-rope, who cry
"Faster! Faster!" She was out of breath, she rebounded of
her own accord like an elastic ball, she let the blows fall
where they would, blinded and exhausted with her vain
search for some safe corner. And the wolf of a father shouted

in triumph, calling her a draggle-tail, and asking her if she had had enough, if she had given up thinking she could get away from him now.

But all at once Gervaise appeared on the scene, drawn by the child's shrieks. She was seized with fury and indignation.

"Ah! you beast!" she cried. "Will you leave her alone, you blackguard! I'll call a policeman!"

Bijard growled like a disturbed beast. He stuttered out:

"Look here, you old hobbler! you mind your own business! Perhaps you'd like me to put on gloves when I give her a dressing? I'm simply giving her a good warning, do you see, that I have a long arm."

And he gave a final cut of the whip, and caught Lalie right in the face. Her upper lip was cut open; the blood flowed. Gervaise caught up a chair and would have fallen upon him. But the child put up her hands entreatingly, saying that it was nothing, it was all over now. She wiped away the blood with a corner of her apron, and quieted the children, who were sobbing as if the blows had all rained down on themselves.

When Gervaise thought of Lalie, she dared not complain. She wished she had the courage of this little child of eight, who suffered by herself as much as all the women on their staircase put together. She had seen that she had been on dry bread for the last three months, scarcely able to eat a crust, and so thin and weak that she had to hold on to the walls to support herself; and, when she had brought her little bits of meat on the sly, she was quite overcome as she watched her swallowing, with her eyes full of tears, a little bit at a time, because her throat was so shrunken, there was scarcely room for food to pass. Despite it all, always affectionate and devoted, wise beyond her age, doing her duty as a little mother, killing herself by these maternal instincts, called out too soon in her little childish innocence. And Gervaise took the dear little creature, so suffering and so forgiving, as a lesson to herself, trying to learn of her to suffer also in silence. Lalie only looked at you silently, with her great, black, patient eyes, in whose depths lay buried a whole night of agony and of distress. Never a word, nothing but those great, black, wide-open eyes.

And in the Coupeaus' household the ravages of the brandy from old Colombe's bar were beginning to make themselves felt. The laundress saw the hour when her man, too, would

take his whip, like Bijard, to set her dancing. And the trouble
that she saw ahead of her made her, naturally, more sensible
to the child's troubles. Yes, Coupeau was getting in a bad way.
The time was past when brandy was accustomed to make him
jolly. He could no longer smack his chest and brag, and say
that the damned stuff only fattened him; for his unwholesome
yellow fat had run down, and he grew lean and fell away,
getting a sort of greenish hue, like a drowned body putrefying
in a pool. His appetite, too, had failed. Little by little he had
lost the taste for bread, and could hardly eat a stew. If you
served up to him the nicest kickshaw in the world, his stomach
turned against it, his teeth refused to chew. He required his
pint of brandy a day to keep him up; it was his daily ration,
his food and drink, the only food that he could digest. In the
morning, when he got out of bed, he sat for a good quarter of
an hour all doubled up, coughing, holding his head, and
spitting up phlegm, something as bitter as gall which came up
in his throat. It had come to be a regular thing with him, you
could have the jordan ready waiting. He was not himself until
he had had his first glass of comfort, which sent the proper
fire down into his inside. But as the day went on he picked up
strength. At first he had felt a tickling sensation, a tingling of
the skin, in his hands and feet; and he laughed and said that
they were tickling him, that the missus must have put something rough inside the bedclothes. Then his legs grew heavy,
the tickling gave place to horrible cramps, which pinched his
chest like a vice. And that seemed far from being as funny. It
was no laughing matter now; he stopped short in the street,
his ears ringing, his eyes blinded. Everything before him
went yellow, the houses danced before his eyes, he reeled for
a second or two, afraid of measuring his length on the ground.
Other times, when he was out in the sun, a shiver, like iced
water, ran down his spine. What pestered him most of all was
that his hands began to shake; the right hand especially must
have been up to something wicked, such a nightmare did it
seem to have. Damnation! wasn't he a man, then, was he
going to get like an old woman? He set his muscles, furiously,
and held his glass in his clenched fist, wagering that he would
hold it motionless, with a hand of iron; but in spite of all his
efforts the glass started dancing, jerked to right, jerked to
left, with a little hurried regular tremble. Thereupon he
drained it off, furious, declaring that he needed dozens of
them, and then he would support a cask without moving a

finger. Gervaise told him that if he didn't want his hand to tremble, he should give up drinking. He merely laughed at her, drained whole bottles, tried again, and then got in a rage and accused the passing omnibus of shaking the liquor.

One evening in March Coupeau came back drenched to the skin; he had come with Mes-Bottes from Montrouge, where they had had a good tightener of eel-soup; and he had been simply soaked all the way from the Barrière des Fourneaux to the Barrière Poissonnière, a good long trot. In the middle of the night an attack of coughing came on; he got flushed, and a frightful shivering fit seized him, setting his sides panting like a broken bellows. When the Boches' doctor came to see him in the morning, and had examined him, he shook his head, and taking Gervaise aside he advised her to have her husband taken at once to the hospital. He had inflammation of the lungs.

This time Gervaise had no objection. Once upon a time she would have let herself be hacked to pieces rather than have her husband in the clutches of the saw-bones. After his accident in the Rue de la Nation she had used up all their little savings in tending him. But fine feelings of this sort don't last when men become sots. No, no, she had no notion of giving herself all that bother. They could take him and keep him; it would be a good riddance. However, when the stretcher arrived, and Coupeau was slung on to it like a piece of furniture, she went pale, and bit her lips; and if she growled and declared that it was good enough, she said it without feeling it, and she would have been only too glad to have had ten francs in the drawer, and to have kept him from being carried off. She went with him to Lariboisière, saw the infirmary people put him to bed, at the end of a long room where rows of sick people, looking like corpses, rose on their elbows to see the fresh comrade brought in; a deathly spectacle it was, the air feverish enought to choke you, and a chorus of consumptives enough to set you coughing and spitting; another room too was like a little Père-Lachaise, with its rows of white beds, laid out like a graveyard. Then, when he lay there with his head sunk into the pillow, she went away, without a word, having, unluckily, nothing in her pocket to comfort him with. Outside, opposite the hospital, she turned and looked back at the pile of buildings. And she thought of old times, when Coupeau, perched at the edge of the gutters, put on the sheets of galvanized, singing there in the sun. He did not drink then; he had a skin like a girl's. She watched him from her window in the Hôtel Boncœur, she saw him there right against the sky; and they waved their handker-chiefs to one another, sending kisses by telegraph. Yes, Coupeau had worked then, little thinking that he was working for himself. Now he was on the roofs no longer, like a gay and amorous sparrow; he was underneath, he had built his nest in the hospital, and he came there with ruffled plumes, to lay his bones there. God! how long ago all that wooing-time seemed today!

Two days after, when Gervaise came to see how he was getting on, she found the bed empty. One of the sisters explained to her that they had to send him to the Saint-Anne Asylum, because, all of a sudden, the day before, he had gone quite off his head. Oh! a regular upset; he had tried to beat his head against the wall, he had howled so that the other patients could not sleep. It was the drink, apparently, that had done it. The drink had been slumbering in his body, and it had seized its chance of gripping him and putting his nerves out of order, when the inflammation of the lungs held him powerless and prostrate. The laundress went home in dismay. Now her man was mad. Nana cried that he had better stay in the hospital, or he would kill both of them.

It was not till Sunday that Gervaise could go to the Sainte-Anne Asylum. It was quite a distance. Luckily the omnibus from the Boulevard Rochechouart to La Glacière passed near. She got down at the Rue de la Santé, she brought two oranges so as not to come empty-handed. It was another huge place, with grey courts, interminable passages, an odour of stale medicaments, which was not quite the sort of thing to put you in a lively mood. But when they had shown her into a cell, she was quite surprised to see Coupeau almost jolly. He was just then on the throne, a very decent wooden box which did not let out the least smell; and they had a laugh at her finding him performing, his backside bare. Then one knows what sick people are. He squatted there like a king, and he had quite his lively old chatter. Oh! he was better now since that went on all right again.

"And the inflammation?" she asked.

"Gone!" he answered. "They cured me of that in a minute. I cough a little, but that rot's over."

Then, as he left his throne to get into bed again, he began joking again.

"You've got a good nose, you're not afraid of its giving you a turn!"

And they had a good laugh together. They were both very happy. It was by way of expressing their satisfaction without going into phrases, that they jested about the matter. One must have had sick people about to realize how glad one is at finding them every way in good working order again.

When he had gone back to bed, she gave him the two oranges, he was quite touched. He was quite nice again, now that he was only taking gruel, and could no longer leave his heart in his glass. At last she ventured to speak to him of how he had been a bit off his head; she was surprised to hear him speak as calmly as usual.

"Ah! yes," said he, laughing, "I was a bit queer. Fancy! I saw rats! I went down on all fours to put a grain of salt on their tail. And you too, you were calling me; there were men after you. Yes, all sorts of silly things, ghosts in plain daylight. Oh! I'm quite myself again now, my nut's solid enough. It's all right now, I dream a bit when I go to sleep, I have nightmares, but then everybody has nightmares."

Gervaise stayed with him till evening. When the house-surgeon came at six, he made him stretch out his hands; they hardly trembled at all, there was only a just perceptible quivering in the tips of the fingers. But as night came on, Coupeau, little by little, became anxious. He sat up in bed twice, looking on the ground, in the shady corners. Suddenly he reached out his arm, and seemed to crush something against the wall.

"What is it?" said Gervaise, in a fright.

"The rats! The rats!" he whispered.

Then, after a silence, half in his sleep, he began to struggle, uttering broken words and phrases.

"Damnation! they are making holes in my coat! Oh! the dirty beasts! Look out! Pull your petticoats about you! Mind that brute there behind you! Damn and blast it! they have knocked her over, and those brutes are laughing! You brutes! You scamps! You blackguards!"

He hit out at the air, pulled up his quilt and rolled it into a bundle on his chest, as if to protect it against the violence of the great bearded men that he saw. A keeper rushed in, and Gervaise went, frightened to death by the scene she had witnessed. But when she came back a few days after, she found Coupeau completely cured. Even the nightmares had

gone, he slept like a child, ten hours on end, without moving
a limb. And his wife was allowed to take him back with her.
Only the house-surgeon gave him the usual good advice,
urging him to pay heed to it. If he took to drink again, he
would get just as bad again, and it would finally carry him off.
It depended entirely on himself. He had seen how nice and
cheerful he was when he didn't drink. Well, he must live at
home just as he had lived at Sainte-Anne's, imagining that
he was under lock and key, and that the public-houses didn't
exist.

"The gentleman is quite right," said Gervaise in the
omnibus, on the way back to the Rue de la Goutte-d'Or.

"No doubt he is right," replied Coupeau.

Then, after a minute's reflection, he added:

"Still, you know, just a glass now and then doesn't kill a
man, it helps him to digest."

And that evening he took a glass of brandy, just for his
digestion. For a week, however, he was very moderate. At
heart he was in a deadly funk; he had no desire to finish his
days at Bicêtre. But his craving had its way with him, the
first glass led to the second, despite himself, and that to the
third, and that to the fourth; and by the end of the week he
had gone back to his usual ration, a pint of brandy a day.
Gervaise was so exasperated that she could have hit him.
How silly she was to have dreamt of living a decent life again,
just because she had found him sober and sensible in the
asylum. Another good moment flown forever, and the last,
certainly the last. Now nothing could hold him back, not even
the fear of death, she swore that she would not bother herself
any more; the household could go at sixes and sevens, she
would let it go; and she declared that she too would take her
pleasure where she could find it. Then the hell of a time began
again, an existence deeper down in degradation than ever,
without a loop-hole open for better times to come. Nana,
when her father boxed her ears, asked furiously why the
blackguard hadn't stayed behind at the hospital. She was
only waiting till she had some money, she said, to buy more
brandy for him and finish him up the sooner. Gervaise, on
her side, completely lost her temper one day when Coupeau
was regretting that he had ever married her. Ah! she had
brought him other people's leavings, had she? she had made
him pick her up out of the streets, with her innocent airs! He
was damned cheeky, he was! As many lies as there were

DRUNKARD   319

words. She didn't want him at all, that was the simplest truth. He went on his knees to her to bring her round, when she had advised him to think it over. And if she had to do it again, wouldn't she say no! she would sooner cut off her arm. Yes, she had seen the moon, before his time; but if a woman had, and is a good worker, she is worth more than a lout of a man who soils his good reputation and that of his family in all the pubs. That day, for the first time with the Coupeaus, they had a regular squabble, and they went for one another so vigorously that an old umbrella and the broom were broken.

And Gervaise kept her word. She sank lower and lower; she stayed away from work oftener, she gossiped away whole days, became as limp as a rag when there was any work to be done. When she let a thing drop, it might lie where it was; she wasn't going to take the trouble to pick it up. She was far too lazy for that. She preferred to save her bacon. She took her time, and never swept up anything now until she could hardly move for dirt. The Lorilleux, when they passed her room, pretended to stop their noses; it was like poison, they said. They kept themselves to themselves, at the end of the passage, keeping free of all the poverty that wailed throughout that part of the house, locking their door for fear of having to lend a franc now and again. Nice, good-hearted, obliging neighbours they were! Any pretext to keep from opening the door. If you knocked and asked for a light, or a pinch of salt, or a glass of water, you were pretty sure to have the door slammed in your face. And regular vipers too. They declared that they had nothing to do with others, when it was a question of helping a neighbour; but they had plenty to do with them, from morning to night, when there was a question of back-biting anybody. When they had shot the bolt and hung a quilt over the door to stop up the crevices and the keyhole, they had a feast of scandal, without ever leaving their gold-wire for a second. Clop-clop's downfall in particular made them purr all day long, like tom-cats when you stroke them. Aren't they hard up, aren't they seedy, my friends! They spied on them when they went to buy provisions, and laughed at the little scrap of bread that she would bring back under her apron. They guessed at the days when she could only dance before the sideboard. They knew just how thick the dust lay in her room, just how many dirty plates were left about, every single thing that she left alone in her growing idleness and destitution. And then her dresses, horrid rags the rag-

pickers wouldn't take! Good Lord! her silks and satins were a
bit off, the beautiful blonde, who had wagged her rump with
such an air once upon a time, in her fine blue shop. That was
what the love of eating and drinking and kissing brought you
to! Gervaise, fancying that they had plenty of bad words for
her, took off her slippers, and put her ear to the keyhole; but
the quilt hindered her from hearing anything. Only one day
she caught them in the act of calling her "big bubs," because
no doubt her bosom was a bit large, despite the little food
that she had to support her. She sent them to their own place;
but she continued to speak to them, so as not to set the neighbours' tongues wagging, not expecting from them anything
but insults, but without the strength to answer them back,
and to send them about their business like the good-for-
nothings they were. And then, what was the use? She only
asked to be allowed to please herself, to live in peace and
quietness, twirling her thumbs, and moving when she felt
inclined, not otherwise.

One Saturday, Coupeau had promised to take her to the
circus. To see ladies galloping about on horseback, and
jumping through hoops, that, at all events, was worth putting
herself out for. Coupeau had just got his fortnight's pay, he
could well afford to split a two-franc piece; and they were
both going to have their dinner out, as Nana was going to be
very late that evening, on account of an urgent order at her
business place. But when seven o'clock came, there was no
Coupeau; at eight, still no one. Gervaise was furious. The
drunken brute was no doubt squandering the fortnight's pay
with his pals, in one pub or another. She had washed a bonnet,
and had been at work since the morning on an old dress, in order
to be presentable. Finally, when it was nearly nine, and she was
famished, and green with rage, she made up her mind to go
down and look for Coupeau somewhere about.

"Are you looking for your husband," said Madame Boche,
seeing the expression of her face. "He is in at old Colombe's.
Boche has just had a cherry brandy with him."

She said thanks. She made her way straight along the
pavement, turning over in her mind whether she should go
for her husband. A little drizzly rain fell, and that did not
add to the gaiety of her promenade. But when she had
reached the bar the fear of being turned out herself, if she
worried her husband, quieted her down and made her careful.
The place was flaring, the gas alight, white flames like suns,

the jars and bottles illuminating the walls with their coloured glass. She stood there an instant leaning forward, with her face against the glass, between two bottles in the window, peering in at Coupeau, who was sitting with his friends at the other end of the place, at a little zinc-topped table, all vague and misty in the smoke of their pipes; and as one could not hear them speak, it had a very odd effect to see them gesticulating, leaning forward, their eyes starting out of their heads. Was it possible that men could leave their wives and homes to shut themselves up like that in a stifling hole! The rain dripped in her neck; she moved away and went on to the outer boulevard, turning it over in her mind, not venturing to go in. Coupeau would give her a nice reception, he so disliked her coming after him. Then, too, it was not at all the place for a decent woman. However, she began to shiver under the dripping trees, and, as she hesitated, she said to herself that she would pick up an illness if she stayed there. Twice she went back and stood outside the window, putting her face against the glass again, vexed to see those infernal drunkards in out of the rain, chatting and drinking. The light of the bar was reflected in the puddles of the pavements, where the rain pattered and bubbled. She stepped back and splashed into it whenever the door opened and shut, creaking on its rusty hinges. After all she was merely coming after her husband; and she had a right to for he had promised to take her to the circus that evening. Well, here goes! she was not going to melt out there on the pavement, like a cake of soap.

"Hallo! it's you, old girl!" cried the tinsmith, roaring with laughter. "Oh! that is a joke, I say! I say, isn't it a joke?"

They all laughed, Mes-Bottes, Bibi-la-Grillade, Bec-Salé, otherwise Boit-sans-Soif. Yes, it seemed to them a joke, and they could not say why. Gervaise stood there, a little taken aback. Coupeau seemed to be in a good mood, and she ventured to say:

"You know, we are going yonder. It's time to be off. We shall get there in time to see something."

"I can't get up, I am stuck; oh! no kid!" said Coupeau, still laughing. "Just feel for yourself; pull my arm as hard as you can. Damnation! harder than that; now haul away! You see that rogue of a Colombe has screwed me to his bench."

Gervaise had entered into the joke, and when she dropped his arm, the other men found it so good that they rolled over one upon another, bawling and rubbing shoulders like asses that are being curry-combed. The tinsmith laughed from ear to ear, such a laugh that you could see right down his throat.

"You little silly!" he said at last, "you might sit down for a minute. We are better here than outside. Well, yes, I couldn't come back, I had business. If you choose to pull a long face, it'll do you no good. Move on a bit, you fellows, will you!"

"If the lady would accept my knees it wouldn't be so hard," said Mes-Bottes gallantly.

Gervaise, in order not to attract attention, took a chair and sat down three feet away from the table. She looked at what the men were drinking, the brandy that shone like gold in their glasses; there was a little pool of it on the table, and Bec-Salé, otherwise Boit-sans-Soif, while he talked, dipped his finger in it, and wrote a woman's name, Eulalie, in large letters. Bibi-la-Grillade seemed to her very much pulled down, as thin as a lath. Mes-Bottes had a flaming nose, a regular blue dahlia. They were very dirty, all four of them, with their wretched little beards, stiff and scrubby as chamber-brooms, their blouses all in holes, their hands grimy and their finger-nails in mourning. But still, one could be seen in their company, for though they had been swilling ever since six, they were decent enough, half on the point of dropping off to sleep. Gervaise saw two others by the bar who were taking their gargle, and they were so tight that they emptied their glasses under their chins, and poured it over their shirts, thinking they were wetting their whistle. Old fat Colombe, reaching out his huge arms, the terror of the establishment, calmly served out drinks. It was very hot, the smoke of pipes went up in the blinding glitter of gaslight, spreading like a cloud of dust, and covering the drinkers with a slowly thickening steam; and out of this cloud there came a deafening, confused hubbub of cracked voices and the clink of glasses, oaths and blows of the fist, like detonations. Gervaise made a wry face, for a sight like that is not a very entertaining one for a woman, especially when she is not used to it; she choked, her eyes burned, her head swam in the alcoholic smell exhaled by the whole place. Then, suddenly, she had an uncomfortable sensation of something behind her back. She turned, and saw the still, the drinking-machine, working away under the glass of the narrow court, with the quivering motion of its wizard's kitchen. At night the coppers looked duller, they had merely a sort of big red star where they were round; and the whole apparatus flung monstrous shadows on the wall at the back, figures with tails, great beasts opening their jaws as if to swallow up everything.

"I say, mealy-mouth!" cried Coupeau, "don't make faces. Wet blankets may go to Jericho! What'll you have to drink?"

"Nothing, certainly," replied the laundress, "I haven't had dinner."

"All the more reason; a drop of something will keep you up."

But as she still kept a glum visage, Mes-Bottes once more came forward politely.

"The lady surely likes liqueurs," he murmured.

"I like men who don't get drunk," she answered surlily. "Yes. I like people to bring back their pay and keep their word when they have made a promise."

"Ah! that's what upsets you!" said the tinsmith, still laughing. "You want your share. Well, you blockhead, why don't you have a drink? You'd better have it, it's all profit."

She looked straight in his face, very seriously, wrinkling her forehead till a black furrow came out all across. And she answered slowly:

"So be it, you are right, it's a good idea. We'll drink the cash together."

Bibi-la-Grillade went to get her a glass of anisette. She pulled up her chair to the table. As she sipped her anisette she remembered all at once how she had had a prune with Coupeau, long ago, there near the door, when he was courting her. At that time she left the brandy sauce. And now here she was drinking liqueurs again. Oh! she knew herself now, she had not a halfpennyworth of will. She only wanted a good kick behind to send her headlong in to the drink. The anisette seemed very nice, perhaps a little too sweet, a little sickly. And she sucked her glass while she listened to Bec-Salé, otherwise Boit-sans-Soif, who was describing his liasion with fat Eulalie, the woman who sold fish in the street, a very artful dodger, a party who scented you out, no matter what pub you were in, as she pushed her barrow along the street; no matter how much his pals gave him warning, and hid him out of the way, she often nabbed him, and only last night she had even smacked his face, to teach him to stay away from work. It was very funny, wasn't it? Bibi-la-Grillade, convulsed with laughter, slapped Gervaise on the shoulders, and Gervaise herself, by this time, joined in the fun, despite herself; they advised her to imitate fat Eulalie, and bring her irons and iron Coupeau's ears on the table of the pub.

"Ah! thanks," said Coupeau, turning over the glass of anisette that his wife had emptied, "you know how to drain it! Look here, old chaps, she means business, doesn't she?"

"You'll have another, madame?" said Bec-Salé, otherwise Boit-sans-Soif.

No, she had had enough. Still, she hesitated. The anisette was not quite the thing. She would rather have had something a little sharper, to settle her stomach. And she glanced sideways at the drinking machine behind her. The blessed object, round as a publican's belly, with its nose that trailed and twisted, sent a shiver through her, half fear, half desire. It might have been the metallic intestines of some sorceress, distilling, drop by drop, the fire that burnt within her. It was a poisonous thing, a thing that should have been hidden away in a cellar, so shameless and abominable was it! But, all the same, she was drawn to the thing, would fain have sniffed at its odour, tasted its bestiality, even if her tongue had burnt and peeled off like an orange.

"What are you drinking there?" she asked the men, in a sly sort of way, her eyes alight as she watched the golden colour of the glasses.

"That, old woman," said Coupeau, "is Daddy Colombe's camphor. Now, don't be silly, you must have a drop."

When they had brought her a glass of brandy, and she made a wry face at the first mouthful, the tinsmith smacked his thighs, and cried:

"Eh! don't it tickle your gills? Toss it off at one gulp. Every drink we have takes six francs out of the doctor's pocket."

At the second glass Gervaise no longer felt the hunger that distressed her. Now she was quite friendly with Coupeau, she was not angry with him for not having kept his promise. They would go to the circus another time; after all, it was no great sight, people galloping about and doing tricks on horseback. They were out of the rain at old Colombe's, and if the wages melted away in the glasses, at all events, one stowed it safely away inside, one drained it down, clear and shining as liquid gold. She sent all her cares packing; there were not so many pleasures in her life; anyway, it seemed some sort of consolation to have her share in cleaning out the cash. She was all right there, and why shouldn't she stay? If you were to set off a cannon, you wouldn't get her to move, when she wasn't in the mood for moving. She simmered away in the nice warmth, her bodice sticking to her back, a sort of pleasant drowsiness coming over her. She laughed all by herself, her elbows on the table, looking about her, highly amused by two men near her, a great hulking fellow and a little shrimp, who were falling on one another's necks in an effusive embrace, so tipsy were they. Yes, she laughed at old Colombe's bar and his full moon, a regular bladder of lard, at the men smoking their cutty pipes, shouting and spitting, at the great flames of gas that lit up the mirrors and liqueur bottles. The odour was not disagreeable to her; on the contrary, it tickled her nostrils, and seemed to her very good; her eyelids half closed, and she drew in short breaths, without any choking sensation, savouring the delight of the gradual drowsiness that crept over her. Then, after the third glass, she let her chin fall on her hands, she only saw Coupeau and his pals; and she sat there face to face with them, quite close, feeling their hot breath on her cheeks, staring at their dirty beards, as if she would count the hairs. By this time they were very drunk. Mes-Bottes slobbered, his pipe between his teeth, with the grave and silent air of a ruminating cow. Bibi-la-Grillade was telling a story, the way in which he emptied a bottle at one gulp, throwing back his head until the beauty was backside up. Meanwhile Bec-Salé, otherwise Boit-sans-Soif, had gone to the counter, and was playing at tee-to-tum for drinks with Coupeau.

"Two hundred! You are swell, you go in for big numbers!"

The hand of the tee-to-tum grated, the figure of Fortune, a great red woman, placed under a glass, turned till it was a mere speck, like a spot of wine.

"Three hundred and fifty! Look here, you've moved it on, you bugger! It's no go, I won't play any more!"

Gervaise watched it with interest. She drank like a fish, and called Mes-Bottes "sonny". Behind her the drinking machine worked away, muttering like an underground torrent, and she was seized with despair as she felt the impossibility of staying its progress, overcome, in spite of herself, with a dull rage, feeling a longing to jump upon the great still like an animal, to trample it under her heels and split it open. Everything grew dim before her, the machine seemed to sway, she seemed to feel herself seized by its copper claws, while the torrent poured across her body.

Then the room danced, the gas-jets were like shooting stars. Gervaise was lit. She heard a furious discussion between

Bec-Salé, otherwise Boit-sans-Soif, and the blackguard of a
Colombe. The old thief was totting up the account all wrong.
After all, one wasn't at Bondy! All at once there was a hustle,
a howl, chairs overturned. Old Colombe had turned them all
out of doors, in a jiffy, without the slightest effort. Outside
the door they slanged him and called him a blackguard. It
was still raining, a little chill wind was stirring. Gervaise lost
Coupeau, found him, and lost him again.

She wanted to go home, she felt her way along by the shops.
The sudden darkness astonished her. At the corner of the
Rue des Poissonniers, she sat down in the gutter, and fancied
herself at the wash-house. All the water that ran everywhere
made her head swim, she felt very sick. At last she got back,
she went quickly past the *concierge's* lodge, in which she saw
the Lorilleux and the Poissons sitting down to table, and their
looks of disgust as they saw her in such a state.

She never knew how she managed to get up the six flights
of stairs. At the top, just as she was turning into the passage,
little Lalie, who had heard her step, came running out, her
arms opened caressingly, laughing and saying:

"Madame Gervaise, papa hasn't come home, come and
see my children asleep. Oh! they do look pretty!"

But when she caught sight of the laundress's stupefied face,
she drew back trembling. She knew that spirituous breath,
those pale eyes, that convulsed mouth. Gervaise staggered
by without a word, and the child stood still in the doorway,
following her with her dark, mute, serious gaze.

CHAPTER ELEVEN

NANA grew; she was now a strapping wench. At fifteen she had shot up like a calf; she was very white-skinned, very full-fleshed, as plump as a pin-cushion. Truly, she was fine and fresh and blooming, as blithe as a bird, as white as milk, a skin as downy as a peach, a funny little nose, a rosy mouth, and peepers that you would like to light your pipe at. Her great mass of blonde hair, the colour of new-mown hay, powdered her forehead with gold, a reddish gold which shone there like a crown of sunlight. A fine doll, as the Lorilleux said, a mere chit of a thing, and yet with the plump round shoulders, the ripe odour, of a grown woman.

Now Nana stuffed no more bundles of paper into her bodice. She had titties of her own now, a pair of titties like brand-new white satin. And they did not come amiss to her, she would have liked her arms full of them, she dreamed of bubs as big as a nurse's, so greedy and inconsiderate is youth. What made her more appetising than anything, was a wicked little habit she had got into of putting out the tip of her tongue between her little white teeth. She had no doubt seen it in the glass, and thought it looked pretty. Thereupon, she put out her tongue all day long, in order to look her best.

"Put your tell-tale in, will you!" cried her mother.

And Coupeau would often join in, with an oath and a bang of his fist:

"Will you put your red rag away!"

Nana was a great coquette. She did not always wash her feet, but she wore such tight boots that she suffered a perfect martyrdom; and if anyone questioned her, seeing her face grow purple, she answered that she had a stomach-ache, so as not to confess her coquetry. When there was no bread in the house, she found it difficult to trick herself out. But she achieved miracles, carried off ribbons from the work-room, worked up wonderful toilettes, dirty dresses covered with bows and rosettes. It was in summer that she had her triumphs. With a six-franc cotton dress she went out every Sunday, filling the whole quarter of the Goutte-d'Or with her blonde

beauty. She was known from the outer boulevards to the
fortifications, and from the Chaussée de Clignancourt to the
Grande Rue de la Chapelle. They called her "the chicken",
for she had in truth the soft flesh and country freshness of a
chicken.

One dress in particular suited her to a T. It was a white
dress with red spots, very simple, without any trimming
whatever. The skirt was rather short, just to her ankles; the
sleeves were large and hanging, and showed her arms to the
elbows; the neck of the bodice, which she pinned back in a
V shape in a dark corner of the staircase, to avoid a box on
the ears from her father, showed a bit of her snowy neck and
just an indication of her bosom. And that was all, all except a
pink ribbon tied round her blonde hair, with its ends falling
and fluttering on her neck. She was as fresh as a rose; she had
the very savour of youth, the beauty of the woman and the
child.

Her Sundays at this time were days of general rendezvous,
rendezvous with all the men who passed her and ogled her.
She longed for them all the week, tickled with all sorts of little
desires, with a feeling of being stifled, of wanting to be out of
doors, out in the sun, in the Sunday bustle of the streets.
Early in the morning she began to dress. She stood in her
chemise for hours together before the bit of looking-glass
hung up over the chest of drawers; and as the whole house
could see her at the window, her mother scolded her, and
asked her if she had nearly finished exhibiting herself in her
chimmey. But she went on composedly plastering down her
kiss-curls on her forehead with sugar-water, sewing buttons
on to her boots, or putting a stitch on her dress, with bare legs,
her chemise slipping off her shoulders, her hair all in a flutter of
disorder. Ah! she was stunning like that! said Coupeau, teasing
and jeering at her; a regular Mary Magdalene. She would do
for a savage woman on show for a penny. He shouted: "Put your
meat under cover, will you, and let me eat my bread in peace!"
And she was adorable, white and fine under the flood of her
golden fleece, raging so furiously that it flushed her skin, not
daring to answer her father back, but snapping off the thread
between her teet with a sharp angry movement, which sent a
shiver through all her beautiful white body.

Then, after dinner, off she went down into the court. The
warmth and peace of Sunday lay over all the house; below,
the workshops were closed; the windows above yawned open,

showing glimpses of tables already laid for dinner, waiting for families who were out gaining an appetite on the fortifications; one woman on the third floor spent the day in washing out her room, rolling up the mattress, shoving the furniture about, singing the same song over and over for hours in a sweet tearful voice. And with everything quiet about, in the midst of the empty echoing court, there would be a game of shuttle-cock between Nana, Pauline, and other big girls. There were five or six of them, all growing up together, who queened it in the house, and divided among them the looks and glances of the men. When a man crossed the court there would be shrill cries of laughter, and the rustle of their starched dresses passed like a breath of wind. Above them the very air seemed heavy and burning, as if mellow with sloth and blanched with the dust of many walkers.

But the shuttle-cock was merely a trick for escape. Suddenly the house returned to its silence. They had slipped into the street and made their way to the outer boulevards. Then the six of them, arm in arm, taking up the whole of the pavement, went on their way in their tight dresses, with ribbons round their bare heads. Their bright eyes shot out tiny sidelong glances from under their lids, nothing escaped them, and when they laughed they threw back their heads, their plump chins in the air. When there was a big splutter of laughter, if a hunchback passed, or an old woman waited for her dog at some corner, the line was broken, some hung back, while others pulled them vigorously, and they swayed their hips, crowded up together, and fell about hither and thither so as to get the people to look at them, and to make their bodices crack under their growing forms. The street belonged to them; they had grown up in it, holding up their skirts along by the shops; they pulled up their skirts now, half way up their legs, to readjust their garters. And they made their way through the slow and pallid crowds, under the slim boulevard trees, from the Barrière Rochechouart to the Barrière Saint-Denis, cutting through groups in zig-zag, turning and flinging phrases and laughter together. And their flying dresses left behind them something of the insolence of their youth; they crowded there in the open air, under the sheer sunlight, with the shameless grossness of the street urchin, delicate and desirable as virgins coming from the bath, their locks yet damp with water.

Nana was in the middle, with her pink dress flashing in

the sun. She gave her arm to Pauline, whose dress, yellow
flowers on a white foundation, glittered too, punctured with
little flames. And as those two were the biggest, the cheekiest,
and the most grown-up, they led the band, swelling with
pride under the looks and compliments. The others the little
ones, tailed off to right and left, trying to swell themselves
out, so as to be taken seriously. Nana and Pauline had deep
plans in mind, all sorts of coquettish ruses. If they ran till
they were out of breath, it was in order to show off their white
stockings, and to set their ribbons and chignons floating.
Then, when they stopped, and pretended to be suffocating,
throwing back their heaving bosoms, you would see, if you
looked round, that there was someone they knew in sight,
some lad of the neighbourhood. And then they would walk
languishingly, chuckling and laughing among themselves, and
looking out of the corners of their eyes. They were always on
the look-out for these chance rendezvous in the crowd and
concourse of the street. Big lads in their Sunday clothes,
jackets and round hats, kept them for a minute at the edge
of the pavement, joking and trying to catch them round the
waist; workmen of twenty, bare-necked in their grey blouses,
chatted with them lazily, their arms folded, puffing the smoke
of their cutty pipes in their faces. They thought nothing of it,
they had all grown up together on the same pavements.
But they were already beginning to make a choice. Pauline
always met one of Madame Gaudron's sons, a cabinet-maker
of seventeen, who treated her to apples. Nana could spot
Victor Fauconnier, the laundress's boy, whom she kissed in
dark corners, the length of any of the walks away. And it
went no further, they were too vicious to do anything without
knowing it. Only they said things straight.

Then, towards sunset, the great delight of the girls was to
stop and watch the tumblers. Jugglers and strong men came
laying out their little carpets worn with much use. Then all
the loungers flocked around, a circle was formed, whilst the
tumbler, in the midst, made his muscles stand out in his
faded tights. Nana and Pauline stood for hours in the thickest
of the crowd. Their pretty fresh dresses were crushed in
between dirty jackets and great-coats. Their bare arms and
necks and heads received all the warmth of those foul breaths,
the odour of wine and sweat. And they laughed, it amused
them, without a feeling of disgust, rosier than ever, on their
native dunghill. About them bad words, the crudest indecencies

the comments of drunken men, fell unheeded. It was their own language, they knew it all, they turned with a smile, calmly, shameless, the delicate pallor of their satiny skin untinged.

The only thing they did not like was to meet their fathers, especially when they were drunk. They watched out for them and gave each other warning.

"I say, Nana," cried Pauline all of a sudden, "there's old Coupeau!"

"All right, and he isn't screwed, oh, dear no!" said Nana, in a disgusted tone. "I'll cut, you know. I don't want him to warm me, I assure you. Look there he has got a dose! Damn! if he'd only break his neck!"

At other times, when Coupeau was close before she had time to run away, she would crouch down and whisper:

"Keep me out of sight, you girls! He's looking for me, he says he'll kick my backside if he catches me here again."

Then, when the drunkard had passed on, she stood up, and they all followed him, bursting with laughter. He would see her! he wouldn't see her! It was a regular game of hide-and-seek. One day however, Boche marched Pauline home by the two ears, and Coupeau walked off Nana with kicks behind.

Night came on, they had a final stroll, coming back in the dim twilight, in the midst of a weary crowd. The dust had thickened in the air, and the heavy sky paled. The Rue de la Goutte-d'Or was like a bit of the country, with its gossips on the doorstep, their sharp voices cutting through the drowsy silence of the quarter, in which there was not even the sound of wheels. They stopped for a moment in the court took up their battledores again, and made a pretence of never having moved from there. And they went upstairs, inventing a story, which they often found it needless to tell, if their parents were too busy smacking one another's faces for a soup not properly cooked or not properly salted.

Nana was now at work, she was getting two francs at Titreville's, the house in the Rue du Caire, where she had been apprenticed. The Coupeaus did not wish her to change, because she would be under the eyes of Madame Lerat, who had been the head woman there for the last ten years. In the morning the mother looked at the clock when the child set out by herself, looking so neat, in spite of the old short black dress that pinched her shoulders; and Madame Lerat had the

responsibility of noting the hour of her arrival, and letting
Gervaise know. They allowed her twenty minutes to get from
the Rue de la Goutte-d'Or to the Rue du Caire, quite enough,
for the little hussies have legs like a deer. Sometimes she got
there just to time, but so red and out of breath that she had
evidently scampered from the barrier in ten minutes, after
having dawdled on the way. More often she was seven
minutes, eight minutes, behind time; and all the time, till
evening, she fawned on her aunt, with eyes full of entreaty,
trying to melt her, and keep her from telling. Madame
Lerat, who knew what youth was, lied to the Coupeaus, but
she read interminable lessons to Nana, speaking of her
responsibility and the dangers that a girl ran in the streets
of Paris. Good Lord! why they followed her enough herself.
She watched her niece with eyes always lit up with sensual
curiosity, and she was quite excited at the idea of watching
over the innocence of the poor little dear.

"Look here," she repeated, "you must tell me everything.
I am too good to you. I should throw myself in the Seine if
anything were to happen to you. See here, my child, if men
speak to you, you must tell me all about it, all, without
forgetting a word. Eh! no one has said anything to you, you
are sure?"

Nana laughed, with a funny curl of the lips. No! men
never spoke to her. She walked too fast. Then, what should
they say? She had no concern with them, why should she?
And she explained her delays with a naïve air, she had
stopped to look at some pictures; or she had been with
Pauline, who had news to tell her. They could follow her if
they didn't believe it; she never even quitted the left pavement,
and she walked at such a rate that she got ahead of all the
other girls, as if she were on wheels. One day, it is true,
Madame Lerat had caught her in the Rue du Petit-Carreau,
standing staring upwards, laughing, with three other little
scamps of flower-workers, because there was a man shaving
at a window; but the child had declared angily that she was
only on her way to the baker's at the corner, to buy a penny
roll.

"Oh! I keep my eye on her, have no fear," said the widow
to the Coupeaus. "I answer for her as if she were myself. If
a blackguard were so much as to pinch her, I would soon be
in the way."

The work-room at Titreville's was a large room on the

first floor, with a big table on trestles filling up all the centre. Along the four bare walls, showing the plaster through rents in the dingy grey paper, there were long rows of shelves, covered with old cardboard boxes, bundles, patterns thrown aside and forgotten under a heavy layer of dust. The gas had left a coating of soot on the ceiling. The two windows were so large and wide that the girls, without leaving the work-table, could see the people pass on the opposite pavement.

Madame Lerat, by way of setting a good example, arrived first. Then the door was opening and shutting for a quarter of an hour, while the girls streamed in one after another, in a confused, sweating, tousled mass. One July morning, Nana turned up last, which, indeed, she was quite in the habit of doing.

"Well!" she said, "I shan't be sorry when I have my carriage."

And, without even taking off her hat, an old black thing that she called her cap, she went over to the window and looked out to right and left, gazing up and down the street.

"What are you looking at?" asked Madame Lerat, suspiciously. "Did your father come with you?"

"No, indeed," replied Nana, composedly. "I'm not looking at anything. I'm looking to see how jolly hot it is. It's enough to make you ill to have to come in such a hurry."

The heat that morning was stifling. The girls had lowered the Venetian blinds, through which they peeped out on what was going on in the street; and at last they got to work, ranged down the two sides of the table, of which Madame Lerat alone occupied the top. There were eight of them; each with her pastepot before her, her nippers, and her goffering cushion. The table was strewn with bits of wire, bobbins, wadding, green and brown paper, leaves and petals cut out in silk, satin, and velvet. In the middle, one of the girls had stuck into the neck of a water-bottle a little penny bunch of flowers that she had worn the night before, and that was now faded.

"Ah! you have no idea," said Léonie, a pretty, dark girl, leaning over the cushion on which she was goffering petals of roses, "well, poor Caroline is awfully unhappy with that chap who comes for her in the evening."

Nana, who was just then cutting out thin slips of green paper, exclaimed:

"By Jove! a man who is false to her every day!"

The girls began to laugh, and Madame Lerat had to show herself severe. She pulled a long face, and murmured:

"You do use nice language, my girl! I shall tell your father, we'll see how he'll like that."

Nana puffed out her cheeks, as if she were keeping back a big laugh. Her father indeed! as if he didn't say that sort of thing himself! But Léonie, all at once, whispered in a quick, low voice:

"Look out! Here's madame!"

It was Madame Titreville, a tall skinny woman, who entered. She generally stayed down below, in the shop. The girls were very much afraid of her, for she never unbent. She went slowly round the table, over which every head was bowed in silent activity. She told one girl she was a bungler, and made her begin a daisy over again. Then she went out with the same starched air with which she had come in.

"Gee-up! gee-up!" cried Nana, in the midst of a general growl.

"Young ladies, really, young ladies," said Madame Lerat, trying to look severe, "you will force me to measures. . . ."

But they paid no attention, they were not at all afraid of her. She was always too easy-going, for the situation tickled her, to be in the midst of all those youngsters with their saucy eyes, and she would take them aside, and try to worm out of them all about their lovers, telling their fortunes with cards when a corner of the table was free. Her leathery skin, her masculine bulk, quivered with the joyous gaiety of a good old gossip, when she could get them on to her favourite subject. She was shocked by crudities of expression; as long as you didn't indulge in that, you could say anything.

And truly Nana's education had its finishing touch in the work-room. Oh! she had inclinations enough, no doubt. But that was the finishing touch, the association with a heap of girls already tainted with vice and misery. They were there one upon another, rotting together; just like a basket of apples, when there are rotten ones among them. Of course there was a certain reserve in public; no one wished to appear too disordered in life, too disgusting in talk. In short, they posed as proper young ladies. But when they could whisper in one another's ears, when they got into a corner, then ribald talk was all the order of the day. You couldn't find two of them together, without their beginning at once to splutter with laughter over some dirty story. Then, as they went off together in the evening, there were confidences and tales, enough to make your hair stand on end, that kept them lingering on the pavement, talking excitedly in the midst of the bustle of the crowd. And for the girls who were still virgins, like Nana, there was a bad air about the work-room, an odour of dancing-halls and scarcely orthodox nights, brought into the place by the girls who went on the loose, in their very chignons, all tumbled, their very skirts, so creased that they seemed to have slept in them. The drowsy idleness that followed a night out, the dark lines under the eyes, what Madame Lerat called discreetly the fisticuffs of love, the lounging gait, the hoarse voices, breathed a certain perversion over the work-table, with the glitter and the fragility of its artificial flowers. Nana sniffed and gloated when she found herself side by side with someone who had already seen the wolf. She had taken her place beside tall Lisa, who was supposed to be in the family way; and she kept looking at her as if she expected to see her swell and burst before her. As for learning anything new, that was a difficult matter. The imp knew everything, she had learnt about everything in the streets. It was merely that in the work-room she saw it before her, and it put into her head, little by little, the wish and the will to do likewise.

"It's stifling," she murmured, going over to the window as if to pull the Venetian blinds down lower.

But she leaned out, and once more looked up and down the street. At the same instant Léonie, who had her eye on a man who had stopped on the pavement opposite, called out:

"What is that old chap doing there? He's been on the mouch here for the last quarter of an hour."

"Some old rake," said Madame Lerat. "Nana, will you be good enough to sit down? I told you not to stand at that window."

Nana went back to the stalks of violets that she was rolling, and all the girls began to talk about the man. It was a well-dressed gentleman of about fifty, wearing an overcoat; his face was pallid, very serious, and very respectable, with a rim of grey beard, carefully trimmed. He waited about for an hour, outside a herbalist's, looking up at the work-room blinds. The girls gave little bursts of laughter, which were drowned in the noises of the street; and they bent busily over their work, glancing up continually so as not to lose sight of the gentleman.

"I say," said Léonie, "he has an eye-glass. Oh! it's a swell. He is sure to be waiting for Augustine."

But Augustine, a tall, ugly, fair girl, answered sourly that she did not care for old men. And Madame Lerat, shaking her head, murmured with her dubious smile:

"You are wrong, my dear; old men are more affectionate."

At that moment Léonie's neighbour, a little plump person, said something in her ear; and Léonie fell back in her chair, gasping and choking with laughter, glancing at the gentleman outside, and laughing more than ever. She spluttered out:

"That's it! oh! that's it! Oh! you are a dirty little thing, Sophie!"

"What did she say? What did she say?" asked all the girls, burning with curiosity.

Léonie wiped the tears from her eyes without replying. When she had quieted down a bit, she went back to her goffering, declaring:

"I can't repeat it."

They insisted, she shook her head, with little bursts of merriment. Then Augustine, her left-hand neighbour, begged her to whisper it to her. And Léonie at last consented to tell her, putting her lips close to her ear. Augustine lay back and went into convulsions. Then she passed it on, and it went from ear to ear, amidst exclamations and stifled shrieks of laughter. When everybody knew Sophie's dirty phrase, they all looked at one another, and there was a general roar, not without some blushes and looks of confusion. Madame Lerat was the only one who didn't know. She was very cross.

"You are very rude indeed, young ladies," she said. "Polite people never whisper when there are others present. It's something indecent, I suppose. You are a nice lot!"

But she dared not ask them to repeat Sophie's dirty phrase, despite her furious anxiety to know it. But while she looked down at her work with an air of offended dignity, she gloated over the conversation of the girls. One of them could not say a word, the most innocent word, apropos of her work, for instance, without the others immediately seeing some hidden meaning in it; they turned the word into another sense, giving it some improper meaning; they put the most extraordinary interpretations upon the most simple words, such as "my nippers are split," or "who has been poking about in my pot?" And they referred everything to the gentleman who loitered about opposite, he turned up in everything they had to say. Ah! if his ears didn't burn! And at last they said extremely stupid things in their anxiety to be witty. But they found the game quite amusing all the same; they got quite excited, their eyes glittered, and they went further and further. Madame Lerat had no cause to be angry, they said nothing crude. She herself sent them all into convulsions by asking:

"Mademoiselle Lisa, my fire is out, hand me yours."

"Oh! Madame Lerat's fire is out!" cried the whole workroom.

She began an explanation.

"When you are my age, young ladies——"

But no one listened; they declared they would call over the gentleman to set Madame Lerat's fire alight.

In this chorus of laughter, Nana took her part finely. Not a double meaning escaped her. She said pretty stiff things herself, emphasizing them with little nods, choking with merriment. She took to vice like a fish to water; and she rolled her stalks of violets admirably while she squirmed on her chair. Oh! she was quite dab at it; she would do it in less time than it would take to roll a cigarette. She would just take up a little strip of green paper, and in a turn the paper ran up around the wire; then a drop of gum at the top to stick it, and it was done, a bit of fresh, delicate verdure, ready to add to any lady's charms. She had the knack of it in her fingers, thin, depraved fingers, which seemed boneless, so supple were they and sensitive. It was the only part of the business she could learn, and she did the stalks so well that she did them all.

Meanwhile the gentleman opposite had gone. The girls quietened down and went on working in the intense heat. When the clock struck twelve, the hour for lunch, they all shook themselves. Nana rushed over to the window; then she said she would do the errands for them if they liked. And Léonie commissioned her to bring a pennyworth of shrimps, Augustine a screw of fried potatoes, Lisa a bundle of radishes, Sophie a sausage. Then, as she was going downstairs, Madame Lerat, thinking it odd that she should have been so drawn to the window that day, came striding after her, saying:

"Wait a minute, I'll go with you, I want to get something."

No sooner was she out of doors than she discovered the gentleman planted there outside, exchanging glances with Nana! The child went very red. Her aunt gave her a little shake as she took her arm and marched her along the street, whilst the party followed them at a little distance. Ah! the old rake was after Nana! Very nice it was, at fifteen and a half to have men running after her! And Madame Lerat questioned her eagerly. Oh Lord! Nana knew nothing; he had only been following her for the last five days, she could not walk a step without meeting him; she believed he was in business, yes, a manufacturer of bone buttons. Madame Lerat was greatly impressed. She turned and glinted at the gentleman out of the corner of her eye.

"He has money," she murmured. "Look here, my dear, you must tell me all about it. Now, you have nothing to fear."

They went on chatting as they ran from shop to shop, the pork-butcher's, the fruiterer's, the cook-shop. And the things, in their greasy paper, grew to quite a pile in their hands. But they smiled and twisted about, casting back bright glances and light laughs. Madame Lerat herself put on some little airs and graces, as if she were a girl, for the benefit of the button manufacturer who still followed them.

"He is quite stylish," she declared, as they returned to the narrow street. "If only he had honourable intentions. . . ."

Then, as they went upstairs, she seemed suddenly to call something to mind.

"By the way, tell me, what were those girls whispering about; you know, what Sophie said?"

Nana made no fuss about it. Only she took Madame Lerat by the neck, and forced her to go two stairs down, because really it was a thing you couldn't say out loud, even on the stairs. And she whispered it to her. It was so gross that her aunt merely shook her head, opened her eyes wide, and screwed her mouth aside. However, she knew now what it was, it no longer worried her.

The girls had their lunch on their knees, so as not to soil the table. They hurried it down, not caring about eating, preferring to spend the time in looking at the people who passed, or in making confidences to one another in the corner. That day they were all wondering where the gentleman they had seen that morning had betaken himself; at all events, he was gone. Madame Lerat and Nana shot covert glances at one another, their lips sealed. And though it was already ten minutes past six, the girls seemed in no hurry to get back to their work, when Léonie, with a *prr!* of the lips, the sound with which house-painters call to one another, announced the approach of Madame Titreville. In an instant they were all in their chairs, buried in their work. Madame Titreville entered and walked severely round.

From that day, Madame Lerat found her entertainment in her niece's first affair. She never left her, she accompanied her morning and evening, putting forward her own responsibility. Nana was a little inconvenienced, but she was proud all the same of being looked after as a treasure; and the conversations that they both had in the streets, with the button manufacturer behind them, inflamed her all the more, and gave her all the more longing to take the leap. Oh! her aunt understood the sentiment; even the button manufacturer, the respectable elderly gentleman, touched her, for a feeling is always deeper with people of mature age. Only, she was on her guard. Yes, they should pass over her prostrate body before any harm should come to the child. One evening she went up to the gentleman, and told him to his face that what he was doing was not the right sort of thing to do. He bowed politely, without a word, like an old practitioner quite used to the rebuffs of relations. She could not really be angry with him, he was so polite. And there were endless counsels in regard to love matters, allusions to the blackguards men were, all sorts of stories of silly girls who had repented of having gone wrong, which sent Nana away languishingly, her eyes shining lustfully out of the pallor of her face.

But one day, in the Rue du Faubourg-Poissonnière, the button manufacturer had ventured to come up close behind aunt and niece, and whisper things that were really quite unseemly. After that, Madame Lerat was frightened, declaring that she was no longer confident on her own account, and she turned over the whole affair to her brother. Then there was quite another story. The Coupeaus kicked up a fine row. First of all the tinsmith gave Nana a good hiding. What was she coming to? the little beggar was going after old men! Well, let him only catch her kissing and cuddling out of doors, and she might look out, he would soon settle that! Did you ever! a little scrub like that who was bringing dishonour on the family! And he gave her a good shaking, saying that, by God, she would have to keep straight in future, for he was going to look after her himself. When she came in he looked her up and down, and carefully scrutinized her face, to see if he could not find the kisses on her eyes, the little kisses that nestle there silently. He sniffed at her, and

turned her round and round. One evening he gave her a
licking because he had found a black mark on her neck. And
she had the impudence to tell him that it was not a sucking-
spot! she called that a bruise, simply a bruise that Léonie had
given her in playing. He would bruise her, he would see she
didn't go on the loose, if he had to break her legs for her.
Other times, when he was in a good humour, he jeered and
made game of her. Oh! she was a nice morsel for the men, as
flat as a sole, and with hollows in her shoulders big enough to
put your fist in. Nana, beaten for the naughty things she had
not done, accused of all sorts of abominations by her father,
had the dangerous and wrathful submissiveness of a trapped
wild beast.

"Let her be," said Gervaise, who was more reasonable.
"You will drive her to want to do it, if you speak to her so
much about it."

And indeed she wanted to! Her whole body itched after it,
if she could only cut and run, as Coupeau said. He kept the
subject so constantly before her that the coldest girl would
have taken fire at it. He even, by his way of jawing her,
taught her things which she did not as yet know, and
that was no easy matter. Then, little by little, she got into
queer ways. One morning he caught her fumbling in a paper,
dabbing something on her cheeks. It was rice-powder, with
which a perverse instinct had taught her to plaster the delicate
satin of her skin. He rubbed her face all over with the paper,
hard enough to break the skin, calling her a miller's daughter.
Another time she brought home some red ribbons to do up
her cap, the old black hat which she was so much ashamed of.
And he asked her angrily where the ribbons came from. Was
it on her back that she had earned them? or had she nabbed
them? Trull or thief, perhaps both. Several times he found
pretty things in her hands, a coral ring, a pair of lace cuffs, one
of those double hearts, the "Come-touch-me's" that girls
put between their two titties. Coupeau tried to take them
from her, but she defended them frantically; they were her
own, ladies had given them to her, or she had exchanged
things for them at the work-room. The heart, for instance,
she had picked up in the Rue d'Aboukir. When her father
crushed the heart under his heel, she stood rigid and white,
and all worked up before him, and something rose up within
her and tempted her to fly at him, and tear something from
him. For two years she had longed for that heart, and now it

was crushed to bits! No, it was too much, she could not stand it much longer.

Meanwhile it was not all outraged honour, but more an instinct for annoyance, that set Coupeau spying on Nana. He was often in the wrong, and his injustice exasperated her. She would stay away from the work-room; then, when the tinsmith gave her a licking, she laughed in his face, declaring that she wouldn't go back to Titreville's, because they put her to sit beside Augustine, who must have eaten her feet, her breath stank so loud. Thereupon Coupeau marched her straight back to the Rue du Caire, and asked the mistress to always put her by the side of Augustine for a punishment. Every morning, for a fortnight, he took the trouble to come all the way from the Barrière Poissonnière in order to accompany Nana to the work-room door. And he waited five minutes outside, in order to be sure that she went in. But one morning, having gone into a pub in the Rue Saint-Denis with a pal, he saw the young hussy, ten minutes afterwards, hurrying down the street at a fine rate. For the last fortnight she had been taking him in, she went up two storeys instead of going into Titreville's, and sat down on a stair, until he had gone. When Coupeau complained against Madame Lerat, she said very tartly that she did not see she was to blame; she had said to her niece all she could say against men, and it was not her fault if the child had a taste for the dirty brutes; now she washed her hands of her, she swore she would never meddle in other people's concerns again, for she knew what she knew, she had heard the nasty things that had been said about her, yes, people who had dared to accuse her of letting Nana go on the loose, and taking a vile pleasure in seeing her do the splits under her very eyes. However, Coupeau learnt from the mistress that Nana had been led astray by another work-girl, the little tart Léonie, who had given up the flowers to go on the loose. No doubt the child was as yet only set on cakes and drinks in the street, and could still wear the orange-wreath at her wedding. But that would have to be jolly soon, if she was to go to her husband without a rent, in good order and condition, in fact, to put it briefly, like all self-respecting young ladies.

In the house of the Rue de la Goutte-d'Or, Nana's old gentleman was spoken of as someone that everybody knew. Oh! he was still quite polite, a little timid even, but deucedly obstinate and patient, following her ten yards off like an

obedient pug. Sometimes he would even come into the court.
Madame Gaudron had met him one evening on the second
landing, making his way stealthily along by the banister, with
his head down, keen and frightened. And the Lorilleux
threatened to move if their snip of a niece brought any more
men about after her, for it had become something quite
disgusting, the staircase was full of them, you couldn't go
down without seeing them on every stair, sniffing and waiting
about; one would think there was a bitch on heat in the house.
The Boches pitied the poor man, such a respectable man,
who had got mashed on a little vagabond. He was a merchant;
they had seen his button manufactory, Boulevard de la
Villette; he could do very well for a woman if he were only
to meet with a decent sort of girl. Thanks to the *concierge's*
details, all the neighbours, even the Lorilleux themselves,
showed the greatest respect for the old gentleman when they
saw him at Nana's heels, with his pallid face, his pendent
lower lip, his rim of grey beard carefully trimmed.

For the first month Nana was immensely amused by her
old gentleman. You should see him, always at her heels, a
regular old messer who would fumble at her skirt behind in
the crowd without anybody noticing it. And his legs! they
were like a bundle of sticks, as thin as laths. And as bald as a
billiard-ball, four hairs drawn across at the back, so that she
was always tempted to ask him for the address of the barber
who combed his parting. The old codger wasn't at all in her
line.

Then, finding him always there, he did not seem quite
such a joke after all. She was desperately afraid of him, she
would have screamed if he had come near her. Often when
she stopped outside a jeweller's she heard him mumbling out
something behind her. And it was true what he said; she
would have liked to have a cross on a velvet ribbon at her
neck, or little coral ear-rings, so small that they looked like
drops of blood. But, even without any great desire for
jewellery, she really could not stay as she was; she was tired
of faking up her things with the refuse of the work-room,
above all, she had had enough of her cap, that hat on which
the flowers she had chivied from Titreville's looked like so
many little clots of dirt. Then, as she made her way through
the mud, splashed by the passing wheels, dazzled by the
splendour of the equipages, she had longings which gripped
her stomach like actual pangs of hunger; longings to be well

dressed, to eat in restaurants, to go to the theatre, to have a
room of her own with nice furniture. She stopped in the street,
pale with desire, a heat seemed to rise from the very streets
of Paris and cling to her thighs, a fierce appetite for all those
enjoyments that hustled her at every step in the pack of the
pavements. And without fail, just at that moment, there was
the old man with his propositions. Ah! how gladly she would
have accepted them but for her fear, a revolt within that
strengthened her refusal, furious and disgusted with the
unknown of man, in spite of all her vice.

But, by winter, existence with the Coupeaus became
impossible. Every evening Nana had her dose. When the
father was tired of beating her, the mother would give her a
clout to teach her to behave herself. And there were often
general scrimmages; when one hit out, another hit back, so
that all three finally rolled on the floor in the middle of the
broken crockery. In addition to that there was never enough
to eat, and often no fire. If the child bought anything pretty,
a bow of ribbon, or some sleeve-links, the parents would take
it away from her and sell it. She had nothing she could call
her own but her daily portion of blows before getting into
bed, where she had only a rag of a sheet, and her little black
petticoat for quilt, over her shivering body. No, that infernal
life could not go on; she did not mean to let it quite finish her
off. Her father, now for a long time, did not count. When a
father drinks as hers did, he is no father, but a dirty beast you
want to be well rid of. And now her mother too was slipping
away from such regard as she had for her. She too drank.
She went now to look for her husband at old Colombe's, really
in order to get drinks offered to her herself. And she sat down
to table very readily, without any of the wry faces she had
pulled that first time, draining down her glasses at one gulp,
dawdling about there for hours together, and coming out with
her eyes starting from their sockets. When Nana passed the
bar and saw her mother there at the back, her nose in her
glass, a soddened spectacle in the midst of the ribald clamour
of the men, she was seized with a blue rage; youth, reaching
after quite another kind of luxury, not understanding the
charms of drink. On such evenings she had a nice tableau
before her, a tipsy father, a tipsy mother, a damned hole of
a crib where there was not a loaf of bread, and which reeked
of liquor. In short, a saint could not stay in such a place. So
much the worse, if she slung her hook one of these days; her

parents would have to make their *mea culpa* then, and say that they had driven her away themselves.

One Saturday Nana came in and found her father and mother in a shocking state. Coupeau, sprawling sideways on the bed, snored. Gervaise, huddled on a chair, rolled her head, with vague troubled eyes which saw nothing. She had forgotten to warm the dinner, the remains of a stew. A candle, which she had not snuffed, lit up the shameful misery of the hole.

"It's you, you snippet," stammered Gervaise. "Your father'll give you a nice dressing."

Nana made no reply; she went quite white as she saw the cold stove, the table without plates, the dismal room on which the pair of drunkards imprinted the chill horror of their besotment. She did not take off her hat; she walked all round the room, then, with her teeth firmly set, she opened the door and went out.

"You're going downstairs?" said her mother unable to turn her head.

"Yes; I've forgotten something. I'll be back. Good-night."

And she did not return. Next day the Coupeaus, quite sober now, came to blows over the responsibility of Nana's flight. Ah! she was far enough away by this time, if she were still running away from them. As they say to children about sparrows, if the parents could put a pinch of salt on her tail they might catch her perhaps. It was a great blow to Gervaise, and it sank her deeper down than ever, for she realized clearly, despite her degradation, that the disaster of the child killed two birds with one stone, and left her now childless, without anyone to respect, ready to fall to any depths. Yes, the un-natural child took from her, in her dirty skirts, the last remnant of her honesty. And she was drunk for three days, furious, clenching her fists, uttering foul words against her whore of a daughter. Coupeau, after having prowled along the outer boulevards, and scrutinized every dirty slut that passed, smoked his pipe again, quite composedly; only when he was at table he got up sometimes, shook his knife in the air, and cried that he was dishonoured; and then he sat down and went on with his soup.

In the house, from which, every month, girls would fly like canaries whose cages had been left open, the mishap at the Coupeaus' surprised nobody. But the Lorilleux gloried in it. Ah! they had foretold that the youngster would piss pepper.

It was only natural, flower-workers always went to the bad. The Boches and Poissons were equally delighted; they made an extraordinary parade and show of virtue. Lantier alone set up a sort of defence for Nana. No doubt, he would say, with his Puritanic air, a girl who cuts and runs is doing very wrong; then he would add, with a glitter in the corner of his eye, that, hang it all! the chit was too pretty to wallow in poverty at her age.

"Do you know?" cried Madame Lorilleux, one day in the Boche's lodge, where the coterie was having coffee. "Well, as sure as the light of day, Clop-clop sold her daughter. Yes, she sold her. I have the proof of it. That old man, who was always about on the staircase, he had already begun to pay in instalments. It was under one's very eyes. And only yesterday someone saw them at the Ambigu, the young miss and her old tom-cat. My word! they hit it off together, you can see that!"

The matter was talked over as they finished their coffee. After all, it was quite possible; one had heard of worse things. And after that, the most sedate of the neighbours declared that Gervaise had sold her daughter.

Gervaise now dragged herself about, without caring what people chose to say. If anyone had called out thief after her in the street, she would not have turned her head. For the last month she had given up working at Madame Fauconnier's; she had had to show her the door, in order to avoid disputes. In a few weeks she had tried eight laundries; she did two or three days' work in each, then she had the chuck, so badly did she mess up the work, careless and dirty, and by this time forgetful of her own trade. At last, realizing that she could only bungle over things, she had given up ironing, and she did washing by the day, at the wash-house in the Rue Neuve; and to have to dabble in all that dirt, to sink to the roughest and easiest part of the business, dragged her one step further down the downward course. And, for one thing, the wash-house did not improve her looks. She looked like a mangy cur when she came out dripping, with her bluish skin. And she grew stouter than ever, despite her dances before the cupboard, and her leg limped so badly that she could not walk by anyone's side without nearly knocking them over.

Naturally, when a woman sinks to that point, her womanly self-esteem goes. Gervaise had dropped her old pride and coquetry, and her requirements in the way of sentiment,

propriety, and respect. You might kick her about, before and
behind, she would never feel it, she had become too flabby
and too sluggish. And now Lantier had left her for good and
all; he did not even make the pretence of paying her any
attentions; and she seemed never to have noticed this end of
a long connection, dragged out to such a length, and let drop
in mutual weariness. For her it was one drudgery the less.
Even the relations of Lantier and Virginie left her perfectly
calm; so indifferent had she become to all that sort of nonsense,
which had formerly made her so furious. She would have
held the candle for them, if they had wished it. Everyone
knew all about it now, they were having a fine time of it. It
was very convenient for them too, old cuckold Poisson had
night duty every two days, and while he was shivering outside
on the deserted pavements, his wife and the neighbour kept
their feet nice and warm at home. Oh! they were in no hurry,
they heard the sound of his boots outside the shop, in the
dark, empty street, without needing to put their noses outside
the quilt for that. A policeman has to attend to his duty,
hasn't he? And they made raids on his property all night
long, while the solemn gentleman watched over the property
of others. The whole quarter of the Goutte-d'Or enjoyed the
joke. It seemed very funny, this cuckolding of the powers that
be. Besides, that little corner seemed to belong to Lantier.
The shop and the shopkeeper went together. He had disposed
of a laundress, now he nibbled up a sweet-seller, and if
haberdashers, and stationers, and milliners, came along, one
after another, he was quite capable of taking in the lot of
them.

Never was there a man who simply wallowed in sweets as
Lantier did. He knew what he was about when he advised
Virginie to go into that line of business. He was too much of
a Provençal not to adore sweets; he could have lived on
jujubes, gumdrops, sugar-plums, and chocolates. Sugar-plums,
in particular, made his mouth water. For a whole year he
had been living on bonbons. He opened the drawers and took
out whole handfuls, when Virginie asked him to look after the
shop. Often, as he **was** talking, when there were five or six
people about, he took off the cover of a jar on the counter,
dipped in his hand, and began to munch something; the jar
remained open, and was soon empty. No one took any notice
of it; it was a mere habit, he said. Then he had invented a
perpetual cold, an irritation of the throat, which he wanted

to soothe. He still did no work, he had bigger and bigger
schemes in view, and he was thinking out a superb invention,
the umbrella-hat, a hat which turned into a gamp on the
head, at the first drops of a shower; and he promised Poisson
half profits, he even borrowed twenty-franc pieces for his
experiments. Meanwhile the shop melted away on his lips;
all the goods of the establishment went that way, the very
chocolate cigars, and red caramel pipes. When he was full
of the sweet things, and took a last tender sip at the mistress
of them, in a corner, she found him all sugary, his lips
like burnt almonds. A delightful man to kiss! He seemed
actually turned to honey. The Boches declared that he
had only to dip his finger in his coffee, and it was turned to
syrup.

Lantier, his heart melted by this endless dessert, became
quite paternal with Gervaise. He gave her advice, scolded
her because she had got tired of work. Hang it all! a woman at
her age ought to know her way about better than that. He
accused her of having always been greedy. But as one is
bound to succour folks, even when they don't deserve it, he
tried to find her little jobs. Thus he had got Virginie to have
in Gervaise once a week, to give the rooms and the shop a
wash out; she was quite used to scrubbing things, and it
would bring her in thirty sous each time. Gervaise made her
appearance on Saturday morning, with her pail and scrubbing
brush, without seeming to find any humiliation in coming
back like this, to do charing, the lowest sort of charing, in the
very place where she had queened it as mistress. It was the
last degradation, the end of all the pride that was yet left to
her.

One Saturday she had a terribly hard job. It had rained
for the last three days, the customers' feet seemed to have
brought into the shop all the dirt of the neighbourhood.
Virginie was at the counter, got up quite in a lady-like way,
with her hair nicely done, and her lace collar and cuffs.
Beside her, on the narrow bench covered with red moleskin,
Lantier lorded it with an air of great importance, as if the
whole place belonged to him; and he dipped his hand negli-
gently into a jar of peppermints, just to crack something
sugary under his teeth, out of habit.

"I say, Madame Coupeau," cried Virginie, who was
watching attentively the washing operations, "you have left
some dirt over there, in that corner. Scrub it a little better!"

Gervaise obeyed. She went back to the corner, and began to wash it over again. As she knelt on the ground, in the midst of the dirty water, she was all huddled up, her shoulder-blades sticking out, her arms purple and rigid. Her old sopping skirt clung tightly about her body. There on the floor she looked like a heap of something not quite decent, her hair all in disorder, the holes in her bodice showing bits of swollen flesh, an overflow of flesh which wobbled and quivered under the rude shocks of her work; and she was so bathed in sweat that great drops guttered off her streaming face.

"The more elbow grease you put into it, the more it shines," said Lantier sententiously, his mouth full of sweets.

Virginie, lying back with the air of a princess, her eyes half closed, kept watch over the work, and made comments now and then.

"A little more to the right. Now, mind the wood-work. You know, I wasn't quite satisfied last Saturday. There were some stains left."

And both of them lolled back as if on a throne, whilst Gervaise dragged herself to and fro on the ground at their feet, in the midst of the dirt. Virginie seemed to gloat over it, for her cat's eyes lit up for an instant with yellow sparkles, and she looked at Lantier with a faint smile. At last she had her revenge for that old thrashing in the wash-house, which she had always had on her mind!

Meanwhile, whenever Gervaise ceased scrubbing, a tiny sound of sawing came from the back room. Through the open door could be seen, against the livid light of the court, the profile of Poisson, who was off duty that day, and who took advantage of his leisure to return to his little boxes. He was sitting at a table, where he cut out arabesques with extraordinary care, in the mahogany of a cigar-box.

"I say, Badingue!" cried Lantier, who had gone back to the nickname, out of friendliness; "I bespeak your box, as a present for a lady."

Virginie gave him a pinch, but the hatter, still smiling, returned good for evil by doing the mouse along her knee under the counter; and he took away his hand quite naturally when the husband looked up, his red moustache and imperial bristling in his ashy face.

"That's just it," said the policeman. "I was doing it for you, Auguste, as a friendly souvenir."

"Oh! the deuce! then I'll keep your little concern!" said

Lantier with a laugh. "I'll hang it round my neck with a ribbon."

Then, all at once, as if this idea called up another:

"By the way," he said, "I met Nana last night."

The shock of the news set Gervaise a-squat in a pool of dirty water. She sat there panting and sweating, her brush in her hand.

"Ah!" she said.

"Yes, I was going down the Rue des Martryrs, and I saw a little person wriggling about on the arm of an old man in front of me, and I said to myself: "There's a behind I seem to have seen." So I hurried along, and there I was face to face with my blessed Nana! Well, you have nothing to complain of, she is nice and happy, a fine woollen dress on her back, a gold cross at her neck, and a saucy little air with it all."

"Ah!" said Gervaise, again in a hollow voice.

Lantier, who had finished his peppermints, took a stick of barley-sugar from another jar.

"She is fly, that child!" he continued. "Just fancy, she beckoned to me to follow her, as coolly as you like. Then she stowed away her old man somewhere, in a café. Oh! a stunning old man; he *is* pumped! And then she came and joined me in a doorway. A regular little serpent! so pretty, and such a little woman, and licking you like a dog! Yes, she kissed me, and asked for news of everybody. I was quite pleased to meet her."

"Ah!" said Gervaise for the third time.

She sat there huddled up, waiting. Hadn't her daughter even sent her a message? In the silence Poisson's saw was again heard. Lantier, very much diverted, sucked his barley-sugar rapidly, with a hissing sound of the lips.

"Well! if I were to see her I should go on the other side of the street," said Virginie, who had again given the hatter a furious pinch. "I should blush up to the eyes to be greeted in public by one of those girls. It is not because you are there, Madame Coupeau, but your daughter is a pretty piece of rottenness. Poisson takes up better than that every day."

Gervaise said nothing, and did not move, her eyes fixed on vacancy. Then she slowly shook her head, as if in answer to the ideas she had in her own mind, whilst the hatter murmured with a dainty air:

"One wouldn't mind an indigestion of that sort of rottenness. It is as tender as chicken. . . ."

But Virginie gave him such a terrible look that he had to

stop short and appease her by a polite attention. He glanced
at the policeman, saw that he was buried in his work on the
little box, and took the opportunity of stuffing the barley-
sugar into Virginie's mouth. At that she had a jolly laugh.
Then she turned her wrath against Gervaise.

"Hurry up now, if you please. It isn't the way to get on with
the work to stick there like a stock. Stir your stumps, I don't
want to dabble in water all day."

And she added in a lower voice, maliciously:

"Is it my fault if her daughter goes on the loose?"

Doubtless Gervaise did not hear. She had begun to rub the
floor again, her back bent, grovelling on the ground, crawling
about with the lumpish motion of a frog. She grasped the
handle of the brush in both hands, and pushed before her a
flood of dirty water, which splashed her with muddy streaks
up to the hair. She had now only to give a final rinsing, after
pouring away the dirty water in the gutter.

Meanwhile, after a silence, Lantier, feeling bored, raised
his voice.

"I didn't tell you, Badingue," he called, "I saw your boss
yesterday, in the Rue de Rivoli. He is deucedly done up, he
hasn't six months' life in his body. Lord! with the life he leads!"

He referred to the Emperor. The policeman answered
dryly, without raising his eyes:

"If you were the Government you wouldn't be so plump."

"Oh! my good chap, if I were the Government," returned
the hatter, with a sudden pretence of gravity, "things would
go a bit better, you bet! Now look at the foreign policy; it's
been a regular job for ever so long. Well now, for my part, if
I only knew a journalist whom I could inspire with my
ideas. . . ."

He began to warm up, and, as he had finished the barley-
sugar, he opened a drawer from which he took some bits of
almond paste, which he munched as he gesticulated.

"It's quite simple. First of all I should reorganize Poland,
and I should set on foot a big Scandinavian state which would
keep the giant of the North in order. Then I should make a
republic of all the little German princedoms. As for England,
it is not at all dangerous; if it made a move, I should send a
hundred thousand men to India. Then I should send the
Grand Turk back to Mecca, and the Pope to Jerusalem, cross
on back. Well, Europe would soon be all right. Look here,
Badingue, look. . . ."

He interrupted himself to take up five or six bits of the paste.

"Well, it would be done as quickly as you swallow that."

And he tossed the morsels one after another into his open mouth.

"The Emperor has a different plan," said the policeman, after two long moments of deliberation.

"Oh, shut up!" said the hatter violently. "We all know his plan. All Europe laughs in his nose. Every day the flunkeys of the Tuileries pick up your boss under the table between two swell society tarts."

Poisson got up. He came forward and laid his hand on his heart, saying:

"You wound me, Auguste. Let us have our argument without personalities."

Then Virginie interfered, and begged them to be quiet. She didn't care *that* for Europe! How could two men who shared and shared alike in other matters fall out about politics? For an instant they growled at one another, and then the policeman, to show that he bore no malice, brought in the cover of his little box that he had just finished; inside, in inlaid letters, could be read: "To Auguste, in friendly souvenir". Lantier, highly flattered, leant over, so that he was almost on top of Virginie. And the husband saw it all, with his face the colour of an old wall, in which his dull eyes said nothing; but the red bristles of his moustache gave a little spasmodic jerk at intervals, in such a queer way, that anyone less sure of his affair than the hatter would have been a bit anxious.

Lantier was a chap who had the cool cheek that always pleases women. As Poisson turned his back, he got the droll idea of putting a kiss on the left eye of Madame Poisson. Usually he was very artful and cautious; but when he had had a quarrel over politics he would dare anything, resolute at all events to be right on the woman question. Those greedy caresses, sneaked so audaciously behind the policeman's back, revenged him upon the Empire which had turned France into a bawdy house. Only this time he had forgotten the presence of Gervaise. She had rinsed and swept out the shop, and she stood in front of the counter waiting until they gave her her thirty sous. The kiss on the eye left her quite calm, a natural thing, which was no concern of hers. Virginie, however, seemed a little confused. She threw the thirty sous on the counter before Gervaise. But Gervaise did not move, seeming still to be waiting for something, still shaking with the washing-up, as sloppy and as ugly as a dog that had been pulled out of a sewer.

"So she didn't say anything to you?" she asked Lantier at last.

"Who do you mean?" he exclaimed. "Oh, yes! Nana. No; nothing else. What a mouth the little beggar has! A regular pot of strawberries!"

And Gervaise went her way with her thirty sous in her hand. Her slippers leaked like pumps, regular musical boxes, which played an air on the pavement, on which they left the imprint of their large soles.

In the neighbourhood, the tipplers like herself declared that she drank to console herself for her daughter's fall. She herself, when she sipped her brandy at the bar, took on melo-dramatic airs, and tossed off the glass with a wish that it might be her last. And when she came back awfully tight, she stammered out that it was her troubles. But honest people only shrugged their shoulders: that was the old story, putting the tipsy bouts at Colombe's bar down to the score of troubles; at all events, they would have to be called bottled troubles. No doubt, to begin with, she had found it hard to stomach the flight of Nana. The honesty that yet remained in her revolted; then, in the general way, a mother does not like to say to herself that her girl, just at that very moment, is being rudely hailed by the first comer. But she was already too stupefied, her head sick, and her heart crushed, to keep much sensation of shame for very long. It came and went with her. She got on very well for a week without thinking of her little trollop of a daughter; then all at once a feeling of tenderness or of anger would come over her, a furious desire to come upon Nana somewhere, perhaps to cover her with kisses, perhaps with blows, according to the inclination of the moment. Finally she came to have no very clear ideas at all on the subject of propriety. Only, Nana surely belonged to her, and you don't care to see your own property melt away.

When these thoughts came over her, Gervaise looked down into the street with the eyes of a detective. Ah! if she were only to catch sight of her peck of dirt, wouldn't she send her home spinning! That year the whole quarter was being pulled about. The Boulevard Magenta and the Boulevard Ornano were brought through what had been the Barrière Poissonnière,

and cut into the outer boulevard. It was scarcely recognizable.
One whole side of the Rue des Poissoniers was pulled down.
And now, from the Rue de la Goutte-d'Or, you had a good
sweep before you, a breadth of sunlight and fresh air; and in
place of the buildings, which blocked the view on that side, a
regular monument had been erected on the Boulevard
Ornano, a six-storey house, carved like a church, with bright
windows, hung with embroidered curtains, a general air of
wealth. That house, all white, standing right opposite to the
street, seemed to brighten it up like a sheet of light. Every day
there was a dispute about it between Lantier and Poisson.
The hatter was never tired of talking about the demolition
of Paris; he accused the Emperor of putting up palaces
everywhere, so as to send the working men into the country;
and the policeman, cold and pale with rage, declared that on
the contrary, the Emperor's first thoughts were about the
working men, that he would pull down all Paris, if need be,
simply to provide them with work. Gervaise, too, seemed
discontented with these embellishments, which were changing
the dingy, out-lying corner to which she was accustomed.
Her discontent came from the fact that the quarter was looking
up just as she was going down. When you are in a dirty state,
you don't like the sun full on you. And, too, when she was
looking for Nana, she was furious at having to get over the
building materials, to paddle along over pavements in course
of being put down, to bump up against scaffoldings. The
beautiful erection on the Boulevard Ornano put her beside
herself. Beastly things like that were for tarts like Nana.

Meanwhile, she often had news of the girl. There are
always kind friends ready to give you bad news. She was told
that the child had given the slip to her old man, a most unwise
thing to do. She was very well off with him, petted, adored,
free even, if she had known how to arrange matters. But
young people are silly, she had gone off with some ninny or
other, nobody knew exactly who it was. What seemed certain
was, that one afternoon, on the Place de la Bastille, she had
asked her old man for three sous for a certain little requirement,
and that he was waiting for her still. In the best society, that
was known as pissing like an Englishwoman. Others swore
that they had seen her since then, dancing the *chahut* at the
"Grand Salon de la Folie", Rue de la Chapelle. And it was
then that Gervaise got the idea of frequenting the low dancing-
halls of the quarter. She could not go past a ball without

stopping and going in. Coupeau accompanied her. At first
they simply went the round of the halls, scrutinizing all the
hussies who kicked up their heels there. Then one evening, as
they had some small change, they sat down at a table, and had
a bowl of wine punch, just by way of a little refreshment,
while they waited to see if Nana turned up. At the end of a
month, they had forgotten all about Nana, they went to the
balls for their own amusement, to watch the dances. They sat
there for hours together, without saying a word, with their
elbows on the table, stupefied in the midst of the quivering
floor, no doubt finding some amusement in following with
their lack-lustre eyes the antics of the street-walkers, in the
dense heat, the red glow of the hall.

One November evening, they had gone to the "Grand
Salon de la Folie" to warm themselves up a bit. Outside, the
cold was sharp enough to cut your face in two. But the hall
was chokefull. There was a regular swarm, people at all the
tables, people in the middle, people above, a very heap of
flesh; those who liked tripe *à la mode de Caen* could have their
fill of it. When they had been right round twice without
finding a table, they decided to stand until some of the people
had cleared out. Coupeau swayed about in his dirty blouse
and old peakless cap, flattened at the top. And, as he stood
in the way, he saw a thin little young man wiping the sleeve
of his overcoat, after having knocked up against him.

"I say!" he cried angrily, taking his cutty-pipe out of his
black mouth, "can't you beg pardon? And you needn't look
so disgusted, because one wears a blouse."

The young man turned and looked him up and down;
he went on:

"Just you learn, bugger of a pimp, that the blouse is the
best kind of dress you can have, yes, the workman's dress!
I'll wipe you down, if you want it, with a couple of good
clouts. Pansies like that insulting a working man!"

Gervaise tried to calm him down. He stretched himself out
in his rags, he smacked his blouse as he shouted:

"That, now, that's the chest of a man!"

The young man disappeared into the thick of the crowd,
muttering:

"What a dirty blackguard!"

Coupeau wanted to follow him. Likely that he would let
himself be sat upon by an overcoat! An overcoat that wasn't
even paid for! A second-hand thing intended to mash a

woman without spending a centime. If he came across him
again he would force him to go down on his knees before the
blouse. But the pack was too thick, there was no moving.
Gervaise and he made their way slowly round the dances;
a triple row of gazers squeezed in tight together, their faces
inflamed when a man showed himself off, or a woman kicked
her petticoats in the air and showed all she had; and as they
were both short, they raised themselves on tiptoe in order to
see something, chignons and hats bobbing up and down. The
orchestra, with its cracked brass, played away furiosly at a
quadrille, a tempest which shook the very roof; whilst the
dancers raised such a cloud of dust with their heels, that it
dimmed the flare of the gas. The heat was overpowering.

"Look there!" said Gervaise suddenly.

"What is it?"

"That velvet hat over there."

They craned up as high as they could. On the left was an
old hat of black velvet, with two threadbare feathers which
nodded; plumes like a hearse. But they could see nothing but
the hat, dancing a very hell of a *chahut*, curvetting, whirling,
dipping, and reappearing. They lost sight of it in the furious
confusion of heads, and they caught sight of it again, wagging
above the others, with such a droll cheek, that the people
about them laughed merely at seeing the way the hat was
dancing, without knowing what there was underneath.

"Well!" said Coupeau.

"Don't you recognize that chignon?" whispered Gervaise
in a choking voice, "I bet my life it's her."

With one shove, the tinsmith made his way through the
crowd. Damnation! it was indeed Nana! And a nice dress she
had on! It was an old silk dress, all sticky with having swept
tavern tables, and flounces from it were strewed all about.
It fitted to her like her skin, she had not a scrap of shawl
about her shoulders, and her bare flesh was visible through
the rent button-holes. To think that the little beggar had had
an old man who was devoted to her, and yet had come down
to this, for the sake of some ponce who probably beat her! All
the same, she was awfully fresh and appetizing, as curly as a
lap-dog, with her rosy little mouth under her great hat.

"I'll make her dance!" cried Coupeau.

Nana, naturally, was suspecting nothing. She wriggled like
anything! A waggle to right, and a waggle to left, curtsies
which bent her double, high kicks right in the very face of her

partner, as if she were going to split herself in two. A circle formed around her, she was applauded, and in her excitement, she picked up her skirts, pulled them up to her knees, carried away by the whirl of the *chahut*, turning and twisting like a top, squatting down on the floor in the splits, then changing to a little modest dance, with an undulation of hips and bust that was simply stunning. You wanted to carry her off to a corner, and devour her with kisses.

Meanwhile Coupeau had got right into the middle of the dance; he upset the figure, and was hustled about.

"I tell you it's my daughter!" he cried. "Let me pass!"

Nana just at that moment was going backwards, sweeping the floor with her feathers, rounding out her posterior and giving it a little shake for effect. She received a whacking kick, admirably aimed, looked up, and turned pale as she saw her father and mother before her. If that wasn't ill-luck!

"Out of it!" yelled the dancers.

But Coupeau, who had recognized in his daughter's partner the thin young man in the overcoat, cared not a straw for anybody.

"Yes, it's us," he growled. "Ah! you didn't expect us, did you? This is where I catch you, and with that greenhorn there, who has just insulted me!"

Gervaise, with clenched teeth, pushed him aside, saying:

"Be quiet! What's the good of explaining all that?"

And she went up and gave Nana two resounding cuffs. The first knocked the plumed hat all on one side, the second left a red mark on her blanched cheek. Nana, half stupefied, received them without a tear or a struggle. The orchestra went on, and the people all round grew impatient, and repeated violently:

"Out of it! out of it!"

"Now then, off you go!" said Gervaise; "march! and don't you try to give us the slip, or I'll have you sent to the lock up!"

The little young man had prudently disappeared. Nana marched stiffly before them, still stupefied by her ill luck. If she seemed inclined to jib at all, a kick behind her sent her on the way to the door. And the three of them went out together amidst the jeers and hootings of the hall, whilst the orchestra finished the dance with such a thundering sound that the trombones seemed to fire out bullets.

The same life began over again. When Nana had had twelve hours' sleep in her old room, she behaved very nicely

for a week. She had faked up a little modest dress, and she
wore a bonnet with strings tied under her chignon. She was
even fired with the idea of working at home; you could earn
as much as you liked, and you were not mixed up with all
the nastiness of the work-room; and she looked about for
work, set up a table and tools, and got up at five o'clock in
the morning, for the first few days, to roll her stalks of violets.
But when she had sent in a few gross, she stretched herself,
and had the cramp in her fingers; she had lost her knack of
doing them, and it felt suffocating to her to stay indoors so
long, she had had such a fine breezy time of it lately. Then the
paste-pot dried up, the petals and the green paper got grease
stains on them, and her employer came himself three times,
and kicked up a row, and demanded his materials back.
Nana lounged about, pocketed her father's blows, was always
nagging with her mother from morning to night, both women
covering one another with the foulest abuse. That sort of
thing could not last long, and on the twelfth day the ragamuffin made herself scarce, carrying off, by way of luggage,
her little modest dress on her back, and her little bonnet on
her ear. The Lorilleux, who had been somewhat put out by
the child's return and repentance, went into shrieks of laughter.
Second performance, eclipse number two; ladies for Saint-
Lazare, this way, please! It was really too funny. Nana was a
regular dab at slinging her hook. Well, if the Coupeaus
wanted to keep her after this, there was only one thing to do,
sew her up and put her under lock and key.

The Coupeaus before people, pretended that it was a good
riddance. Inwardly they were furious. But furious feelings
cannot last forever. They soon heard, without manifesting the
least concern, that Nana was on the ran-tan all over the
neighbourhood. Gervaise, who declared that she did it for
the purpose of bringing them into disgrace, professed to
disregard all the scandalous reports. If she were to meet her
girl in the street, she would not soil her hand by so much as
giving her a clout. No; it was all over. If she found her naked
and famishing on the pavement, she would pass by without
saying that the dirty slut was her own flesh and blood. Nana
was the great attraction of all the balls in the neighbourhood.
She was known from the "Reine-Blanche" to the "Grand
Salon de la Folie". When she entered the "Elysée-Montmartre"
people mounted on the tables to see her do the *écrevisse qui
renifle*, in the *pastourelle*. As she had twice been turned out of

the "Chateau-Rouge", she only prowled before the door, on the watch for people she knew. The "Boule Noire", on the boulevard, and the "Grand-Turc", Rue des Poissonniers, were uppish sort of balls, to which she went when she had decent under-linen. But of all the balls of the neighbourhood the ones she preferred were the "Bal de l'Ermitage", up a damp court, and the "Bal Robert", Impasse du Cadran, two beastly little halls lit up by half a dozen lamps, very free-and-easy, happy-go-lucky places, where the ladies and their partners were allowed to embrace in the corners without being disturbed. And Nana had her ups and downs, regular transformation scenes, now furbished up like a swell lady, now trailing in the dirt like the lowest draggle-tail. Ah! she led a fine life!

Several times the Coupeaus fancied they caught sight of their daughter in very unseemly sort of places. They turned tail and decamped forthwith, so as not to be obliged to meet her face to face. They were not inclined to stand the jeers of a whole hall for the sake of taking home a baggage of that sort. But one night, as they were going to bed, they heard a banging at the door. It was Nana, who calmly asked if she might come in and have a bed; and, good Lord! what a state she was in, bare-headed, her clothes in tatters, her shoes in rags, a toilette bad enough to be marched off to the police-station. She had a good hiding, naturally, then she fell greedily upon a morsel of hard bread, and fell asleep, quite worn out, with her last mouthful still between her teeth. Then she went on in her usual way. When she had faked together some new clothes, off she went, one fine morning. The bird was flown, no one knew where. Weeks, months, rolled by, she seemed lost for good, when all at once she turned up again, without ever saying where she came from, sometimes so dirty that you wouldn't touch her with a pair of tongs, her body scratched all over; at other times nicely dressed, but so limp and worn out, that she could hardly stand. Her parents had to get used to it. The hidings she got made no difference to her. They gave her a good drubbing, but that did not prevent her from making use of their lodgings as a sort of inn, where one could put up by the week. She knew that she would have to pay for her bed by a thrashing, and she came and took her thrashing, when there was anything to be gained by it. However, people get tired of dealing blows, and the Coupeaus finally came to take Nana's escapades as they came. She came in, or she did not come in; as long as she did not leave the door open, it was all right. Good heavens! decency, like anything else, wears out in time.

There was only one thing that put Gervaise beside herself. It was when her daughter reappeared in dresses with trains, and hats covered with feathers. No, she could not stomach that sort of luxury. If Nana must go on the loose, let her; but when she was with her mother, she might at least dress as a work-girl ought to be dressed. The dresses with trains set the whole house in commotion. The Lorilleux sneered, Lantier, quite elated, came sniffing about; the Boches told Pauline that she was not to speak to the draggle-tail, with all her tinsel. And Gervaise, too, was angry with Nana for her way of sleeping on till noon after one of her escapades, her night-dress all open, her hair undone and still full of hair-pins, so white, and breathing so short, that she seemed dead. She shook her five or six times of a morning, threatening to empty a pail of water over her. The lovely, lazy girl, half naked, buxom with sex, exasperated her, as she lay there sleeping off the lusts that seemed to fill out her flesh, unable even to waken herself. Nana opened one eye, closed it again, and stretched herself out more comfortably than ever.

One day Gervaise, scolding her very crudely for the way she carried on, and asking if she had turned the red-coats' tart to come back so done up as all that, carried out her threat by shaking her streaming hand over her. The child was furious; she rolled herself up in the sheet, and cried:

"That's enough, now mamma! Don't you talk about men; you'll be wiser not to. You did what you liked, I shall do what I like."

"What? what?" stammered the mother.

"Yes, I never said anything to you about it, it was none of my business; but you didn't use to be so very particular. I saw you often enough going about in your nightdress, down below, when papa was snoring. Now you don't care for it, but others do. So you shut up, and don't preach to me!"

Gervaise stood there pale and trembling, turning about without knowing what she was doing, whilst Nana, flat on her face, clasping her pillow in her arms, fell back into the torpor of her leaden sleep.

Coupeau growled, but he had now lost his habit of knocking her about. He was getting a bit weak in the upper storey. And really he was not to be regarded as an immoral father,

for the drink had taken from him all distinction of right and
wrong.

Now it was a regular thing. He was drunk constantly for
six months, then he got knocked up and was taken to Sainte-
Anne's; it was a sort of country outing for him. The Lorilleux
said that my Lord Tipple-well went to his family-seat. After
a few weeks he came out again, patched up a bit, and he began
to undo all the good that had been done, until he was again
in need of patching-up. In three years he was seven times at
Sainte-Anne's. In the neighbourhood it was said that they
kept his cell for him. But the worst of it was that the inveterate
drunkard got worse each time, so that in fall after fall one could
foresee the final caper, the last crack of the shivering cask, as
hoop after hoop gave way.

And he had become too quite a sight, a very spectre. The
poison made awful ravages. His body, soaked in alcohol,
shrivelled up like a fœtus in a chemist's jar. When he stood
in front of the window, you could see daylight through him,
he was so thin. His cheeks were hollow, his eyes ran with
rheum, wax enough to supply a whole cathedral; only his
flaming proboscis, fine and florid, stood out like a carnation
in the midst of his wasted visage. Those who knew his age,
just forty, shivered as they saw him pass, bent and shaky, and
as old as the streets. And the trembling of his hands had
increased, his right hand in particular kept up such a ticking,
that, on certain days, he had to take his glass in both hands
to lift it to his mouth. Oh! that infernal trembling! it was the
only thing that really frightened him, in the midst of his
general collapse. Sometimes he would growl out all sorts of
abuse against his hands. Other times he would sit for hours
watching his hands as they danced, seeing them jump like
frogs, without a word, not angry, but seeming to be trying to
find out what piece of inner mechanism set them frolicking
like that; and one evening Gervaise found him sitting thus
while two big tears trickled down his inflamed cheeks.

The last summer during which Nana still spent the fag-end
of her nights at her parents', was a very bad one for Coupeau.
His voice changed completely, as if the spirits had set a new
tune going in his throat. He became deaf in one ear. Then, in
a few days, his sight began to go; he had to hold on to the
banister of the staircase, to keep from falling. As for his
general health, it was so-so. He had frightful headaches,
dizziness which made him see specks dancing before him.

All at once he was seized with acute pains in his arms and legs; he went pale, and was obliged to sit down, and keep his chair for hours together; once, after one of these crises, his right arm had been paralysed for a whole day. Several times he had to take to his bed; he curled himself up under the clothes, breathing hard and fast like an animal in suffering. Then the extravagances of Sainte-Anne's began over again. Restless, suspicious, parched with fever, he rolled over and over in mad accesses of rage, tore his blouses, bit the furniture with his convulsive jaws; or he fell into a lachrymose state, complaining like a girl, sobbing and lamenting that no one loved him. One evening Gervaise and Nana, coming in together, found he was not in bed. In his place he had put the bolster. When they discovered him, crouching between the bed and the wall, his teeth were chattering, and he told them that men had come to murder him. The two women had to put him to bed again, and comfort him like a child.

Coupeau knew only one remedy, to toss off his tumbler of brandy, which set him up like a kick in the ribs. It was in this way that he cleared his phlegm every morning. His memory had long since gone, his skull was quite empty; he was no sooner on his feet than he laughed at illness. He had never been ill at all. Yes, he had come to the point at which a man who is at his last gasp declares that he is perfectly well. Then, too, he had got quite childish. When Nana came back, after six weeks' wanderings, he seemed to think that she had just been out on an errand. She often met him when she was going along on the arm of a gentleman, and she laughed in his face without his recognizing her. But he did not count at all; she would have used him for a seat, if there had been nothing else to sit upon.

With the first frosts, Nana took to her heels again. She had pretended that she was going to the fruiterer's to see if there were any stewed pears. She felt the approach of winter, and she had no mind to hear her teeth chatter before a cold stove. The Coupeaus called her a jade, because they had to wait for the pears. No doubt she would come back again; the other winter she had stayed out three weeks when she had merely gone down for a pennyworth of tobacco. But months went by, and the girl did not return. This time she had evidently set off on a fine gallop. June came, but she had not returned with the sun. Evidently it was all over now, she had made her nest somewhere. One day the Coupeaus, when they were hard up, sold her iron bed for six francs, which they spent in drink at Saint-Ouen. The bed was in the way.

One morning in July, Virginie called in Gervaise who was passing, and asked her to lend her a hand with the plates and dishes, because, the night before, Lantier had brought in two friends for a little feast. And as Gervaise washed up the plates and dishes, thick with grease after the hatter's little feast, he called to her from the shop, where he was still digesting his meal:

"Look here, mother, do you know I saw Nana the other day?"

Virginie, who sat at the counter, pulling a long face as she looked at all the empty jars and drawers, shook her head furiously. She restrained herself, so as not to show her disgust, for it looked bad. Lantier saw Nana very often. Oh! she wouldn't have gone through fire for it, he was capable of doing worse than that when a petticoat came into his head. Madame Lerat, who had just come in, and who was now on the most confidential terms with Virginie, gave her ambiguous grimace, and asked:

"What do you mean, you saw her?"

"Oh! in a good sense," replied the hatter, very much flattered, laughing, and curling his moustache. "She was in a carriage; I was dabbling along the pavement. Fact, I assure you. There would be no defending one's self; for the swells whom she has about her now are awfully lucky."

His eyes glittered, and he turned towards Gervaise, who was standing at the other end of the shop, wiping a plate.

"Yes, she was in a carriage, and dressed all in style. I didn't recognize her, she looked quite the society lady, with her little white teeth in her face as fresh as a flower. It was she who sent me a little wave of her glove. She has mashed a viscount, I fancy. Oh! she's all right now! She can get on without us well enough, she has as good a time as you like. A little love of a thing! Oh! you have no idea what a little love!"

Gervaise went on wiping her plate, though it had been shining for some time. Virginie was thinking, anxious about two bills that she did not know how to meet the next day; whilst Lantier, plump and comfortable, exuding the sweet-stuff on which he lived, filled the shop with his enthusiasm for nicely-dressed little loves, the shop now two-thirds devoured, in which there was already a sort of odour of decay. Yes, there

were only a few more burnt almonds to crack, a few sticks of
barley-sugar to suck, and the Poissons would be cleaned out.
All at once he saw the policeman on the pavement opposite;
he was on duty, and he went by buttoned to the chin, his
sword flapping at his side. And that tickled him all the more.
He made Virginie look at her husband.

"Ah, well!" he murmured. "He looks funny this morning,
the good Badingue! Mind! he's buttoned in too tight, he's
been prying somewhere, and finding out something or other."

When Gervaise went upstairs, she found Coupeau sitting
on the edge of his bed, in the stupefaction of one of his crises.
He stared at the floor, with his extinct eyes. Then she sat
down herself on a chair, tired out, her arms hanging idly by
the side of her dirty skirt. And she sat there in front of him for
a quarter of an hour, without saying a word.

"I've heard some news," she muttered at length. "Someone
saw your daughter. Your daughter is all in style now, she
doesn't need you any more. She is awfully lucky, that girl.
By God! I only wish I were in her place."

Coupeau still stared at the floor. Then he raised his
haggard face, with an idiot's laugh, stammering:

"Well, you know, ducky, I won't hinder you. You're not
too bad till, when you wash your face properly. You know
they say there's no pot too old to find its cover. Damn all I
care, if it's money for jam!"

CHAPTER TWELVE

IT must have been the Saturday after quarter day, somewhere about the 12th or 13th of January, Gervaise was not quite clear about it. She lost count of things, it was so long since she had had anything warm to eat. Ah! that infernal week! a regular squeeze, two four-pound loaves of bread on Tuesday, which had lasted till Thursday, then a dry crust from over night, and not a crumb since for thirty-six hours, a veritable dance before the side-board! What she was quite clear about, however, what she felt in her very bones, was that it was frightful weather, a black cold, with a sky like the ashes under the grate, big with snow that would not fall. When you have winter and hunger in your inside, you may tighten your girdle as much as you please, it is no resource.

Perhaps Coupeau would bring back something that evening. He said that he had got work. Everything is possible, and Gervaise, no matter how often she had been deceived already, had come to count upon that money. After all sorts of experiences, she could find nowhere now where there was even a dish-clout to wash; even an old lady for whom she cleaned up the place had turned her off, accusing her of drinking her liqueurs. No one would have anything to do with her, her credit was completely gone; and she was half glad of it in her heart, for she had fallen to that point of degradation in which you would rather die than move your ten fingers. Well, if Coupeau brought home his wages they could have something hot to eat. And meanwhile, as it was not yet noon, she lay stretched out on the mattress, because you are less cold and hungry when you are stretched out.

Gervaise called it the mattress; but, in truth, it was merely a bundle of staw in a corner. Little by little the bed and its belongings had found their way to the second-hand dealers. First of all, when she was hard up, she had unsewn the mattress and taken out handfuls of wool, which she took out in her apron and sold at ten sous a pound in the Rue Belhomme. Then, when the mattress was empty, she made thirty sous on the canvas, one morning, to pay for the coffee. The pillows had followed, then the bolster. Only the bedstead was left, and that she could not put under her arm, for the Boches would have raised the whole house if they had seen the landlord's guarantee vanish. However, one evening, with the aid of Coupeau, she kept watch on the Boches, who were having a little feast, and coolly took the bed out in bits, the sides, the back, the bottom framework. With the ten francs they made out of this, they had a jolly time for three days. Was not the straw mattress enough? Even the covering of that had gone the way of the rest; they had thus succeeded in disposing of the bed, not without getting an indigestion of bread, after a fast of twenty-four hours. They turned the straw with the broom; it was one way of turning the mattress, and it was no dirtier than other things.

Gervaise lay huddled up on the heap of straw, her feet tucked up under her rag of a skirt, to keep them warm. And as she lay there in a heap, her eyes wide open, she turned over all sorts of ideas that day. No, no, it was quite impossible to go on living like that without anything to eat. She did not feel hungry now; only she had a leaden weight in her stomach, and her brain seemed empty. Sure enough, it was not in the four corners of her wretched little hole that she was likely to find subjects for mirth. A very dog-kennel now, where the grey-hounds who wore overcoats in the streets would not have stayed for a minute. Her lack-lustre eyes gazed at the bare walls. Everything now was at uncle's. The chest of drawers was left, the table, and one chair; but the marble and the drawers of the chest of drawers had gone the way of the bed. A fire would not have made a cleaner sweep of everything, all the little things had gone, from the ticker, a watch worth a dozen francs, to the family photographs, of which a dealer had bought the frames; a nice friendly dealer, who would take a saucepan, an iron, a comb, and give her five sous, three sous, two sous, according to the value, with which she could buy a little bread. Now there was nothing left but an old pair of broken snuffers, for which the dealer would not give her a copper. Oh! if she had known of anyone who would buy dirt, and dust, and filth, she would have opened shop straight away, for the room was appallingly dirty. She could see nothing but spider's webs in the corners, and spider's webs may be good for cuts, but there are no merchants as yet ready to buy them. Then, turning her head, abandoning all hope of doing business, she drew herself closer together on her straw mattress, preferring to look out of the window at the sky laden with snow, a desolate light which chilled her to the very marrow.

What a nuisance it all was! What was the use of working herself up into a state, and worrying her brain for nothing? If she could only get a wink of sleep! But the thought of her rotten crib went over and over in her head. M. Marescot, the landlord, had come himself the day before to tell them that they would be turned out if they did not pay up the last two quarters within a week. Well, let them be turned out, they would certainly be no worse off in the streets. But here was this hulking brute in his great-coat and his woollen gloves, coming up to talk to them about their quarter's rent, as if they had a mine of gold somewhere about. Damn him! if instead of patting his own stomach he had only stuffed a little something into theirs! He was really too big a brute, with his pot-belly; she wished him to hell. And there was her old fool of a Coupeau, who could not come in now without giving her a tanning; she sent him after the landlord. By this time she could have peopled hell, she sent everyone packing off there, she only wanted to be rid of them and life together. She had become now a regular boxing-booth. Coupeau had a cudgel which he called his fancy fan. And he fanned the poor woman like anything, leaving her all in a sweat. And she was not too amiable herself either, would bite and scratch. Then there was a hurly-burly in the empty room, dressings and drubbings enough to turn your stomach. But at last she got used to this too, as to all the rest. Coupeau might make Holy Monday for weeks together, might go on the booze for whole months, might come in mad-drunk and batter her as much as he pleased, she was used to it now, it was a bore, that was all. And it was on days like this that she wished him to hell. Yes, to hell, her bloody fool of a man! to hell, the Lorilleux, the Boches, and the Poissons! to hell the whole lot of them, who looked down on her! to hell with all Paris! And she gave herself a sounding whack, with a gesture of infinite contempt and disgust.

Unluckily, however, though you can get used to many things, you cannot acquire the habit of doing without eating. It was that that ruffled Gervaise. She was ready to admit that she was the lowest of the low, the last leakings of the gutter, and she did not care if people drew aside when she came near them. Bad words break no bones; but hunger certainly gnaws at your vitals. Oh! she had said good-bye to dainty dishes, she would devour anything she could lay hands on. It was a feast-day for her now when she could buy from the butcher, at fourpence a pound, the leavings of the meat that had been lying blackening in a plate; and she put with it a handful of potatoes that she boiled in a saucepan. Or she would fricassee a bullock's heart, a delicacy which made her lick her lips. Other times, when she had wine, she would buy the washiest stuff, just to sop her bread in. Two penn'orth of pigs' chitterlings, a bushel of white potatoes, a quart of dry beans cooked in their own gravy, these were feasts to which she could not often treat herself. She came to be thankful for the broken meat that you could get in low eating-houses, where, for a copper, you could get a mess of fish-bones with the refuse of burnt meat. She fell lower still, begged crusts from a charitable restaurant-keeper, and made bread soup of them, letting them soak as long as possible over a neighbour's oven. When she was absolutely starving, she would even prowl with the dogs in front of the shopkeepers' doors, before the scavengers made their round; and in this way she sometimes found rich dishes, rotten melons, mackerel a bit off, chops that she examined at the thin end, to see if there were any maggots in them. Yes, she had come to that; that revolts one's dainty notions, no doubt; but if one had eaten nothing for three days, we should see if dainty notions would hold their own against the needs of the stomach; or if one wouldn't rather go on all fours and eat dirt like the rest. Ah! the starvation of the poor, the empty bellies that cry for food, the want that turns men into beasts, and sets their teeth gnashing, and crams them with foul things, in this huge Paris, all gold and glitter! And to think that Gervaise had once had enough and to spare of fat goose! Now she hardly dared think of it. One day when Coupeau had sneaked away two bread tickets, to sell them again and spend the money on drink, she nearly killed him with a blow from a shovel, for she was famishing, and the theft of a morsel of bread set her beside herself.

She had stared at the dim sky until at last she sank into a short, disturbed slumber. She dreamed that the snow-laden sky broke over her, she was so pinched with cold. All at once she sat bolt upright, awakened with a start by a great shiver of anguish. Good God! was she going to die? Haggard and shaking, she looked out and saw that it was still light. Would the night never come? How time drags, when you have nothing inside you! Her stomach too seemed to awake, and began to torture her. She sank on a chair, her head drooping, her hands between her legs in order to keep them warm, and she set to thinking what they would have for dinner when Coupeau brought back the money; some bread, a bottle of wine, and two portions of tripe, *à la Lyonnaise*. Three o'clock struck on old Bazouge's clock. It was only three. At that she burst into tears. Never would she have the strength to wait till seven. She rocked her whole body to and fro, like a little girl who is in pain, all doubled over, crushing her stomach flat, so as not to feel it any more. Ah! the pangs of child-birth are nothing to the pangs of hunger. And, feeling no better, she got up in a rage, and moved about the place, hoping to send her hunger to sleep, like a child whom one carries about in one's arms. For half an hour she banged herself against the four corners of the empty room. Then all at once she stopped short, her eyes fixed. Yes, they might say what they pleased, she would lick their feet if they liked, but she would borrow ten sous from the Lorilleux.

In winter time, on that staircase, the lousy staircase, there were continual loans of ten sous, of twenty sous, little services that these starving people rendered to each other. Only, they would all have died rather than go to the Lorilleux, because they were so notoriously close-fisted. Gervaise needed all her courage in knocking at their door. She was so frightened on the way that she felt a sudden relief when she had done so, like people ringing at the dentists'.

"Come in!" cried the sharp voice of the chain-maker.

How comfortable it was in there! The forge flamed, lighting up the narrow work-room with its white flame, whilst Madame Lorilleux put over some gold-wire to heat again. Lorilleux, at his work-table, was so hot that he sweated as he soldered the links to the stem. And there was a nice smell, some cabbage soup was simmering on the stove, sending out a steam that turned Gervaise half-sick and half-dizzy.

"Ah! it is you," growled Madame Lorilleux, without so much as asking her to sit down. "What do you want?"

Gervaise did not answer. She was not on bad terms with the Lorilleux that week. But the request for ten sous stuck in her throat, for she had just caught sight of Boche, planted in front of the fire, retailing his usual scandal. He had a free and easy sort of air, the brute! He laughed like a bum, his mouth rounding out, and his cheeks puffing up till they hid his nose; a veritable bum!

"What do you want?" repeated Lorilleux.

"You haven't seen Coupeau?" faltered out Gervaise, at length. "I thought he was here."

The chain-makers and the *concierge* laughed. No, indeed, they had not seen Coupeau. They were not able to offer him drinks enough to see much of Coupeau. Gervaise made an effort, and stammered:

"He told me he was coming back. He was going to bring back some money, and as I am absolutely in want of something . . ."

Silence reigned. Madame Lorilleux blew the bellows vigorously in front of the fire. Lorilleux had bent his head over the bit of chain that grew under his fingers, whilst Boche still laughed like a full moon, showing such a great round of mouth, that one was inclined to put one's finger into it to see what was there.

"If I had only ten sous," murmured Gervaise in a low voice.

Still silence.

"You can't lend me ten sous? Oh! I'll let you have them back in the evening."

Madame Lorilleux turned and stared straight in her face. It was no use trying soft soap on them. Today she was down on them for ten sous, tomorrow it would be twenty, and there was no reason why it should not go on for ever. No, no, none of that. Once in a blue moon.

"Why, my dear," she cried, "you know perfectly well that we haven't any money. Look here, look at the lining of my pocket. You can feel it as much as you like. Of course I should have been delighted."

"One is always delighted," growled Lorilleux; "only, when one can't, one can't."

Gervaise nodded, very humbly. However, she did not go, she kept her eyes fastened on the gold, the gold thread hung up on the walls, the gold wire that the wife pulled through the draw-plate with the full force of her short arms, the gold links heaped up under the bony fingers of the husband. And it seemed to her that the tiniest scrap of that metal would be enough to pay for a good dinner. That day the work-room might be dirty enough, with its old iron, its coal-dust, its oil-stains only half effaced; she saw it shining with riches, like the shop of a money-changer. So she ventured to repeat, softly:

"I will let you have it back, I will let you have it back, you may be sure. Ten sous won't inconvenience you."

Her heart was full, she could not confess that she had not broken her fast since the day before. Then she felt her legs give way under her, she nearly burst into tears, and she faltered:

"It would be so kind of you. You don't know. . . . My God! I've got to that point. . . ."

At that the Lorilleux bit their lips and exchanged a glance. Now Clop-clop had turned beggar! Well, the fall was complete now. They certainly didn't approve of that kind of going-on. If they had known, they would have shut themselves in, for you must always keep your eyes on beggars, people who would make their way into rooms under some pretext or other, and go off with valuable things. All the more so, as, in their place, there was something to steal; you could lay hold on things all about, and carry off thirty or forty francs by merely shutting your hand. Several times already they had been suspicious of the queer way in which Gervaise looked at the gold when she planted herself before it. This time, at all events, they would be on their guard. And as she came nearer, and put her feet on the squares of wood put to catch the dust, the chain-maker called out roughly, without taking any further notice of her demand:

"I say, mind what you are about, you'll carry off bits of gold on your shoes. One would think that you have greased them on purpose."

Gervaise slowly drew back. She had leant for an instant upon a shelf, and seeing Madame Lorilleux examining her hands, she opened them out, and said with her drawling voice, without seeming at all offended (she had fallen so low that she accepted everything as it came):

"I haven't taken anything; you can look and see."

And she went out, for the strong odour of the cabbage-soup and the pleasant warmth of the work-room made her feel quite ill.

Ah! the Lorilleux were far from keeping her back. Good riddance, and the devil if they ever opened to her again! They had seen enough of her, they didn't want other people's poverty within their doors when that poverty was deserved. And they gave way to a regular jubilation of selfishness at finding themselves nicely off, nice and warm, and with the propect of a famous soup before them. Boche, too, gave himself a stretching, puffing out his cheeks until his laugh became quite indecent. Clop-clop was well paid now for her old goings-on, her blue shop, her guzzling, and the rest of it. It was only too thorough; it showed well enough what came of caring too much about your prog. A good riddance to all gluttons, and idlers, and brazen-faced hussies!

"Fine cheek! coming begging ten sous on the sly!" cried Madame Lorilleux as Gervaise went out. "I like that! Fancy me lending her ten sous right away, for her to spend in drink!"

Gervaise dragged her feet wearily along the corridor, her shoulders heavy and drooping. When she reached her door she did not go in, her room frightened her. If she went on walking she would get warmer, and would be able to wait better. On her way she looked in on old Bru's hiding-place, under the staircase; here was someone like herself who ought to have a fine appetite, for he had been dining by heart for the last three days; but he was not there, the place was vacant; and she felt a sort of envy as it occurred to her that someone might have invited him out. Then as she reached the Bijards', she heard groans, and, finding the key in the door, she went in.

"What's the matter?" she asked.

The room was very neat. It was evident that Lalie had swept and straightened it that very morning. Poverty might breathe upon it as it chose, strip it of everything, cover it with dirt and disorder, Lalie came after, set things straight, and made them all look neat again. If it was not well-to-do, her place always showed a good housekeeper. That day her two children, Henriette and Jules, had found some old pictures, which they were quietly cutting out. But Gervaise was quite surprised to see Lalie lying on her narrow strap bed, the sheet pulled up to her chin, very pale. She, lying down! she must be very ill indeed!

"What is the matter with you?" said Gervaise, anxiously.

Lalie had ceased groaning. She slowly lifted her white eyelids, and tried to smile with her convulsive lips.

"Nothing," she said, in a very faint voice, "oh! really nothing at all."

Then, her eyes closed, and she said with an effort:

"I have been too tired these last few days, so I'm taking it easy, I'm petting myself a bit, you see."

But her little childish face, streaked with livid spots, had
such an expression of supreme anguish, that Gervaise, forgetting her own distress, clasped her hands and fell on her
knees beside her. For the last month she had seen her obliged
to support herself by the wall as she walked, all broken by a
cough which rang as hollow as a coffin. Now the child could
not even cough. She gave a gulp, and a streak of blood
trickled from the corners of her mouth.

"It isn't my fault; I don't feel strong at all," she murmured,
as if relieved. "I crawled about a bit, and put things in order.
It looks all clean, doesn't it? And I wanted to clean the
windows, but I couldn't keep on my legs. It's so silly! But
when you're done up, you have to lie down."

She broke off to say:

"Just see that my children don't cut themselves with the
scissors."

Then she stopped, trembling, for she heard a heavy step
on the stairs. Old Bijard flung the door brutally open. He had
his usual dose, his eyes flaring with the raging madness of
alcohol. When he saw Lalie in bed he slapped his thighs with
a snigger, and took down the big whip, growling:

"Damnation! that's coming it a bit too strong! That is a
good joke. The hussy goes to bed now in the middle of the day,
eh? Are you making game of a fellow, you bloody dawdler!
Now then, get up, stir your stumps!"

He cracked the whip over the bed. But the child implored
him:

"No, papa, please, don't hit. I'm sure you'll be sorry.
Please don't hit."

"Will you get up?" he yelled, "I'll tickle your ribs for you!
Will you get up, you bloody jade?"

But she said softly:

"I can't, you see. I am going to die."

Gervaise threw herself on Bijard and wrenched the whip
from his hands. He stood stupefied before the little bed.
What was the youngster talking about? People don't die so
young as that when they haven't been ill! Some trick to coddle
herself a bit. Ah! he'd teach her, if it was a lie!

"You'll see, it's the truth," she went on. "I haven't given
you any more trouble than I could help. Do be kind, and say
good-bye to me, papa."

Bijard made a grimace. He was afraid they would lock him
up for it; for she certainly did look very queer, her face was

as long and solemn as a grown person's. The wind of death seemed to pass through the room, it sobered him all at once. He looked all around with the air of a man wakened out of a long sleep, saw the whole place all tidied up, the two children with their clean faces, laughing and playing. And he sank on a chair, faltering:

"Our little mother, our little mother."

That was all he could say, and that, for him, was quite affectionate. Lalie had never been so spoilt before. She comforted her father. What particularly distressed her was to be taken like that, before she had finished bringing up her children. He would look after them, wouldn't he? With her dying voice she gave him details as to how they were to be managed, and kept clean. The besotted creature, overcome once more by the fumes of drunkenness, rolled his head as, with his staring eyes, he watched her sinking. All sorts of things stirred in his mind; but he found nothing more to say, and his skin was too scorched to weep.

"Listen, now," said Lalie after a silence. "We owe four francs seven sous to the baker; that has to be paid. Madame Gaudron has an iron of ours that you must get back from her. Tonight I wasn't able to make the soup, but there is some bread left, and you can put the potatoes over."

To her last gasp, the poor little thing remained the little mother of all her folks. There, now, was one whose place would never be filled up! She died because she had had, at her age, the instincts of a real mother; her little body was too fragile and too small to contain so large a motherhood. And, if he lost this treasure, it was the fault of her wild beast of a father. After having killed the mother with a kick, had he not slowly done to death the daughter? His two good angels would be in the grave, and there was nothing for him now but to die like dog in a ditch.

Gervaise had to restrain herself, or she would have burst into sobs. She stretched out her hands, longing to relieve the child in her pain; and, as the rag of a sheet slipped, she picked it up to rearrange the bed. Then the poor little body of the dying child appeared. God of mercy! what a sight, a sight at which the stones would have wept. Lalie was stark naked, a scrap of bodice round her shoulders by way of chemise; yes, stark naked, and it was the bleeding and sorrowful nudity of a martyr. On her sides thin purple weals covered her to the thighs, where the lash of the whip had

stamped them. A livid streak circled her left arm, as if the
jaws of a vice had crunched the fragile limb, no bigger than a
match. On the right leg there was a half-closed wound which
had never healed up, a wound which had opened every
morning as she went about the house-work. From head to
foot she was one livid mass. Oh! that slaughter of the innocents,
the heavy heels of a man trampling the poor little love under
foot, the abomination of it all, so desperate a weakness bowed
beneath so intolerable a cross! There are scourged saints in
churches whom men adore, whose nudity is less pure than
that. Gervaise sank down by her side, forgetting to put back
the sheet, overcome by the sight of such a little pitiful nothing-
ness, sunk into the bed there; and her trembling lips felt after
forgotten prayers.

"Madame Coupeau," whispered the child, "please. . . ."

With her little arms, too short to reach it, she tried to pull
up the sheet, confused, ashamed for her father's sake. Bijard,
stupefied, his eyes fixed on the corpse that he had made, still
rolled his head, with the slow movement of a bewildered
animal.

And when she had covered up Lalie, Gervaise could stay
there no longer. The dying child grew feebler, could no
longer speak; only her eyes lived, those black infantile eyes,
so resigned and meditative; and she fixed them on her two
children, busy cutting out their pictures. The room filled with
shadow; Bijard slept his drunken sleep, while the child lay in
her last agony. Life was too horrible! Ah! the vile thing, the
vile thing! And Gervaise went out, went downstairs, she knew
not how, heedlessly, so bowled over by all this misery, that
she could have thrown herself under an omnibus, and so
ended it.

Hurrying on, cursing Fate, she came to the door of the
yard where Coupeau pretended to be working. Her legs had
brought her there, her stomach took up its old burden,
hunger's lament in ninety verses, a lament that she knew by
heart. In this way, if she could catch Coupeau on the way out,
she would lay hands on the money, and buy some provisions.
It was only an hour's waiting, at the outside; she could stand
that, after sucking her thumbs all day.

It was the Rue de la Charbonnière, at the corner of the
Rue de Chartres, a miserable cross-road where the wind
caught you on all four sides at once. It wasn't warm work,
walking up and down the pavements, not even if one had had

fur things! The sky was still that desolate leaden colour, and the snow, piled up there, covered the whole place with its icy helmet. There was nothing falling, but there was a dead silence in the air, the promise of a fine new disguise for Paris, a new white lovely ball-dress. Gervaise looked up, praying that it might not be just yet. She stamped her feet, looked into the grocer's opposite, then turned away, for there was no use getting too hungry beforehand. There was nothing much to look at about. The few people who passed went by in haste, muffled up to the eyes, for, naturally, one doesn't lounge about when the cold pinches one. However, Gervaise observed four or five women who mounted guard, like her, at the master tinsmith's gate; other unhappy women, sure enough, wives waiting for the wages, to keep them from taking wings in at the pub. There was a great virago, with a face like a policeman, squeezed tight against the wall, ready to jump upon her man. A little woman, in black, with a meek, refined face, walked to and fro on the other side of the street. Another, a lumpish creature, had brought her two urchins with her, and she dragged them along on each side of her, crying and shivering. And all, Gervaise and her comrades on guard, passed and repassed one another, giving side glances, without speaking. A pleasant meeting-place, or something else! They had no need to become acquainted, in order to know who they were. They all lodged under the same sign, Poverty & Co. It was more chilling than ever, to see them on the move, passing one another in silence, in this terrible January weather.

So far, there was not a cat to be seen in the yard. At last a workman appeared, then two, then three; but those, evidently, were good chaps, who took home their pay, for they shook their heads when they saw the shadows prowling before the door. The great virago kept closer to the gate, and, all at once, she fell upon a little pallid man, who was cautiously craning out his neck. Oh! that was soon settled; she simply searched him, and collared the money. He was caught, the tin was taken in a trice, without leaving him the where-withal for a single drink! Then the little man, vexed and disheartened, followed the big woman, crying like a child. Workmen kept coming out, and as the poor soul with the two urchins had come forward, a big dark man, who looked a bit of a dodger, and who had caught sight of her, went quickly back to warn the husband; when the latter came swaggering out, he had stowed away two brand-new five-franc pieces, one in each shoe. He took one of the kids under his arm, and went off cramming his wife with fibs, as she began scolding him. There were some droll chaps, who darted into the street in hot haste to go and spend their fortnight's pay on a big feed with their friends. Others were haggard and squalid, clenching their fists over the three or four days' pay out of the fifteen that they had earned, accusing one another of idleness, and making drunkard's vows. But what was saddest was the distress of the little woman in black, so meek and refined; her man, a fine young fellow, made off under her very eyes, and so brutally, that he nearly knocked her over; and she went off alone, tottering along by the shops, crying her heart out.

At last the stream had ended. Gervaise stood in the middle of the street, and stared at the gate. It looked rather bad. Two workmen more came out, but no Coupeau. And when she asked them if Coupeau was not coming out, those who twigged the situation replied jeeringly that he had just gone out with Thingumbob by the back-door, to lead the fowls to water. Gervaise understood. It was another of Coupeau's lies, bringing her there under false pretences. Then, slowly, dragging her down-at-heel shoes, she went down the Rue de la Charbonnière. Her dinner seemed further and further away, and she watched it dwindle into the yellow twilight, with a little shiver. This time, it was ended. No help or hope now, only the night and hunger. Ah! the night it was to starve in, this dingy night that weighed down her shoulders!

She went laboriously up the Rue des Poissonniers, when all at once she heard Coupeau's voice. He was in at the "Petite-Civette", and Mes-Bottes was standing him a drink. Mes-Bottes, the joker, towards the end of the summer, had had the brilliant idea of marrying, really marrying, a lady, who it is true was a little gone off, but with nice remainders; oh! a lady of the Rue des Martyrs, not a street hussy. And you should see the lucky mortal, now quite the gentleman, his hands in his pockets, well clothed and well fed. You could scarcely recognize him now, he was so plump. The mate said that his wife had as much business as she wanted with the gentlemen of her acquaintance. A wife like that, and a country house, what more do you want to make things comfortable? And Coupeau gazed at Mes-Bottes admiringly. The josser had even got a gold ring on his little finger.

Gervaise put her hand on Coupeau's shoulder as he came out of the "Petite-Civette".

"I say, I'm waiting for you. I'm hungry. Won't you give me anything?"

But he drove home her argument in a very summary fashion.

"You're hungry; eat your fist then. And keep the other for tomorrow."

It seemed to him a pretty piece of affectation, to go for that sort of melodrama in public. Well, whether he had worked or not, the bakers baked their bread just the same. Who did she take him for, coming after him with such ridiculous stories?

"Do you want to drive me to steal?" she murmured, in a hollow voice.

Mes-Bottes caressed his chin in a conciliating sort of way.

"No, that isn't allowed," he said, "but a woman who knows how to fake things about a bit . . ."

Coupeau interrupted him with a bravo! Yes, a woman ought to know how to fake things about a bit. But his wife had always been a slut and a sloven. It would be her own fault if they both died in a ditch. Then he recurred to his admiration of Mes-Bottes. Wasn't the chap a swell! He looked quite the householder, with his white shirt, and his tricky shoes. No second-hand stuff that! Now there was a man whose missus kept things going!

The two men went down towards the outer boulevard. Gervaise followed them. After a silence she said, behind his back:

"I'm hungry, you know. I depended on you. You must find me something to eat."

He did not answer, and she repeated in a heart-rending voice:

"Then you won't give me anything?"

"Damnation! when I tell you I haven't anything," he roared, turning on her furiously. "Let go, or I'll hit!"

He raised his fist. She recoiled, and seemed to decide on something.

"All right, you can, I'll find a man."

The tinsmith burst out laughing. He pretended to take it in joke, and urged her on, without appearing to. Why, it was a fine idea! At night, under the gas, she might still make conquests. If she picked up a man, he recommended her to go to the "Capucin" restaurant; there were nice little private rooms there, where you got an excellent dinner, And as she turned down towards the outer boulevard, white and haggard, he called after her:

"I say, bring me back some of the dessert, I like cakes. And, if your gent is well dressed, ask him for an old overcoat; I'll get my share out of it."

Gervaise, followed by this infernal chatter, went quickly onwards. When she found herself alone in the crowd, she slackened her pace. She had quite made up her mind. Between stealing and doing that, she preferred to do that, because at all events she did no wrong to anyone. She was only going to dispose of what was her own. No doubt, it wasn't the proper thing to do; but proper and improper clashed together in her head then in mere confusion; when you are starving you don't philosophize, you eat the bread that comes to hand. She went up as far as the Chaussée Clignancourt. The night would never come! While she waited she walked along the boulevards, as if she were having a little stroll before going in to have dinner.

The neighbourhood that gave her such a feeling of humiliation, so gorgeous had it become, lay open now in all directions. The Boulevard Magenta, running up from the heart of Paris, and the Boulevard Ornano, stretching out into the country, had cut through the old barrier, a lordly pile of buildings, two huge avenues still white with plaster, with, on either side of them, the Rue du Faubourg-Poissonnière and the Rue des Poissonniers, which dwindled off into dreary, winding intricacies. The city wall had long since been pulled down, for the extension of the outer boulevards, which had now side-walks and a central alley for pedestrians, planted with four rows of small plane-trees. It was an immense cross road, stretching out into the horizon endlessly, with its seething crowds, amidst all the chaos of buildings in course of erection, But, side by side with tall new houses, there were old tottering buildings still standing; between carved façades gaped black hollows, and old hovels displayed the destitution of their window-frames. Under the rising flood of all this new wealth coming up from Paris, the poverty of the suburb forced itself to the front, like a foul blotch on this brand-new, jerry-built city.

Lost in the midst of the crowd under the plane-trees, Gervaise felt lonely and forsaken. Merely to look along that vista of avenues made her feel hollower than ever; and how strange it was that in all this flood of people there was not a Christian soul to see the state she was in, and slip sixpence into her hand! Yes, it was all too large and splendid, her head swam, and her legs gave way, under the immeasurable breadth of grey sky, stretching over such a breadth of ground below. The twilight had the dirty yellow of Parisian twilights, a colour which makes you long to die out of hand, so hideous is the life of the streets. The light grew dubious, the distance faded into an indistinguishable dinginess. Gervaise, wearied out, found herself suddenly in the midst of the workmen coming home from work. At that hour the ladies who wore hats, the nicely-dressed gentlemen, belonging to the new houses, were lost in the midst of the working people, processions of men and women, already pale with the foul air of work-shops. Along the Boulevard Magenta and the Rue du Faubourg-Poissonnière there were streams of them, panting with the climb. Amidst the duller rumble of public vehicles and cabs, the drags, covered carts and wagons, galloping along empty, an ever-increasing swarm of blouses and jackets covered the side-walk. The porters came by, their porters' knots over their shoulders. Two workmen strode along, taking great steps, talking very loudly, and gesticulating, without looking in one another's direction; others, all alone, in cap and great-coat, walked on the edge of the pavement, with their heads sunk; others came in fives and sixes, one after another, not exchanging a word, their hands in their pockets, their eyes dull. Some of them had their pipes, which had gone out, still between their teeth. Some masons in a covered van, four of them, with their hods rattling on the roof, showed their whitened faces at the window. Painters swung their paint-pots; a tinsmith carried a long ladder, with which he was in danger of knocking out people's eyes; whilst a belated mender of water-taps, his box slung across his shoulders, played the air of the "Bon Roi Dagobert" on his little trumpet, an air full of sadness in the dreary twilight. Ah! the sad music, to which all this herd seemed to keep step, these tired-out beasts of burden, dragging themselves homewards. Another day over! The days were so long, and they began again so soon. There was scarcely time to fill up, and sleep off the meal, before it was broad daylight, and time to take up the yoke of misery again. There were jolly chaps, however, who whistled as they went, hurrying onwards with sounding footsteps, as if they already smelt the soup awaiting them. And Gervaise watched them pass, indifferent to the jostling, elbowed to right, elbowed to left, carried along in the midst of the crowd; for men have no time to be polite when they are worn out with fatigue and sinking with hunger.

All at once, as Gervaise raised her eyes, she saw before her what had once been the Hôtel Boncœur. The little house, after having been a thieves' haunt, which was closed by the police, had been left untenanted, the shutters covered with placards, the lamp broken, crumbling and rotting away under the rain from top to bottom, its wretched dark-red paint all mouldy. And nothing in the neighbourhood seemed changed. The stationer's and the tobacconist's were still there. Behind, over the low buildings, could be seen the same five-storey houses with their leprous frontages, looming up with their tattered silhouettes. Only the hall of the "Grand-Balcon" had gone; the hall with its ten flaring windows had been turned into a sugar-cutting establishment, from which came a continuous hissing sound. And it was there, in that dirty hole, the Hôtel Boncœur, that all the misery of her life had begun. She stood gazing at the window on the first floor, from which hung a shutter, half wrenched off, and she recalled her young days with Lantier, their first bickerings, and the shameful manner in which he had left her. No matter, she was young then, it all seemed cheerful enough, seen from far. Only twenty years ago; God! and she had fallen to this. The sight of it made her ill; she turned back, and went up the boulevard towards Montmartre.

On the sand-heaps between the seats, there were still some children at play, though the night was gathering. The march past still continued, work-girls went by, on the run, hurrying along so as to make up for the time they had spent in looking into shop-windows; one tall girl had her hand in the hand of a youth who accompanied her to within three doors of her own; others, as they left one another, made appointments for that evening at the "Grand Salon de la Folie", or at the "Boule-Noire". In the midst of groups there would be now and then a tailoring hand with his materials under his arm. A chimney-sweep, harnessed to a hand-cart filled with rubbish, was nearly run over by an omnibus. And now, in the crowd which had somewhat melted away, bare-headed women hurried by; they had been up and lit the fire, and gone out again to fetch the dinner; they hustled people out of their way, dashed into the baker's and the pork-butcher's, and out again, without losing a minute, their provisions in their hands. Little girls of eight, sent out on errands, went along near the shops, clasping in their arms great four pound loaves as tall as themselves, like big yellow dolls, stopping in ecstacy, for five minutes at a time in front of pictures, resting their cheeks on their great loaves. Then their was a lull, the groups grew fewer and fewer, the workmen had all gone home after their work; and the glare of the gas, marking the end of the day that was over, seemed to strike a light for the sloth and dissipation that awoke with the coming of night.

And for Gervaise too the day was over. She was more utterly worn than all this army of workers, whose passing had shaken her. She could lie down now and die, for there was no hope for her in work, and she had laboured hard enough in her lifetime, to be able to say: "Next one's turn! I'm done." And now everyone was eating. It was the end, the end, the sun had put out her candle, the night would be long. God! just to lie down and never get up any more; to say to one's self, now I have laid down my tools for good, I can go on dozing for ever and ever! How good that would be after having slaved for twenty years! And Gervaise, while the cramp twitched her stomach, thought, despite herself, of those old feast-days, the big feeds and jollifications of her life. Once in particular, one sharp winter day, a Thursday in mid-Lent, she had had a fine time of it. She was pretty then, blonde and fresh. Her wash-house, in the Rue Neuve, had declared her queen, in spite of her limp. Then they had promenaded along the boulevards, in cars decked with greenery, all in the midst of the people; and how they had looked at her! Gentlemen put up their eye-glasses as if she were a real queen. Then, at night, what a tightener they had had, and they danced till dawn. Queen, yes, a queen, with a crown and scarf, for twenty-four hours, twice the round of the clock! And now, in her stupefaction, in the tortures of her hunger, she looked down on the ground as if she would find the gutter into which her queenship had slipped and fallen.

She raised her eyes again. She was opposite the slaughter-houses, which they were pulling down; the front was gone, and it left bare the dark, evil-smelling courts, still humid with blood. And when she had gone further down the boule-vard, she saw too the Lariboisière Hospital, with its steep grey wall, above which spread the gloomy wings, pierced at regular intervals with windows; there was a door in the wall

that was the dread of the whole neighbourhood, the door of
the dead, whose solid oak, without a crack, had the rigid
silence of a tomb-stone. Then, to escape from herself, she went
on further, on as far as the railway-bridge. The high cast-iron
parapets hid the line from sight; she could only see, against
the luminous horizon of Paris, the large angle of the station,
with its immense roofs, black with coal-dust; she heard,
inside this immense open space, the whistle of locomotives,
the rhythmical shock of the turning-plates, a whole world of
activity hidden from sight. Then a train passed, coming from
the city, with its panting breath, its rumble growing louder
and louder. And she saw nothing of it but a white plume, a
sudden puff of smoke that streamed over the parapet and was
gone. But the whole building had trembled, and she herself
still felt the quiver of the rapid passage. She turned, as if to
follow the invisible locomotive, the sound of which died
away in the distance. That way must lie the country, under
the free sky, down in a hollow, with tall houses to right and
left, scattered, set about at random, with unplastered walls,
walls painted with huge advertisements, stained with the
same yellowish stain from the soot of the engines. Oh! if she
could only have gone there too, right away, away from these
houses of misery and suffering! Perhaps she might have started
on a new life. Then she turned and gazed blankly at the posters
stuck on the wall. There were posters of all colours. One, a
little one, a pretty blue one, offered fifty francs' reward for a
lost dog. How someone must have loved that dog!

Gervaise went slowly on her way. In the midst of smoky
shadow that settled in, the gas-lamps burst into light, one
after another; and the long avenues that had gradually
darkened, flashed out again, lengthening out, shearing
through the night, till they were lost in the dark depths of the
horizon. A great wind passed, and the widening vista sprang
into life, filleted with little flames under the immense,
moonless sky. It was the hour when, from end to end of the
boulevards, public-houses and dancing-halls flared with the
jolly gaiety of the first drink and the first *chahut*. Pay-day
filled the pavements with a pack of idlers on the booze.
Booze was in the air, and plenty of it, but as yet decent
enough, just a trifle of elevation, no more. In the eating-
houses people were stuffing; inside all the lighted windows one
could see people eating, their mouths full, laughing without
taking the trouble to swallow. In the public-houses drunkards

had already taken up their positions, shouting and gesticulating. And there was an infernal noise, the yapping of voices, thick voices, heard through the continual trampling of feet on the pavement. "I say! come and have a bite? . . . Come along, lazy bones! I stand drinks. . . . Hallo! there's Pauline! no, not taking any!" Doors opened and shut, sending out odours of wine and puffs of music. There was a whole string waiting outside old Colombe's bar, which was lit up like a cathedral for high mass; and, by God! you would have said there really was a ceremony going on in there, for the jolly good fellows inside were singing away like choristers, puffing out their cheeks and rounding out their corporations. It was in celebration of the patron saint of pay-day, a nice good saint, who ought to have charge of the cash-box in paradise. Only, hearing how heartily they had struck in to it, now at the beginning of the evening, the little householders who trotted out their wives, shook their heads, and declared gravely that there would be a deuce of a lot of men drunk in Paris that night. And the night was very dark, frozen and lifeless above all this turmoil, pierced only by the lines of light along the boulevards, at the four corners of the sky.

Planted there before the bar, Gervaise mused. If she had had two sous, she would have gone in and had a drop of drink. Perhaps that would have kept her from feeling so hungry. Ah! the drinks she had had there. It seemed good to have had them. And, from a distance, she gazed at the drinking machine, realizing that all her misfortune came from that, and dreaming of ending it there too, when she had the money to do it. But a shiver passed through her hair, she saw that the night was dark. Now was the time. Now she must take heart and show herself at her best, if she was not to die of starvation in the midst of the general jubilation. To watch others eat was not precisely the way to fill her own belly. She moved more slowly than ever, and looked about her. Under the trees the shadow was darker. Few people passed, now and then someone hurrying across the boulevard. And on this great, dark, deserted causeway, where all the gaiety of the other pavement had died out, there were women standing waiting. They stood for long moments motionless, patient, rigid as the little meagre plane-trees; then, slowly, they moved on, dragging their feet over the frozen soil, made ten steps and stopped again, rooted to the ground. There was one, with an enormous trunk, and the arms and legs of an insect, rolling in her own fat, in an old rag of black silk, with a yellow handkerchief round her head; there was another, tall, lean, bare-headed, who had on a servant's apron; others again, old plastered hags, dirty young ones, so dirty and shabby that a rag-picker would not have picked them up. Gervaise did not know what to do, she tried to pick it up, to do as they did. She felt frightened, like a little girl; she did not know if she felt shame, she acted in a bad dream. For a quarter of an hour she stood still. Men went by without turning their heads. Then she too moved, she ventured to accost a man who passed with his hands in his pockets, whistling, and she murmured in a choking voice:

"Hallo, dearie. . . ."

The man glanced at her and went on, whistling more loudly.

Gervaise grew bolder, forgetting herself in the fury of the chase, so hollow did she feel, so greedily set on the meal that fled farther and farther from her. She walked for a long time at random, unconscious of the hour and the way. About her travelled silent black forms, under the trees; they went to and fro with the regularity of wild beasts in a cage. They came out of the shadow, slowly, vaguely, like apparitions; they passed under the light of a gas-lamp, and their pallid masks suddenly surged into view; then they were lost again, they relapsed into the shadow, balancing the white line of their petticoats, fading back into the tremulous charm of the darkness. Sometimes men would stop and chat, just for a lark, and go on again laughing. Others, prudent and careful, turned aside, ten yards behind a woman. There were loud whispers, squabbles in stifled voices, furious bargainings, which sank all at once to a dead silence. And Gervaise, as far as she went, saw these women spaced out like sentinels in the night, as if women were planted from end to end of the outer boulevards. Always, twenty yards after another, she found yet another. The file was lost in the distance, it guarded all Paris. Angry at being passed by, she changed her position, and went from the Chaussée de Clignancourt to the Grande Rue de la Chapelle.

"Hallo, dearie. . . ."

But the men passed her by. She left behind her the slaughter-houses, with their walls reeking of blood. She gave a look at what had once been the Hôtel Boncœur, uninhabited and equivocal. She passed before the Lariboisiére Hospital, and

counted mechanically the lighted windows in front, burning
like night-lights set beside the dying, with a pale and tranquil
glimmer. She crossed the railway-bridge, shaken by the passing
trains, rumbling and tearing the air with the desperate cry
of their whistles. They were the night's making, all these sad
things! Then she turned, she stared again and again at the
same houses, the monotonous repetition of this part of the
avenue; and she passed ten, twenty times, without interval,
without a minute's rest on a seat. No, no one would have her.
Then she went down once more in the direction of the hospital, she went back towards the slaughter-houses. It was her
last promenade, from the courts of blood where they slaughtered, to the ghastly cells where death stiffened men out in
the poor man's common bed. All her life had lain there.

"Hallo, dearie. . . ."

And all at once she saw her shadow on the ground beside
her. When she came near a gas-lamp, the vague shadow drew
together and grew definite, a huge squat shadow, ridiculously
round. It spread out, the stomach, the chest, the hips, running
into one mass. She limped so badly with one leg, that, on
the ground, the shadow collapsed at every step, a regular
Punch and Judy show! Then, when she got further away,
the shadow grew larger, grew gigantic, filled the boulevard
with curtsies which knocked her nose against the houses and
the trees. Lord! how funny, how frightful she was! Never
had she realized before the depth of her degradation. And
she could not keep herself from looking at it, watching out for
the gas lamps, following with her eyes the *chahut* of her shadow.
Ah! a nice slut it was who walked beside her! It was a beauty!
That ought to catch the men straight away. And she lowered
her voice, she dared no more than falter after the passers-by:

"Hallo, dearie. . . ."

It seemed to be very late. Everything was shutting up.
The eating-houses were shut, the gas shone with a reddish
light in at the pubs, from which came the sound of the thick
voices of drunkards. Jollity had turned to quarrels and blows.
A great tattered object roared: "You count your bones; I'll
knock you to bits!" A girl had come to blows with her lover,
at the door of a dancing-hall, and she called him a dirty
beast and a bloody fool, while the man repeated, "And
your sister?" without finding anything else to say. The drink
breathed out a breath of slaughter, a something savage which
gave a pale convulsed look to the faces of the few passers-by.

There had been a fight, and one drunken chap had been knocked flat, whilst the other man, thinking he had done for him, took to his heels, with a clatter of his heavy shoes. Bands of men howled ribald songs, there were long silences, broken by the hiccup and the dull fall of drunkards. The fortnight's booze always ended like that, the wine had been flowing so freely since ten, that it had to extend itself to the streets. Oh! there were nice splashes all over the pavement; dainty folk had to take long strides across them, so as not to step in. A nice neighbourhood it was indeed! A stranger who was to see it before it was swept up in the morning would carry away a charming impression. But, at this hour of the night, the drunkards had it all to themselves, and precious little they cared for Europe. Knives, too, came out of pockets, and the little holiday ended in blood. Women walked fast, men with wolfish eyes prowled about, the night thickened, big with abominations.

Gervaise still limped along, going up and down with the one idea of going on walking for ever. Slumber overcame her, she half slept, rocked to sleep by her leg; then she looked around her with a start, and saw that she had gone on a hundred yards without knowing it, as if she were dead. Her feet seemed to grow larger in her tattered shoes. She lost consciousness of herself, she was so fagged and empty. The last clear idea that she had was that her wretched child, at that moment, was perhaps eating oysters. Then all became confused, she kept her eyes open, but it was too great an effort to think. And the single sensation that persisted in her, in this annihilation of all her being, was that of freezing cold. such a sharp and deadly cold as she had never felt before. Sure enough, the dead were not so cold in the earth. She raised her head, an icy lash seemed to cut her in the face, It was the snow that at last decided to fall from the smoky sky, a fine, thick snow, that a light wind whirled in eddies. It had been expected for the last three days. Now was the time for it to fall.

The first fall awoke Gervaise, and she walked more quickly. Men ran by, hurrying home, their shoulders already white. And, as she saw one who came along slowly under the trees, she went up to him, and said again:

"Hallo, dearie. . . ."

The man stopped. But he did not seem to understand her. He held out his hand, he murmured in a low voice:

"Please, have pity . . ."

They looked at one another. Good God! they had come to that, old Bru begging, Madame Coupeau on the streets! They stood speechless before one another. Now they could clasp hands. All the evening the old workman had been prowling about, not daring to speak to anyone; and the first person that he stopped was starving like himself. Lord! was it not pitiful? to have worked for fifty years, and to beg! to have been known as one of the best laundresses of the Rue de la Goutte-d'Or. and to come down to the gutter! They gazed at one another hard. Then, without a word, they went their way, under the snow that buffeted them.

It was a regular tempest. On those heights, in the midst of those large open spaces, the fine snow whirled, as if it blew from the four quarters all at once. You could not see ten steps before you, everything was buried under the flying dust. The houses had disappeared, the boulevard seemed dead, as if the fall of snow had laid the silence of its white sheet over the hiccups of the last drunkard. Gervaise still made her way onward, painfully, blinded, and lost. She touched the trees to find out where she was. As she went forward, the gas-lamps stood out of the pallid air like extinguished torches. Then, all at once, as she came to a cross-road, the lights themselves failed her; she was seized and enveloped in a dense whirlwind; she could distinguish nothing to guide her. Under her the ground seemed to retreat, vague and white. Grey walls hemmed her in. And, when she stopped short, hesitating, turning and looking round her, she could only guess, behind that icy veil, at the endless avenues, the interminable lines of gas-lamps, all the black and desolate infinitude of sleeping Paris.

She was at the point where the outer boulevard joins on to the Boulevard de Magenta and the Boulevard d'Ornano, thinking of making her bed on the ground, when she heard the sound of footsteps. She ran, but the snow blocked her eyes, and the footsteps grew fainter, without her being able to tell whether they went to the right or left. At last she saw the large shoulders of a man, a black, dancing bulk, dwindling into the mist. Ah! she would have this one, she would not let him go! And she ran harder, she caught him up, and clutched his blouse.

"Hallo, dearie. . . ."

The man turned. It was Goujet.

And now she had hooked on to Gueule-d'Or! What had

she done, what had she done, to be tortured like this to the
very end? It was the last stroke, to have flung herself into
the blacksmith's arms, to be seen by him in the ranks of the
street harlots, haggard and suppliant. And they were right
under a gas-lamp, she saw her misshapen shadow as if it
danced with glee upon the snow, caricaturing her. She must
seem like a drunken woman. God! to pass for a drunken
woman when you have not had bite or sup for the whole day!
It was her fault, why did she get drunk? Goujet must certainly
think she had been drinking, and had gone out on the loose.

Goujet meanwhile, gazed at her, whilst the snow scattered
its daisies in his golden beard. Then, as she lowered her head,
and turned away, he held her back.

"Come," he said.

And he walked first. She followed him. The two of them
passed silently through the sleeping streets, silently along by
the walls. Poor Madame Goujet had died in October, of
acute rheumatism. Goujet still lived in the little house in the
Rue Neuve, desolate and alone. That day he had been watching up by the bedside of a mate who had been injured. When
he had opened the door and lit a lamp, he turned towards
Gervaise, who stood humbly on the landing. He said, very
low, as if his mother could still hear:

"Come in."

The first room, Madame Goujet's, had been religiously
preserved just as she left it. Near the window, on a chair, was
the lace-making frame, by the side of the great arm-chair
which seemed to await the old lace-maker. The bed was
made, and she could have slept there, if she had left the
cemetry to spend the night with her child. The room had a
cloistered air, an odour of goodness and simple piety.

"Come in," repeated the blacksmith in a louder tone.

She entered, timidly, like a prostitute who finds herself in a
respectable quarter. And he too was pale and trembling, at
the thought of bringing in a woman, there in his dead mother's
room. They passed through the room, stepping softly, as if
they feared to be heard. Then, when he had pushed Gervaise
into the room, he shut the door. Now he was in his own
domain. It was the little narrow room that she knew, a room
like a school-girl's, with a little iron bed with white curtains.
Only against the walls the pictures had spread further, and
now reached the ceiling. Gervaise, in all this purity, dared
not come forward; she slunk back, away from the lamp.

Then, without a word, in a sort of fury, he would have seized her and crushed her in his arms. But her strength failed her, and she murmured:

"Oh, my God! oh, my God!"

The stove, covered down with coke, still burned, and the remains of a stew, which the blacksmith had put over to warm, expecting to be back earlier, smoked before the ash-pan. Gervaise, overcome by the heat, could have flung herself on all fours and eaten out of the saucepan. It was more than she could stand, her stomach seemed torn within her, and she stooped down with a sigh. But Goujet had understood. He put the stew on the table, cut some bread, poured out some wine.

"Thanks! thanks!" she said. "Oh! you are good! Thanks!"

She stuttered, she could scarcely bring out the words. When she took up the fork, her hand trembled so that she let it fall. The hunger that choked her made her head waggle like an old woman's. She had to use her fingers. At the first potato that she put into her mouth, she burst into sobs. Big tears rolled down over her cheeks, on to her bread. She still went on eating, devouring greedily her bread soaked in tears, breathing heavily, her chin convulsed. Goujet forced her to drink, so that it should not choke her; and her glass made a little sound against her teeth.

"Will you have some more bread?" he asked, in a low voice.

She wept, she said no, she said yes, she knew not what she was saying. God in heaven! how good and sad it is to eat when you are starving!

And he, standing in front of her, gazed at her. Now he saw her clearly, under the bright light of the lamp shade. How aged and faded she was! The warmth melted the snow on her hair and her dress, and the water streamed off her. Her poor shaking head was all grey, grey locks all blown about by the wind. Her head was sunk in upon her shoulders, she sat there huddled up, ugly and clumsy enough to make you weep. And he recalled how they had loved each other, when she was all rosy, ironing away and showing the baby-crease that put such a pretty collar round her neck. Then he would gaze at her for hours, content merely to look at her. Later on she had come to the forge, and they had tasted huge delights, while he hammered his iron and she stood there, caught up into the dance of his hammer. Then how many nights he had bitten his pillow, longing to have her and hold her, so, in his room! Oh! he would have broken her in pieces, if he had had her, so ardently had he desired her. And now she was his, he could take her. She finished her bread, she wiped up her tears, big silent tears that fell upon what she was eating.

Gervaise rose. She had finished. She hung down her head for an instant, confused, not knowing if he would have her or not. Then, thinking she saw a flame light up in his eye, she put up her hand to her bodice, and undid the first button. But Goujet went down on his knees, and took her hand, saying softly:

"I love you, Madame Gervaise, oh! I love you still and in spite of all, I swear to you!"

"Don't say that, Monsieur Goujet!" she cried, beside herself at seeing him there at her feet. "No, don't say that, you hurt me too much."

And as he repeated that he could not love twice in his life, she was more distressed than ever.

"No, no, I won't have it, you shame me too much. For God's sake, get up! It is my place to kneel before you."

He got up, trembling all over, and in a faltering voice he said:

"May I kiss you, Madame Gervaise?"

She was lost in wonderment and overcome with emotion, and she could not find a word. She nodded for yes. Good heavens! why, she was his, he could do with her what he pleased. But he merely stretched out his lips.

"That is all between us, Madame Gervaise," he murmured. "It is all our friendship."

He kissed her on the forehead, on one of her grey locks. He had kissed no one since his mother's death. Only his good friend Gervaise was left to him in the world. Then, when he had kissed her, with such respect, he stepped backwards and fell upon his bed, his chest torn with sobs. And Gervaise could stay there no longer; it was too sad, too abominable, to meet again like that, for people who love one another. She cried out:

"I love you, Monsieur Goujet, I too love you. Oh! it isn't possible, I know. Good-bye, good-bye, it would kill us both."

And she ran out, across Madame Goujet's room, and found herself once more in the street. When she returned to herself, she had rung at her door in the Rue de la Goutte-d'Or, and Boche was releasing the catch. The house was all in darkness. She went into it, as if she were going into mourning.

At that hour of the night, the porch, gaping and dilapidated, seemed like great jaws opened to swallow her. To
think that she had once had the fancy to find foothold in
that great hulk of a barracks! Had her ears then been stopped
from hearing the wail of despair that echoed behind those
walls? From the very day when she had put foot there, she had
begun her downward course. Yes, it must bring misfortune,
to be heaped up one on top of another like that, in those big
beggarly workmen's houses; one was sure to get the cholera
of poverty there. That night, all life seemed extinct. She
heard only the snoring of the Boches on the right; whilst
Lantier and Virginie, on the left, made a sort of purring sound
like cats who lie curled up, awake and warm, with closed
eyes. In the court she seemed to be in the midst of a cemetery;
the snow laid a pale covering over the ground; the steep
walls rose up, a livid grey, without a light, like blocks of a
ruin; and there was not a breath stirring, a whole village
seemed to be buried there, stiff with cold and hunger. She
had to step over a black runlet, the dyer's stream, smoking
and opening a muddy passage in the midst of the whiteness
of the snow. The water was of the same hue now as her
thoughts. Those beautiful streams, pale blue and pale pink,
had all run to waste.

Then, as she climbed the six flights in the dark, she could
not help laughing; a wicked laugh which hurt her. She
thought of her old ideal: to work quietly, have always bread
to eat, a decent place to sleep in, bring up her children well,
not be beaten, and die in her bed. It was really ridiculous
how it all came out! She no longer worked, she slept on
filth, her child was on the streets, her husband thrashed her;
it only remained for her to die in the road, and it would be
soon, if she had not the courage, on going in, to throw herself
out of the window. One would have thought that she had
prayed heaven for thirty thousand francs a year, and to be
looked up to. Well, in this life you may be modest enough in
your demands, and still go a-begging! Not even food and
house-room, that is the common lot. And what brought back
her wicked laugh again, was to recall her fine hopes of retiring
into the country, after twenty years of ironing. Ah, well, she
was on her way there, she was on her way to the country. She
would have her bit of greenery at Père-Lachaise.

When she reached her corridor, she was half crazy. Her
poor head turned. Deep in her heart she felt a great sorrow,

because she had said good-bye for ever to the blacksmith. It was all over between them, they could never see each other again. Then, on top of this, came all her other distresses: it was the finishing touch, the last stroke. On her way she looked in at Bijard's, and saw that Lalie was dead, her face happy at being laid out, where she could take her ease for ever. Ah, well! children had better luck than grown people. And, as old Bazouge's door let out a streak of light, she went straight in, seized with a mad longing to go on the same journey as the child.

The old joker Bazouge had come back that night in a state of extraordinary jollity. He had such a dose, that he snored on the ground, despite the temperature; and it did not prevent him, evidently, from having a lovely dream, for his sides seemed to shake with laughter as he slept. The light was left burning, and it lit up his black hat, squashed up in the corner, his black cloak that he pulled up over his knees, like a bit of quilt.

Gervaise, at seeing him, began to moan so loudly that he awoke.

"Damnation! will you shut the door! It's so beastly cold! Ah! it's you! What's up? what do you want?"

At that, Gervaise, stretching out her arms, not knowing what she was uttering, began to entreat him passionately.

"Oh! take me away, I have had enough of it, I want to go away. Don't be hard upon me. I didn't know; my God! how should one know till one is ready? Oh, yes, one is glad to go, one day or other. Take me, take me; how I will thank you if you will take me!"

And she fell on her knees, shaken from head to foot with a desire that blanched her visage. Never had she so cast herself at the feet of a man. The face of old Bazouge, with his wry mouth, and his skin black with the dust of burials, seemed to her beautiful and shining as the sun. But the old man, only half awake, took it for some bad joke.

"I say," he muttered, "you needn't try to seduce me!"

"Take me away," repeated Gervaise more ardently than before. "Don't you remember, one night, I knocked at the wall; then I told you I hadn't, because I was still too stupid. But now, give me your hands, I am not frightened now! Take me away, where I can sleep; you shall see, I'll never move. Oh! I want nothing but that, oh! how I will love you!"

Bazouge, always polite, felt that he ought not to be harsh

with a lady who had such a fancy for him. She was getting a
bit childish, but she still looked well, when she was excited.

"You are jolly well right," he said with an air of conviction;
"I packed up three, only today, who would have given me a
fine tip, if they could have put their hands in their pockets.
Only, my little woman, it can't be done like that."

"Take me away, take me away," cried Gervaise again.
"I must go. . . ."

"Lord! there's a little operation first. You know, couic!"

And he made a sound in his throat as if he were swallowing
his tongue. Then, thinking the joke was a good one, he
chuckled.

Gervaise got up slowly. Even he could do nothing for her.
She went back into her own room, blankly, and flung herself
on her straw, sorry that she had had anything to eat. Ah, no,
poverty killed too slowly!

CHAPTER THIRTEEN

THAT night Coupeau was out on the booze. Next day, Gervaise received ten francs from her son Étienne, who was stoker on an engine; the child sent her five-franc pieces from time to time, knowing that they were not over-rich at home. She put over a *pot-au-feu*, and ate it all by herself, for the brute of a Coupeau did not come in the next day either. Monday, no one; Tuesday, still no one. The whole week passed. Damn it all! if it was a woman who had taken him on, it was quite a piece of good luck. But on Sunday Gervaise received a printed paper, which at first frightened her, because it looked like a communication from the police. She was relieved to find that it was only a notification that her bloody fool of a husband was in Sainte-Anne's, very ill. It was put in politer language, but it came to the same thing. Yes, it was indeed a woman who had taken on Coupeau, and the woman was called Sophie Turneye, the drunkard's last sweetheart.

Good gracious! Gervaise was not at all concerned at that. He knew the way, he would come back by himself all right; they had cured him so many times, that they would be sure to do the same old joke once more, and put him on his legs again. Had she not just heard that very morning that, for the last week, Coupeau had been seen as tight as tight could be, going the round of the pubs of Belleville, in company with Mes-Bottes? Precisely, it was even Mes-Bottes who financed the affair; he seemed to have got his missus' little store into his clutches, savings earned in a nice way too! Ah! they drank a proper sort of money, enough to give them all the diseases under heaven! It served Coupeau right if it had given him a colic. And Gervaise was particularly angry when she thought that those two selfish buggers had not even thought of asking her to have a drink with them. Did you ever hear of such a thing! a week's booze, and not so much as a little attention to a lady! When you drink by yourself, you may perish by yourself!

However, on Monday, as Gervaise had a nice little dinner for the evening, the remainder of a stew and a glass of wine, it occurred to her that a little walk would give her a good appetite. The letter from the hospital, there on the chest of drawers, worried her. The snow had melted, it was charming weather, soft and grey, with an invigorating sharpness in the air. She started at mid-day, for it was a long walk, right at the other end of Paris, and her lame leg hindered her a bit. And there was a whole heap of people in the streets; but the people amused her, and she got there pleasantly enough. When she gave her name, they told her a pretty stiff story; it appeared that they had fished Coupeau out from under the Pont-Neuf; he had leapt over the parapet, fancying he saw a big-bearded man who barred his way. A nice jump, was it not? and as for finding out what Coupeau was doing on the Pont-Neuf, that was a thing he could not explain himself.

Meanwhile, an attendant escorted Gervaise upstairs. On the way up she heard yells which chilled her to the very bone.

"He makes a jolly row!" said the attendant.

"Who?" she asked.

"Why, your man! He has been yelling like that since the day before yesterday. And he's dancing, you'll see!"

Heavens! what a sight! She stood stupefied. The cell was padded from top to bottom; on the ground there were two straw mattresses, one on top of the other; and, in a corner, there was a mattress and a quilt; that was all. And there Coupeau danced and yelled. A regular street rough of La Courtille, with his blouse in tatters, and his legs fighting the air; but a street rough, not amusing at all, oh no, a street rough whose frightful *chahut* made your hair stand on end. He was disguised as a moribund. Good God! what a *pas seul!* He pitched against the window, returned to it backwards, beating time with his arms, shaking his hands as if he wished to snap them off and fling them in the face of everybody. You see jokers in the dancing-halls who imitate that; only they imitate it badly, you have to see the real thing danced by a real drunkard, if you would realize how dashingly it can be done, when it is done properly. The song too has its own special character, a sort of carnival howl, a wide-open mouth uttering, for hours together, the same husky trombone notes. Coupeau had the cry of an animal on whose paw you have trodden. And it was, orchestra ahead! round with partners!

"Good Lord! what is the matter with him? What is the matter with him?" said Gervaise, in a deadly funk.

A house-surgeon, a big, fair, rosy-cheeked young man, in

a white apron, was quietly seated, taking notes. The case was curious, and he never left the patient.

"You can stay here a few minutes, if you like," he said to the laundress; "but be quiet. You can speak to him, he won't know you."

Coupeau, indeed, did not seem even to see his wife. She had not properly seen him when she came in, he was flinging himself about to such an extent. When she saw him full face, she could scarcely believe her eyes. Could it really be he, with that face, those bloodshot eyes, those scabby lips? She would not have recognized him. First of all, he made so many meaningless grimaces, his phiz all awry, his nose contracted, his cheeks drawn like the nozzle of a beast. His skin was so hot that the air about him steamed; and it looked as if it had been varnished, streaming with sweat that dripped off. In his dance, an eccentric dance gone mad, you could see that he was in distress, his head heavy, his limbs paining him.

Gervaise went up to the house-surgeon, who beat a tune with his fingers on the back of his chair.

"I say, Monsieur, is it serious, then, this time?"

The house-surgeon nodded, without replying.

"I say, isn't he muttering something to himself? Do you hear? What is it?"

"Things he sees," murmured the young man. "Be quiet, let me listen."

Coupeau spoke in a staccato voice. But there was still a spark of jollity in his eyes. He stared at the ground, to right and left, turning, as if he were strolling in the Bois de Vincennes, talking to himself.

"Ah that's pretty, that's awfully good. . . . There are booths, quite a fair. And the music's ripping. What a spread they've got there, they're breaking the glasses. . . . That's fine! Hallo! there's a flare-up; fire balloons in the air; don't they jump, don't they cut! . . . Oh! oh! what a lot of lanterns under the trees! . . . It's quite jolly here! Water everywhere, fountains, cascades; how the water sings, oh! like a chorister. . . . Stunning, those cascades!"

And he pulled himself together, as if to hear better the delicious song of the water; he drew in deep breaths, as if he were drinking in the fresh spray of the fountains. But, little by little, his face was over-clouded with anguish. Then he crouched, he ran round the walls of his cell, faster, with dull threats.

"It's some dodge, all that! . . . I'm on my guard. . . . Silence, you set of louts! Yes, you cheek me, do you? You want to make a fool of me, with your drinking, and your jawing, and your drabs! . . . I'll give you beans! . . . Damnation! will you stow that blasted row!"

He clenched his fists; then he gave a shrill cry, and ran crouching along the ground. And he stuttered, his teeth chattering with fright.

"You want me to kill myself! No, I won't throw myself over! . . . All that water, that means that I haven't the courage. No, I won't throw myself in!"

The cascades, that fled at his approach, advanced when he retreated. And, all at once, he gazed stupidly about him, and faltered, in a hardly intelligible voice:

"It's impossible, they've set the doctors against me."

"I'm going, Monsieur; good-night," said Gervaise to the house-surgeon. "I can't stand it; I'll come again."

She was quite white. Coupeau continued his *pas seul*, from the window to the mattress, and from the mattress to the window, sweating and toiling, always to the same time. And she went out. But all the way downstairs she could still hear the infernal *chahut* of her man. Oh Lord! how good it was to be outside, and breathe again!

That evening all the house in the Rue de la Goutte-d'Or was talking of the strange illness of old Coupeau. The Boches, who looked down on Clop-clop now, offered her a cassis in their lodge, all the same, so as to hear all the details. Madame Lorilleux came in, and Madame Poisson. There were interminable comments. Boche had known a carpenter who had stripped himself stark naked in the Rue Saint-Martin, and who had died dancing the polka; he drank absinthe. The women shook with laughter, for it seemed such a funny idea, sad as it was. Then, as they did not quite understand, Gervaise pushed them back, and cleared a space; then, in the middle of the lodge, while the others looked on, she did Coupeau, bawling, leaping, wriggling, with frightful grimaces. Yes, honour bright! it was just like that! At that the others marvelled: impossible! a man could not last for three hours, going at that rate. Well! she swore by all that was most sacred, that Coupeau had been at it since the day before, thirty-six hours already. They could go and see him for themselves if they didn't believe her. But Madame Lorilleux declared that she was much obliged, but she had no desire to go to

Sainte-Anne's; she would not even allow Lorilleux to go there. As for Virginie, whose shop was going from bad to worse, and who looked as gloomy as a funeral, she merely muttered that life wasn't all smiles, good heavens! by no means. They finished up their cassis, and Gervaise wished them all good-night. When she was not speaking, she looked half imbecile, with her staring eyes. No doubt she saw her man still waltzing. Next day, when she got up, she declared to herself that she would not go there again. What was the use? She didn't want to go dotty herself. Nevertheless, every ten minutes she fell to thinking; she was on it, as they say. It would be curious if he were still kicking up like that. When twelve o'clock struck, she could restrain herself no longer, she never noticed the length of the walk, so fully was her brain occupied by the desire and the fear of what awaited her.

Oh! she had no need to ask for news. From the very bottom of the stairs she could hear Coupeau's song. Just the same tune, just the same dance. She could almost fancy that she had only just come down, and was going right up again. The attendant she had seen the day before, who was carrying basins of gruel along the corridor, winked at her, by way of being polite.

"Well, just the same!" she said.

"Oh! just the same!" he replied, without stopping.

She went in, but she stood by the door, for there were people in the room with Coupeau. The fair, rosy-cheeked house-surgeon was standing, he had given up his chair to an old gentleman, who had the ribbon of the Legion of Honour; he was bald and lantern-jawed. Evidently he was the head-physician, for he had a look that was as keen and piercing as a gimlet. All the ministers of sudden death have that look.

Gervaise, however, was not there for that gentleman's sake, and she peered over his bald cranium, devouring Coupeau with her eyes. The madman danced and yelled more vigorously than ever. She had seen, long ago, in mid-Lent balls, strapping wash-house men go it the whole night through; but never, never would she have dreamed that a man could amuse himself so long; when she said amuse himself, it was a way of speaking, for there is no amusement in taking flying-leaps without meaning to, as if you had swallowed a powder-magazine. Coupeau, bathed in sweat, steamed more than ever. His mouth seemed to have grown larger by force of screaming. Oh! it was well that women with child were not there to see. He had travelled so often from the mattress to the window, that she saw his trail on the ground; the straw-mattress was worn away by his slippers.

No, in truth, it was not a pleasant sight, and Gervaise, trembling, asked herself why she had come. The idea that at the Boches, the night before, they had accused her of exaggerating! Why she had not done it half! Now she saw better what Coupeau was doing, she would never forget him, with his eyes wide open upon vacancy. Meanwhile she caught some phrases of the house-surgeon and the physician. The former gave details about the night, with words she did not understand. All night long, her man had talked and pirouetted; that was what it all came to. Then the bald old gentleman, not too polite in his ways, seemed at length to notice that she was there; and when the house-surgeon had told him that she was the wife of the patient, he began to interrogate her, with the unpleasant air of a police inspector.

"Did the father of this man drink?"

"Yes, Monsieur, just a little, like everybody. He was killed by a fall from a roof, when he was tipsy."

"Did his mother drink?"

"Lord! Monsieur, like everybody, you know, a drop now and again. Oh! it is quite a good family! There was a brother, who died very young in convulsions."

The physician looked at her with his piercing glance. He continued, in his brutal voice:

"And you drink too?"

Gervaise stammered, denied, put her hand to her heart to give her sacred word.

"You drink! Take care, you see what drink leads to. One day or other you will die like that."

She stood as if pinned to the wall. The physician had turned his back. He bent down, not caring if he picked up some of the dust of the straw-mattress on his frock coat; he studied Coupeau's trembling for a long time, waiting for him as he came along, following him with his eyes. By that time the legs too jumped, the trembling had gone down from the hands into the feet; a regular Punch, with someone drawing the string, setting the limbs in motion, and leaving the trunk as stiff as wood. The disease gained ground little by little. It was like a music under the skin; it started every three or four seconds, shook for an instant; then stopped, and then started again, just like the little shiver that runs through a lost dog,

when the winter cold bites it, in a doorway. Already the belly
and the shoulders quivered like water when it is all but
boiling. What a funny way to break down, wriggling about
like that, like a girl who is ticklish!

Meanwhile Coupeau uttered low moans. He seemed to
suffer much more than the day before. His incoherent
complaints indicated all sorts of distresses. Thousands of
needles pricked him. He had something heavy all over his
body; some cold, damp beast dragged itself over his thighs,
and dug its claws into his flesh. Then there were other beasts
that clutched at his shoulders, and tore bits out of his back
with their claws.

"I'm thirsty, oh! I'm thirsty!" he muttered continually.

The house-surgeon took a jar of lemonade from a shelf, and
gave it to him. He seized it with both hands, greedily took a
great gulp, spilling half of the liquid over himself; but he
spat it out at once with a furious disgust, crying:

"Damnation! it's brandy!"

Then the house-surgeon, at a sign from the physician, tried
to make him drink some water, without letting go the water-
bottle. This time he swallowed the mouthful, howling as if he
had swallowed fire.

"It's brandy, damnation! it's brandy!"

Since the day before, whatever he drank was brandy. It
redoubled his thirst, and he could drink nothing, for everything
burned him. They had brought him some soup, but they
evidently wanted to poison him, for the soup smelt of brandy.
The bread was sharp and musty. There was nothing but
poison all about. The cell stank of sulphur. He even accused
them of rubbing matches under his nose to infect him.

The physician stood up and listened to Coupeau, who now
once more saw phantoms in daylight. Did he not see spiders'
webs on the walls, as big as the sails of ships? Then their
webs became nets, with meshes that grew smaller and bigger,
a queer sort of plaything! Black balls travelled up and down
the meshes, regular jugglers' balls, first as large as billiard-balls,
then as large as cannon-balls; and they swelled and they
shrank, simply to annoy him. All at once he cried:

"Oh! the rats! look at the rats, there!"

The balls had turned to rats. The filthy animals swelled,
sprang through the net, leapt upon the mattress, where they
evaporated. There was an ape, too, which came out of the
wall, and went back into the wall, coming so near him every

time that he recoiled, for fear he would have his nose bitten off. Suddenly, it changed again; the walls seemed to caper, for he cried, choking with terror and rage:

"That's it, ah-h! you can shake me, I don't care! . . . Ah-h! the crib! ah-h! there, on the ground! . . . Yes, yes, ring the bells, you pack of priests! play the organ to keep me from calling the guard! . . . And they've got a machine there behind the wall; oh! the rabble! I can hear it, it snorts, they'll blow us all up. . . . Fire, damnation! fire! They're calling fire! see how it flames! Oh! it's all lighting up, it's lighting up! the whole sky's a-fire, red fires, green fires, yellow fires. . . . Help, help, fire!"

His shouts died away into a rattling in his throat. He muttered now only inconsequent words, foaming at the mouth, his chin dabbled with saliva. The physician rubbed his nose with his finger, a little movement which was doubtless habitual with him before grave cares. He turned to the house-surgeon, and asked him in a low voice:

"And the temperature, still a hundred and four?"

"Yes, Monsieur."

The physician made a grimace. He remained there for a couple of minutes, his eyes fixed on Coupeau. Then he shrugged his shoulders, adding:

"The same treatment, broth, milk, unsweetened lemonade, fluid extract of cinchona as a draught. Don't leave him, and have me called."

He went out, Gervaise followed him, to ask him if there was no hope. But he walked so fast that she dared not follow him. She stood there for an instant, hesitating whether to go back and have another look at her man. But the sight had been quite as much as she could stand. When she heard him shout again that the lemonade smelt of brandy, she went her way; she had had quite enough of the performance. In the streets, the gallop of horses and the noise of wheels made her feel as if all Sainte-Anne's was at her heels. And that physician who had threatened her! She felt as if she were already taken ill.

Naturally, at the Rue de la Goutte-d'Or, the Boches and the others were waiting for her. The moment she appeared at the door, they called her into the lodge. Well, did old Coupeau still last? Yes, he still lasted. Boche seemed stupefied and amazed: he had laid a bet of a bottle of wine that old Coupeau could not last till night. And he still lasted! The whole company smacked their thighs, and declared that they were

astonished. Madame Lorilleux calculated the number of
hours: thirty-six hours and twenty-four hours, sixty hours.
Good Lord! he had been working his pins and his jaws for
sixty hours! Never had anyone heard of such a feat. But
Boche, who laughed on the wrong side of his mouth on account
of his bottle of wine, questioned Gervaise with an air of
doubt, asking her if she was sure he hadn't hopped the twig
the moment her back was turned. Oh! no, he was jumping too
vigorously, there was no chance of it. But Boche pressed her
more and more, begging her to do them what he was doing,
so that they could see. Yes, yes, just a bit! to oblige them all!
They all declared it would be so nice of her, for there were two
neighbours there who had not seen it the day before, and who
had come down expressly to see it. The *concierge* told them all
to stand around, and they left the middle of the lodge clear,
elbowing one another in a spasm of curiosity. But Gervaise
shook her head. She was really afraid of making herself ill.
However, to show that she was not merely wanting to be
pressed, she began two or three little starts; but it made her
feel quite queer, she drew back, no, word of honour! she
couldn't. There was a murmur of disappointment: What a
pity, she imitated it to perfection. However, if she didn't feel
able! And, after Virginie had gone back to her shop, old
Coupeau was forgotten, and they began to chatter about the
Poisson household, now all at sixes and sevens; the bailiffs had
come yesterday; the policeman was going to lose his situation;
as for Lantier, he was now after the daughter of the restaurant-
keeper close by, a magnificent woman, who talked about
setting up as a tripe-seller. Lord! what a joke it was, they
already saw a tripe-seller installed in the shop; after the sweets
came the solids. The cuckold Poisson looked very queer in
connection with it all; how the devil could a man whose very
business it was to be on the alert, be such a simpleton in his
own home? But suddenly all hushed, as they saw Gervaise,
whom they had ceased to look at, and who was practising,
all by herself, at the other end of the lodge, setting her hands
and feet trembling, doing Coupeau. Bravo, that was just it,
it couldn't be better done, She stopped with an air of stupefaction, as if waking out of a dream. Then she hurried away.
It was good-night all; she would try and get some sleep.

On the following day the Boches saw her set out at twelve
o'clock, as she had done the two preceding days. They wished
her a good time of it. That day the corridor at Sainte-Anne's

shook with the yells and stamps of Coupeau. She still had her
hands on the banisters, when she heard him howl:

"Look at those bugs! . . . Just you come here! I'll bone
you! . . . They're all over me, ah! the bugs! . . . I'm a match
for the whole lot of you! Off with you, damnation!"

For an instant she lingered at the door. He seemed to be
fighting with a whole army. When she entered, the sight was
more astonishing than ever. Coupeau was raving mad, a very
lunatic! He struggled in the middle of the cell, struck out in
every direction, at himself, at the walls, at the floor, tumbling
down, hitting out at vacancy; and he tried to open the window,
and he hid away, put himself on guard, called, replied, making
a regular inferno all by himself, with the air of fury of a man
who is set upon by a whole host of people. Then Gervaise
saw that he fancied himself on a roof, engaged in putting on
sheets of galvanized iron. He imitated the bellows with his
mouth, he stirred the irons in the brazier, went down on his
knees, to run his thumb along the edge of his mattress,
fancying that he was soldering. Yes, his trade came back into
his head at the last; and he yelled so loud and clung on to his
roof, because there were blackguards who hindered him from
doing his work properly. On all the neighbouring roofs there
were scamps who were annoying him. And the vagabonds set
bands of rats at his legs. Ah! the dirty beasts, he saw them
wherever he looked. It was all very well to stamp them out
with his foot, new gangs of them turned up, the whole roof
was black with them, and there were spiders too. He slapped
his hand on his trousers, to kill the big spiders that had lodged
there. What the blazes! he would never finish his day's work,
his master wanted to get him into trouble, and send him to
prison. Then, as he hurried on with his work, he fancied
that he had a steam-engine in his belly; and with wide-open
mouth he puffed out steam, a thick steam which filled the
cell and floated out of the window; and, leaning over, still
puffing, he watched the tail of steam unroll, float up into the
sky, where it hid the sun.

"Hallo!" he cried, "it's those chaps from the Chaussée
Clignancourt, disguised as bears, just to show off."

He crouched before the window, as if he were watching a
procession in the streets, from the top of a roof.

"What a cavalcade, lions and panthers all grinning. . . .
There are urchins dressed up as dogs and cats. . . . There is
Clémence, with her hair stuck all over feathers. Ah! damn!

there she goes head over heels, she's showing all she has! . . .
I say, ducky, you'd better slope! . . . Eh! you bloody
cops, just let her alone! . . . Don't fire, what the hell! don't
fire. . . ."

His voice rose, shrill with fright, and he crouched down out
of sight, declaring that the slut and the redcoats were there
below, men aiming at him with muskets. In the wall he saw
the mouth of a pistol pointed at him. They had dragged away
the girl.

"Don't fire, damnation! don't fire. . . ."

Then the houses crumbled away, he imitated the crash of a
collapse; and everything disappeared, they were all gone.
But, he had no time to breathe, other tableaux passed, with
extraordinary rapidity. A furious need of speaking filled his
mouth with words, which he spluttered out incoherently, his
chest heaving. He cried louder and louder.

"Hallo! it's you, good-day! . . . None of that now! don't make
me eat your hair."

And he put his hand in front of his face, he breathed hard
to drive away the hairs. The house-surgeon questioned him.

"Who do you see?"

"My wife, of course!"

He looked at the wall, with his back turned to Gervaise.

Gervaise gave quite a start, and she too examined the wall,
to see if she could see herself. He went on talking.

"Look here, don't entangle me . . . I don't want to be tied
up. . . . You do look well, that's quite a swell dress. Where
did you earn that, you bitch? You've been on the loose, you
hussy! I'll give it to you. . . . Who on earth is that? Look and
see. . . . Damn! it's him again!'

With a terrible bound, he dashed his head against the wall;
but the padded wall softened the blow. One heard only the
rebound of his body upon the straw mattress, on which the
shock had thrown him.

"What do you see?" repeated the house-surgeon.

"The hatter! the hatter!" howled Coupeau.

The house-surgeon questioned Gervaise, but she only
stammered, without being able to give an answer; the scene
brought up again all the worries of her life. The zinc-worker
shook his fists.

"Let's have it out, old chap! I'll wipe you out! Ah! you're
going off now, are you, with that rep on your arm, to make
game of me in public! I'll strangle you, yes, yes, I, and I

won't put on my gloves to do it. . . . None of your swaggering! . . . Take that, and that, and that, and that!"

He pummelled away at the air. Then a frenzy seized him. He had come against the wall as he recoiled, and he fancied that he was being attacked from behind. He turned, and furiously attacked the wall. He leapt in the air, sprang from one corner to another, banged his belly, his buttocks, one shoulder, rolled over, got up again. His bones grew soft, his flesh sounded like damp tow. And he accompanied his performance with fiendish threats, savage and guttural cries. But the battle seemed to turn against him, for his breath came short, his eyes almost started out of their sockets; and he seemed gradually to turn as timid as a child.

"Murder! murder! . . . get out of it, both of you! Oh! the brutes, they're laughing at me. Look at her, the wanton with her legs in the air! . . . She must go that way, it's certain. . . Ah! the brigand, he's killing her! He's cutting off her leg with his knife. The other leg's off, the belly's split open, it's all full of blood. . . . Oh! my God, oh! my God, oh! my God. . . ."

And, bathed in sweat, his hair standing on end, a fearful sight, he went backwards, waving his arms violently, as if to push the abominable scene from him. He uttered two piercing groans, and fell backwards on the mattress, in which his heels had got entangled.

"Monsieur, Monsieur, he's dead!" said Gervaise, clasping her hands.

The house-surgeon went forward, and pulled Coupeau into the middle of the mattress. No, he was not dead. His shoes and stockings had been taken off; his bare feet stuck out at the end of the bed; and they danced, all by themselves, one beside the other, keeping time, a little quick, regular dance.

Just then the physician came in. He brought with him two colleagues, one thin and one fat, both, like himself, decorated. All three bent over, without saying anything, scrutinizing the man all over; then they talked rapidly, in whispers. They had laid the man bare from the loins to the shoulders, and Gervaise, by standing on tip-toe, could see the naked trunk. It was complete now, the trembling had gone down the arms and run up the legs, the trunk itself had got lively now. Positively the creature danced now with the belly as well. There were little laughs all along the sides, the whole body seemed to shake with laughter. And it all kept time, naturally, the muscles took up their positions, the skin vibrated like a drum, the hairs waltzed and bowed. It was the final kick-up, like the last gallop, at break of day, when the dancers all hold one another's hands, and stamp their feet.

"He's asleep," murmured the head-physician.

And he pointed out the man's face to both the others. Coupeau, his eyelids closed, had little nervous shocks which drew his whole face aside. He was more awful still, thus weighed down, his jaws protruding, like the shapeless mask of a dead man who has had nightmares. But the physicians, catching sight of the feet, began to observe them with an air of profound interest. The feet still danced. Coupeau might sleep, but the feet danced on. Oh! their master might snore, it was no concern of theirs, they continued their even course, without hurrying or lingering. Regular mechanical feet, feet which took their pleasure where they found it.

When Gervaise saw the physicians laying their hands on her man's chest, she wanted to feel too. She came forward softly, and put her hand on one shoulder. And she left it there for a minute. Good heavens! what was going on there? The dance seemed to go through and through him; the very bones danced. Shivers, undulations, came from a distance, and ran like rivers under the skin. When she pressed on it a little, she felt the piteous cries of the marrow. To the naked eye there were only little waves dimpling out, as on the surface of a whirlpool; but, inside, it was a terrible destruction that was going on. It was like a mole working underground, sapping the whole structure. And it was the brandy of old Colombe's bar that hammered away like a pick-axe. The whole body was soaked in it, and it had only to finish its work, crumbling down, bearing the man away in the general, continuous trembling of the whole carcase.

The physicians had gone. At the end of an hour Gervaise, who had remained with the house-surgeon, repeated in a whisper:

"Monsieur, Monsieur, he is dead."

But the house-surgeon, looking at the feet, shook his head. The bare feet, outside the bed, danced on. They were far from clean, and they had long nails. Hours passed. All at once they stiffened, motionless. Then the house-surgeon turned to Gervaise, and said:

"There you are."

Only death had quieted the feet.

When Gervaise returned to the Rue de la Goutte-d'Or,

she found a whole crowd of gossips in at the Boches', chattering excitedly. She thought that they were waiting to hear her news, as they had been the other days.

"He's gone under," she said, opening the door composedly, with a weary and stupefied air.

But no one heard her. The whole house was in a state of excitement. It was a story that was simply immense! Poisson had nabbed his wife with Lantier. No one knew exactly how things had happened, because they all had their own way of telling the story. However, he had come upon them just at the moment when they were least expecting him. Such a sight, naturally, had put Poisson beside himself. A very tiger! The man who spoke so little, and walked as if he had swallowed a poker, had roared and danced with rage. Then nothing more had been heard. Lantier had evidently explained the matter to the husband. However, it could go on no longer now. And Boche announced that the daughter of the restaurant-keeper close by was really going to take the shop, and set up a business in tripe. The hatter, sly dog, adored tripe.

Meanwhile Gervaise, seeing Madame Lorilleux come in with Madame Lerat, repeated in a dull tone:

"He's gone under. . . . Fancy! four days kicking and yelling. . . ."

At that the two sisters felt bound to take out their handkerchiefs. Their brother had not been all he might have been, but still he was their brother. Boche shrugged his shoulders, and said, loud enough for everybody to hear:

"Bah! one drunkard the less!"

From that day, Gervaise was often a little wandering, and it became one of the sights of the house to see her do Coupeau. There was no need to press her, she gave the performance gratis, trembling in hands and feet, with little involuntary cries. No doubt she had taken up the trick at Sainte-Anne's, through watching her man. But she had not the luck to die like him. She only made horrible grimaces, like an ape, and had cabbage-stalks thrown at her by the boys in the street.

Gervaise went on like that for some months. She went down and down, accepted the last insults, starved a little every day. When she had scraped together a copper or two, she spent it in drink, and got drunk. She did all the dirty work of the neighbourhood. One evening, there had been a bet that she would not eat something disgusting; and she ate it, to earn sixpence. M. Marescot had decided to turn her out of the room on the sixth floor. But, as old Bru had just been found dead in his hole, under the staircase, the landlord let her have that niche. Now she lived in old Bru's niche. It was there, on some old straw, that she fasted, empty within and cold without. The earth would have none of her, apparently. She became silly, she never even thought of throwing herself out of the sixth storey on to the pavement of the court below, to end things. Death took her little by little, bit by bit, bringing her to the bitter end of the damnable existence she had made for herself. No one ever knew exactly of what death she died. It was put down to cold and heat. But the truth was that she died of poverty, of the dirt and fatigue of a life that had run to waste. She died like a pig in a sty, as the Lorilleux said. One morning, as there was a bad smell in the corridor, the neighbours remembered that they had not seen her for two days; and they found her already green, in her niche.

It was old Bazouge who came, with the poor people's coffin under his arm, to lay her out. He was awfully drunk that day, but a jolly good fellow all the same, and as blithe as a lark. When he saw who his customer was, he made some philosophical reflections, as he set about his work.

"Everybody goes that way. . . . You've no need to hustle, there's plenty of room for everybody. . . . And it's silly to be in too much hurry, because you don't get there so soon. . . . For my part, I only want to give satisfaction. Some want to go, and some don't. Let's have a look now. . . . Here's one who didn't want to, then she did want to. So she had to wait. . . . Now, here she is; she's got her way. Gently does it!"

And, when he had seized Gervaise in his great black hands, he was touched by a certain tenderness, he lifted her gently; she had fancied him for so long. Then, as he laid her out in the coffin with paternal care, he stuttered, between two hiccups:

"Now here . . . listen . . . it's me, Bibi-la-Gaieté, called the ladies' comforter. . . . Now you're all right. Sleep sound, my beauty!"

THE END